In this series:

The Witches of Karres by James H. Schmitz

The Wizard of Karres
by Mercedes Lackey, Eric Flint & Dave Freer

Also by Mercedes Lackey, Eric Flint & Dave Freer:

The Shadow of the Lion

This Rough Magic

The Wizard of Karres

Mercedes Lackey
Eric Flint
Dave Freer

THE WIZARD OF KARRES

This is a work of fiction. All the characters and events portrayed in this book are fictional, and any resemblance to real people or incidents is purely coincidental.

A Baen Books Original

Baen Publishing Enterprises
P.O. Box 1403
Riverdale, NY 10471
www.baen.com

ISBN: 0-7434-8839-3

Cover art by Stephen Hickman

First printing, August 2004

Library of Congress Cataloging-in-Publication Data

Lackey, Mercedes.
  The wizard of Karres / Mercedes Lackey, Eric Flint, Dave Freer.
    p. cm.
  "A Baen Books Original."
  ISBN 0-7434-8839-3 (hc)
  1. Interplanetary voyages--Fiction. 2. Space ships--Fiction. 3. Witches--Fiction. 4. Circus--Fiction. I. Flint, Eric. II. Freer, Dave. III. Title.

  PS3562.A246W56 2004
  813'.54--dc22

                                                              2004009766

Distributed by Simon & Schuster
1230 Avenue of the Americas
New York, NY 10020

Production by Windhaven Press, Auburn, NH
Printed in the United States of America

10 9 8 7 6 5 4 3 2 1

CHAPTER 1

The shrill screaming from inside made Captain Pausert open the cabin door with some caution. Not that screaming was necessarily unusual around his present company—just that it was a good idea to meet screaming with due care.

He ducked reflexively as something went whizzing past his head. Vermilion splattered all over the wall of the *Venture*'s second-best stateroom. It didn't make things look much worse. The eggshell blue paint that Goth had picked out with such care during their refit on Uldune was scarred and splattered with mute testimony to the savageness of the battle that was going on inside.

In the center of what had once been an ankle-deep pale cream carpet was the perpetrator of the ghastly destruction.

The Leewit, the younger of the two witch girls of Karres aboard the ship, stopped drumming her heels on the floor, sat up and glared at him. "What are you doing here, stupid?" she demanded, weighing the next paint bottle in her hands.

Like the sound of sunlight, like seeing a scent, he was aware of the insubstantial thing somewhere in the room: a thumb-sized vatch, filling Pausert's head with tinkling vatch-giggles. Then he saw it. Around the light, a sheet of paper dragged by that tiny piece of impossible blackness fluttered like a demented moth.

Throw it at the Big Dream Thing! squeaked the vatch, inside his head, its silvery eyes wide with delight. **Throw, throw!**

"Shan't!" said the Leewit, changing her mind.

1

Spoilsport! Throw at me again, then! The vatch swooped down at her, fluttering what had obviously been the Leewit's artistic endeavor inches from the Leewit's nose.

The Leewit snatched at it furiously, nearly dropping the paint bottle. "Mine! Give it!"

The vatch and the picture twitched away from her fingers, and then disappeared, and then reappeared—in four different localities at the same time.

Life with vatches was interesting. So was life with Karres witches. Life with both was . . . *complicated.*

Captain Pausert's life had been very, very complicated for some time now.

The Leewit impotently threatened the dancing vatch quartet with the paint bottle. Then she turned on the captain. "You! You can even handle a giant vatch. Get my picture back from the stinkin' little thing!"

"Seeing as you asked so nicely, child, I will." Captain Pausert was careful to keep a straight face. It amused him to see the Leewit persecuted, for a change, since the Leewit was ever so capable of doing a fair amount of persecuting herself.

Still, vatches were too capable of creating havoc for him to leave one on the loose here. Forming hooks of the invisible stuff that was klatha force, Pausert began to reach with them for the tiny vatch . . . or vatches.

There were four of them and they all looked the same—less than an inch of blackness and a pair of slitty silver eyes. They all seemed to have the Leewit's picture, too. That was confusing. But vatches did odd things to time and space in human dimensions. He'd just try each one in turn.

He did. To no avail.

"It's doing a light-shift, Captain." That observation came from the Leewit's older sister, Goth, from where she lounged in a formfit chair on the far side of the room. "Splitting its image. Neat trick. Hadn't thought of that," she said, rubbing her sharp chin.

Pausert stared at the four. "So where is it actually?" Light-shifts were one of Goth's klatha skills.

"Got to be somewhere between them, Captain."

Pausert "felt" with the klatha hooks . . . encountered nonmaterial resistance. Suddenly there was only one tiny speck of whirling midnight, and the Leewit's artwork fluttered towards the floor. The little blond witch snatched it out of the air.

Pausert was a vatch-handler. He'd taken on Big Windy, the giant vatch. He could pull them inside out and make them jump through hoops, if he had to. Only . . .

There was one kind of these nonmaterial klatha creatures that was supposed to be unmanageable—and, unfortunately, you couldn't tell which kind of vatch you had until you had it. Then it could be too late. Klatha was powerful, but also dangerous.

Tickles, giggled the vatchlet.

Pausert tried to make the little creature move. It was like pushing smoke. With a sinking feeling, he realized that the silvery-eyed mischief must be one of the kind of vatch that none of the witches of Karres could make do anything.

I like this place. It's fun! The vatchlet whizzed around his head, then—into his chest.

Pausert's heart stopped for a moment. But nothing else happened, and it restarted again.

Well, at least it hadn't turned on him. And it sounded and acted awfully young. He'd—

Suddenly, the ship-detector alarms sounded through the intercom system. Pausert had set them up to do so when the *Venture* had made her run through the Chaladoor, that region of dangerous space between Emris and Uldune. He'd never gotten around to undoing it.

The baby vatch and the Leewit would just have to sort out their own problems. This could be something far worse. The captain left at a run, with Goth hard at his heels. They nearly collided with Vezzarn, the old spacer-cum-spy who was one half of their crew. The other half, Hulik do Eldel, former Imperial agent and citizen of the pirate planet Uldune, was barely moments behind.

The captain focused the viewscreens on the object—no, objects—the detectors had picked up. They were still almost at maximum range, but were coming in fast.

"Imperial cruisers, Captain," said Goth, looking at the heavily armed spacecraft.

Pausert's heart began doing complicated calisthenics. Pirates would have been preferable. Infinitely preferable.

"There is another one up there coming in the upper quadrant," said Hulik, pointing.

"And another one, dead ahead," added Vezzarn. "I think they've got us boxed in, Captain."

They did indeed. Pausert realized that this meant that someone back at the governor's palace in Green Galaine on Emris must have passed on details of their plans, including their exact trajectory. This was not good, and he had the feeling it was going to get a great deal worse.

"Do you want me to unseal the nova guns, Captain?" asked Vezzarn nervously.

"Not sure it'll do much good," replied Pausert grimly. The guns were very effective when they worked, but they were also old and erratic—and sometimes downright dangerous to use.

Nevertheless, he nodded his head. "May as well, though. In the meantime, Hulik, try the communicator."

The slim, elegant Miss do Eldel set it to the Empire's general beam length.

A young man in the neatly pressed uniform of an Imperial lieutenant stared out at them from under his regulation cap. " . . . instructed to stop firing your thrust generators and allow us to match velocity and trajectory, and board for inspection."

The man paused, obviously about to repeat. Pausert leaned over and hit the send button. "This is Captain Pausert of the *Venture*. What are you looking for?"

The officer looked faintly startled, as if he hadn't expected them to reply. "Ah. Captain Pausert. Can you give us visuals, please?"

"Our visuals *are* on," said Pausert smoothly. "Sorry. We might be having a malfunction with the screens. Or perhaps you are. But what seems to be the problem, Lieutenant? What are you looking for? We're a civilian spacecraft, on a course from the Empire planet of Emris to the provincial capital of the Regency of Hailie. We're not a pirate vessel, I assure you. In fact, we have a letter of safe conduct with the seal of the Empress Hailie herself."

The lieutenant was definitely looking more respectful now, but Pausert was not going to drop his guard. A good half of the people aboard the *Venture* were *persona non grata* so far as the Empire was concerned. The last thing he wanted was to have any Imperials aboard.

The Imperial lieutenant hesitated for a moment. Then said: "I'll give you to Commodore Fleser, sir. If you'll just wait a moment. He'll answer your questions."

Pausert flicked the toggle. "What do you think, Goth? Hulik?"

"Better play along, Captain. Me and the Leewit will get the Sheewash Drive ready." Goth headed for the hatch leading out of the control room. "We can outrun them if we have to, but Threbus said to keep a low profile."

Hulik nodded. "We can outrun them, but they do outgun us. Let's see what they want first."

The captain decided their advice was good and toggled on the buzzing communicator. The screen now showed a jowl-faced gray-haired man with commodore's insignia.

" . . . Fleser of the Imperial cruiser, ISN *Malorn*. Reduce thrust or be fired on."

Pausert realized that the Imperials weren't going to pussyfoot around. He reached out and began cutting the thrust. "This is Captain Pausert of the *Venture*. Why are you interfering with a vessel in the legitimate pursuit of business?"

"We have orders to investigate the possibility that you may be carrying a dangerous criminal, as well as one of the infamous witches of Karres," said the commodore grimly. "Cut thrust further, Captain. You're within range of our guns now and they're locked onto your ship. Any attempt at escape and you will be fired on. Out." He cut the communicator-link.

Pausert shook his head at the blank screen. "Great Uncle Threbus was dead wrong about one thing. That commodore knew who we were, and he was still prepared to fire on us. Looks to me like the Empire doesn't plan to leave us alone after all." He stood up. "They're looking for our passengers. I'm going to have a word with Goth."

"Ought to be all right," said Goth. "I can hide myself in no-shape. You got that safe-conduct signed by the Empress Hailie for the passengers. And they won't be looking for the Leewit at all."

"I don't think letting them find Hantis and Pul is a good idea, safe-conduct or not. You know smuggling them past any Imperial security agents is what we're supposed to do."

"Guess you're right, Captain. I can try a shape-change on them, except . . . I'm still not really good enough at that to use any shape except one I already know well. Not and keep it up for more than maybe a minute. Like I did when I made myself and Leewit look like Hantis and Pul on the Worm World. But any shape like that might also be in Imperial records."

"What about no-shape?" Goth could bend light around herself so she was invisible.

"Got to do that to yourself." Goth shook her head regretfully. "It's too bad I can't do an age-shift yet, like Toll and Threbus can."

Pausert scratched his chin, dubiously. A younger—or older—Hantis and Pul would still look like a Nartheby Sprite and a grik-dog. That was too close for comfort. Still . . .

"What about this: could you do a shape-change that *imitates* an age-shift? You'd still be working with shapes you know well, just changing their age. That might be enough to fool the Imperials, if we combined it with disguises."

Goth thought about it for a moment, then smiled. "I think so. That's a good idea, Captain!"

"We'll have to hope so. I don't see anything better, in the time we've got. The Imperials should be in boarding range in a few minutes. You go and talk to Hantis and explain things. What about the Leewit?"

"Can look after myself," scowled the Leewit, gray eyes peering up at him from under lowered brows. "So long as you keep that smelly little vatch away."

The captain couldn't rell the little silver-eyed piece of klatha-blackness anywhere. Even if he couldn't detect it, though, he suspected it was still around somewhere.

"I bet you can, brat." He rumpled the Leewit's hair, which she hated, and ducked around the doorway before she could purse her lips to form one of her supersonic whistles. She could literally bust machinery with them.

Back in the control room he found Vezzarn, returning from the nova guns. "They're all ready, Captain. They might be old but I wouldn't want to have them fire on me at this short range, even if those are cruisers."

"Let's sight them on the nearest of the Imperials. It might remind them of their manners."

The little old spacer gave a crooked smile. "I kind of figured on that, Captain. I've been tracking them in with the rear turret. I reckon we could bring the forward turret to bear too, once they're alongside."

"Do that."

The communicator buzzed insistently. It was Commodore Fleser of the ISN *Malorn*. "Captain Pausert. You will deflect your guns from my ship!" he demanded angrily.

"Commodore Fleser," replied Pausert in an even tone of voice, "we've had a lot of pirate trouble. We do not, in fact, have any proof you are who you say you are. So our guns will stay locked onto your vessel. Before we open our airlock we'll put the lock-bar in place, and seal up the access codes. Make a false move and you won't have a command any more. At this range—you might destroy us, but we'll take you with us."

The Imperial officer looked like he was going to explode

himself. "Over and out," said Pausert, before the man had a chance to reply.

What fun! squeaked the vatch.

Pausert groaned. That was one complication he could have lived without.

"You agree, our papers are in order," said Pausert stiffly. "You are welcome to inspect our cargo. None of our passengers or crew even resemble these descriptions and holo-plates." He handed back the pictures of Goth, the Nartheby Sprite Hantis, and the grik-dog Pul. "You've been misinformed and sent on a wild-goose chase, Commodore."

Pausert was trying to keep calm. To him, the air in the cabin practically reeked of vatch. He could rell that little quicksilver-eyes in here somewhere.

Bulldog-faced Commodore Fleser in his blue-black gold-braided uniform, of course, would not be able to see the vatch. But he wouldn't be immune to its mischief. At the moment the officer was rather off his stride, knowing his vessel was locked by electromagnetic hull clamps into a death-grip with the *Venture*. That could change in a vatch-inspired instant, though. From what the commodore had said, the Imperials wanted Karres witches even more than the supposed criminal Hantis.

"We have specific orders from ISS headquarters," said Fleser, equally stiffly, "to stop this ship. They are absolutely certain you have these miscreants aboard."

Pausert hoped the Imperial commodore took the sudden widening of his eyes for a reaction to the mention of the dreaded Imperial Interservice Security . . . and not to the glass of water that the captain could see slowly lofting from his desk. He shrugged. "Go right ahead and search, Commodore. But I'll be making an official complaint to Duke Abelisson, the Empress' comptroller."

The vatch was quite capable of creating trouble just for the fun of it. Likely to, in fact. Vatches regarded human space as little more than an aspect of their dreams, and they regarded people as dreamed-up pieces in their games. It hardly mattered to them what happened to the pieces, when the game got boring.

The Imperial hadn't seen the glass. He turned towards the hatch. "Humph. My men will conduct a thorough search and—"

Pausert practically pushed him through it. "Well, you must see to them, then! A good commander always leads from the front, sir. Let us take you to it."

Water trickled down Pausert's back. There had to be some way of dealing with the little menace!

CHAPTER 2

Sedmon the Sixth, Daal of Uldune—sometimes called Sedmon of the Six Lives by the witches of Karres—listened silently to the communicator relaying the subradio report from his agent on Emris.

Sedmon bit his knuckle.

Sedmon patted him on the back.

Sedmon sighed in sympathy.

The fourth Sedmon flicked the screen controls to show the star maps of the route between Emris and the Regency of Haile.

The other two Sedmons continued looking out of the one-way windows of the western tower of the mighty House of Thunders, the ancient castle in the highlands south of Uldune's capital city of Zergandol. They knew what the others were doing and thinking anyway. Ruling the web of power hierarchies and fierce business interests that made up the former pirate planet of Uldune was no sinecure. In fact, it would have been too much for most humans. But the hexaperson was the best six people for the job. The telepathically linked clones spoke only because words helped formalize their shared thoughts. Also, it was a good habit. Whichever one was on public duty that day would have to speak to ordinary people.

"A Nartheby Sprite! It would help if we could contact the Wisdoms of Karres."

"Karres has done its disappearing trick again, unfortunately."

9

"No idea where or why?"

"None. But the rumor of the Worm World having destroyed them is almost certainly a falsehood emanating from the ISS."

"Pausert is in great danger, however. The Agandar's fleet are certainly in hot pursuit."

The Sedmon left unsaid the fact that Captain Pausert being in danger meant that a certain member of his crew was in danger also. They all knew that. They also knew that it had surprised them to discover just how upsetting that was.

"Not to mention the ISS."

"Unfortunate about the subradio beeper."

"It has been policy to have it fitted to all ships assuming new personalities here for near on a century. It is the first time it has served us so ill. The fact that the Agandar's pirates had discovered it, and that the late Jonalo had sold the information to the Imperials is unfortunate. But that is where things stand. We must make the best of it."

"We're going to have to take action ourselves."

"I suppose we are the only one we can trust."

Two of the hexaperson got up and went to the door. It was unnecessary to discuss the mission and who would go. Or to bid the others farewell. They all knew that the Nanite plague had to be stopped. The other four would have to manage without them.

The Sedmons' ship, *Thunderbird*, did not look like the vessel belonging to a wealthy, powerful planetary ruler. But then, it wasn't supposed to. The ship did have a number of features that were unusual even for a full-size battleship, and simply unthinkable in a scruffy-looking cargo tramp. Right now, what it had that was important was speed. And also a subradio tracker, fixed to the frequency of a certain signature transmission given out by the engines of the *Venture*. Even at this range, the signal and direction indicators were giving readouts. Emris, the world from which the *Venture* had lifted, was three dangerous weeks travel from Uldune, across the zone of space called the Chaladoor. To go around took the better part of a year. However, the *Venture's* course headed her inward towards the Empire's heart at a tangent which the Sedmons' ship could intersect in little more than two months. The hexaperson could only hope that that would be soon enough.

CHAPTER 3

A full platoon of Imperial Marines were busy with the search. They were being impeded at full volume by the Leewit. The Marines did not know quite how to deal with this miniature empress. In a lacy girl's party-dress, the Leewit looked to be a little blond girl of somewhere between three and four. With her stuffed fluffy stiff-legged toy puppy under one arm, she stood in the center of the cabin and berated them at the top of her voice. *How dare they make such a mess of her room!*

Her nursemaid was stooped over, as she had been since the Marines entered, trying to put everything in order. She was a skinny old woman with sharp features, wearing a baggy ship's suit. Her head was covered in something like a turban, even her ears and eyebrows. If any of the Marines had noticed something oddly young looking about the nursemaid's very large, grass-green eyes, the ruckus being caused by the Leewit had distracted their attention.

Commodore Fleser looked at the carnage. He turned to the saluting sergeant. "What happened here?" he demanded.

The NCO gestured helplessly. "Honest, sir, I don't know. It was like this when we came in, I swear."

"Was not!" squealed the Leewit. Her accusing finger swept across the squad of Marines. "They did it!"

"My best stateroom!" bellowed Pausert. "There is going to be trouble about this! I gave you permission to search, not to destroy the place."

11

"We have to find the criminal and the witch. We will take whatever steps we need to!" But even Fleser looked a bit aghast at the paint-splattered walls and the tumbled furniture.

"And I will lodge an official complaint with Duke Abelisson, be sure of it. *Another* one." Pausert scowled ferociously. "Miss Seltzer, take the young lady into the empty stateroom next door. You have finished with that one, Sergeant?"

"Er. Yessir."

"One moment," said the bulldog-faced Fleser. "These people . . ." He pointed to the Leewit, with her stuffed toy, and the nursemaid. Pausert just hoped he didn't put a hand on them. Goth's light-shift illusions didn't stand up to touch. "They are not listed by the officials at Green Galaine. Who are they?"

Captain Pausert looked at the sergeant and his Marines. "I will explain, Commodore. But confidentially, please. It is an Imperial matter."

The commodore drew himself up. "I am an officer of the Imperial Space Navy, sir. You can trust me."

"Good," said Pausert cheerfully. "Then I'll reserve it for your ears only. Sergeant, escort Miss Seltzer and her charge next door, please."

To his horror he began to rell vatch again. "*Vatch*erly there is a good explanation," he added. Goth, cloaked in no-shape, would rell the vatch also. But Hantis might not be able to. Best give her some warning that mischief was around.

All but the commodore and one rather slimy-looking individual in plain black coveralls left.

Pausert looked questioningly at the man. "And you are?"

"This is Micher," said the Commodore. "Imperial Interservice Security."

"Ah. Now I understand." Pausert's tone was decidedly frosty. "What I have to say is not for his ears, Commodore."

"This is my assignment," said the ISS man, in a rather whiny voice. Pausert knew the type. A bully to those below him and a bootlicker to those above. There was something odd about him, though. Pausert couldn't quite put his finger on it, but the man gave him an uneasy feeling.

"I have orders from the regional chief of Imperial security about this, Commodore," said Pausert firmly. "Goodbye, Micher."

Micher blinked. "But my orders . . ."

The commodore propelled him firmly out of the door and closed it. "Now, what is this about, Pausert? Whatever it is, the ISS is not going to like it." His expression made clear his own low opinion

of the ISS. Fleser was an officer in Imperial service, and thus had
to put up with them. Yet, here was Pausert, ostensibly on Imperial service himself, chasing them away. The commodore was plainly
fascinated by such apparently contradictory behavior.

Pausert glanced uneasily at the door. "This is strictly between
ourselves, Commodore. A very important Imperial lady's honor
hangs on it."

Now the commodore's curiosity looked about ready to sit up
and beg. "Of course. You can trust me."

Pausert did his best to look even more uneasy. It wasn't hard.
"Ask yourself just how a nursemaid and a child could get onto a
ship in Green Galaine without being on any passenger list, Commodore. Without being observed by security cameras. In total
secret. Just who has the influence to do that?"

It was the commodore's turn to look uneasy. "Something like
that could be organized, Captain. But not to keep it secret from
the ISS. They have agents everywhere."

Pausert bit his lip and said nothing. Just raised his eyebrows
and drew the Charter and Seal of Haile out of his pouch. Tapped
it meaningfully.

The commodore's mouth fell open. "You mean . . ."

"The ISS doesn't handle *quite* everything. The royal family's
security is handled by . . . But I never said a word, Commodore
Fleser. And if you take my advice, you won't either. The little girl
is very *imperious*, though, isn't she?"

He smiled, allowing the commodore to put his own interpretation on that smile. "The ISS is very jealous about the situation.
Speaking personally, I'd be quite happy to hand the whole thing
over to them. The girl's a little monster, frankly. I don't doubt for
an instant that your Marines were just grossly slandered."

He drew himself up stiffly. "However, that's not my decision—
nor yours—and duty is what it is. But that's what this is all about,
Commodore. Not some hogwash about mythical witches of Karres
and criminals. The ISS is trying to cause embarrassment within—"

A pregnant pause, here, designed to make the commodore even
more uneasy. "—certain quarters."

Someone knocked, and then entered the stateroom without
waiting for a reply. It was the security agent. His moist eyes were
alive with suspicion. "A message for you, Commodore. The Chief
Engineer from the *Malorn* has come across. He insists on seeing
you." The ISS agent looked as if he would have liked to kiss the
engineer. "He's waiting. Won't let me pass the message on."

As he spoke, the burly engineer gave up waiting and came in anyway. "Commodore, the *Malorn*'s air recycler is not working," he said bluntly.

Even Captain Pausert was stunned by this news. Air recyclers never failed. Never. They were the most reliable piece of equipment on any ship. Without them, space travel would be impossible.

The commodore looked as if someone had kicked his legs out from under him. All the bulldoggy bluster was gone in an instant. "Can you fix it?" he asked.

The chief engineer looked at him gloomily. "It's mostly solid-state engineering, sir. That's why they don't go wrong. I've got my men busy stripping what can be stripped. But we can't get to a lot of it." He took off his cap and ran fingers through close-cropped gray hair. "The auxiliary plant is running, sir. But you know that only gives us thirty-six hours."

At least they had a standby of some sort, thought Pausert. But of course military craft did have, in case of combat-damage. The *Venture* didn't.

"Suit-bottles," he said, thinking back to his own military training with the Nikkeldepain Space Navy. "You've got Marines on board. They must have air-cylinders. At least a couple of hours each. And the other cruisers must have the same."

The engineer looked gratefully at him. "I hadn't thought of that. We could transfer all but a skeleton crew to the other ships, too."

The commodore nodded. "We're still six days from base. We'll have to move. Sergeant Harris!" he bellowed.

The sergeant came at a run, Blythe rifle at the ready. "Sir." He took in the scene and realized that he wasn't being called to arrest anyone, or shoot it out with a dangerous criminal. He lowered the barrel of the rifle.

"Round up your men and get them back onto the *Malorn*. At the double."

"But the search!" protested the ISS man. "The witches must have done this."

"That's enough of that rubbish!" snapped the commodore. "Move, Micher, before I leave you behind. I'm not abandoning my new command for the ISS's bit of spite. Besides, if these so-called witches can put my air recycler out of order, then I certainly don't want to fight with them."

Unfortunately, the sergeant had left open the door leading to the next cabin. As they passed by in the corridor, Pausert got another scent of sunlight and the sound of violets. He glanced in and saw that the little vatch was here—and was playing light-shift with the Leewit's head. Making it look like she was wearing an Imperial crown . . .

Even more unfortunately, the commodore had glanced through the floor also. Fleser stopped in his tracks.

"That enough fooling around, my little lady!" said Pausert sternly. He shouldered the commodore aside and stalked into the cabin, obscuring Fleser's view. "That thing is supposed to stay out of sight."

Pausert readied his klatha hooks for the little brute. Even if he couldn't catch it, he could maybe squelch it long enough . . .

Behind him, he heard the commodore mutter something. It sounded like "—glad I don't have to deal with the spoiled—" Fleser's heavy footsteps led away down the corridor.

Pausert sighed with relief. Alas, his klatha hooks once again seemed to be able to nothing worse than reduce the little vatch to giggles.

A few moments later the outer locks clanged. When Captain Pausert arrived back in the control room, the communicator beebled insistently.

The commodore's red face was glaring at him. "Damnation, Pausert. Can you deflect your guns?"

"Oh. Yes, certainly. Good luck, Commodore."

After Pausert deflected the guns, he saw that the vatchy patch of darkness was now above the coffee dispenser in the control room.

What was it going to do this time? He began the klatha-reach. It darted away.

I've got to go, Big Dream Thing. But I'll be back! Back . . . Baaaack . . .

That was really *not* what he needed to hear. But at least he could see in the screens that the Imperial flotilla was receding. Quite rapidly, in fact.

"I hope," he said to the indentation on the couch, "that you'll give them back their piece of air recycler. That was cruel. I think you frightened the commodore out of ten years of life. Being stuck in deep space without air is enough to terrify anyone."

"I've teleported it back already. When they try it again it'll be working. And it served them right. You told some awful fibs."

He tried to look innocent. "Just false suggestions. The commodore fooled himself."

Goth laughed. "Just so long as the Leewit doesn't find out she was supposed to have imperial blood. She's already impossible!"

"Just like that little vatch." He grimaced. That had been a near thing. And the vatch hadn't even been *trying* to create mischief. It had said it would be back; without a doubt it would return at the worst possible moment.

Goth appeared out of no-shape. "They're hunting for us pretty hard, Captain," she said seriously.

"Yes. It's not what Threbus led to me expect."

"I guess this must be more important than they told us," said Goth, biting a strand of hair.

The captain took it gently out of her mouth. "I guess you're right, girl. And I don't like being kept in the dark."

The Leewit and the grik-dog trotted into the control room. Pul was looking even more sour-faced than usual.

"My legs are still stiff," growled the grik-dog. "Posture like that's unnatural."

"You complain?" sneered the Leewit. "Try holding yourself up sometime, pretending you're a third your real size. I'm the one had to do all the work. Fatso."

"That information," said the Nartheby Sprite, making a small moue and wrinkling her foxy brows, "is available strictly on a need-to-know basis. And I don't think you need to know, Captain."

"Well, I beg to disagree!" snapped Pausert. "And as the captain of this ship—"

Pausert felt something close on his leg. Just firmly, but with a hint of immense unused strength. "Shall I gnaw his leg off, Hantis?" asked the grik-dog out of the corner of his mouth.

"Do that and I'll swing you around my head by your tail, Pul," said Goth, crossly. "The captain has to know what he's dealing with, Hantis. Even if you don't tell him everything, you have to tell him *something*."

The Nartheby Sprite laughed musically, and twitched her long, pointed ears. "Very well. To save my Pul's tail and the captain's leg, I will tell you some of it. Not all of it, mind. I *can't*. There is a mind-block so I don't remember parts of it, and won't until I speak to the Empress. It can't even be tortured out of me."

"We grik-dogs bite people who swing us by the tail," gruffed Pul. He had, however, released the captain's leg. And the look he gave Goth was a tad uneasy.

"Let's just have the story," said the captain peaceably.

"But it goes no further than you and Goth, understand? We don't want to cause alarm and panic. That would serve them better than us."

"I give you my word."

"Very well." She sat down, arranged her graceful legs, and began. "My kind are the last remnant of an old, old civilization. Nartheby is our home-world where almost all of our kind now live, but once we roamed widely, even to your Yarthe itself. There are stories about our people visiting—although as you were a young and developing culture we largely left you alone. Then we were afflicted by a plague. It wrecked our culture, our colonies and our star travel. We only saved ourselves by retreating to Nartheby and destroying any ships that came near our world, for a period of five centuries. Then it appeared that the danger was over. But the only Sprites that survived were on Nartheby." She pinched her fine nostrils. "Now . . . The plague has resurfaced. It is spreading, fast, through the Empire."

Pausert and Goth stared at her. The captain was the first to find his tongue. "But . . . Surely we shouldn't be keeping it a secret? We should be quarantining the infected areas."

Hantis had always seemed to be smiling. Now, as she shook her head, she just looked sad. "It's not that kind of plague, Captain. That's what we thought it was too, at first. It's an invasion. The invaders are just very small. Although we've never determined their exact nature, they are at least partly klatha creatures and seem to have a collective mind. They attack the way a plague would, but they're intelligent. They invade a host, breed billions of operatives, and then take over their hosts and control them. No quarantine can stop an intelligent disease."

"Does Karres know of this?" asked Goth.

Hantis nodded. "Yes. That's why they've gone into hiding. There are no Karres witches out in the Empire at all right now. Except those on this ship."

"But why?" demanded Pausert. "Why have they just run off and left us to deal with this?"

Hantis shook her head. "They haven't. But they have to be very careful. The Nanite plague feeds on and uses klatha energy. Klatha energies are also the only way to fight them. That makes Karres and her witches the greatest danger in human space to the Nanites. They've been trying to get Karres destroyed. So Karres is preparing a number of defenses—but after the fight with the Worm World they're pretty battered."

Goth nodded. "Threbus and Maleen both kind of hinted at this. So what is it you have to do, Hantis?"

"Yes," agreed Pausert. "Why is getting you to the Empress Haile so important?"

"Because of Pul."

"Pul? Him?" Captain Pausert looked at the blue-furred animal with its impressive mouthful of teeth.

Hantis patted the grik-dog affectionately. "Yes. Grik-dogs were bred to smell out Nanite exudates. Pul here can tell if someone has been infested. No Nartheby Sprite would ever consider leaving home without one."

"And I can tell you that ISS agent from the Imperial cruiser had been invaded and taken over," growled Pul. "It was all I could do not to bite him."

"Grik-dog fangs can inject a venom that kills Nanites. Unfortunately it kills the host too, and also takes quite a long time." Hantis looked even sadder.

"Which means that anyone who is infected can't be saved." Pausert felt very cold, suddenly.

"The Empress Haile is going on her procession through her territories and dependencies soon. We've learned—suspect, at least—that there is a Nanite plot designed to reach fruition when she returns to the Imperial Capital. It is essential that Pul and I get there before then. Unfortunately, the Nanites have obviously taken over some of our own agents. They know who I am and where we are going. They will stop at nothing to prevent us from getting there."

CHAPTER 4

"Captain, that fleet is still following us," said Vezzarn worriedly. "They'd be out of detector range if you hadn't had that new stuff fitted on Uldune."

Captain Pausert looked at the small blips on the detector screen. One large and fifteen smaller spots of light, traveling in formation. The fleet was still outside the range of the visual screens. He wished he could see them.

"Let's try stepping up the power—slowly, so it isn't obvious— and changing vector slightly. This is the most direct route to the Sheris system. It is possible that they aren't actually following us . . . I suppose."

Two hours later they were able to say for certain the fleet was following them. Moreover, the fleet could also follow them despite their slow increase in speed to the *Venture*'s maximum.

"I don't like it, Goth. I think you and the Leewit should get ready to use the Sheewash Drive," said Pausert finally. Getting rid of their followers was worth the risk.

Goth nodded. "Good idea, Captain. Let's lose them while we can. I'll go and get the Leewit."

"And I am going back to my cabin," announced Vezzarn. Witch-stuff made the old spacer nervous. If it couldn't be explained in terms of space-time physics, he wanted to be elsewhere when it was happening,

A few minutes later, a globe of orange fire danced above some twisted black wires in the control cabin. Outside, the viewscreens showed that space suddenly blurred. Captain Pausert eyed the process with interest. During the *Venture*'s last voyage, Vezzarn, Hulik do Eldel and Laes Yango—who had also gone by the name of "the Agandar" and had commanded a fleet of pirates that were fast becoming a navy—had all wanted to steal the Sheewash Drive. They had all thought that it was something technological, and could be stolen. What they hadn't known was that it didn't work without a witch; all they had known was that it was really, really fast.

The Sheewash Drive wasn't something Pausert had mastered yet and with klatha powers you had to be ready . . . or you could get hurt. You could even be killed—or, as one witch had said, darkly, "worse." Pausert wasn't prepared to contemplate what "worse" could mean, though sometimes he had uneasy images of being turned inside-out for trying. But the pattern of the Sheewash seemed to be almost in his grasp. The two witch sisters kept it up for about a minute, but that would be enough to make the *Venture* disappear from tracking screens. As the wire collapsed and the globe of orange fire winked out of existence, the captain was already setting another course-vector and pulling the engines back to normal cruising speeds. This detour would avoid their next scheduled stop, the Sheris system, and take them on a rather odd tangent to the Alpha Dendi stars instead. That was quite a dense cluster which ships in a hurry avoided. There was a lot of intersolar dust there, and that would make visual tracking difficult. Captain Pausert relaxed, and went to fix the two young witches some food. Using klatha energies, especially for something as powerful as the Sheewash Drive, left the young witches exhausted and starving. So it had to be used judiciously. Neither Goth nor the Leewit could do the Sheewash Drive again too soon.

It was two days later, just as they were entering the first of the dust-veils around the Alpha Dendi cluster, when Hulik do Eldel paged the captain. He got up, and, still sleepy, headed into the control room.

"Vezzarn told me about our followers, Captain." She pointed an elegant finger at the detector-screen. There was one large and fifteen smaller blips, in the same formation. "Looks like they're still behind us."

Pausert blinked at them. This was only a couple of hours into his sleep period, and he wasn't at his brightest. It certainly looked like the same pattern. But how could the Imperials possibly have caught up with them, or even followed them at all?

"Shall I try hailing them, Captain?"

Pausert shrugged tiredly and flopped into the command chair. "It can't do any harm, I suppose. But I don't think they're chasing after us to buy Councilor Rapport's tinklewood fishing-poles."

There was no response on the Empire general beam-length, but as Hulik flicked the dials, they picked up a jabber of some unknown language. "Ship-to-ship communication over there, I think," said Hulik. "They've obviously forgotten to switch over to narrow beam."

Pausert had already hit the ship's intercom.

"What is it, Captain?"

"Goth, we need the Leewit's translation skills down here. Fast. We've got ships on our tail and they're talking to each other on broad-beam."

"We're coming."

"I'm recording, Captain," said Hulik. "Also trying to get visuals, but they're at long range."

Goth and the Leewit tumbled into the control room. The Leewit, besides her equipment-shattering whistles, was also a klatha-translator. She could instantly translate any language, even robot and machine tongues.

She started immediately. "They say . . . tubes overhot. This pace very much longer cannot be kept to."

She paused, before continuing. Obviously, only the communication officer of the ship in trouble with its tubes had forgotten to set his equipment to narrow beam. They were only getting half the conversation. "The one who spoke earlier says it matters not. If their tubes blow they will get none of the Agandar's loot anyway."

She paused again. "Oh! He says he hopes . . . *Beelzit* . . . I'm not going to translate that. Filthy mind! Should wash his mouth out with soap." She reached for the transmitter-switch, without a doubt, to give the com-officer a lesson.

Hastily, Captain Pausert slapped his hand over it. "Easy now. Let's save it. They don't know we know their ship-channel. That could be useful."

The Leewit scowled at him. "S'pose so," she said reluctantly. "But I was looking forward to it. That was really filthy."

Hulik shook her head in amazement. "The Agandar's loot! But . . . *what* loot, Captain? Did he leave anything on the ship?"

Pausert tried to think. "Well, there was his personal gear, and the crate the Sheem robot was in. We dumped the crate. I think his gear is stashed in the corner of the hold, with a few bales of unsold cargo. I've got a few of those educational toys, some tinklewood fishing poles and those allweather cloaks left over from the cargo I loaded on Nikkeldepain."

He saw that Hulik, Goth and the Leewit were all heading for the door. "Go and look then," he said crossly. "It'll be nothing more than his clothes and toiletries. You can't hide a ton of loot in a couple of holdalls."

"He did raid the Star diamond concession on Coolum's World," pointed out Hulik.

Goth grinned at the captain. "I remember Wansing, that crook of a jeweler you rescued me from on Porlumma, talking about it. They found some top-quality stones there as big as your head."

"And if you do find them there, I'll return them to their own-ers!" he called after them, irritably. There were times that he felt at a distinct disadvantage, being an honest man. Then he rather determinedly turned to face the screens again.

The twenty or so suns in the cluster marked on the charts were never all visible at one time. Planetoids, asteroids and intersolar dust hung in gravity-whirled skeins. It was, the captain admitted, the perfect place for an ambush. He'd been planning on being well-slept and alert when they went into it, but, thanks to Hulik's call when she'd spotted the following ships and the excitement that followed with searching the Agandar's gear, he'd never gotten it.

Ha. Some treasure! No alien crowns or head-size diamonds. Toiletries and clothes, as he'd predicted. A few personal items. The most exciting thing was a pack of cards with hand-painted face-cards that the Leewit had appropriated to play with. The captain supposed that it was all right for her to do so. After all, the late Agandar still owed him for damages his war-robot had done to the ship. A pack of cards was a pretty cheap exchange.

What was worrying Pausert far more was that they'd had to cut speed here in order to dodge all the space-debris. And they'd lost sight of the Agandar's fleet. The captain had tried every dodge in the book to make sure that they weren't actually being followed, but the dust, rocks and moonlets made this a perfect place for the enemy to hunt, rather than the *Venture* to hide. The pirates had a number of ships to cover the possible routes through the lenticular cluster.

The captain had gambled on the most difficult route also being the one least likely for them to encounter an ambush. So far, he'd been right. But it was slow going, and the trip was taking a toll on the ship's crew. Even at reduced speed, they had very little time to react to obstacles. The ship simply couldn't run on automatic systems. One of the senior ship-handlers, either Vezzarn or Pausert himself, had to be there. Pausert had been teaching Goth and Hulik—even, when he could get her attention, the Leewit—but none of them were good enough yet for this kind of seat-of-your-pants flying, with all the instant decision-making it took.

On the other hand, the Leewit was bidding fair to become a superb shot with the nova guns. She seemed to have a gift for anticipation; which, considering her witch background, could actually be real precognition starting to develop.

Looking ahead, Pausert realized he might just need her gun skills. That was definitely a ship's drive registering on the detectors. Some of the Agandar's fleet must have gotten in front of them, perhaps taking a course that had less debris to avoid. A few seconds later, there was a second blip from the detector. Pausert decided he'd had enough. He was tired and angry. The *Venture* had her nova guns and more speed and maneuverability than they would expect. He held to his course.

A third set of blips appeared.

That was too much. In the maze of dust-walls and drifting asteroids and moonlets, there had to be a way of avoiding the pirates. The captain turned the *Venture*, running back the way they had come.

The detectors began squalling again. More ships, this time coming up the *Venture*'s course.

"I thought space was supposed to be empty," groused Pausert, hitting the communicator switch. "We've got bandits!"

With all the obstacles, the Sheewash Drive couldn't get them out of trouble. But using it for a few seconds could make a lot of difference to their success in evading their enemies. An opportunity, in the shape of a light-second-wide gap in the drifting debris, presented itself off to the starboard. The captain took it. The ships had all been at extreme detector range. They might still be able to lose the pursuing bandits.

"It's impossible! Wherever we go they seem to follow us, or get there before we do. It is almost as if they know our vectors and they're anticipating us."

Hulik do Eldel grimaced. "Captain, I think we must have a leech."

"A leech?"

"Imperial security hooks them onto suspicious ships, if they get a chance. I suspect these pirates must have got hold of one, and put it onto the *Venture*'s hull, somewhere. It's a simple subradio transmitter. All they have to do is follow their signal-strength indicators."

"How do we find it and get rid of it?"

"We search the outside of the ship."

Pausert chewed on his lip. "Which we can't really do, while we're running. And we can't stop running because they're nearly on top of us."

Vezzarn looked thoughtful. "I could use the spare communicator unit and a couple of directional aerials to pinpoint it, Captain. When we get the chance," he added, a bit lamely.

The communicator buzzed again. "Empire hailing frequency," commented Goth, not touching it. "Want to talk to them, Captain?"

Pausert shrugged. "Why not? We might convince them to leave us alone if we drop the Agandar's gear out of an airlock."

He clicked the communicator on. An officer in the uniform of the Imperial Space Navy appeared in the screen.

"This is ISN patrol vessel *Saraband*. You are ordered to halt and be searched."

Captain Pausert gaped at the speaker. Then recovered. "Not a chance, pirate! We're not being fooled that easily. The Empire takes a hard line on those who impersonate her officers."

Now it was the other man's turn to gape. "How dare you, sir!"

Pausert snapped the communicator off. "That told the fraud where to get off!"

"Except that was no fraud, Captain," said Hulik do Eldel wryly. "I did my Imperial Security marksmanship course with that man. He was a pompous prig then and it doesn't sound as if he's improved." She smiled. "He was a terrible shot, too."

"Let's hope that that hasn't improved either!" exclaimed the captain. "I suppose I'd better try and explain."

Balls of purple fire exploded in space to portside. "I think it's too late for that. Great Patham! Those ships ahead are also firing on us, Captain." Goth's eyes widened. "Look at the size of that thing!"

"It must be the Agandar's flagship," said Pausert, hastily programming in evasive action. "He boasted about how big it was. It's terrifying!"

The crew of the Imperial ships must have had a similar reaction. A hasty "What ship? What ship?" came over the general hailing frequency that Pausert had been about to use to call the ISN *Saraband* on.

The captain snapped his fingers. "What was that frequency that you got the ship-to-ship talk from the pirates?"

".00g53," said Hulik. "But . . ."

Pausert had already changed to it. He put a hand on the Leewit's shoulder. "Tell them it must be a trap. An ambush. That the quarry has led them into the Empire's clutches."

She nodded, seizing the microphone and began jabbering away. The captain recognized one word. *Beelzit.* She said it with great satisfaction. Pausert had the feeling that it was just as well he couldn't translate or he'd have had to go through a lot of kicking and biting to wash her mouth out with soap.

Pausert wished he'd managed a better landing. The *Venture* stood at an awkward angle on the ice-moonlet which was now following its orbit away from the combat zone. Still, things could be worse.

"Great Patham! They're clumping well giving it to each other, aren't they," said Goth in delight.

The Leewit pounded his shoulder. "See what I did!" she said proudly. It was true enough. When orders came pouring out of the Agandar's flagship, she'd added to them. In the resulting confusion, the firefight had spread between the pirates themselves, as well as between the Imperials and the pirates.

"Neat idea of yours, landing here, Captain," said Vezzarn. "It'll fool their mass-detectors anyway."

"And it'll give us a chance to suit up and go out and look for this leech." Pausert rose to his feet. "Just as soon as I know we've slipped away safely and don't need to blast off immediately."

Hulik nodded. "They certainly seem to have lost us, or lost interest in us. It could be that the leech is one of the kind that doesn't have a power-pack and relies on drawing its current from the ship. They used to use those once upon a time, but they found it meant that they could lose ships coasting on inertia. I guess I'd better suit up, too. I've placed a few leeches and I know what to look for."

"How big are they, Miss Do Eldel?"

The do Eldel made motions with her hands. "About like this,

Captain—say the size of three fists. And they're hull-metal color. They're usually put somewhere near the drive tubes, where the area is too hot to spend long looking."

"Makes sense." Pausert looked at the viewscreens and detector array. "And it appears that we have one that relies on our power, because we seem to have escaped notice. The fight is definitely moving off. We'd better suit up, take radiation meters and go hunting. It's going to be a big job, but we'd better leave . . . Vezzarn in the command chair and the Leewit on the nova guns. The rest of us can go out a-hunting."

The Leewit rubbed her hands in glee. "Hope they find us!"

Pausert didn't feel that way about it at all. There were an awful lot of ships out there.

The moonlet was made up of gray-blue water-ice imbedded with rock fragments. The surface was jagged with impact craters and tricky to walk on, being either uneven or glassy smooth with shards of sharp rock sticking up like daggers out of it. True, the suits were tough. But if someone went sliding in among those rocks— well, those rock-edges looked very sharp. The rock seemed to be volcanic glass and there was no atmosphere here to erode the splintered edges.

Pausert, Hulik and Goth, roped and suited, made their way cautiously onto the surface from the ramp. Gravity was perhaps a hundredth of ship-normal. They had to be careful not to make sudden moves or even to step too high, as they edged their way cautiously along the hull. The captain had a blaster at the ready. It wasn't likely that the planetoid would have any dangers, but the one thing humans had learned since leaving old Yarthe was that life in space took myriad forms and cropped up in the most unexpected places.

However, other than the fact that the surface was difficult to move on, with low gravity and very little friction, there were no problems. Only . . . there seemed to be a trace of vatch around. Pausert could rell it somewhere, though he couldn't say exactly where the thing was.

They searched patiently and carefully around the tubes. Suddenly the ground shuddered.

Pausert fell.

They all did, tumbling on the ice among blades of rock. The airless space above the moonlet was full of flying shards, too. Looking upwards as he spun across the ice, the captain saw to his horror that the *Venture* was toppling off her unstable landing point . . .

Towards him. He was on his back, slithering and skidding help-lessly closer. The bulk of the hull would squash him like a bug. There was a terrible, helpless inevitability about it all.

The rope linking him with Hulik and Goth suddenly went taut. Hulik and Goth, wrapped around a stone monolith, were haul-ing at it.

It was a small ice-lump moon they'd landed on. There was not much gravity here. The *Venture* was falling over in a kind of ultra-slow motion, and Hulik and Goth were exerting a terrific pull on the rope. A pull that would have dragged him on Karres or Nikkeldepain or even old Yarthe.

Here, it sent him flying. Hurtling between the stone edges, steering frantically with his feet and arms, whizzing past Goth and Hulik . . . and right up a steep ridge and into space.

The *Venture* coughed; the briefest flicker of her laterals. Vezzarn must have taken action to stop her fall. He must have desperately weighed up frying them or crushing them.

Pausert realized that his flight had had a rather unexpected consequence. He'd plucked the other two into space after him. Well, there had been pretty little holding them down on the moonlet. They were quite safe . . . except they were going one direction and the *Venture* and the moonlet and a number of asteroid fragments other directions. They'd just have to use reaction pistols to get back.

Then, with a sickening feeling, the captain realized it wasn't going to be that simple. They'd set out to walk around the *Venture*'s hull. Walk. Not spacewalk. Still, there should have been a reaction pistol at his belt.

There wasn't. Just a completely recoilless and useless blaster. And the moonlet, along with the *Venture*, was proceeding on its merry way. They were heading in the opposite direction: three tiny sparkle-figures in the vastness of space.

The vatch giggled. **What fun!**

Drifting away from them, dark against the dust veils, Captain Pausert saw three reaction pistols.

Vatches thought of the human universe as a sort of dream-game, with humans as pieces. The fun lay in challenging the pieces . . . so there had to be a solution. Besides, the little vatch seemed more inclined to mischief than anything more malicious.

Goth seized the initiative. The guns were well within her weight limit and she teleported them back.

The vatchlet squeaked indignation. **It's not supposed to be that easy!**

"Quick. Before it thinks of something else. Back to the ship."

The leech search was abandoned in their flight back to the *Venture*.

Pausert studied the screens. "It looks like our landing jarred this little moonlet a bit off-course. In a crowded zone of space like this, it only takes a tiny fraction of a degree to cause other collisions. We'd better abandon the search, because this iceball is almost bound to hit something else. I'd like to take off before that happens, and not after."

The Leewit scowled. "Captain, I was listening in to the pirates— they'd lost us, but they picked up the signal the moment that Vezzarn kicked the engines."

Hulik bit her lip. "The leech must definitely draw its power from the ship's drive, then."

Pausert shrugged. "We have to use them sometimes."

"We could use the Sheewash Drive," pointed out Goth.

"Not all the time. You and the Leewit would get too tired. And we couldn't use it very well here, anyway, in this part of space. There are too many obstacles."

"Yes, but we could hop for the edge of this cluster now. Even if they follow us, they're too far off to catch up before we get there and . . . oh-oh. Vatch."

It wasn't the little silver-eyed mischief, this time. It was a much bigger vatch, almost the size of Big Windy. Pausert wasn't surprised. The *Venture* had drawn much klatha force to her, and vatches were attracted by klatha. The captain had a feeling of big slitty eyes peering at them in delight. He hastily formed the pattern in his mind of a vatch lock, which would at least stop the creature reading his mind.

A BLOCKED ONE! AND SUCH A SITUATION, SUCH POTENTIAL!

And then . . . **Go 'way. Mine! Mine!** The tiny vatch was not amused. The words were almost glowing in Pausert's mind.

YOU ARE FAR TOO YOUNG FOR THIS GAME, PUNY ONE.

Pausert could see the tiny blackness dancing in front of the greater bulk of nothingness. **Am not! They're mine! Go 'way!**

PLAY YOUR PATHETIC GAMES ELSEWHERE. I AM GOING TO SEND THESE BACK.

The *Venture* moved, abruptly, to the center of the conflict. The hull shuddered and rang like a bell as the *Venture* took a hit.

With an effort of will, Pausert forced himself to ignore the terrifying noise, and formed his klatha hooks. He reached for the bigger vatch, hooking great lines of force into it and pinning it down.

The internal spinning maelstrom of blackness seethed. It began yowling. YAAAH. THE MONSTER! The vatch desperately strained against the bonds. The captain pulled out pieces of it, flinging them at the pirate vessels.

LET ME GO! LET ME GO, I BEG—THIS IS KILLING ME!

Pausert thought sternly at the squalling creature. *We need to be outside this cluster. Do that and you can be free.*

The *Venture* knew a moment of disturbed reality which left them sitting outside the cluster. CAN I GO? pleaded the creature. THIS HURTS, DREAM CREATURE! I HAVE DONE NOTHING TO YOU.

Yet, said Pausert. *But be gone. And don't come back!* The captain reeled in his klatha hooks and the big vatch fled.

Bravo! The little one squeaked triumphantly. **Go, you bully! And don't come back!**

The big vatch didn't pause to reply. In fact, it fled in such haste that the captain was left with a whirling black fragment of vatch stuff, still attached to the klatha hooks. Well, from previous experience, Pausert knew that this stuff could be useful. It could be set to work.

The little vatch moved towards it. The vatches could reabsorb the stuff at will, though pieces also seemed to survive outside of them.

Mine, said Pausert.

Suppose so, said the little vatch amiably. **This is fun, Big Dream Thing! The big ones always chase me away. Now I've got you all to myself!**

Pausert wondered if he should have waited just a little bit longer.

"We've got trouble still, Captain," Vezzarn said, wringing his cap in his hands. "That hit we took. Straight bad luck, sir. It damaged the outer airlock. We're losing pressure. It's a slow leak but a steady one. We'll never reach a planet with atmosphere to set down on, before we asphyxiate."

"Or before the other ships catch up with us." Goth pointed back at the cluster. "It's time for the Sheewash Drive, Captain."

Pausert could only nod.

CHAPTER 5

The two Sedmons looked at each other thoughtfully. The choice of courses available to Captain Pausert from the Alpha Dendi cluster were just too numerous. Without some sort of clue to guide the Sedmons' ship, they would have difficulty in guessing the best interception course.

If the *Venture* had made it out of the Alpha Dendi cluster . . . The signal had stopped. Then briefly, just for a second, it had registered again. There had been nothing since.

Of course, Pausert might be using the witches of Karres to move the ship. Or Pausert might really be a witch himself. When the *Venture* had come to Uldune, the Sedmons had been of the opinion that Captain Pausert and Goth were Threbus and Toll, doing an age-shift. When the agent on Green Galaine on Emris had later reported Threbus and Toll meeting Pausert and Goth, the Sedmons had realized that they had been mistaken. But it was still not clear if Pausert was a Karres witch himself or not. It seemed as if the captain was nothing more than a citizen—with a price on his head, to be sure—from a small and stuffy republic called Nikkeldepain.

But the witches could do that kind of substitution very successfully. You couldn't trust superficial appearances when dealing with them. And now the Sedmons realized they had a problem, even when they were far off.

"We'll have to go to the Alpha Dendi system. Just to check."

"It'll lose us time."

31

"Can't be helped. I think we'd better try to slow them down if they're ahead somehow. They still bank with the Daal's bank back on Uldune. We could intervene there."

"That could be a bit awkward for Pausert."

"We could set it up so that when credit checks are run, the account comes up as requiring our clearance."

"Well, that would make for a delay."

"Which is what we want, after all."

Subradio messages were sent. The Sedmons' ship turned to the Alpha Dendi cluster.

CHAPTER 6

Above the twisted, truncated cone of black wires, a ball of orange fire danced. Captain Pausert looked intently at it, wishing, not for the first time, that generating it was one of his klatha powers. But his klatha abilities had been slowly developing, growing and changing, almost as he'd needed them. Perhaps one of these days he would draw this skill from inside his mind too. Squinting with concentration, he looked at the "Sheewash Drive" on the floor between the two young Karres witches. The pattern almost made sense. Almost . . .

The wires fell inward, and the ball of fire winked out. Goth pushed back her brown fringe and blinked tiredly at him. "What's up, Captain?"

"Came to see how you were doing," said Pausert carefully. He didn't want his worry to upset them.

The Leewit scowled fiercely. "We're not! It feels like we're pushing this crate through clumping toffee."

Goth nodded. "It's not like anything we've encountered before, Captain. It's as if the *Venture* was as big as a dreadnaught. She just seems to be dragging a whole weight of klatha force."

Pausert checked the readings. "So it seems. We're doing about twice our normal drive speed, but nothing like the velocity we've gotten under the Sheewash Drive before. I wonder what's wrong."

"You aren't feeding us enough," said the Leewit grumpily. "I need breakfast."

Pausert waved at the door. "It's waiting for you."

"How is the oxygen supply holding out, Captain?" asked Goth, getting slowly to her feet. That wasn't like Goth. She was normally as lithe and springy as a jungle-miffel.

Pausert shrugged. "We've done what we can to the lock. But the seals are damaged beyond repair. They'll have to be replaced. So we have another thirty hours or so. We should make it at this rate . . . but not with a lot to spare."

The Sheewash Drive had brought them this far. Far, far from the pursuit in the crowded space of the Alpha Dendi cluster. Goth and the Leewit had taken three bursts at it, but the two little witches were exhausted. The Leewit had actually fallen asleep during the last session, which seemed to have severely sapped Goth.

But now, even if Goth and the Leewit had been in a fit state to do it, they could go no closer to planetfall without advertising the Sheewash Drive. They really didn't need to show that ability to all and sundry in this region of the spiral arm. So, despite the leaking airlock, they would have to proceed by more conventional means. Of course, that meant that those who followed by the leech's signals would be able to get on their trail again. Pausert just hoped he'd have a chance to find and detach the device on their next planetfall, on the world of Pidoon. If they could get in, do repairs, fuel up, get rid of the leech and head out before the pirates caught up with them, they'd show them all a clean pair of heels.

Pidoon was a busy trading hub, with a number of landing ports set into its rolling plains, in fierce competition with each other. The planet didn't have a lot to offer except for being conveniently on the way to everywhere, and having a good supply of raw materials for rocket-fuel manufacture. It was a sort of filling station and trading depot.

Hulik, Goth and the captain peered at the map on the screen. Hulik pointed. "If we land here at Gerota Town . . . it's just big enough to justify a single ISS operative. He or she will be a no-hoper farmed out somewhere they can't do too much harm. The major cities will have dozens of operatives, and one of the smaller places is more likely to be watched. Here we'd just have one to deal with."

"It's a popular choice for that reason, sir," Vezzarn said wryly. "I went there, twice, when . . . my former boss wanted more information on one of the smuggling routes. It's a small city, with nothing but a lot of prairie for a thousand miles all round it. The customs officials are so sleepy, they put pillows on their desks."

"Sounds good to me, eh, Goth?"

Goth wrinkled her forehead. She should have been asleep, Pausert knew. But something was plainly troubling her. "I wish we had someone who could premote," she said uneasily.

"I wish we didn't have to land at all, but we've got to." Pausert pointed at the fuel readout, which was distressingly close to empty. "I'm afraid we're quite low on choices around here."

Now he pointed to the display charts. "Within range before we run out of recyclable air . . . There's Pidoon, or there's the Dictat of Telmar—and every second person there is supposed to be a spy. Or, right on the edge of our fuel range, never mind air, Imperial sector headquarters. Pidoon does so well because this sector of space is quite empty of habitable worlds."

"What about this one?" Goth pointed to the chart and a beacon number right on the margin. It was out of their way, but within range.

The captain called up the star map. There was just one habitable world on that beacon, in among a cluster of red dwarfs and dead suns. "Vaudevillia," he read.

Hulik began to chuckle.

"What's so funny?" asked Vezzarn, who had stepped across to check some readouts.

"They were suggesting going to Vaudevillia," said Hulik, trying to smother her laughter.

Vezzarn grinned. "Your home, this Nikkeldepain place, is pretty far away, eh, Captain?"

"I threatened to run away to Vaudevillia when I was ten," said Hulik. "It's the circus-world, Captain Pausert. All the old showboats go there."

Pausert blinked. Just one of the fabulous lattice ship showboats had ever come to Nikkeldepain in his youth. He could still remember it clearly, however. It had seemed so bright and so wild and exciting compared to life on stuffy Nikkeldepain. He'd thought of running away to join the show himself. The Nikkeldepain Council had turned down the next one's landing permit. Apparently a number of councilors had lost quite a lot of money when the first one had abruptly departed.

Vezzarn grimaced. "Especially when they're broke. No port charges—because there is no proper port. Mind you, it's a bad place to try to buy fuel, Captain. Cash money only, and at a twenty-five percent premium. The fuel-sellers have had so many bad debts, they won't provide fuel on any other terms. It sounds very romantic to kids, but believe me, Captain, it's a dump. It's barely habitable. Can't even grow its own food. And it rains non-stop."

The captain looked at Goth, who was looking very speculative. "Well, we're not going there. And we don't need to tell the Leewit about this place, do we? Let's stick to Pidoon and this Gerota Town."

Goth shrugged. "I'm too tired. But it doesn't feel right."

Gerota Town was seedy and run-down. "Not the kind of place you'd want to buy a used flyer in," said Vezzarn with a sly grin.

The captain looked at the shabby sprawl of two- and three-story buildings that stretched out towards a flat horizon. "It's a whistle-stop for us. So long as the fuel is okay and we can find that leech, and do some repairs on the airlock . . . within the day we should be out of here."

They soon found out that this was not to be the case. The fuel available in Gerota Town was Empire standard. But . . .

"Captain Pausert, could you please come across to our offices?" asked the elegantly coiffured, platinum-blond secretary of Pidoon Fuels and Lubricants. There was a faint furrow between her brows, and her tone was quite unlike her earlier obsequious one.

Goth looked tiredly at the captain and rubbed her nose tip. "Feels like trouble, Captain."

"Probably papers that need filling in."

"I don't think so," said Goth, rubbing her eyes now. "I'll go with you."

"You're exhausted. I'll take the Leewit. She slept the last bit."

Goth nodded.

Ten minutes later, Captain Pausert and his tow-headed "niece" walked towards the cluster of offices at Port Control. Above them, the sky was a cloudless and chilly blue. Their reception in the offices of Pidoon Fuels and Lubricants was even colder.

The secretary ushered them in to a sumptuous office. From behind the flamewood desk a man with a baggy face glowered at them. He didn't bother to stand up. "Captain Pausert, there seems to be some problem with your banking account."

Pausert leaned over the half-acre of flamewood desk. "I happen to know that account is at least a half million maels in

the black, sir. If you don't want our business, we'll take it elsewhere."

"Not on Pidoon you won't," said the jowl-faced executive, grimly.
"We've already put out a credit warning to the other companies,
in case you took off and put in a landing elsewhere."

"But we're very solvent!"

Jowl-face leaned back in his formfit chair. It groaned quietly in
protest. "Oh, you've got the money all right. But your account is
blocked. You can't draw as much as a single mael of those ill-gotten
gains."

Pausert gaped. "Ill-gotten gains?"

"Don't try to come the innocent with us, Captain Pausert." Jowl-
face smirked triumphantly, cocking his head, hearing something
outside. It sounded suspiciously like the squeal of groundcar tires.
"The ISS informed the Pidoon police of your nefarious crimes.
We were told to delay you here as long as possible. I have elec-
tronically locked the door and I have a blaster here." He raised a
Glassite 366 from beneath the desk. "Don't even think of attempting
to escape."

There were shouts outside. "That'll be the troopers now."

The Leewit gave an earsplitting whistle, just as someone pounded
on the outer door yelling, "Open up in the name of the law!"

An entirely satisfactory shattering of glass and small electronic
components followed that whistle. Jowl-face, looking in alarm at
the trickle of dust flowing from where his blaster's trigger mechanism had been just moments before, pressed a remote door-key
frantically. Smoke curled up from the button.

"Havta break it down, Sergeant!" bellowed the voice outside.

Pausert realized just how right Goth's feelings had been. The
captain hauled the jowled executive out of his seat. "Is there another
way out?" he demanded.

The man had gone from unpleasant triumph to quivering terror, since he'd discovered that he was trapped—and now dis-
armed—in here with the two of them. He had a lot of jaw to
tremble. It made his speech unintelligible, but they could follow
the shaking pointed finger to the door beside the cabinets. While
the shoulders of Pidoon's finest pounded against the manager's
office door, Pausert and the Leewit crammed their way out of the
bathroom window.

It was only after the captain had landed awkwardly on his
feet that he realized that the Leewit wasn't whistling or calling a warning because she was too busy biting an oversized

uniformed man's hand. And there were ten more of them in the alleyway.

Bruised, with a swelling eye and a bloody nose, gagged and with his hands forcecuffed, the captain sat between two huge guards in the back of the groundcar. He'd seen the Leewit, similarly gagged and forcecuffed, dragged kicking into the second vehicle. They seemed to be heading out across the landing field back towards the *Venture*.

The two vehicles pulled up beside the *Venture*, along with a third transporter which was painted in the colors of the Imperial Customs and Immigration inspectorate. One seldom had trouble with them deep inside the Empire, but their orange-and-gray vehicles always inspired caution.

The Pidoon troopers threw open the doors of the groundcars and pushed the prisoners out. "March them in front of us," snapped the customs official. "The Agandar's accomplices are desperate men, but they're not likely to shoot his chief lieutenant."

Clearly, Imperial Interservice Security had woven quite a net of lies around them. The Leewit's eyes were as wide with outrage as Pausert felt his mouth would like to be, if he hadn't been gagged. He noticed that the troopers, while making the Leewit into a very small human shield, were being extremely careful to keep their shins away from her.

Obviously, someone in the *Venture* was watching. The damaged airlock opened.

"That's spacegun damage," said one of the customs men, pointing to the ragged burn in the hull-metal. "This is the ship we're after, all right!"

They paused, waiting for the ramp to finish extending. "Better keep her out here," snapped one official, pointing at the Leewit. "We don't want to end up as captives and hostages on their ship."

The Leewit managed to kick two of the policemen and very nearly squirmed free. But she was pushed back into one of the groundcars, and Pausert had to continue into the *Venture* without her.

They were met by Goth, Hulik and Vezzarn. The captain's heart fell when he saw Goth. He'd been hoping she'd have hidden in no-shape.

"What is going on, sirs?" asked Hulik.

"We're acting on information received," said the customs official who seemed to be in charge. "Seize them. We need to conduct a thorough search for the other two."

"You can't do this!" protested Hulik. "We have rights! And this ship is acting under charter from the Empress Hailie!"

The official tapped the folder under his arm. "Your little fraud has gone on long enough. We have information that this ship was involved in setting up an ambush of an Imperial patrol in the Alpha Dendi system, as part of the pirate fleet of the infamous Agandar."

"Honest, officer, we had nothing to do with that," said Vezzarn. "It was an accident. We were just caught up in the middle of it and got our ship damaged. Look at our crew, sir. No desperados. A couple of children, a young woman and me. I'm just an old spacer, sirs. Not a pirate."

"Shut your gab," snapped the official. "Forcecuff these people's hands and search the ship. Bring them with us. I want to observe them closely for any possible reactions. I want every conceivable place searched and all personnel seized."

The customs man, in his orange-and-gray uniform, saluted smartly as his men hastily grabbed Goth, Vezzarn, and Hulik do Eldel. "Yessir! This will put Gerota Town on the map! This is our lucky day!"

Captain Pausert's heart sank closer to his boots. This certainly wasn't his lucky day. No matter what shape change Goth had managed on Pul and Hantis . . . they'd be hauled out of here. If only he could talk to Goth.

They were shepherded along the *Venture*'s passages, as the customs men displayed their expertise. They inspected absolutely everything, vibro-sensors probing the walls for hidden chambers, the officers peering everywhere, even into drawers too small to hide an infant, let alone a person. At length they came to the stateroom which the Nartheby Sprite had occupied with her grik-dog. There was no sign of either Hantis or Pul. But the customs men began with searching under the beds, chairs and cupboards.

Something, the captain felt, was odd about this room.

It was only when he glanced upwards that he realized what it was. The elegant central light-fittings were off-center. The room was not quite the right shape! Goth must be creating an illusionary bulkhead. Pausert did his level best not to look at the wall. But what would it help? Goth's illusions could fool the eye, but the vibro-sensors in the custom inspectors' hands would see right through them, so to speak.

The inspectors began on the first wall.

When they reached the end of it, Pausert saw Goth calmly nudge Hulik. The do Eldel stepped with all her weight on one spike-heeled foot . . . onto the toes of the obnoxious customs officer.

Hulik do Eldel was a slimly built aristocratic-looking woman. It was still a lot of weight to concentrate on one small square half-inch of heel.

"Yow!" The customs officer yelled and pushed her off.

Hulik's look of surprise and her apology were masterful. "I am so sorry, sir! It's these heels. I was just getting ready to disembark, and after wearing ship boots for weeks . . . I just lost my balance. I really am sorry. I do hope your foot is all right?" With a per-formance like that, if Hulik had actually run away to that show-boat planet, she'd have been the queen of the galactic stage by now.

Naturally all the customs officials and police officers had turned to look. Facing as he was, Pausert had to keep a poker-face as the wall they'd been about examine . . . appeared to slide around to the wall that they had just finished with.

"You did that on purpose!" grumbled the customs officer, massaging his foot through his polished shoe. "You won't distract us! Check that next wall carefully."

They did. Very carefully. Eventually they finished and began on the next. And to his absolute horror, Captain Pausert began to rell vatch.

Little silver slit-eyes and vatch laughter.

Troubles never came singly.

He could see Goth knew about it, too.

The illusionary bulkhead began to develop a window. None of the customs officials were looking at it just then, concentrating their attentions on the opposite wall. But they would be sure to turn any moment now. And the window in the illusion revealed the startled face of Hantis, with Pul in her arms. It was a charming cottage window complete with leaded diamond panes and lace trimmed chintz curtains, neatly framing the fugitives' faces.

As Captain Pausert stared, unable to tear his eyes away, two things happened. First, he felt the forcecuffs on his wrists vanish. The field that had held them disappeared, and the small metal force-generator fell to the floor. And, second, looking at the window that the mischievous little vatch had created—all Pausert saw, briefly, were the Nartheby Sprite's elegant boots, moving rapidly upwards and out of view.

Plainly the little vatch thought it would have some fun with the captain trying to fight his way free, before the Imperial customs officials saw the "window" it had created in Goth's light-shift illusion.

Well, he wouldn't do what the vatch expected. And it looked as if the Nartheby Sprite had helped him to avoid having to do so. She obviously had klatha skills of her own. Or had Goth lifted her with her teleportation skill? No. Goth could manage objects of a few pounds in weight, but despite her delicate elfin appearance the Nartheby Sprite must weigh far more.

Pausert hastily concentrated on finding the vatch. He couldn't catch or control this little one with his klatha hooks, but it did seem that he could tickle and distract it.

His resistance to taking the course that the little vatch had tried to trick him into had saved them from a fight. It had also caused one of the customs officials to squint at the fading window. It was a good thing the official couldn't hear the vatchlet giggling and squeaking. **Stop it, Big Dream Thing!**

The man rubbed his eyes, and then very deliberately turned away shaking his head. Pausert went on "tickling" furiously. The last thing they needed now was more complications. With any luck, the vatch would go away. Pausert was so intent on tickling that he had to be herded out of the room by his captors, who weren't gentle about it. But he had his reward. The relling of vatch presence grew fainter and then vanished.

The search went on, relentlessly. The customs men got very excited about the big safe, and the secret compartment in the engine room. And became very disappointed when both proved absolutely empty of people. They did confiscate the Totisystem Toy inside it. It was a very badly designed educational toy, which Pausert and Goth had fitted there in the vain hope of fooling spies. The spies who had tried to steal the spacedrive for the Empire or the Agandar's pirates had not been taken in.

The customs officials, however, were more gullible.

Pausert grinned through his gag. If he hadn't been so mad at Gerota Town customs men, he would have felt sorry for them. He just hoped that the Totisystem Toy didn't explode on them, as the rather fiendish educational device was inclined to do. The toy was another one of the odd unsellable items that his one-time about-to-be father-in-law, Councilor Onswud, had dumped on Pausert in lieu of a decent cargo. Looking back, Pausert could see that he'd been set up to fail. Well, he'd succeeded, beyond their wildest dreams—and gotten lucky, too. He could have ended up married to the insipid Illyla. Instead she'd married Councilor Rapport while he was away. That was real luck, although it hadn't seemed like it at the time.

But right now, in the back of a smelly paddy wagon bouncing over the cobbles towards what would doubtless be an even smellier jail, Pausert didn't feel all that lucky. Hantis and Pul were still hidden on the ship, but the rest of them were being taken away from the *Venture*. And Pausert still hadn't had a chance to talk to Goth. Maybe they'd put them all into one cell together and . . .

Nobody had noticed yet that his hands weren't forcecuffed. That wasn't too surprising, since forcecuffs just didn't fall off. Pausert wondered if he could gain any advantage from his free hands, but it didn't seem so. The others had been transported together, but he was apparently considered more dangerous. He had a transport all to himself. It seemed unfair. It was hardly his fault that the Leewit had somehow got her guards to take her gag off. The destruction that she'd caused with her whistles had wrecked the groundcar, and had meant that the customs officers had had to call for another.

The captain's gag was only taken off after he had been transported from the jail to the courthouse. The judge wasn't particularly interested in hearing their side of the story, but the prisoners had to answer when their names were read onto the record.

"Ungag him, officer," ordered the judge. He was a lean man whose face seemed to have been colonized by a rampaging tribe of thick black eyebrows. The eyebrows crawled together and the judge peered at Pausert. "Now. Have you been correctly identified?"

This judge looked very different from the one who had soaked him for the release of Maleen, Goth's sister, in what seemed another lifetime. "Yes, Your Honor. But those charges are a pack of trumped-up lies."

The judge's heavy eyebrows seemed to twitch upwards of their own accord. "When I wish to hear from you, Captain Pausert, I will ask you to speak. Be silent or be silenced."

He peered more closely. "Why is this man not forcecuffed?"

It was some time later, and after some consternation in the court, that the judge cleared his throat. "Ahem. Now let us consider the first of the charges brought against you. You've got quite a list to answer to. Call the first witness."

"Athon Laag."

The jowl-faced Laag was the local manager for Pidoon Fuels and Lubricants, when he wasn't being first witness.

"Oh, yes, Your Honor. He's a desperate rogue. I wrestled with him for vital minutes until the police Miz Snodder had called got there. Clearly he intended to commit fraud on my company, as well as his unprovoked brutal assault on an honest businessman. When he discovered the law was outside, he finally overpowered me and fled."

"Lies!" yelled Pausert. "He threatened me with a blaster and accused me of being a pirate."

The judge waved a threatening gavel at the captain. "I told you that you would be silenced, and if you speak without permission again you will be, Captain. Continue, Laag. How did you decide he was attempting to commit fraud?"

The self-proclaimed honest businessman continued, after a fearful look at the captain. "His credit statement, your honor. His account has been blocked. He has an account with the Daal's Bank on Uldune. The one-time pirate-world, Your Honor. "

The judge steepled his fingers. "I am aware of Uldune's unsavory history."

Laag nodded. "Well, when we got the order for fuel and the banking details, we sent a notification to ISS headquarters in Pidoon City. It's routine. Imperial Security looks carefully at money coming from that source."

The judge snorted. "Hardly surprising."

"Yes, Your Honor," nodded Laag. "We got a call from them about three minutes later, revealing that that man"—he pointed to Pausert—"was one of the notorious Agandar's closest associates. We were asked to delay them as much as possible, as it was believed that he had two wanted and dangerous assassins on board his ship."

The judge's caterpillarlike eyebrows did a rapid crawl inward and out again. "Bankrupt, charged with assault, attempted fraud, consorting with criminals. Well, Captain Pausert? Now you may speak."

Captain Pausert didn't think it would help him much. "Your Honor, I am not one of the Agandar's associates. In fact we are being pursued by his fleet, because we were responsible for his death! You can confirm that with the Governor of Green Galaine province on Emris."

The prosecutor stood up, waving a piece of paper. "Your Honor, we have here a transcript of a report from Captain Benit of the Imperial Space Navy Cruiser *Saraband*. It states clearly that one

Captain Pausert of a ship identified as the one now on Gerota Town landing field, did not only refuse to halt, but decoyed them into a pirate ambush."

The judge looked sternly at the captain. "Did you or did you not disobey a lawful order from an Imperial Navy vessel to halt?"

"Yes, but . . ."

Pausert was right. Being allowed to talk wasn't helping much at all. Within twenty minutes he was being herded away to start his fifty-five-year sentence. The extra three years that he'd gotten for the injury of a customs official, because of the Totisystem Toy's self-destruction, was merely the most unfair of a number of injustices. He wondered what they'd do to the others, and just how they could get out of this mess. He had noticed that Hulik do Eldel wasn't with the others in the holding pen at the back of the courtroom. But he'd had no chance to find out why, or even to exchange a word with them.

The captain explored his cell very carefully. That used up half a minute. Only fifty-four years, eleven months, thirty days, twenty-three hours, fifty-nine minutes and some change to go . . .

After that, he alternated between pacing, staring at the bars while sitting on the bed, and staring at the bars while standing up. It went well with his mental state, which alternated between fuming about how they'd been caught, worrying about the others, worrying about their mission, and worrying about Hantis and Pul, left sitting inside the *Venture*.

His worrying was interrupted by the click of heels coming down the concrete floor of the passage. With any luck it would be some food, and maybe a chance to ask the jailor about the others.

"Good evening, Captain."

Captain Pausert sat down on the bed, gaping at Hulik do Eldel in a freshly pressed ISS uniform.

"You! You . . . you . . ."

"Traitor?" she supplied. "Turncoat?" She casually flicked a folded piece of paper into his cell. "I suggest you keep your temper and cooperate with me."

Was that the flicker of a wink? What was going on?

"I think 'rat' was the word I was looking for," said the captain grimly. "And, as for cooperate! Great Patham's seventh hell! I'll see you rot first, do Eldel."

She smiled coolly. "Come now, Captain Pausert, mind your temper and your language. You're the one who will rot in here—

unless you cooperate. We want the two alien passengers you have hidden on the *Venture*. You are going to tell us, Captain. You or one of the others."

Now the captain was sure that it had been a wink! Hulik had known where the Nartheby Sprite and the grik-dog had been hiding.

Well, if Hulik wanted him to play along he'd do his best. He shook the bars furiously. "What have you done with the others, you devils! Where are my nieces? You know that these are ridiculous trumped-up charges! You know we should be back on our ship and on our way. When word of this gets back to the Empress Hailie, heads are going to roll. Even heads within the ISS!"

Hulik curled her lip, disdainfully. "Your threats, while you and your companions are behind bars, are not exactly terrifying, Captain. I'll leave you with the thought that you are a bankrupt prisoner, unable to pay landing fees, and your ship has been impounded. If it is not redeemed within thirty-six hours, it'll be towed out into space and used as a target hulk by the Imperial Space Navy. Even if we can't find the villains we're looking for, we'll destroy them along with their hiding place. Think about that for a while. I'll be back in an hour or so to see if you've decided to cooperate."

She turned and left, and Captain Pausert went on clinging to the bars. It was a good thing he'd been holding on when she'd told him about the *Venture*. That had helped to keep him on his feet. Did their troubles only ever seem to get worse? It took him a few minutes to let go of the bars and remember the tiny piece of folded paper Hulik had flicked so casually into his cell. He walked over towards it, pretended to stumble and picked it up.

Lying on his bed, with the paper hidden in a flap of his gray prison blanket and masked by the lumpy pillow, Captain Pausert read: *You are under constant observation by a spy ray.* That didn't surprise him. But could he really trust her? She was apparently an agent of Imperial Security, after all. How else could she have gotten her liberty restored?

The next line of the tiny message was more startling. *V and I will be coming for you at midnight. Be ready. Destroy this.*

V? Vezzarn? But the little spacer had been with the other prisoners. Hulik had plainly talked her way free, but Vezzarn was sure to be imprisoned.

Well. He could only wait and see.

✳   ✳   ✳

It was a long wait. He got a bowl of prison stew, which he ate, even though the gray chewy lumps weren't very appetizing and the wooden spoon looked as if might give him a dangerous disease. It still tasted better than the piece of paper he'd swallowed earlier.

"Yum, yum!" he said to the jailor. He got no more reply to that than he'd gotten to his query about the others. If the man could talk, he certainly showed no interest in doing so.

Later, Hulik came back with another ISS agent. By his flat nasal accent he was a local man, and this was plainly the biggest thing that had ever happened in his career. He cracked his outsize knuckles, while attempting an intimidating stare. "You *will* tell us where they're hidden!" he yelled abruptly.

"Your customs men searched my ship from stem to stern," said Pausert. "There is nothing and no one hidden on it."

"Lieutenant do Eldel, get me the keys for this cell. I'm going to beat it out of him."

The captain looked at the ISS agent. The fellow was big, but he was definitely pudgy. Maybe now would be good time to depart from this cell, especially if Hulik was ready to help. Pausert put his hands on his hips. "You and which army?"

Hulik hadn't moved. "Lieutenant do Eldel!" snapped the ISS man.

"Yes, District Officer?" Hulik asked, cocking her head in polite enquiry.

He held out his hand. "The cell key."

"Sir, we know that the officer commanding in Pidoon City has sent an aircraft to fetch this man. It's a long flight but they'll be here by three A.M., and they'll be questioning him."

"I know that!" snapped local officer in annoyance. "But *I* want to get the answers."

"I advise against it, sir. The Agandar's lieutenant is a notorious killer, reputed to be very skilled at unarmed combat. I believe he is trying to provoke you into going into his cell."

The local ISS man snatched back the hand he'd been holding out for the key, as if it had been burned. He tried to look nonchalant, and only succeeded in looking foolish. "Humph. Consider yourself lucky," he told Pausert. "Or unlucky. The fellows from headquarters will bring tools that will make you sing, all right."

They left, and the evening wore on.

There were no lights in the cell, and the passage lights had long been switched off. Pausert had nothing by which to judge the passage of time. They'd confiscated his chronometer along with

his belt and his boots. Time did seem to be passing exception-
ally slowly. Pausert became increasingly convinced that Hulik had
either been caught or hadn't been able to come. Once the ISS men
came to take him to their headquarters, escape would be even more
difficult and he'd be a long way from the *Venture*.

And then he began to rell vatch. Like the sound of a scent, like
the smell of music.

You're in trouble again, Big Dream Thing. The familiar little
silver-eyed vatch seemed quite delighted.

Pausert was desperate enough even to be pleased to see it. *You
don't know where the others are, do you?* he thought at the vatchlet.

**They're in a cell in the next passage. They asked me where you
were!** The vatch apparently found this quite funny. **Even the little
one asked nicely. You're not going to tickle me again, are you?**

Can you get me out of here?

Yes, but I can't stay. And I want to watch!

*Please? I chased the big one for you, didn't I? And they're com-
ing to take me away. I won't be able to save Hantis and Pul, or my
ship if they take me off to Pidoon City. That would finish your fun.*

The little slitty quicksilver eyes considered him. **Oh, all right.
If you give me that piece of vatch stuff you took from the big
one. It's not doing well on its own.**

Pausert had forgotten about the fragment of vatch stuff. The
tiny piece of blackness was still there, in his pocket. A black fragment of nothingness was not something that the warders who had
confiscated the rest of his property would have seen. Or been able
to move or touch. *I'll lend it to you.*

'Kay.

The vatch took it. The silvery-eyed little thing grew a tiny fraction.

Have fun, Big Dream Thing. I'll see you later. And the vatch
was gone to wherever small vatches went.

He was about to curse it for a rotten cheat, when the lock on
the cell door clicked open.

Captain Pausert was free—and on his own in the darkened
passages of Gerota Town prison. Free, without boots, belt or any
real idea of where to go. He stood in the passage, listening, straining
his ears for the sound of patrolling warders. Instead he heard,
faintly, the Leewit's voice. When she was yelling like that, faintly
and far-off was the best way to hear it. But the sound still cheered
the captain immensely. He set off to see if he could find them.

CHAPTER 7

Pausert found himself blessing the Leewit. Her voice was very easy to follow—and the passages were dark. He also found himself cursing the loss of his boots. He'd been very proud of those boots. They'd come from the hands of Mister Hildo of Hildo and Naugaf, Nikkeldepain's finest cobblers, back in the days when it had seemed he was going to be the first of Nikkeldepain's miffel-fur millionaires. Right now what he missed most about them was the fact that they protected his feet. Not only was the concrete floor of the jail-block brutally cold, but he had stubbed his toes a couple of times already.

Bare feet did make him walk a lot more quietly than the jailor who was also heading down the passage, which was still echoing with the Leewit's voice. "If you don't shut up, you'll get no food in the morning!" threatened the jailor angrily. When he reached the Leewit's cell, he rapped on the bars of the cell with his nightstick, as he shone his torch around the cell. "Some of us are trying to sleep!"

The Leewit blew him a magnificent raspberry. The warder was lucky. At least she didn't whistle *at* him. And she did shut up. Pausert knew the Leewit too well by now to believe that was likely to be without reason. So he shrank back into the shadows and waited for the warder to head back towards the desk he had been sleeping at.

He was dead right. The man had hardly been gone a minute

when the captain heard a clink of keys and Goth's whisper. "Here. You try. The door only unlocks from outside and your hands are smaller than mine. You'll have to reach through the bars."

He walked quietly over to the cell door. "Let me help you. It'll be easier from this side," he whispered.

"Captain!" both girls squeaked.

"Hush. We don't want the guard coming back here now that you have teleported his keys, do we?" Pausert took the key from the Leewit and opened the door.

The girls piled out of the cell. "Knew you were coming," said Goth, gruffly, squeezing his arm.

"Do either of you have any idea of the time?"

"No," said Goth. "They took our watches before they put us in the cell. I thought it must be pretty late, so we got the Leewit to call the guard."

"They took mine, too." Pausert worried a little that he might have misestimated the time. "Did Hulik come to see you?"

"Yeah. With that creep of a local ISS officer friend of hers. She'd better hope we never catch up with her," said the Leewit nastily.

"It's not as simple as all that," said the captain. "I'm not too sure what game she's playing. She was supposed to come and let us out at midnight. The ISS have sent their agents from the capital of this mudball to come and fetch us. They should be here around about three in the morning."

"We'd better get out of here then, Captain," said Goth decisively. "It's got to be well after midnight by now."

"I suppose so. I'm inclined to trust her, myself, but . . . there are so many things that could have gone wrong. I reckon we should head for the old *Venture*. They're planning to use her as a target hulk. Leaky airlock, low fuel or not, I think we'd better run. Are you two rested enough to do the Sheewash Drive again?"

"Yep. Count on us. It's a pity you can't help, Captain. You're a hot witch."

"Believe me," said Pausert, "you can't want me to do it any more than I do. I feel as if I'm almost getting it."

"You can try too hard with klatha stuff," said Goth sternly. "Sometimes it comes when you need it, rather than when you want it."

That sounded like her mother Toll's pattern talking, rather than Goth herself. The young Karres-born witches had a guiding "pattern," a nonmaterial partial replica of the personality of an adult similar in nature to help and steer them. The instructor resident in their minds took a hand when they were ready to learn new klatha skills. Captain Pausert wished that he also had one. But he simply had to muddle along on his own. And some of the klatha manipulation was dangerous, if you got it wrong. It could dismind you or burn you up. Make you burst into flames and combust yourself.

"Do you have any idea what happened to Vezzarn?" asked the captain, changing the subject back to their immediate problem. "I think Hulik meant to bring him along with her. He could know more about what is going on."

"He got a twelve year sentence for aiding and abetting dangerous criminals," said the Leewit, seeming to relish the words. "That's us, you know. He was put into a cell about three down."

But when they got there, the cell was empty, the door just ajar. There was a pillow and a rolled-up blanket under the covers, roughly shaped like a man. But of the little old spacer there was no sign.

"Well, I guess we'd better get going without him," said Goth. "Who knows. He might be back on the *Venture* already."

"Or trying to spring us," said Pausert.

"Nope. He knew where we were, just as well as we knew where he was," said the Leewit. "I guess he decided to rat."

Pausert couldn't help thinking that when the Agandar and his Sheem war-robot had been hunting them, Vezzarn had decided to betray them. The little man had seemed genuinely remorseful and reformed afterwards, but it did indicate the potential for that kind of behavior. "Maybe he did. Either way, we haven't got the time to go and look for him. Let's see if we can find our way out before the ISS agents arrive to find us gone."

Moving quietly through the corridors, they tried to find their way out, without awakening any warders. After a while they came to double metal swing-doors. In the dim light of various indicator globes, Pausert surveyed what could only be the prison kitchens—a gloomy hall of square-edged shadows and great cauldrons—smelling of grease and old boiled greens . . . and full of things that skittered and chittered from the dark corners. He began regretting that he hadn't stuck to just eating Hulik's piece of paper. "I suppose there might be a back door," he whispered. He could just make out Goth's nod.

The first door proved merely to be a coldroom. But the next door they came to was invitingly ajar. A cool night breeze licked into the smelly kitchen. Pausert peeped around the door. It opened into a shadowy little courtyard full of garbage cans. That the air from out there could smell sweet, spoke ill of the prison kitchen. True, the courtyard would probably be locked. But with the girls' klatha powers they should manage to get through them. Hopefully.

They crept out, the captain waiting for a powerful searchlight and the howl of sirens with each wary step. It never came.

And the heavily chained gate was ... open. Someone had sheered the links of the chain. The cut links gleamed in the wan moonlight. Hulik must have prepared this. . . .

He swung the gate open just wide enough for them to slip out.

Too late, Pausert smelled a huge rat, even above the garbage stench. But as he realized that something was wrong, the waiting men had already dropped a paralyzer web over them. Someone was also standing by with a hypodermic darter.

The captain was just aware of being hastily loaded into a groundcar, like a sack of meal, before oblivion took him.

Hulik do Eldel fumed. Her cover as a loyal ISS agent was blown now, and all for the want of a few minutes. She looked at the unconscious body of the ISS district officer. Well, she had had to do it. He'd have raised the alarm for certain. She'd better get down there, find Captain Pausert and get him, Vezzarn, Goth and the Leewit into the ISS van she planned to take them to the spaceport in.

She glanced up at the monitors from the spy-eyes . . . and realized that it wasn't going to be quite that simple. The infrared showed the girls trying to unlock their cell. Hastily she turned the sound gain on that spy circuit back up. The Leewit's shrieks had persuaded Officer Jayelo to turn the sound off, and stopped him noticing the captain's breakout until it was too late. She was just in time to hear Captain Pausert say: "I'm not too sure what game she's playing. She was supposed to come and let us out at midnight . . ."

Hulik took a deep breath. It was still ten minutes short of that. She listened further. Well, she'd just have to find them at Vezzarn's cell. Opening that would hold them up a bit.

But when she got there, they'd already left. Hulik was left to play a silent kind of hide and go seek with them, trying to guess where they might have gone.

She was dismayed to find the prison warders at the central desk . . .

Dead.

For a moment she was horrified that Pausert could have been so brutally efficient. It wasn't as if the warders of this sleepy little prison, in this sleepy little town, on this sleepy little planet, had posed any real threat. Then she realized that someone had blasted the far door. The remains of it showed unmistakable blaster burns. A Mark 20 cannon, to judge by the damage.

Where would the captain have got a military-grade blaster cannon from? Was this Karres witchcraft?

Or was this something else? Or maybe . . . *someone* else. Not bothering about quietness now, Hulik ran down the passage, her own issue blaster in her hand.

As she went into the kitchen she heard a strangled yell from outside. That was Goth's voice . . .

She was just in time to see a black groundcar speed away from the forced gates. She took aim, bracing her arm.

"Don't shoot!" hissed Vezzarn from the wall-top.

She nearly shot him instead.

He dropped down onto the dustbins, and into the courtyard. "Phew. That was close!"

"I'd have stopped the vehicle at least, if you hadn't interfered!" snapped Hulik. "How are we going to track them now? Great Patham! I had it all organized and then the captain broke out ten minutes early."

Vezzarn pointed. "There was a second vehicle in the alley. If you had fired, they'd have got you. This was very professional, Hulik. They've been monitoring the cells with a spy ray."

Hulik shook her head. "That was us, Vezzarn. The local ISS man and myself."

Vezzarn gave her a crooked little grin. "I took my tools in with me, Hulik. Imperial Security on these backwater planets is pretty sloppy. There was more than one spy ray being worked. I mirrored it out of my cell, before I went to work on the lock, and then I was just doing a little pathfinding snoop when the guys with the heavy artillery broke in. I was really worried at first, until I overheard them saying that they needed all of them alive."

"Well, that's a relief."

"Alive for now, anyway. Once they get what they want out of the captain there will be no point in keeping him. Or the little girls."

Hulik took a deep breath. "We'd better get hunting then, Vezzarn. If you're coming?"

The little wizened old man nodded. "I still owe the captain. Besides, we're free for now, but this planet isn't big enough for us to hide from the kind of trouble we've ended up in, Hulik. If these guys'll break into the jail and kill warders, they'll hunt us down and kill us sooner or later."

Hulik holstered the issue blaster. "And the ISS agents from Pidoon City will be here soon. They'll make it even hotter."

Vezzarn stretched his short legs to match her stride. "Besides, ten to one the authorities will blame the captain—and us—for murdering the prison warders."

Hulik nodded. "I think you could bet on that at one hundred to one. So we should get off-world as fast as possible . . . which means we've got find where they've taken the captain, Goth, and the Leewit."

"I got a tracer on the spy ray. It was sending back between us and the spaceport. About a mile off. I've been here before, remember. That's Port-town. I've got a contact we can try."

Hulik do Eldel was expecting to be taken to a seedy bar, but Vezzarn's smuggler contact was not the proprietor of some portside dive. She was the very high-nosed keeper of a little gift shop, obviously aimed at propitiating the wives of long-absent spacers. Vezzarn must have given some special signal, because they were invited to look at "some special merchandise, for the discerning customer."

They stepped through the door into a second little room, with more expensive knickknacks on the crowded shelves.

"This place is about as well shielded as possible," said the lady proprietor, looking worried. "What brings you here, Illa? We haven't had any consignments moved through here for months. I haven't seen you for years." Hulik was not surprised at the assumed name Vezzarn was known by. She had several herself.

Vezzarn shrugged. "I'm on another run these days, Thora. I just need some information in a hurry."

Thora raised an eyebrow. Hulik knew that they were on dangerous ground.

"I just need to know who some people are and where to find them," said Vezzarn reassuringly. "You know I'm trusted. I won't bring any trouble to you. That would be more than my life's worth."

"Ask, then," the gift-shop proprietress said, guardedly.

Vezzarn described the groundcars that had taken part in the snatch of the captain, Goth and the Leewit.

"Fullbricht," she said. "The second vehicle is pretty distinctive. But you really don't want to find him, Illa. He runs most of the crime in this town these days. He started off as an informer for someone, but he's moved up. He's got control over several of the other small towns. You really don't want to cross him."

Vezzarn grimaced. "He's bad news, huh?"

The gift-shop proprietress pulled a face. "No. It's worse. He *wants* to be bad news. He's a small-time operator who wants to be thought big. He'll go too far one day, but at the moment he's like a kill-mad miffel. His trademark is making statues."

Hulik blinked. "Statues?"

Thora regarded her with a jaundiced eye. "That's what they're called around here. Statues . . . humans cast in ferroplast," she said dryly. "Then they get dropped into the lake."

Hulik took a deep breath. "We need to find him anyway, Thora."

The woman looked at the two of them. "Well, the fake ISS uniform might help," she conceded. "His headquarters are in the Myamosa building, but that's just the front office. The place where they do most of their business is in an old hazardous materials warehouse off Thirteenth Street."

CHAPTER 8

Pausert awoke with a stunning headache. When he tried to cradle his head in his hands . . . he very rapidly realized that a headache was the very least of his problems. He was in a barrel that came to just below head height. The barrel had been filled up to his chest with fast-setting ferroplast. The stuff was already in the thick and glutinous stage. And his hands were tied behind his back.

Inevitably, his nose began to itch.

Twitching his nose desperately, he looked around the cavernous room. The twitching did nothing to alleviate the irritation of his nasal membranes. He realized that the sensation wasn't entirely psychological. The smell in here would make any self-respecting nose itch. The air was ammoniacal. That could be why the people standing between him and the two other barrels were wearing rebreather masks.

The masks hid most of their faces, but Pausert didn't think that they were worried about being identified. They were carrying, between the seven of them, enough heavy weaponry for a regiment . . . well, a platoon anyway. One of the biggest men Pausert had ever seen was carrying a Mark 20 blaster cannon—the kind of weapon normally mounted on sand-scouts. This man had it slung across his back as if it were an ordinary rifle.

Two of their captors were busy cutting one of the other barrels shorter with a steel-grinder, with the metal screaming. If that was the level of noise accepted around here, then shouting for help was not going to do any good.

One of the masked men noticed that Pausert was starting to look around. "He's stirring, Captain Elin."

Pausert had expected the big man with the Mark 20 to turn, but instead a short, stocky woman did. She had one of the most perfect gambler's faces that Pausert had ever seen. Absolutely and totally expressionless. Pausert realized that that could be even more frightening than someone who looked either threatening or mad.

"Captain Pausert." Her tone too was nearly expressionless; a casual, greet-you-without-pleasure-in-the-street tone of voice—not "I-have-you-bound-and-up-to-the-chest-in-ferroplast" nasty. Somehow, that was even more intimidating.

And she knew who he was, obviously. "We need some information out of you. You are going to tell us."

Another figure bustled up, a wristphone pressed to his ear. A big, plump, sloppy-looking man, but nothing like the size of the giant with the Mark 20.

"The prison is crawling with cops. I've got two of my men monitoring the ISS channels. They're planning to set the launching of his ship forward. It'll be in space as a target hulk within two hours. If the information is on the ship, it'll be space dust soon. You've got to get it out of him. We've got to get out of here." There was both fear and greed in the whiny voice.

"Shut up, Fullbricht. You're a penny-ante bungler. Don't let your delusions of local importance let you think that you can give orders to me."

"It's all very well for you, Captain Elin," he said sullenly. "You'll be out of here. I'll be left to carry the can. Your men used my vehicles. Someone is bound to have seen them."

"Then you'll have to leave your comfortable little nest here, Fullbricht. How likely are they to know of this place? Should we move the captives to our ship?"

"No one comes here. It was a radioactive materials store, before the mines played out. Then they used it for guano, until that was exhausted."

Well, that explained the ammonia smell, thought Pausert. But a radioactives store would be built like a fortress. No wonder they weren't worried about noise. The men who had been cutting the drum hauled the cut section off to reveal a tousled blond head sticking out above the ferroplast. The Leewit was obviously still unconscious. And Pausert was pretty certain that the third barrel contained Goth.

The woman referred to as Captain Elin turned back to Pausert.

Her eyes were inhumanly cold, Pausert thought. "How fond are you of the two children, Captain?" A vibro-knife appeared in her hand. She walked over to the unconscious Leewit. "Do you want her to have a quick death or a slow and painful one? It's your choice. We want the Agandar's codes. And we want them now."

"Codes?" Pausert tried to sound less dumbfounded than he felt.

She slapped the unconscious Leewit, hard. "Access codes to his vaults in the Daal's bank on Uldune."

Fury boiled up in Captain Pausert. Incandescent anger. It was all the worse for being helpless. "She's a child! I'll . . ."

"You'll tell us what we wish to know. We know you have drawn funds from his accounts."

Pausert forced himself to be calm. He hadn't done anything of the kind! He had to think his way out of this dilemma. Someone had set this up. Someone who was out to destroy the *Venture* and her crew or passengers.

"Stubborn, eh?" she said. "Well, you have that reputation, Captain." She slowly raised the vibro-knife. The blade glittered and shimmered in the harsh factory lighting of the storehouse.

Pausert wished, desperately, for some way to protect the unconscious Leewit. If only she was conscious! If only there was some kind of klatha shield he could raise around her. Olimy, the top Karres witch they'd transported from Uldune to Emris had been protected like that. Olimy had disminded himself, protected himself from the horror of the Worm World with a kind of stasis. If only . . .

A complex klatha pattern came to his mind, unbidden. What was it that Goth's Toll pattern had said? *When you need it, not when you want it.*

But what would it do? Dismind him? That could only be reversed with difficulty on Karres. Or dismind the Leewit? The glittering knife drew closer to the Leewit's face. There was no time for doubts now. The captain traced the klatha pattern with his mind. It was an intricate one, full of strange dimension-turning twists which made him feel both giddy and cold. He directed it at the Leewit and had the satisfaction of seeing the pirate captain pull her knife hand back as if stung.

The watching Fullbricht hissed "Witchcraft!" and backed off fearfully.

Captain Elin turned towards Pausert, her eyes glittering. "So. You're also one of those Karres witches. We were told it was just them! That we just had to keep them doped."

"They told you wrong," said Pausert with a confidence that he didn't feel. He didn't know that he could reverse what he'd done on the Leewit, or how good a protection it was. For that matter, he didn't really even know exactly *what* he'd done. It had certainly left him feeling physically drained.

"You'd better let us go. Or else."

"Keth. Blast her."

To his horror, Pausert saw that the huge man with the Mark 20 bring his weapon to bear on the Leewit. Before Pausert had a chance to protest the man let loose with it.

It should have blown her head off her ferroplast-encased shoulders.

It didn't. A puff of wind might have had more effect.

The glittering eyes of Captain Elin didn't blink. "Let's see how good you are with machinery, witch. Fullbricht, set the pourer running." The man, wild-eyed, backed up against the wall and pressed a green button. High above them, machinery clanked and whirred to life. Riding along a roof-rail came a mechanical bucket. Pausert didn't need to be told that the bucket was full of ferroplast. This was presumably a leftover machine from when this place processed radioactives for shipping. He'd bet that the machine had been set up to seal these drums.

What should he do now? If he sealed himself and Goth in with the pattern, they might be unreachable and unhurtable. But they'd be unreachable in a state from which there might be no return at all—and certainly in a state in which they could neither help Hantis, Pul nor themselves.

Indecision nearly paralyzed Pausert as the suspended bucket rolled closer. Pausert was very aware that the Mark 20 was now pointed at himself. Better there than at Goth. But what was he to do?

He tried focusing his newly discovered klatha shield on the suspended bucket. It had no effect at all. Perhaps it needed something living, or something he cared about. The bucket clanked closer . . . well, there was nothing for it but to shield Goth.

The chest of the big man with the Mark 20 disappeared in a sear of blaster fire. The lights went out.

"Witchcraft!" yelled someone in a huge voice, and cackled maniacally.

Hulik watched as Vezzarn tickled the lock at the back of the hazardous materials warehouse with a tool from his tiny set. It clicked open most obligingly, and they slipped inside and up the stairs to the office that overlooked the warehouse.

Looking down at Captain Pausert, Goth and the Leewit, each trapped in their barrel, with the hard-bitten, heavily armed captors surrounding them, Hulik did not see how they could get them out.

"I've found the switch box," said Vezzarn quietly, just as the captain successfully created a klatha shield to protect the Leewit.

Hulik had found a switch, too. For the intercom. She switched it on in time to hear someone below exclaim "Witchcraft!"

That would do. That would just have to do. "Have you got a gun, Vezzarn?"

He shook his head. "No. They took it away. To be honest, I'm not a very good shot anyway."

"I am. We'll just have to chance it. The captain and the girls will be quite well protected in those barrels. I'll take out the guy with the Mark Twenty. You cut the power to the bucket, and the lights. And see if you can cause some panic with the intercom microphone. Then cut the lights back on so I can get some more shooting in."

Vezzarn grinned wryly. "It's a pity that the little Wisdom can't be here to give them some of her whistles. I'll do my best, Hulik do Eldel."

The shrieks and blasterfire prompted Pausert to go right ahead and shield Goth. He put a lot of force into that klatha pattern. He wanted it strong and big. He gave it his everything.

There was the sound of tearing metal; then, a hideous metallic whine and an explosive crashing sound. The lights came on again. Captain Pausert saw Goth, no longer in a barrel and no longer encased in ferroplast, slowly topple over like a round-bottomed skittle. She lay about two arms-length above the floor . . . on nothing. And there was a substantial hole in the side of the building. As blasterfire from the roof-suspended office hissed down into the warehouse, Pausert realized what he must have done. The shield around Goth was so thick that it had torn the barrel seam and exploded it.

Some of the pirates had fled, and at least one was dead. But most of them had sought cover behind the vehicles at the main door, except for two who were crouched beside the barrel that held the Leewit. One of them began firing at the stanchions that held the office. If they could burn through it then the rescuers up there would fall.

Pausert concentrated on the klatha shield around the Leewit, hoping that he'd be protected by his own barrel. He concentrated his effort on the lower part of her shield. Suddenly, the bottom half of the Leewit's barrel split with a tortured metal scream even the Leewit herself would have been proud of. Barrel shards and ferroplast flew all over like shrapnel. The eruption killed the two pirates beside the barrel instantly, and it was enough to send the remaining ones scrambling towards one of the groundcars or racing towards the heavy double door.

Someone obviously had a remote door control because the doors opened as they reached it, then swung shut behind them.

Hulik and Vezzarn came running down the stairs. In the distance, Pausert heard the sound of police sirens.

"Captain, are you all right?" Vezzarn attempted to haul Pausert out of the barrel.

"Well, I'm alive. Am I glad to see you two. How did you get here?"

Hulik had now taken the other shoulder and the two of them hauled. She was slightly built but lithe and strong. Slowly, he began to move. "We followed you. Not without difficulty, Captain. You bolted the coop ten minutes before I was ready for you."

Captain Pausert was grateful to be hanging over the edge of barrel. It helped to hide his embarrassment. "They took my chronometer. I thought you must have been captured."

"Just as well, in a way," said Hulik, as Pausert half fell, was half-dragged out onto the floor, dripping ferroplast. "We'd all have been captured. These guys were watching your cell too."

Vezzarn went to work on the captain's bonds with the vibro-knife. "Now all we've got to do is get out of here, Captain. What's up with the little Wisdoms?" He was using the Uldune term for the Karres witches.

"I put them into some kind of shield. I just hope I can get it off." With difficulty and with the support of Vezzarn and Hulik, the captain struggled to his feet. Partly, his weakness came from having been tied up in the ferroplast. Partly he was just dead tired. He knew now how Goth and the others felt after the Sheewash Drive. As Goth said, it sure took it out of you.

"I'm not very experienced at this Karres witchery. I think we'd better try and get them back to the *Venture*. I might need to find another Karres witch—and that could be difficult, seeing as how the ship isn't likely to be going anywhere without these two."

Hulik shook her head. "It's worse than that, Captain. We may already be too late to save the *Venture* or the lives of Pul and Hantis. I've been listening in on the communications on the ISS band. As soon as the team arrived to pick you up, they discovered that the prison warders were dead."

"Dead?" exclaimed Pausert.

"Yes, dead," said Hulik, grimly. "You were captured by some local hoodlum called Fullbricht."

"And some of the Agandar's pirates," added Pausert. "They definitely considered this Fullbricht as a sort of bungling minor functionary."

"Yes. He was probably a local spy for the Agandar, once. Well, that explains the heavy weapons and the brutality! Anyway, they murdered the prison warders. But the local police and the ISS are blaming you. So they've sent an order to have enough fuel run into the *Venture* for a take-off. Then they're going to use her as they'd planned, for a naval training exercise, and blow her apart."

Pausert shook himself, scattering gobs of ferroplast. "Come on. Let's get Goth and the Leewit into that groundcar. I'll have see what I can do. We'd better try to get to the *Venture*."

"I'll bring the groundcar over here, Captain."

As Hulik moved across to the showy groundcar, Pausert looked around. "How do we get out of here? Can we just crash through those doors?"

Vezzarn shook his head. "This is a hazardous material store, Captain. Those will be especially hardened doors. Guess I better go to work on the locks."

Pausert tried to shake more ferroplast off himself, while he reflected that having an expert safe-breaker and lock-pick in your crew could be very useful. He set his mind to work undoing whatever it was that he'd done to Goth and the Leewit. He had no idea on how or where to start.

Hulik brought the car over. She'd picked up Vezzarn. "Someone is trying to open the doors. I guess Vezzarn wasn't the only one who could trail Fullbricht back here by the cars, Captain. But I think that hole the exploding barrel made in the wall over there is big enough for this groundcar."

They loaded the slickly smooth invisible eggs containing Goth and the Leewit into the car. Hulik eased the vehicle forward and they bumped out through the hole in the side wall. The warehouse plainly hadn't been used for some time. There were plenty of weeds and some rusting stacks of a very familiar barrel. As they drove further, the reflection of flashing lights on the surrounding concrete wall revealed that Gerota Town's finest were at work on the warehouse door.

Hulik clicked the groundcar lights off. By the light of Pidoon's moons, they quietly edged away from the building, following the trail cleared by Goth's flying barrel. Pausert realized just what an intensely fast and powerful reaction he must have caused by his klatha use. The barrel had finally smashed into the concrete wall. The wall was only partially flattened, but, short of going out past the Gerota Town police, there was no other escape route.

"Shall we charge it?" asked Hulik, making the groundcar's motor growl.

"Let's just try pushing, " said Vezzarn. "It looks weakened."

It was, and a section fell in. They bumped and bounced their way down onto the deserted adjoining street and turned the powerful vehicle towards the spaceport. As they did so, they listened in on Hulik's ISS-issue communicator to the reports coming in concerning the search for them.

Apparently, the Agandar's pirates had done them something of a favor, as the vehicle they'd fled in had been spotted and was being pursued. There were also reports from the ISS man and the local space-pilot they'd rounded up to get the *Venture* into space. The ISS man had had some trouble getting fuel out of Pidoon Fuels and Lubricants. Pausert, despite the fact that he was having absolutely no luck in reversing his klatha shield around Goth and the Leewit, found that that was worth laughing about.

The spaceport was bustling. As bustling, at least, as the spaceport of a small town of a minor backwater planet could be just before dawn. There were seven vehicles in the groundcar park. One was an ISS-liveried loader. At least there were no police waiting. Perhaps they assumed that now that the ISS men were aboard the *Venture* and that she was getting ready for take off, there would be no need for them to watch the spaceship any more.

"How will we get onto her?" asked Vezzarn, as they drew into the parking lot.

"Borrow the ISS loader," said Pausert. "Hulik, contact the agent to let him know that we've got a load of explosives, intended to make doubly sure that the *Venture* is totally destroyed."

Hulik looked at him in surprise. "That's not like you, Captain."

Pausert shrugged. "I don't like to break the law. But I'm wanted here already for murders I didn't do. Stealing an ISS vehicle can't add more than another execution to the list. If we live through this and get to explain, we can always pay for it. Provided we get to use the *Venture*'s money again."

Vezzarn was already out of the vehicle, working on the door lock of the loader. Breaking in took him barely a minute. The captain and Hulik manhandled Goth and the Leewit out of Fullbricht's groundcar and onto the lowbed of the loader. There was a tarpaulin which he and Vezzarn tossed over the top of the girls. Pausert would have sworn Goth's eyes were now open. But the light was bad and time was pressing. Hulik was already on the communicator.

"Agent Sboro. We've dispatched a load of explosives to make sure that the vessel is completely destroyed. See that your pilot doesn't attempt to leave before it's aboard," snapped Hulik into her ISS communicator.

There was a pause. "Yes, ma'am. I will open the cargo hatch."

Agent Sboro sounded a little breathless, thought Pausert, as they drove across the concrete to the old *Venture*. Pausert looked lovingly but fearfully at her. If he couldn't work out how to get Goth and the Leewit out of the trap he'd put them into, then they were in even more trouble. It seemed, right now, that the *Venture* and her crew had only been lurching from disaster to disaster since the beginning of their mission.

They hastily unloaded the Leewit and Goth. Then, because it was quickest way to do it, rolled the transparent egg shapes up into the cargo hatch.

The captain saw the flaw in his plan. There was no way out of the cargo hold into the ship—unless, like the Agandar, you had a Sheem war robot that could cut through the bulkheads.

The ship intercom crackled. "Get off the ship. We're about to launch!"

"We've got a confidential message for you. It must be delivered in person," said Pausert smoothly. "We can't get off until it is delivered. Orders."

"I repeat, get off. If you're not out of the cargo hatch by the count of five, I'm sealing it and we'll blast anyway. One. Two . . ."

"It is essential!"

"Three. Four."

"We have information about the hidden passengers. We know where they are."

The hatch began to close. "I'm coming down. You're about to take a ride into space. Line up against the back wall with your hands away from any weapons."

"What do we do?" asked Hulik.

Vezzarn and Pausert looked at each other. Hulik was a fine marksman, and a good companion. But she was no spaceman. Pausert shrugged. "Cooperate," he said. "We have to strap in on acceleration couches for launch."

"Oh."

"If this agent Sboro is humane enough to let us." Pausert looked at Goth's definitely open eyes. "We'll just stand behind Goth and the Leewit. We know that the shield can stop even a Mark Twenty blaster bolt." He felt guilty about it all the same. "Put your gun on the floor, Hulik. If need be you can drop and shoot."

Goth was awake in there. Was she all right? Could she breathe? Or was it like traveling by the Egger Route . . . did she need to?

The door to the hold opened cautiously. A figure with a Blythe gun in hand stepped though.

Hantis smiled foxily. "I couldn't be really sure it was your voice, Captain."

"Hantis!" exclaimed the captain.

She bowed slightly. "Pul is in the control room with the prisoners. We're in trouble, Captain Pausert."

The captain pointed to Goth and the Leewit. "You're telling me. I've put them into some kind of shield. If I can't get them out, then we can't use the Sheewash Drive."

Hantis drew her brows together. "That actually makes it worse. But the problem's immediate. The ISS heard your call to Sboro about the explosives. They just attempted to contact him on the ship communicator rather than his ISS device. They warned him that they think that there may be fake ISS operatives trying to board this ship. I think we can be sure that atmospheric craft have been scrambled and are on their way here."

Pausert pushed wearily off the wall. "Well, let's get everyone into acceleration couches and show them what the old *Venture* can do. We'll go down fighting if we can't get away. Come on, we need to carry Goth and the Leewit."

"She's moving around in there," said Vezzarn looking at Goth. "Do you think the little Wisdom will be able to free herself?

"We haven't got time to find out right now," said Hulik. "If we use a blanket we can make it into a stretcher of sorts. That will be quickest."

Up in the control room they found an ISS agent and a nervous-looking pilot.

On the floor.

Pul was standing over them with a long piece of ISS uniform collar in his jaws. "The churls called me a dog, Hantis. Can I rip their throats out?"

"It's no use, lady," said the pilot, looking nervously at the grik-dog's powerful jaws. "I won't fly this craft. Not even if you kill me."

"Dead men don't pilot spaceships anyway," said Pausert tiredly. "Tie them up. We can go and dump them in their loader."

Two to a prisoner, they hastily carried the pilot and agent out to the ISS vehicle, and tossed them onto the loadbed. Vezzarn hopped into the cab, engaged the vehicle's engine and leaped out. At a run, they sprinted back to the *Venture*. A bolt of blasterfire licked out at them, adding impetus to their pace.

Once into the control room Pausert scrambled for the control chair, and began initiating the blast-off sequence. "Sorry, Goth, this is an apology in advance. This is going to be one of my bad take-offs."

It was. But it was also too fast for the two atmospheric craft that came racing in from an airfield several thousand miles off. The *Venture* staggered into space, farther and farther from Pidoon. As the planet dropped away below them Pausert felt relief. But he was aware that the fuel gauges were dropping fast. They were already using the reserve tanks.

The detectors started to bleep. "Imperial Navy ships, Captain," said Vezzarn grimly.

They didn't even make an effort to hail the *Venture*. They were already firing. Even yelling that there was an ISS man on board helped not at all. Pausert pushed the thrust down to maximum.

The *Venture*'s drive surged. And stuttered. A wall of navy fire fell just short. The three Imperial vessels that were racing towards them would be in range for their next salvo. "The nova guns, Captain . . ."

The *Venture* suddenly surged again, leaping as if a wasp had stung her. Pausert felt the wonderful, familiar surge of the Sheewash Drive. Looking across at Goth he saw the acceleration nets still covered her couch. Covered an invisible cocoon, in fact. But inside that cocoon, the twisted black wires and strange orange fire of the Sheewash Drive danced. He was almost too tired to wish he knew how it worked. Relief—and exhaustion coming like a wave—overcame him.

CHAPTER 9

When he awoke, with a start, the captain found that someone had covered him up with a blanket. He was still sitting in the command chair in the *Venture*'s control room. Looking out of the forward viewscreens showed nothing but an emptiness of space.

So they'd gotten away. Away in a leaking-hulled vessel with absolutely no fuel. There might be a drop or two in the lateral rocket tanks but other than for docking, those were next to useless. He looked sideways. Goth was still lying above the acceleration couch, surrounded by a layer of nothingness.

"I see you are awake, Captain," said Hantis. "Good. We must try to undo this shield you have put around Goth and the Leewit." She looked curiously at him. "I was not told that you were such a powerful klatha operative."

"I'm not. I seem to learn how to do things by accident," admitted Pausert. "I don't know what I've done, or how to undo it." He looked at the Nartheby Sprite. "Goth said you were klatha-skilled too, Hantis. Can you get her out of there?"

Hantis shook her mane of foxy hair. "No. It is very difficult for one klatha operative to undo the work of another. Each person's skills seem to be unique, even if they sometimes achieve the same thing. My skills, anyway, lie with levitation, truth hearing and music. They would be of little help to you. But perhaps Goth herself can help."

Pausert sat up hastily and looked at Goth. "But how? I mean . . ."

"The same way she got the wires necessary to run the Sheewash Drive. She teleported them across the barrier. She can do that with notes even if she can't talk to you."

"And the Leewit?" asked Pausert.

Hantis smiled impishly. "Has been awake, and, by her expressions, whistling and screaming. We can't hear her, of course. Oh, and she's been showing you a number of rude signs. Your little vatch came earlier too. Even it can't get into the shield. Anyway, the Leewit is asleep again."

Pausert blinked. "Again? Have I been asleep long?"

"About fifteen hours," Hantis said. "Most klatha use is demanding on the user's energy. It looks like you came pretty close to burning yourself out, Captain Pausert. Sometimes new klatha users die like that. You must be careful."

"I only did it because there seemed no alternative. I feel as if I haven't eaten for a week, never mind slept for fifteen hours. I'll just see to Goth and then it's food!"

Goth smiled up at him from her shield cocoon. She held up a sheet of paper she'd prepared. It read: *Hello, Captain.*

Pausert started to reply, realized what he was doing, and looked for writing materials. They were sitting ready on the console next to Goth. Painstakingly he wrote down what he had done and asked for advice.

He waited. Goth was plainly consulting with her inner "teacher," the pattern of her mother Toll.

She wrote: *You could try doing it backwards, Captain. See the pattern and then trace it backwards.*

He nodded, and took a deep breath. She scrawled something hastily. *Eat first.* Then, when he'd seen that, she scrawled: *Dangerous.*

Pausert realized she was right. Using klatha in ways that you weren't sure about could be very dangerous—and it certainly wasn't something he should try when lack of food made him feel quite light-headed. Besides, he just couldn't visualize the pattern.

So he ate. He also took a quick shower and changed into fresh clothes. He cursed the loss of his best boots, and dug a spare pair out of his locker. They didn't fit as well as the his old ones, but he supposed he'd just have to live with it. He wasn't going to get back to Nikkeldepain and Hildo and Naugaf for another pair, ever. Not while his erstwhile about-to-be father-in-law lived, anyway.

On the positive side, he consoled himself, ill-fitting boots were more comfortable than life with Illyla would have been. Pausert still wasn't taking seriously Goth's placid assumption that they'd eventually get married once she was old enough—well, not *very* seriously, anyway—but the time he'd spent in the girl's company had made clear to him just how utterly unsuitable a wife Illyla would have made for him. Illyla was ultimately just plain boring— something that could never be said about Goth.

Pausert could see that now. A bit of distance lent clarity...

And maybe that would work here, too, he thought. The captain forced himself to try to visualize, not the details of the klatha pattern, but the whole thing.

All of a sudden, it burned clearly in his mind's eye. So, walking back to the control room by habit and feel, he concentrated on it until he got back to Goth.

Now ... he traced it backwards ... erasing it. Carefully. Precisely.

Goth fell to the couch. The cocoon of force around her was gone. She scrambled to her feet and hugged Pausert fiercely. "You're a hot witch, Captain. That's powerful klatha, that."

Pausert blushed. That was not from modesty so much as his recent thoughts contrasting Goth to Illyla. The girl was still much too young for him to be thinking about such things as how she might compare to anyone as a wife. On occasion, though, that was hard not to do. And he suddenly realized, uneasily, that the occasions seemed to be coming more often of late.

He shook his head forcefully. "I didn't know what I was doing and I nearly got us all killed because of it. Thank goodness you thought of teleporting the wires for the Sheewash Drive. That was smart, Goth."

She gave him that sly little Goth-smile that he had come to know so well. "Neat trick, huh? It worked too. At first, there was that drag we've been getting with the Sheewash Drive. And then ... it was back to normal." She suddenly started giggling. "Look, the Leewit is awake. And she's mad. Yelling her head off by the looks of it. Shall we pretend we haven't noticed?"

"I'm tempted. But I guess we'd better let her out." Pausert concentrated.

A few moments later the Leewit fell to the couch. Still yelling. She jumped up, waving a small finger threateningly under the captain's nose. "What you do? Clumping idiot! What did you do to us?!"

"Only saved your life," said Hulik, who had come into the control room. "That shield of the captain's stopped a Mark Twenty blaster bolt. You were lucky he did it, and he only did it in the first place to stop your face getting sliced up with a vibro-knife."

The Leewit had the grace to look embarrassed. "Well. I didn't know. I just woke up trapped in that, that *stupid* cocoon."

Hulik smiled coolly at her. "You can hear about it later, but right now we have other problems." She turned back to Pausert. "I'm glad you're up and have the little Wisdoms out, Captain. Hantis had Pul on guard at the door. We weren't allowed to wake you. She reckoned if you didn't rest you might not wake up at all, and that only you could ever get Goth and the Leewit out. But the doorseal is still leaking. We're going to have to go somewhere with an atmosphere pretty quick. And we've no fuel."

Goth made a face. "We got a real problem, Captain. Maleen was the only one of us who could handle the Sheewash Drive for landings. It takes really fine control. The Sheewash Drive is just too powerful and fast. We need fuel to land."

Pausert scratched his chin; which reminded him that he needed a shave. "I guess we'll just have to get around it. How much fuel have we got, Hulik?"

"In the main drive tank, Captain? Maybe a few seconds worth, that's all. The tank for the lateral rockets is about half full. We could pipe it to the main tank, but that still won't give us very much. Not enough to land on, that's for sure."

"Then we either take to piracy, find a space refueling point or . . . if worse comes to worst, hitch a ride."

Hulik wrinkled her forehead. "Hitch a ride? What do you mean, Captain?"

Pausert stood up. "I don't much like the idea of piracy, unless we find the Agandar's fleet and cut a ship out of that, and space refueling is pretty rare in the Empire. Most inhabited worlds outlaw it, because if ships can bypass landing it cuts down on trade. That leaves hitching a ride . . . so you'll have a chance to find out first hand, Hulik."

He clapped Goth and the Leewit on the shoulders. "We need the Sheewash Drive to take us to Vaudevillia. We're going to join a circus, if we can find one coming in to land."

The idea so distracted the Leewit that she entirely forgot that she was mad with him. They got the charts up on the display consol and worked out where they were, and where they needed to go.

Sheewash!

*   *   *

"We've lost them," said Sedmon, to his self. "Not so much as a blip since the ship left Pidoon." There was no hiding the anxiety in his voice. The other understood only too well, anyway.

"They could be using the secret drive."

"They have done so before. We've always picked them up on the detectors within a few hours."

Neither said what they both feared: that one of the other parts of the pursuit might have caught up with the *Venture* first.

"It wouldn't be easy for anyone to catch them," said one of the selves, doubtfully. "We all know just how fast the *Venture* can be, with its secret drive."

"We'd better land on Pidoon and see what we can find out. Vezzarn is likely to send them to the port at Gerota Town. Remember that one of the smuggling networks we have taken over goes through there."

"At least we have contacts."

Between the selves they knew exactly who was involved in the gemstone smuggling ring Vezzarn had so painstakingly investigated for them. It was now quite a profitable sideline for Uldune.

Even after the unrewarding search in the Alpha Dendi cluster, they were catching up on the *Venture*. The two Sedmons on the ship had been sure they'd finally reach Pausert and his companions on Pidoon. Especially after they received word from their selves back on Uldune that a query on the *Venture*'s credit status had been made by Pidoon Fuels and Lubricants. They'd thought that there would be a day or two of subradio queries and negotiations before the Daal's Bank would allow the account to be accessed. But it appeared that Pausert must have had other funds. The *Venture* had been tracked leaving Pidoon.

Since then, nothing. They decided to set the ship down in Gerota Town.

Into a hornet's nest.

In the typical fashion of officialdom the galaxy over, the customs officers and the police of Gerota Town were now on high alert. Well after the fact, of course, but no one wanted to look as if they could have been the slackers and sluggards who had allowed such a notorious criminal as the infamous Captain Pausert to escape.

"My papers are in perfect order," said the Sedmon who was on public duty.

Which, of course, they were. The very best members in the Daal's extensive staff of forgers on Uldune had worked on those papers. As for finding the secret compartment in which the second Sedmon sat, patiently . . . that was unlikely. One of the side effects of running an extensive smuggling ring into the Empire as a state enterprise, was that the Empire's customs techniques and equipment were well known to the Sedmons. And well countered. The vibro-sensors Captain Pausert had feared would certainly not reveal the second Sedmon's chambers.

The search was still exhaustive.

And still found nothing, although while Sedmon stood patiently watching, the chief customs officer called the ISS offices in Pidoon City to inform them how suspiciously heavily armed and cargo-less the *Thunderbird* was.

The Sedmons didn't much care. They intended a very brief stop, anyway. While the one in hiding monitored the detectors, still searching for the signal-trace from the *Venture*, the other would make an unobtrusive visit on foot to a near-port gift shop.

Unfortunately, he made a simple error. The Sedmons had all walked, lightly disguised, around the environs of Zergandol. But they knew Zergandol; knew what the streets looked like, knew where they were going. The Sedmon wandering around the seedier parts of Gerota Town's port area got lost.

The Sedmon then got a firsthand experience of the difference between being the all-powerful and slightly sinister Daal of Uldune, where his word was life or death and his spies and secret police were remarkably efficient, and being an arbitrary spaceman in a foreign port.

There were certain elements in common. Any of the Sedmons going out incognito on the winding hilly streets of Zergandol had a number of the Daal's secret police watching. Here, too, the Sedmon was being watched by the secret police. However, there the similarity ended. The Daal's agents—the Sedmon was quite sure of it—were never as clumsy and obvious as this idiot. And he had never been shadowed by just one man.

The Sedmon stepped around a corner and slid into a convenient alleyway, toggling a button on his collar. The pale blue suit he was wearing became a strident green, and he raised himself up a further two inches with platform soles. His dark complexion he could not alter as easily, but with the addition of a curling beard and moustache he had become a different person.

None of which helped him at all. He hadn't walked more than

twenty feet farther down the alley before someone hit him very expertly across the base of the skull.

When the Sedmon awoke, he was aware that the other hexa-person on the ship was already locking certain key aspects on the *Thunderbird* and coming to his assistance. He also realized that his wallet, ship-key and chronometer were all missing. Being, as it were, one with the Sedmon who was leaving the *Thunderbird*, he discovered he was in something of a predicament there, too. The ship must have been under close observation because he hadn't even crossed the tarmac when a groundcar with five heavily armed ISS agents screeched to a halt in front of him. The five heavily armed agents grabbed and forcecuffed the Sedmon.

"What's this all about?" demanded the Sedmon, who had just emerged from the ship.

"Shut up," said the ISS officer. He held the Sedmon at blaster-point, as two others systematically searched and removed various items from his person that the customs officials had not discovered in their search.

The part of the hexaperson who was attempting to get up in the alley borrowed from his other selves to control his feet. Back on Uldune in the House of Thunders, the Daal got up abruptly from where he had been presiding over a court hearing in the Little Court. He went hastily to join his brothers in the tower. At times like this, physical closeness was comforting if not necessary.

In the office in the port building that the ISS had appropriated for their own use, one of the hexaperson was being strapped into a chair equipped with electrodes. The Daal had such a chair, too. The hexaperson had never anticipated being strapped into it, however. It administered shocks when the instrumentation detected the telltale signs of a lie. It was a very effective way of getting the truth out of a suspect.

"We want to know just how you managed to get back to your ship after you had evaded our agent," stated the ISS interrogator. "If you lie, this is what will happen."

Agony washed through all six of the Sedmons.

CHAPTER 10

The air in the *Venture* was getting thin. The trip had taken longer than they'd thought, even with the Sheewash Drive.

"Whatever was dragging at us is back, Captain," said Goth, tiredly. "Maybe we should try using that shield you put us in again. That seemed to work."

"NO WAY!" shouted the Leewit. "Not never! I couldn't stand it. I won't help if you do that again! I'll whistle at you!"

So they'd plodded on. By the time they got to Vaudevillia, they were gasping almost constantly.

The space around Vaudevillia was fairly crowded—everything from great lattice ships to small tramps. No planetary control greeted them, and the space traffic seemed to be left to look after itself.

"It's a pretty chaotic place, Captain," said Vezzarn. "There's no planetary authority. Nor any real ports. No defenses neither. It doesn't need none. Even the most desperate bunch of raiders wouldn't waste their time on Vaudevillia. It's nothing more than a giant gypsy encampment. There are no real towns. You land anywhere. It rains so much that wherever you choose would be muddy and flat, sir."

"Well, let's try and get some fuel to land with, before we try doing it the hard way. Let's try the communicator. We're low on air and fuel. Surely someone will help."

They might as well have shouted into space. No one was coming near them; although, by the way some of the tramps were hovering, they were just waiting for the *Venture*'s crew to die.

"Well, if no one will help, we'll have to help ourselves," said Captain Pausert.

The lattice ship looked far more like an umbrella that had lost all of its fabric, than a spacecraft. And it was big. Huge was a better word. Gigantic.

Pausert remembered the excitement of one of the great lattice showboats landing on Nikkeldepain; standing, watching in delight as the great metal skeleton became covered in tinsel bright synthasilk, as the showboat transformed an empty fifteen acre field into a paradise of stages, freak shows and strange stalls. He could almost hear the music again . . .

But now he had to concentrate. It was difficult when you were gasping.

This was a seriously tricky bit of ship-handling. It had been something they'd done in his Navy time with one-man interceptors on empty tanker ships. But the *Venture* was a lot bigger and less maneuverable than a one-man interceptor. The timing was crucial.

Pausert had come as close as he dared to the spiderweblike lattice showboat that they were planning to catch a ride on. There were the remains of several other space-craft hung around in the lattice's skeletal arms. They weren't the crashed hulks of other ships that had tried to ride down on her. Rather, they were cobbled onto the lattice—stores, props, extra living quarters. An old ship made a convenient air-tight addition to the giant lattice.

The lattice showboat began its descent. Pausert used the laterals to begin the drop after it. He closed in on the upper stage. Gravity began to tug at the *Venture*.

"Stand by the magnetic locks, Vezzarn," he snapped. They were falling fast now. There were squawks of protest from the lattice showboat—but it was too big and cumbersome to take evasive action. Now, it loomed large and terribly, terribly close. Atmosphere was beginning to buffet the *Venture* too, making steering even more difficult. Plainly the lattice ship was trying to drop faster to get away from a potential collision.

Everyone was in the control room. If they failed now . . . they could kill themselves. Pausert held that last bit of fuel in the *Venture*'s tanks in reserve against the possibility of impacting the lattice showboat. But of course those on board the lattice ship wouldn't know that.

At the last possible moment—just when collision seemed inevitable—Pausert swung the *Venture* over on the laterals. "Now, Vezzarn!"

With a barely audible click, the *Venture* was magnetically locked onto the upper stage of the lattice showboat.

Never had anything on that stage been quite so enthusiastically applauded.

The lattice ship continued her descent. "Right," said Captain Pausert. "Acceleration couches everyone. We're going to have to leave our host in a hurry. They're going to be plenty mad at us. We'll skip as soon as we're a hundred yards above ground level. Full thrust. We've got a tiny bit of fuel and we're going to use every drop. We really don't want to land right next to them."

Vezzarn chuckled. "That's for sure. Judging by the language coming out of that speaker, the captain wants to do some very interesting things to us."

"I didn't even know some of those words," said the Leewit gleefully. "I don't think they even really exist except as cuss words in his own mind. They must be *really* filthy."

"If you use so much as one of them, I won't even wash out your mouth with soap," said Pausert sternly. "I'll put you into my shield cocoon again."

She stuck her tongue out at him and made a very rude noise. But she didn't use the words.

Two minutes later, in rain and sheeting lightning, Captain Pausert gave the *Venture* full thrust. She took off like . . . a damp squib. Then the drive coughed and flung them forward. Pausert frantically tried to see where the hiccupping drive was sending them. Then it died. Using the laterals and the detectors, the captain set the *Venture* down.

Vezzarn was right. It was pretty flat and yes, it was muddy. The storm hissed and poured rain down at them. But at least there was breathable air out there, even if it was rather moist.

"I can see why no one wants this place much," said Hulik, gazing into the gloom. "To think I actually wanted to come here."

"It does slack off sometimes," said Vezzarn, chuckling. "I came here with a smuggling consortium. They thought an unpoliced planet sounded just perfect. Well, we were here a week. At the end of that, the captain said it was one of the best planets in the universe to leave."

The old spacer scanned the area. "The lattice showboats don't mind. It's a place where there are no port fees, and no debt collectors. And they've got a few acres of dry inside them. More than a few. But no one actually lives here. The fuel companies send in mobile tankers, and sell fuel at a cash-in-advance premium. And that's about all there is."

"But every planet has *some* permanent residents—even glorified filling stations like Pidoon."

Vezzarn shrugged. "The showboats recruit. They tried to recruit from us, twice. The second time was an armed stand-off. I know the world of the lattice showboats is where every kid in the galaxy thinks they'll run away to, but the truth is they want the showboats and not Vaudevillia. And along the way some people go off to live more normal lives, I guess."

Pausert looked out at the rain. It was easing slightly. "Well, we might need to get recruited. We've got air, now. But we've got no fuel, no money and no way out of here." He patted the console of the old *Venture* affectionately, almost apologetically. He loved her and he hated the idea of leaving his ship here to rust. "What were all those tramps and other little vessels doing around the planet, Vezzarn?"

"Food and fuel and drink, I suppose, Captain. You can get fish here, but not a lot else. A small operator can turn a pretty tidy profit out of it, if he's lucky. But it's quite risky to land with no ground-control and bad weather, unless you're a big lattice ship. Even the showboats don't land here more often than they really need to."

"Picking up atmospheric craft on the detectors, Captain," said Hulik, warily. "They could come from the ship we caught a ride down on. They should be here in about three minutes."

Pausert looked at the display. "Great Patham! I never thought of them having atmospheric craft on board. I suppose it makes sense. And I suppose if I were that captain, I'd be out looking for the idiots who endangered my ship, too. I hate the idea of shooting at them, but we'd better get the nova guns ready."

"We could always hide," said Goth.

"Where?" asked Pausert. "I mean, what we can see of this place doesn't offer much cover. There doesn't even seem to be any vegetation, never mind a nice deep valley."

"Light-shift," said Goth. "They'll be searching hull-metal on their detectors. When they get closer they'll try for a visual examination. Let's see if I can fool them that this is just an old wreck."

Pausert nodded. "It does seem fairer than blowing them out of the sky."

A few minutes later two aircars dropped through the clouds. Pausert could dimly make out the craft circling the *Venture*.

"See if you can pick them up on the communicator."

Hulik put the communicator on search, and a few moments later they heard a voice " . . . seems to be an old wreck. We've got the position marked down. You can send a team out later to bring it in. We'll go on searching."

Outside the fliers cut their way away through the misty rain.

The captain took a deep breath. "You can stand down on the guns. We'll have to get the *Venture* up on her laterals and move her."

"Excuse me, Captain, but why?"

"You heard them. They've got the position and they're sending a team out later. We don't want to be here."

"Perhaps we do," said Hulik, slowly. "Perhaps that would solve our problems. They want the 'wreck'? Well, let them have it. You saw what they do with them—weld them into the lattice. They're always recruiting, so we should be able to get ourselves a berth. We can get ourselves *and* the *Venture* off this world."

There was a silence. "It could work," said the captain grudgingly. It hurt to think of the old *Venture* being welded onto the lattice like so much scrap, but it did make sense.

"It's brilliant!" said Goth.

"And the leech won't work because the drive won't be running," pointed out Vezzarn.

"We're going to join the circus! Yay!" The Leewit bounced cheerfully off the walls.

Pausert took a deep breath. "All right. What are we doing here, and how long have we been here, and what are we going to do when they find the *Venture* isn't a wreck?"

Goth grinned. "I can keep the light-shift up."

The captain shook his head. "Not indefinitely, Goth." He sighed. "What do you think, Hantis? This mission is about you."

She gave him her enigmatic smile. Her pointed ears twitched. "The most important thing is getting to the Empress Hailie. Actually getting there. Not being killed trying. If that means Pul and I must take roles in a human freak show, then we will do that too. If we can get away with it, that is. The men on that lattice ship were very angry. And the captain is right. Goth cannot keep the light-shift going indefinitely."

"We can do a little disguise work," said Hulik, "and make sure that the *Venture* won't fly until we take a few pieces out of the safe. And maybe deal with the communicator so it won't function. We could claim to have been here for weeks. Have you got any plausible cargo for this place, Captain?"

"Tinklewood fishing poles and some really ugly allweather cloaks, and a few Totisystem Toys. They're what's left of the cargo I set off from Nikkeldepain with. I couldn't sell them anywhere."

Hulik held up her hands. "Perfect. This would be the ideal place to bring both. It has got fish in the streams and it has got rain."

Pausert knew he was beaten. Besides, he didn't have any better ideas. "There is some paint in the stores. Plenty of mud out there. We can make it look like we've been here a while. I'm going to make it look as if we have fuel, and also that the systems won't work. And somebody find me a lump of ash to put into the spot where I take the main transponder out of the communicator. And we need to think about the story. We all need to sing the same tune, about when we got here, where we're from and why."

"You let us deal with that," said Hulik. "You're too honest and truthful, Captain."

"I guess someone has to be," said Pausert, sourly. He got to work on the communicator. "How do we know that these showboat people won't try any funny stuff? Slaves are still legal in the Empire."

"A hot set of witches like us should be able to deal with that," said the Leewit with a grin, and skipped off.

By the time a dilapidated lifter from the lattice showboat arrived nearly twelve hours later, the *Venture* looked like a pretty genuine wreck that had been lying there for a fair while.

She wasn't called the *Venture* any more, either, since they'd used that name while they'd been in orbit around Vaudevillia, appealing for help. She'd gone back to being the *Evening Bird*, a name Uldune's masters of ship's paper fakery had provided for her run into the Chaladoor.

The lifter, like some gigantic long-legged insect, settled over the body of the *Venture*. Except for Vezzarn, who was sitting quietly at the nova guns, they all trooped out into the rain and waved at the lifter.

The two people in the lifter gaped at them. They flicked the cockpit open. Captain Pausert noted that the short, rotund, glistening-faced one had a Blythe rifle pointed at them. "What are you doing here?" the skeletally thin pilot demanded, his sharp-planed face taut with suspicion, his voice harsh.

"This is our ship. We crashed here a couple of weeks ago," said the captain, as sincerely as he could.

The thin man relaxed visibly. "You're not from one of the other showboats?"

"No. We're traders with a load of tinklewood fishing rods and allweather cloaks. We had a systems malfunction while we were landing. We haven't been able to fix it. Our communicator got trashed, too."

"Hmm. Mind if we come on board?" asked the thin man, still sounding suspicious.

Captain Pausert shrugged. "Sure. If your friend stops pointing that rifle at us."

The rifle muzzle shifted not one micron. "It makes me feel more secure," said the plump man, his face scintillating oddly in the cloud-filtered light. "There ain't much law here on Vaudevillia."

Captain Pausert shrugged again. "Suit yourself." He pointed up at the nova gun turret which was locked onto them. "It does seem a bit pointless, though."

The glistening-faced one nearly dropped his rifle. "It's a trap!"

Pausert held up his hands pacifically. "No. We are just being careful. Like you are. You leave the Blythe rifle there and we'll get Vezzarn to deflect the turret."

"All right. We just want to call our ship first, huh? You try anything and the guys from the *Petey, Byrum and Keep* will fix you."

"Sure, go ahead," said Hulik. "We have some allweather cloaks and fishing rods for sale. Or to trade for some extra rations."

A brief call to the lattice ship, and the two men disembarked and came out of the rain and into the *Venture*. Viewing them now in good light, Captain Pausert thought that if he'd been some alien captain meeting these members of the human race for the first time, he'd have been inclined to think that they were from two different species. The thin man was so thin you could see every strap of sinew across his bones. He was not actually particularly tall. He just looked that way with the stiff blue-dyed upright comb of hair on his head. The short plump man was entirely hairless, and his skin seemed to shimmer with different color-patterns gleaming, coming and going.

The Leewit stared admiringly at him. "How does it work? How does your skin go like that?"

That broke the ice. He bowed and winked. "I'm Mannicholo the chameleon man," he said with a grin. "Half-lizard, half-man, that's me. The strangest creature in the Universe!"

"I bet I could do it," said the Leewit firmly, "if I knew the trick. Go on, tell me how it really works. Please?" She cocked her head and tried to look cherubic.

"Trade secret, dearie." Mannicholo chuckled, revealing rainbow striped teeth.

"He's tattooed with various temperature-sensitive crystals," explained the blue cockscombed man superciliously. "And he has tiny bits of reflective stuff imbedded in his dermis. As the crystals get warm they change color, and that color radiates heat better so they change color back again." Then he ducked, folding himself under the swing of Mannicholo's arm, with almost boneless ease. "And he hates me telling people."

"I'll fold you into shapes even you can't get into, Timblay," growled Mannicholo.

"Impossible," said the man with the blue cockscomb, bowing to them. "As you may have gathered from my compatriot Mannicholo, I am Timblay, otherwise known as the Incredible Folding Man." He looked around the control room. There were parts of one of the panels artistically strewn about, along with an array of tools. "You do seem to have something of a problem."

"Main drive firing sequencer won't work," said Vezzarn, having gotten up from the nova gun controls. "We had a massive lightning strike just as we were trying to touch down. It fried that, and fried our communicator."

"Ah. That can happen here," said Timblay, understandingly. "This your first trip to Vaudevillia?"

Pausert nodded. He noted that Timblay had eased over to the fuel gauges. He flicked a glance down at them before asking, casually. "Repairable?"

"With a few spares we're not carrying," said Hulik. She pointed to the electronic components on the floor. "We've tried cannibalizing other stuff, but so far it hasn't worked."

"Ah. Well, maybe we can help each other. Exchange things, as it were."

"We have allweather cloaks to offer. Very good line. Remarkably effective . . ."

"I'm sure the outside crews will buy some," said Timblay smoothly. "But that doesn't really get around your problem, does it? You've got a fried communicator and drive sequencer, and here you are stuck on a planet where you just can't buy spare parts.

No, I'm afraid we can't sell them to you, not even in exchange for your truly magnificent allweather cloaks. But . . ."

He smiled, all teeth. "We can perhaps still reach an accommodation with each other. Help each other out. Get you off this damp spot and benefit us, too."

"What do you mean?" asked Pausert suspiciously.

"Well, this ship is useless to you. It's not going anywhere. You're stuck on one of the wettest planets in the Galaxy. Now, in exchange for the ship—which we'll use as a store—and some short-time labor contracts, we'll take you to another world with a spaceport."

Pausert was surprised to see the glistening-skinned Mannicholo, who was standing behind Timblay, shake his head warningly. Well, when it came down to it, Pausert had absolutely no intent of agreeing too easily anyway. And, while he was a reasonably skilled trader, he had a past-master in his crew. Goth could get the better of anyone.

"It doesn't sound like much of a bargain to me," said Pausert. "We're just short a few electronic components. We're armed. We've got a locally valuable cargo and we've still got our laterals firing. We'll be able to start moving around on them. Find a fuel seller and arrange for the parts we need for the communicator at least. After that we'll have to fight off customers. Sooner or later we'll get the spares we need. No, I don't think you've got a deal. Now, if you'd like to give us a lift back to Pidoon—for a small fee, of course—I'm sure we'd be grateful."

Timblay waved his hand dismissively. "I don't think we'd be very interested. Pidoon's not on the itinerary. But why don't you come and talk to Master Himbo? Maybe he can reach a more mutually equitable deal with you. We'll transport your craft there . . ."

Pausert shook his head. "We'll come, but under our own steam. I'm not having you claim salvage on the *Evening Bird*."

Timblay pinched his narrow mouth. "Up to every trick in the book, are we, Captain . . ."

"Aron. From Mulm."

"Well, Captain Aron. I see you have damage around your main airlock."

"You aren't the first would-be salvagers," admitted Captain Pausert.

The *Venture* proceeded to follow the lifter to the lattice showboat on the last dregs of fuel in her laterals. In the gray, driving rain, the showboat loomed like a small dark mountain. The lattice skeleton of triangular hull-metal girders was covered over, not with the bright synthasilk of Pausert's memories, but a utilitarian black. A small yellow digger was busy trenching and a work team was repairing a small exposed section of the lattice. The showboat looked very workaday ordinary, except . . .

It was very, very big. Had it been a solid hull-metal thing it would have dwarfed a fair number of battle-dreadnaughts—and cost a small fortune in fuel to fly. As it was, the round, plump half dome, ringed with attendant smaller half-domes, could take crowds of thousands—and fly between planets at minimal cost.

The *Venture* set down in front of the entry portal. Here on their home-world, with no customers to draw, the showboat hadn't bothered to clad the two towers and arch in bright bunting and flags. Instead, a guard with a disrupter cannon huddled in the small metal box above the rippling array of colors that formed fifteen-foot-high red-and-gold ornate letters.

PETEY, BYRUM & KEEP
THE GREATEST SHOW IN THE GALAXY

"Clumping awesome!" said the Leewit.

CHAPTER 11

Vezzarn stayed to man the guns. Mere fabric and I-beams would be a poor defense against the unpredictable might of the nova guns. Yes, they could be taken hostage, but the captain had made sure he'd said loudly, in earshot of their two escorts: "Vezzarn, if they try to take us captive just blow the lattice apart until they let us free. They're in a weaker position than we are."

"We've got guns on *Petey B* too, you know," snapped Timblay. "More than a match for those antiquated novas."

Pausert snorted. "At this range? Vezzarn's only got to hit a couple of I-beams and the whole thing would fall over. And we're not threatening, it's just better being careful, eh?" Mannicholo definitely gave him a wink and a glance of amusement at Timblay.

They formed a very small procession coming in, out of the rain, into the great cavernous interior. "Where are all the levels? Where are all the stalls?" demanded the Leewit.

"Don't put them up here on Vaudevillia, little 'un," said Mannicholo, with a wry grin. "The stages"—he pointed to several stages hung on girders higher up in the structure—"are there for rehearsals and practices. But what's the use in setting out the bleachers for no one to sit on?"

"But . . ." The Leewit blinked a tear away, showing she was not as old, or as tough, as she pretended to be. "I thought it would be like . . . like I'd seen it. Oh, look!" She pointed. Across the space, various of the show's animals were being exercised. "Telebars! Cute!"

Mannicholo chuckled. "You should try mucking out their cages!"

"They'll probably get a chance to," said Timblay sourly, and strode off ahead.

The rotund, color-shifting man spat. "Never mind him, he's just sour because he never suckered you. Miserable fellow. He's an 'artiste,' " he said sarcastically. "Doesn't like working with mere freak show folk like me. You'll be all right dealing with Himbo Petey. He's mean but fair. Timblay would have tied you into a manual labor contract for the circus section if he could. That's the hardest work. Any of you have an act? That's best money."

"We weren't planning on joining the show. We just wanted a lift off-world," said Hulik.

Mannicholo grinned, making colors dance and sparkle across his cheeks. "That's the only way off Vaudevillia, honey. And Himbo will never agree to a one-stop hitch."

The showboat boss was a small, dapper man with a little goatee and a pair of elegantly curled mustachios that Pausert secretly envied. He plainly loved his own appearance, and had several full-length mirrors in his office. He paced as he spoke, and paused occasionally to admire himself, especially when he made dramatic gestures.

"But no one," he said calmly, "is a passenger on the Greatest Show in the Galaxy. In fact no one does just one job. I myself am ringmaster, I do a magic show in the sideshows, I am the accountant and chief navigator, and I play certain roles in the thespian section. I also stand in on the harpsicordium from time-to-time. Even our leading lady—and Dame Ethulassia is an exacting woman—controls the costumery. We simply can't afford passengers. We'll take your ship along, but she'll also have to work her passage. Props is in desperate need of more storage space. You can have her back when your contracts expire—provided you replace her with a space-tight hulk of similar size. But if you want off Vaudevillia, it's as part of the troupe or not at all."

Pausert shrugged, hiding his thoughts. A space-tight vessel . . . Even a derelict from a scrap merchant was going to cost at least a hundred thousand maels. They could manage that, easily enough, if they could draw on their funds; but, as the experience on Pidoon had revealed, right now they couldn't. That was a lot of money to try to earn, otherwise.

And then they'd still have to refuel and to repair the *Venture*. They'd have to earn as much as they possibly could. "We're multi-skilled too. For instance my niece Dani here does great stage magic, and is a skilled negotiator, Master Petey. She'll dicker with you about our worth and how long we'll travel with you and at what rate."

Himbo Petey was plainly amused. "Amateur stage magic isn't good enough for the Greatest Show in the Galaxy, Captain Aron. I dare say the thespians will want you for crowd scenes and the animal trainers will want you for grooming and mucking out. The lady with the pointed ears and the doggie"—Pul growled—"aren't even weird enough for the freak show."

Goth sat down cross-legged on the office floor, clapping her hands. A ball of flames suddenly balanced on the upstretched fingertips of each hand. She flicked them and they leapt from hand to hand. Captain Pausert knew that it was just a light-shift, but it certainly was very impressive. Then she clapped her hands again. The balls disappeared in midair. On her palms rested a paperweight from the showboat boss' desk.

Himbo Petey grinned. "I take it back! That's very good. The flame-balls are a neat one. Great distraction! I almost didn't see you slip my paperweight from your sleeve, and I am a professional. Can you juggle more than two flame-balls? How do you get them to go out when you clap?"

Goth shook her head. "Trade secret. But timing is pretty important."

"Ah!" Himbo nodded. "Misdirection! Excellent! We'll get you a stall of your own or include you into one of the bigger shows. Do any of the rest of you have acts?"

"He called me a doggie. Can I bite him, Hantis? Just once?"

"Ha! A ventriloquist! A good one, too. We don't have a talking dog act at the moment. Any more talents?"

Pul stalked forward. "You're a dead man, churl."

"Now, Pul," said Hantis. "He's never met a grik-dog before." She gave the showboat boss an enigmatic smile. "I believe we are strange enough for your so-called freak show after all."

At this point the door was flung open. A woman with a vast, upstanding coif of brassy hair paused in the doorway, making a grand entrance. It was plainly something she did often and well. "Himbo!" Her voice was a rich contralto, so strong it seemed to make the walls vibrate.

He sighed. "Yes, Ethulassia. You'll get some of them. You've told me you need them, oh, several hundred times already. You'll get even more staff, though the thespian section gets far more resources than its financial contribution justifies."

It was plainly a well-rehearsed argument. And by the way she was drawing breath, about to become a loud one.

Pausert began to rell vatch. Things could get worse, after all. The witches all stiffened. **Hello, Big Dream Thing! This is a fun place, this!**

He hardly heard Dame Ethulassia's salvo. Something about adding quality and real worth to a tawdry show, and drawing punters to the stalls that they would never visit otherwise.

He cleared his throat as Himbo puffed himself up for the return volley, and stepped between them. "I, um, have an act, too. When we came to Vaudevillia we thought we might join one of the shows."

He sent a quick thought at the little silver-eyed vatch. *This will be far more fun if you actually help me.*

All right, Big Dream Thing.

Both the Showmaster and the Leading Lady stopped, perhaps surprised that anyone would dare to interrupt them. But with that little mischievous destructive vatch around . . . it was a case of ride the Dire-beast or be devoured by it. In a moment of madness, Pausert had chosen to ride the thing. Now, as the two most powerful figures on the showboat stared at him, he wondered if he might not have been better off letting the vatchlet just do its worst.

Dame Ethulassia surveyed him rather like a housewife choosing a piece of meat from a butcher's counter. She looked him up and down very slowly. Pausert felt himself blushing. She raised a perfectly curved eyebrow.

Then, her expression seemed to soften considerably. "And just who are you, sweetie?" she purred, giving him the benefit of the full out-thrust expansion of her frontage.

Pausert felt himself blush some more. "Captain Aron, at your service." No sooner had he said this than Pausert wished he'd chosen some other phrase.

" 'Service,' is it? That sounds intriguing. You've got talent, I can see. You've felt the Call of the Stage, haven't you?" She had very red lips. And long nails that matched.

By the look on her face, Goth didn't think much of Dame Ethulassia.

That could get even worse than the little vatch on the rampage.

"Oh, yes, I have often wanted to be on the stage, but my real skills are in, in escapology."

At the moment, he wished he could escape from here. Ethulassia seemed be some sort of magician, herself—*The Incredible Expanding Bosom*—and Goth's expression had gone from sour to that blank-faced look which meant she was already plotting and scheming in ways that Pausert really didn't want to think about.

"I do some stage magic too," Pausert said hurriedly. He pointed at the two girls. "With my nieces as assistants."

The Leewit stuck her tongue out at him. "I'm a clown. I don't *assist*."

The showboat boss had plainly recognized Pausert's intervention for what it was, even if he thought Pausert was saving him from the leading lady and not vatch-trouble. After all, as a stage magician himself, Himbo knew the importance of distraction. He shifted his cigar. "Well, show us something, then."

"Er. I'll need some props . . ."

Himbo stepped across and opened a locker. It was a large walk-in locker, meticulously arrayed with everything a conjurer might desire. "What can I offer you? Forcecuffs? Strong rope? Chains? A lockable chest?

"I . . . I'll skip the chest. I'll take the ropes, forcecuffs and chains. You, sir, and the good lady, would you be good enough to tie my hands and feet—attach the cuffs as well—and then wrap the chains around me and padlock them? And then put the keys in your pocket."

He sat down on the office floor and offered his hands and feet. Himbo and Ethulassia tied and chained Captain Pausert up, with considerable showmanship—and a speculative gleam in the Leading Lady's eyes which made him still more uneasy. Goth's face now had that utterly blank expression which meant the little witch's brain had gone into overdrive. It was a pretty fiendish brain, when it wanted to be.

Himbo displayed the ten feet of rope carefully, engaging in a little tug of war with the Leading Lady. Ethulassia clicked the locks closed and then challenged Hantis to open them, displaying that they were indeed locked as they appeared to be. And Himbo insisted on tying his hands behind him. "There is no science to escaping if they're in front of you," he said cheerfully. Then he wrapped rope around Pausert's chest in some seven or eight turns.

Captain Pausert thought having his hands behind him was a poor idea. But he couldn't exactly say so and he wasn't too concerned about it, anyway. The little vatch had proved able to undo forcecuffs and locks before.

"Now . . . if you could just drape two of those allweather cloaks over me, Dani."

He was covered from head to toe in voluminous allweather cloaks. And, sure enough, the keys for the locks and the forcecuffs were in his hands a moment later, thanks to Goth's teleportation skills . . .

The little vatch was giggling furiously. And so, Pausert realized, was everyone else. Well, he'd show them. Even if the vatch was not going to cooperate he had the keys. Now . . .

Pausert began realizing that having the key in your hand was not the same as actually being able to get it into the lock of a forcecuff behind your back. Especially when your hands were tied. He strained. And twisted his hands . . . And finally got the key to the keyhole . . .

It didn't fit. It must fit the one on his feet. With difficulty he managed to exchange keys. He was concentrating fiercely by this time, and was hardly aware of the laughter. It was only when he'd just managed to reach the lock the second time—and the key somehow twitched out of his fingers with more vatchy laughter— that he realized that while the rest of him was stifling and hot, his back and hands were cold. By the breeze blowing on their sweatiness, they weren't covered up!

No wonder everyone was laughing. Cringing with embarrassment, with no thought except to get out of there, Captain Pausert stood up, clumsily, as a man whose hands are manacled behind his back will, the hot allweather cloaks falling away. It was only when he was on his feet, that Captain Pausert realized that his feet were no longer manacled. Or tied. Or even chained.

"Brilliant misdirection, boy! Brilliant! I didn't even notice you doing the legs."

Pausert blushed. This had gone so wrong. He brought his hands up to hide his face.

It was only when the length of chain still on his wrist hit him on the head that he realized that his hands were free too. All that remained of his bonds were the loops around his chest. He realized that the little vatch had kept its promise after all. He was free!

Well, almost. There were just the loops of rope around his chest. If he could pretend it was all planned . . . He sent begging thoughts at the little vatch. All he got was the tinkle of laughter. He strained desperately at the rope. Strained and strained. He felt the veins stand out on his forehead.

The ropes stayed as tight as ever. Pausert wilted. "I'm afraid . . . something has gone wrong with this stage. I'll have to ask you to undo the knot. Or cut it," he said lamely.

Himbo got up from his perch on the edge of his desk and walked across. "Never mind. A fine performance anyway. As good as any I've seen. You'll just have to practice that part. And we'll need to find something better in the way of a cloak than those silly things. Turn around." A moment later: "Ho ho! Very clever. Very good indeed!"

Pausert wished that he knew just what piece of naughty-minded witchery had again sent everyone, from that pestilential little vatch to Dame Ethulassia, into gales of laughter. Of course, he couldn't see it. With a sinking heart, Pausert knew that just as Pul and Hantis had to sacrifice their dignity to being part of the "freak" show, he would have to make a fool of himself in front of audiences across the Empire. Well. At least they probably wouldn't be going to Nikkeldepain.

He was too gloomy at the thought to pay any real attention to the rope falling around his ankles. Or the little twist of flowers where the knot had been.

Pausert sat in the control room talking to Goth. The *Venture* was safely snugged into the latticework on the second tier. Her hold was now full of an assortment of ropes, screens, fake treasure chests, feather-light swords, and an eclectic collection of bric-a-brac furniture ranging from ornate ancient chairs to stools some showperson might just have stolen from an ultramodern bar somewhere.

"You got us a good deal," said Goth, hugging her knees and grinning. "You're a hot witch, Captain. I wouldn't have thought of that trick with the flowers. And I nearly died when the back of the allweather cloak lifted up so that we could see you and the keys." She started laughing again. "It was so neat! You had them all fooled."

"Actually, Goth, I didn't plan any of that. It was that dratted little vatch. It was playing its tricks on me. We were just lucky, I guess."

"Luck's a klatha thing too, Captain."

Pausert sighed. "We're going to need it, Goth. Everything has gone haywire on this trip. We expected an easy voyage . . . and look at it. We've lost our money, we've nearly lost our ship. I've even lost my best boots. I'm getting used to these new ones now, but they're not the same."

Goth examined the boots. "They're pretty spiffy ones, Captain. Looks like Lambidian iguana leather."

The captain looked at the boots in question. They were smarter looking than he remembered. "They're a spare pair I've had for years. I certainly never had the money for Lambidian iguana. Even my best pair were just tanned miffel-hide, but made to measure. Anyway, I think boots are going be the least of my problems. I'll have to try to get that bit of vatch stuff I gave to the little one back. I might be able to rely on that. I can't rely on the little vatch. I'll be all chained up on stage and it'll think it a capital joke to disappear."

"I wonder if I can talk Dame Ethulassia into being chained up in one of your performances?" asked Goth, innocently.

"You stay away from her," Pausert said sternly.

"You do the same, then," Goth growled. "Even if I'm not marriageable age yet, I don't want you fooling around with anybody else."

The captain rolled his eyes. "Great. Not only does it seem I've gotten myself a pint-sized fiancée—and how did that happen, exactly? I don't remember anybody asking me—but she's jealous as Medea to boot."

"Don't need to ask, not on Karres," Goth replied firmly. "What's bound to happen is bound to happen. Besides, fair's fair. I'm not fooling around with anybody else either."

"Of course you're not. You're only twelve years old!"

"Still. Fair's fair."

CHAPTER 12

"Well," Dame Ethulassia said, archly, surveying Pausert and the rest of his crew. "I suppose you want to know why I asked you— *here*."

She waved her hand at the rows and rows of theater seats beyond the stage. At least, Pausert *thought* there were rows and rows of seats out there; he could only see the first few.

Goth was paying no attention to the Dame at all. Instead, she was peering into the darkness. "Who's that?" she suddenly demanded.

"*Richard Cravan*," replied a rich and powerful voice from the darkness. The voice seemed to echo, as if in a great cavern.

"*Sir* Richard Cravan," said Dame Ethulassia, "The founder and director of our theatrical company."

To the captain's surprise, she dimpled. The smile made her seem a lot younger. A lot more attractive, too, than her earlier Great Vamp performance. For a moment, The Incredible Bosom even seemed to belong to a real woman.

"Poor Himbie! He thinks I make all the decisions about casting! But if he knew it was Sir Richard, he'd never let us have half the resources he gives me."

"My dear Lassia," chuckled The Voice, "You make as many decisions as I."

"But you are the heart and soul of the Company," Dame Ethulassia replied. Pausert would have expected her to simper, but

95

she simply seemed serious, almost reverent. "Miss Hulik, would you step to the front of the stage, please?"

With a look of surprise, Hulik did so. As she did, Pausert saw words appearing in the air between them and the theater. "This is a love-speech, Miss Hulik," said The Voice. "The lady in question is very young, and so is her lover. They just met this evening, and fell instantly in love, even though their families are involved in a deadly feud. He has come to see if she feels as strongly as he does—as *you* do, Miss Hulik. He stands below you, beneath your balcony. Let me hear you speak to him, please."

Hulik stepped forward—and to Pausert's delight and surprise, seemed to shed years and become someone else altogether.

He had known, of course, that the do Eldel was an agent of the Empress, and as such, was capable of many roles. What he had not really understood was that she could *act*. Hulik started reading her lines from the words projected in the air without seeming even to pause.

"What man art thou," she whispered, "that thus bescreen'd in night so stumblest on my counsel?"

"By a name," The Voice replied, sounding impossibly adolescent, breathless and excited all at once, "I know not how to tell thee who I am: My name, dear Saint, is hateful to myself, because it is an enemy to thee. Had I it written, I would tear the word!"

Hulik clasped her hands before her, gasping with mingled consternation and delight. "My ears have yet not drunk a hundred words of thy tongue's uttering, yet I know the sound. Art thou not Romeo, and a Montague?"

Pausert listened and watched, holding his breath, and he was not the only one. Goth and even the Leewit were doing the same; the grik-dog actually lay down and was gazing up at Hulik soulfully. And when he looked out of the corner of his eye at the Dame, expecting to see her eyeing Hulik with jealousy, he was shocked to see a tear trickling down her cheek and an odd little smile playing on her lips.

Then Hulik finished a very long speech that ended: "And not impute this yielding to light love, which the dark night hath so discovered."

The Voice said, "Enough, Miss Hulik. Thank you. My dear Lassia? I believe you are correct. Historically, it should be the handsome young lady beside Captain Aron, of course, but—no. There are some things it is better not to be accurate about, and allowing Juliet to be portrayed by a young adolescent is one of them."

"It's been too long, dear Richard, since our little troupe has been able to stage *Romeo and Juliet*," the Dame said, with a passion that surprised Pausert. "I am many things, and capable of many roles, but I will no longer attempt to play a fourteen-year-old girl. It would be foolish."

"And you are no fool. Captain Aron?"

"Sir?" Pausert stepped forward.

"May I ask if you have ever handled a sword?"

As it happened, he had. Fencing was one of the sports provided at school on Nikkeldepain, and he'd tried it out of curiosity. He'd kept it up in the Nikkeldepain Navy, since swordsmanship was something of a tradition there. "I fence a bit, sir," he replied cautiously.

"Well! You surprise me pleasantly! A captain who actually knows how to use a sword. I thought that was illegal, these days."

In fact, The Voice *did* sound extremely pleased. But given that whoever The Voice belonged to was obviously a consummate actor, Pausert didn't know if he was or not.

"Come, Captain, step forward. You are Romeo's best friend Mercutio—older, something of a bully-boy, and just a little mad. It was a favored role of mine, but alas! I have accumulated too many years for it. Now, our hero has not met his Juliet at this point—he believes himself in love with another girl, and his friend Mercutio is trying to jolly him out of his depression by coaxing him to go to a party."

The Voice changed, somehow sounding again like that younger self that had spoken with Hulik. "Give me a torch, I am not for this ambling. Being but heavy I will bear the light."

Pausert had been looking at the words in the air, and tried to put on a "jollying" tone. "Nay gentle Romeo, we must have you dance!"

"Not I, believe me! You have dancing shoes with nimble soles, I have a soul of lead so stakes me to the ground, I cannot move."

Romeo sounded like a moping little teenaged fool. *If I were his older friend, what would I sound like when he's in a mood like this?* Pausert wondered. He made himself sound impatient; more than a little tired of this theatrical depression. "You are a Lover, borrow Cupid's wings, and soar with them above a common bound!"

The Voice was finished with him much quicker than with Hulik. "Good, good, you'll do. You're no Barrymore, mind—but if you can handle a sword at all, you're head and shoulders above anyone else we might use for the part. Now, Miss—Hantis, is it? Please step forward."

New words appeared in the air.

"You are something very different, my dear. Your appearance suits you ideally for a creature known as Puck. He is not human, is in fact a sort of magical spirit. He's also exceedingly mischievous. Begin, please?"

Hantis threw herself into the part with more enthusiasm than Pausert had expected—more enthusiasm than talent, perhaps, but The Voice did not interrupt her too quickly. "Good, good, that will do. Your appearance is half the thing, and when I've explained what all that seeming nonsense you've been reciting actually *means*, I believe you'll do very well. And the . . . grik-dog, I believe he is called? With jaws like that, it behooves me not to offend him."

"Pul," growled Pul.

"So it is. Pul, indeed. I mean to have you play one of Titania's attendants, and perhaps, if you do well, a much larger role in another play later on. You might make an interesting Caliban."

Pausert hadn't a clue what all that meant, but the Dame clapped her hands with glee. "Wonderful! And Miss Hantis for Ariel?"

"That was my thought. Now, let me see what the others can do."

The Voice ran through the rest of them in fairly short order. Goth did not seem to be at all unhappy that she was dismissed with: "A Fairy, an attendant on Juliet, and some crowd scenes, I think." But, then, she wouldn't be. Goth took a sly pleasure in being overlooked by people, as long as the captain wasn't one of them.

The Leewit, of course, scowled when she wasn't picked for a larger role, but she didn't make any open protest. Her lips didn't even start to purse for a whistle. Pausert would have been surprised, since the Leewit's self-esteem normally fell in the Mistress of the Universe range. But there was something immensely authoritative about The Voice that even seemed to affect her.

Vezzarn, however, completely declined to even audition, The Voice be damned. "Not me!" he declared, red-faced. "Couldn't recite at school, won't do it now."

Finally: "House Lights," said The Voice. The lights came up beyond the stage, showing a tall, gray-haired man sitting in the fourth row back.

As he stood, it was clear that he had a couple of inches on Pausert, and that he had the sort of face that people would remember.

"Miss Hulik, I hope you understand just what Dame Ethulassia is sacrificing here," he said gravely. "She is giving over the title role to you, a newcomer, not even a classically trained actress, when it is *she* who has been the leading lady of our company."

Pausert wondered if he had been the only one to hear the emphasis on the word "classically." Clearly, Richard Cravan was well aware that Hulik was an actress, even if he wasn't sure just what sort of actress she was.

"Believe me, I'm grateful," Hulik said, sounding as if she were.

"Piff!" said Ethulassia, with an exaggerated wave of her hands. "I still have Titania, Lady Macbeth, and Portia! And Lady Capulet is not so bad a role, anyway."

The Great Vamp returned, alas, and The Incredible Bosom underwent another suprahuman transformation. Ethulassia eyed Pausert through lowered lashes. "I shall be able to play her with that hint of suppressed passion that I've always wanted to do."

Cravan laughed. "Well, Captain! I believe that I can assure Himbo Petey that your crew is going to fully pay its way without anyone being relegated to roustabout or janitorial duty too frequently. Dame Ethulassia will see to it that you all have copies of the four plays we will be doing, with my explanations and annotations so that you can understand some of the archaic languages. There will be a prompter in your ear, and as you saw, we have LiteTitles to be sure that if you forget your lines, they will appear before you. They can be adjusted so the audience can't see them. Our first rehearsal will be tomorrow morning."

That seemed to be a dismissal, and Pausert set at example by turning and exiting the stage. He was followed by Goth, and then, belatedly, by the others.

"Commanding sort, isn't he?" Pausert remarked.

Goth wrinkled her nose. "He didn't even consider that any of us might not *want* to be in his plays."

"Of course he didn't," said Hulik with a smile, coming up behind them. "I've seen his type before. Born actors, and he simply can't even imagine that anyone in his right mind *wouldn't* wish to be on the stage."

Goth didn't seem put out, though. "As long as it means less sweeping, I'll learn to like it well enough."

"If it means less playing the fool, I'll definitely like it," said Pausert.

❋　　❋　　❋

When the *Petey B* lifted off, Pausert scarcely noticed. He was used to the roar and acceleration of his own ship; but, of course, a delicate structure like the lattice ship could not take such stresses and so was using obsolete but still perfectly functional Orris-Jawl engines. The *Petey B* simply elevated, as gracefully and slowly as a puff-seed.

Slowly was indeed the hallmark—no fast getaways here! They took hours to get into space, with the ground of Vaudevillia slowly growing farther and farther away. Pausert would have liked to watch, but he was too busy.

When he wasn't learning his parts for the plays or rehearsing them, he was practicing his escapism, or he was dragooned into any one of a number of odd jobs that called for strength. Over the course of the *Petey B*'s return to space, for instance, he could have been found moving and stowing cargo, bracing a ladder for one of the riggers in the "Big Top," or helping that same rigger haul up the net for the aerialists.

That experience was enough to convince him that "actor" was indeed the best job he could ask for on the ship. Truth to tell, he was hoping he wouldn't even have to spend too much of his time on Sideshow Alley.

So, he was pleased to discover that he had parts in all four of the new plays that Cravan's company was going to perform: He was a character called "Bottom" in *A Midsummer Night's Dream,* Mercutio in *Romeo and Juliet,* a servant called Launcelot in *Merchant of Venice,* and King Duncan in *Macbeth.*

Goth and the Leewit were particularly taken with *Macbeth,* for, with some amusement, Sir Richard had cast them at their own request as two of the three Witches. He had no idea why they wanted to play Witches, until at the first rehearsal, Goth played more of her light-shifts and levitated the potion ingredients into the huge cauldron, adding a very interesting bit of "business" to the scene.

Cravan said nothing more than "hm," but he agreed that they could have the coveted roles, and added Hantis as the third Witch. Since this also meant that none of them would be doing as much mucking-out for the animal-trainers, they were delighted.

Pul wasn't delighted at all. True, no one expected him to do any mucking-out work. But he was beginning to darkly suspect that he'd soon be consigned to the mucking end of the business— locked in a stall himself, as if he were a mere animal! Fortunately for the limbs of all concerned, he stopped growling and baring

✳ THE WIZARD OF KARRES ✳   101

his teeth after Sir Richard allowed that the Bard's Sacred Work could be tweaked enough to permit one of the witches to have a familiar.

Pausert was sorely puzzled by the Dame. She was almost two people: One, flamboyant and flirtatious—and still making sly innuendos regarding "service"—outside the theater; the other, when inside the theater, was serious, careful, and clever, treating everyone with respect and Sir Richard with near-veneration.

He said as much to Goth and Hantis.

"She's an actress," Hantis replied immediately, as if the answer was self-evident. "'Actress' with a capital 'A.'"

"Well yes, but—"

"So, she doesn't confine her acting to the stage."

He thought about it. "But which one is the act?"

Hantis smiled but didn't answer the question. Goth just sighed, shook her head, and started muttering. Pausert didn't quite catch it all, but some of it sounded like: *stupid useless klatha . . . oughta be a way to get older quicker . . . it's not fair . . .*

The Leewit joined the clowns—or "joeys," as they called themselves—fitting in as if she had been one all her life. A group of four, alike as clones, took her into their tumbling act, making her into a kind of human ball that they tossed about. Oddly enough, the Leewit didn't seem offended by the business. The captain was surprised. As a rule, he would have thought, the Mistress of the Universe does not take well to finding herself the Beach Ball of the Galaxy.

Himbo Petey was certainly much happier about it. A little girl being tossed about he could understand; real witches he couldn't.

But however much Himbo was puzzled by Pausert and his companions, it soon became obvious to the captain that he didn't understand the thespians at all. He truly didn't understand the plays that Sir Richard was putting on, or what motivated them to do it.

Pausert walked in on the tail end of one of his arguments—his, because it was entirely one-sided. Sir Richard might look as if the Showmaster was about to drive him mad, but he clearly wasn't going to budge.

"But the audiences won't *like* it if the lovers are dead in the end!" Himbo protested unhappily. "They'll walk out! Wait and see!"

"By the time they walk out the play will be over, Himbo. So I hardly see where it matters."

"But why can't you change the ending?"

"Because then it wouldn't be a *tragedy*, would it?" Cravan waved a playbill under Himbo Petey's nose. "Look there—it's in four colors and full process: *The Great Tragedy of Romeo and Juliet*. I hardly think that the audience is going to arrive expecting jokes!"

"And that's another thing—you've got *clowns* in this play of yours, but they aren't wearing—"

"They're only *called* 'clowns,' Himbo," Cravan said, wearily. Pausert got the feeling this was something that Himbo Petey had been told many times before. "I've explained this to you in the past. They are not circus clowns. They do not wear paint, or clown-suits, or red noses, or big shoes. It is a term that means—"

"Well, if it means *dunces and fools*, then why don't you call them that?" Petey asked resentfully. "Oh, never mind. I still think you should rewrite the ending of that Julioff and Rominette thing. People aren't going to like it, I tell you, and not even all those sword fights are going to appease them!"

After Himbo Petey bounced off, indignation in every step, Cravan put his head in his hands. "One of the greatest classical tragedies of all time, and he wants me to rewrite the ending! Bad enough that I've changed the language to something less archaic, to satisfy him, now he wants me to rewrite a masterpiece!"

Pausert felt he understood why Himbo Petey was so upset. It was clear enough the Showmaster really didn't understand *any* plays, much less these. Petey couldn't grasp why people would be willing to sit for hours and watch live actors on a stage, with limited effects and scenery, when they could see the same story on holo, replete with special effects—and with no human actors who might forget their lines.

In truth, Pausert wasn't sure he understood it either, no matter how many times Dame Ethulassia tried to explain it to him. Petey was certain that displaying something that was going to make people cry instead of laugh was a bad idea; and while Pausert didn't agree with him entirely, he wondered just how many people would be willing to watch something so primitive, and so full of archaic language.

He reminded himself that, fortunately, the *Petey B* didn't often set down on sophisticated worlds where there were holo-theaters and threedee parlors, and a vidscreen for every room in your house. So maybe the audiences wouldn't have any objections.

Certainly the staged sword fights were exciting things. Richard Cravan plotted every single one of the moves and had all of the participants learn them to background music, so that it was all like a complicated dance, with the music telling you what to do. And if something happened and you missed a move, you didn't have to think about what was coming next; all you had to do was pick it up at the next beat.

When he wasn't worrying, Pausert was enjoying that part, far more than he'd expected to, but he was certain that his other act, the escapist act, wasn't going to come up to Himbo Petey's standards. He hadn't relled vatch in days, and while he thought he'd probably be able to replicate what the vatch had done, with Goth's help, he was afraid by this time that *not* relling vatch meant that the wretched little creature would turn up at the worst possible moment.

He was worried about a lot of other things, too. The ISS, for one. This new Nanite plague that Hantis had told them about, for another. The pirates. Why Karres had disappeared again. If he was ever going to get the *Venture* back.

Meanwhile, Hulik was also enjoying the situation—far more, in his personal opinion, than she should be. She had thrown herself into her four roles with astonishing enthusiasm, but it was the role of Juliet that she was really reveling in. She seemed to have forgotten all about their plight, the poor old *Venture*, and the urgent need to get to the Empress with whatever information that Hantis had.

As for Hantis herself, well, Pausert never had been able to tell what the Sprite was thinking anyway. He hoped she was as worried as he was, because everyone else, even Goth and the Leewit, was acting as if they really *were* children who had run away to join the circus.

Even Vezzarn! He didn't have an act at all, and as a consequence, didn't have much choice but to muck out animal cages to earn his way. But when Pausert asked him, in the middle of shoveling out several tons of fanderbag manure, if he wasn't nearly dying with eagerness to get the *Venture* fueled and fixed and get gone, he looked up with astonishment.

"What, Captain? And give up *show business*?"

Pausert could only throw up his hands and walk away.

Their first planetfall after Vaudevillia was a little agro-world called Hanson's Reach. Pausert was a little astonished by the backwardness of the place. Once you got a few miles from the port, people actually used *animals* for transportation.

Not farming, though. That was business, and animals couldn't do the work that an all-purpose combine could do. But the precious and expensive fuel was saved for farm machines. No one wasted it on the unimportant matter of getting people from here to there.

The *Petey B* set down just outside the port, landing as slowly as she'd taken off from Vaudevillia. Her descent was announced by a shower of bright-colored leaflets as they drifted over the landscape—or to be more precise, while the landscape drifted by underneath the *Petey B*. Using the lattice ship's inertial drives meant that Hanson's Reach rotated under them and they slowly matched up to the planetary rotation.

The leaflet were vivid bits of butterfly-bright paper that were cut and shaped to fly like little wings in all directions, They spread the word that the *Petey B*, home of **PETEY, BYRUM AND KEEP, THE GREATEST SHOW IN THE GALAXY**, was beginning a limited engagement on Hanson's Reach, setting down by special arrangement just outside the main center of population and commerce.

"Limited?" Pausert asked, since he'd heard of no set departure date.

Mannicholo shrugged. "Limited to as long as their money holds out."

The *Petey B* certainly provided a spectacle that was as good as a parade as they set down. And, once they were down, the set-up was a show in and of itself.

If Pausert hadn't been busy helping, he'd have wanted to watch. It looked as if every man, woman, and especially child that could possibly get to the showboat was standing out there, gawking. Stages were deployed, the stays and struts that held up the synthasilk of the tents popped open, tents were hauled up, canopies unfolded, bleachers and benches arrayed, rigging rigged and ropes winched tight, bunting and flags strung out to flap and snap in the breeze, and lastly, the huge banners depicting all the delights to be found within were dropped down to hang from every vertical surface—and all of it was done to a chant of "*Push* 'em back! *Haul* 'em back! *Take* 'em back! *Ho!*"

What that was supposed to mean, nobody seemed to know. But it was effective, because it wasn't all autowinches and robot-pulleys that did the work, it was muscle and sweat of people and beasts. The huge fanderbags were hitched in teams to pull up the biggest tent-poles; grumbling and complaining, the humpies did the same for the smaller poles. And every hand that might be useful was put on a rope for the several hours it took to get the show-boat up and running.

And when they were all finished, the *Petey B* looked very like the showboat of Pausert's memories: all bright-colored flags and banners and synthasilk veiling the workaday exterior of the lat-tice ship, so that it hardly looked like a thing that could go to space at all. And for the first time since they'd hitched up with the *Petey B*, Pausert began to feel a tingling sensation of dread and fear and excitement that had nothing whatsoever to do with all of the predicaments that had brought them here.

CHAPTER 13

The free Sedmon, still in the portside alleys of Gerota Town, had to pause and lean against the wall to cope with the nausea and the pain.

"What's up, chum?" said one of a pair of crop-haired spacers who had just turned the corner. "Too much of the local rotgut?"

The Sedmons were now very wary of even the most innocuous seeming encounter. The free Sedmon watched these two with some caution. "Just stomach cramps. I ate some dodgy local food."

The other spacer grinned. "Stick to the grog next time. At least you've got a decent excuse for being sick. You need any help?"

The Sedmon was still far from trusting. The two of them were coming a little too close, and something in the second fellow's voice sounded a bit off. "Just trying to find the rest of my crew. There are ten of us off the *Vanel*. Have seen a bunch of guys—one of them the size of two of me—trundling around? They're probably looking for me by now. Or do you know where 'Voyager Smiles' is? It's a posh little gift-shop we were heading for."

If they had been thinking of any funny stuff, the two weren't anymore. "Thora's place? It's just around the corner to your left," said the first speaker, tugging at his friend's arm. "Come on, Merk. We've got things to do."

Sure enough, the Sedmon found what he'd set out to look for. The gift shop was an expensive-looking establishment in a considerably more respectable street a mere two blocks from the spaceport. A much safer street, too, from its appearance.

Inside, the Sedmon gave the haughty proprietress a near heart-failure. The Daal's agents did have certain code recognition symbols—individual ones, so not a bit of good came of torturing or drugging them out of someone. The words that Thora Herrkin heard from the lips of the slightly shaky-looking man were not something she was prepared for. But she knew that she'd better give him the best cooperation and help possible.

The Sedmon in the truth-shock chair, on the other hand, was giving his captors as little help as possible. It was possible for him to do that, because, now that he was aware of what was coming, he could split the electroshock between the selves of the hexaperson. The sensation made all of them feel more than a little ill, but it was bearable.

So, he just resigned himself to a period of unpleasantness. Indeed, he was almost serene about the whole matter. One of the great advantages of being a hexaperson was that he had complete and total confidence in his closest associates. And why not? They were him, after all.

Evening and the local ISS headquarters were both close. For the sort of money the Daal had on call, recruiting a few ex-troopers willing to do a great deal with no questions asked had been an easy enough task. And from Thora, who was now very eager to oblige, the Sedmons knew of the disastrous happenings on Pidoon—and that the *Venture* had, once again, abruptly and mysteriously disappeared.

"Some of them are still on the run, sir. It's a bit confusing but a woman reputedly called Captain Elin and a couple of her men are hiding out somewhere—along with a local hoodlum called Fullbricht. The ISS can't find them, but my partners know where they are. They're in a small farm just outside town next to the lake. Fullbricht keeps a boat there he uses for dropping, ah, ferroplast 'statues' into the water."

The Sedmon scowled—not at the ruthlessness involved in submerging corpses, but at the pettiness of the whole situation. Local criminals and their pitiful attempts at being murderous. Bah. In times past, the Daals of Uldune had terrified entire star sectors. They were moments—not often, but this was one of them—when the Sedmons regretted their modern civilized ways.

The hexaperson cheered himself up with the thought that, on the other hand, they still weren't all *that* civilized.

"We'll arrange a visit, then," he said coldly, "just as soon as we have the matter in hand dealt with."

A shifty-looking man in spacer's clothes was ushered into the back office of the gift shop where the Sedmon had set up his makeshift temporary headquarters. The man handed over a spaceship lock-key and a chronometer. "The chronometer got brought to the hock-shop about twenty minutes back. One of the boys extracted the key from Slick Wullie."

"Ah," said the gift shop proprietress. "Do you want him dealt with?"

The free Sedmon winced. His captive clone was being tortured again. "No, there is no point in drawing attention to the matter any further. Is my ship still being watched?"

"Not since about ten minutes back," said the ever-efficient Thora.

"Good. Let us proceed, then."

The Sedmon, along with Thora and the hired mercenaries, went back to the *Thunderbird* in a nondescript van. A few minutes later, they set off for ISS headquarters with a cutter and two cylinders. One had a highly illegal anesthetic in it. It was nearly odorless, and fast acting. The other was a rather unpleasant standby. But the Sedmons were rather tired of taking the pain, and they'd never been fond of the ISS to begin with.

There was a small basin in the corner of the ISS rooms, where a fastidious torturer could wash his hands between beatings. The drainage pipe from the basin bubbled as the gas was pumped through. But, as Sedmon inside was cued by Sedmon outside, his screams hid the noise quite well. The hexaperson encountered the strange sensation of having one of themselves gently pass out.

Somewhat regretfully, the Sedmon satisfied himself with simply extracting his clone. If he'd had the time and the additional space in his vehicle . . . A number of ISS agents would have become ferroplast statues providing shelter for fish at the bottom of a lake.

But, he simply left them there. He consoled himself with the thought that recovering from that particular anesthetic was an excruciating experience if you didn't possess the antidote—of which he had enough for his clone but no one else. That was partly why he'd picked it. Well. That was *mainly* why he'd picked it.

Not all that civilized, even the modern Daal of Uldune.

✳　　✳　　✳

Fifteen minutes later, the plain van and two other vehicles were making a visit to a small farm by the lakeside.

One of the ex-soldiers, a former sergeant in the Imperial Naval Infantry, studied the place through his nightscope. Then, he offered the device to the awake Sedmon, while the clone in the car went through waking up with the help of a well-paid medical assistant. If Thora thought the two looked remarkably alike, she was sensible enough not to say anything. Or question the money in her account.

The Sedmon using the nightscope examined the farm carefully. The incredibly expensive device's sophisticated thermoimaging even allowed him to study the farm's inhabitants. Quickly, he was able to determine that there were three people in the building. The crew of the *Venture*—including the one the Sedmons were particularly concerned about—were not among the inhabitants. The Sedmons would have been surprised if they had been, but having the assumption confirmed caused a momentary—and most disconcerting—spike of anguish.

Across light-years, the hexaperson issued a collective sigh. Not because of the disappointment, so much as the simple fact of it. They had lived a life of splendid isolation, after all, and the recognition that they now intended to give it up—if at all possible— produced very mixed feelings.

The Sedmon watching through the nightscope didn't personally recognize the trio in the farm. But the Sedmons back in the tower at the House of Thunders had access to a great many records.

They found her. And her associates.

The Sedmon turned to Thora. "There is an Imperial bounty on her head. A million maels, I believe. Her real name is Nairdoo Sheyan. Among other things, she's wanted for the mass murder of the miners on Coolum's World. The second one, Henry Bagr, is worth a mere fifty thousand. The third, I believe, is your local Fullbright fellow. He'll be worth something too, I imagine, though not much."

"Do we get a cut?" inquired Thora. She looked as if she regretted the words almost as soon as she said them.

But Sedmon smiled at her. "You can have it all, Thora. You've been most efficient and helpful, and I believe in rewarding those of my subordinates who are. Your talents are clearly wasted, anyway, just smuggling and spying and selling expensive trinkets."

A thought came to him. "Although, before I leave the planet,

I'll want to purchase a suitable trinket for . . . ah, someone. A young lady."

"I have just the thing."

"Good. And now, let's finish this business."

The smile was still on the Sedmon's face, but it had become a very grim sort of thing. He had no way of knowing it, but at that moment Thora had no doubt at all that her boss was in the direct line of descent from the Daals of Uldune who had committed far worse crimes than even such as Nairdoo Sheyan.

"The reward specifies 'dead or alive,'" he murmured. "Make that 'dead,' if you please. The Sheyan creature has been threatening certain, ah, interests of mine. And I'm not in a charitable mood."

CHAPTER 14

"Who's that?" Pausert asked Mannicholo sharply, pointing to a sausage vendor strolling among the audience. The man looked perfectly ordinary, with his hotbox of sausages slung over his shoulders and not a sign of manner, costume, or oddity to mark him. That was suspicious, for it meant he was too ordinary to be one of Himbo Petey's people.

"Eh? Oh. Local. Petey has all the real food here sold and made by locals."

"Locals? But I thought we sold—"

Mannicholo shook his head vigorously, so that his facial colors swirled like oil on the water. "All we sell are CarniSnax, that come straight out of the replicators. CarniCorn, CarniFluff, CarniPops, CarniCreme, CarniBars, CarniBites, and CarniSlurps. Fat, sugar, starch, water and salt, is all that's in them; one hundred percent artificially flavored and nutritionally null, packed with enough preservatives that if you pick up a Pak in a thousand years it still won't have passed its sell-by date. The stuff's pure garbage but it's guaranteed not to poison any sapient in the known universe. Real food gets sold by the locals and we take a cut. That way *we* don't have to store and cook real food for more than the crew, and if anybody gets poisoned, or wants to claim he has been, he has to take it up with one of his own people."

Pausert eyed the vendor with disfavor. It was going to be hard enough to try and pick out possible crooks, ISS agents, freelance spies and piratical agents out of the crowd as it was. With a lot of loose locals being given carte blanche to run around backstage for the purpose of selling sausage rolls and funnel cakes, it was going to be even harder. You could hide almost any sort of spying mechanism in one of those food boxes! And you could hide weapons, too.

He tried to convey his concern to the rest of the *Venture*'s crew as they waited for the stagehands to set things up for a final dress rehearsal. Hulik just gave him an opaque look, saying, "It will be just as hard for any spies to find out who *we* are, Captain. We are part of the showboat family now, and they are notoriously close mouthed around strangers, especially when someone has come around asking questions about one of their own."

Hantis said nothing. "I can smell a spy a mile away," growled Pul. "Don't you worry about that."

The Leewit looked positively bored. "We're smarter than they are," she said, with the absolute confidence of a seven-year-old Mistress of the Universe. "They haven't caught us before, and they won't now."

Pausert decided not to remind her that being encased in ferroplast didn't fall in with *his* definition of "not being caught."

Goth, at least, looked as worried as he felt. "I don't like it either," she admitted. "But we can't keep them off the ship. We'll just have to be careful."

That didn't fit his definition of a solution either. Pausert worried about it so much that all through rehearsal, he kept missing cues and his marks. He'd have thought that Richard Cravan would be so angry with him that he'd be fired from the thespians outright—but nothing whatsoever was said.

In fact, Cravan looked guardedly pleased. Pausert couldn't figure out why, and said so aloud.

Alton Morrisey, the male romantic lead who was playing Romeo to Hulik's Juliet, looked up from his script. "Bad dress, good opening," he said abruptly.

It took Pausert a moment to decipher that. He decided that it must be another of the thespians' superstitions, like never whistling in the theater and always referring to *Macbeth* as "The Scottish Play" and *Richard the Third* as "Dick Three-Eyes." Presumably, it meant that a bad dress rehearsal resulted in a good opening performance. He hoped that was right, although for someone like himself who had been trained as a space pilot, the logic was downright bizarre.

But Pausert decided not to worry about it. He was feeling more relaxed, anyway, since now that every single one of them was in stage makeup most of the time he realized that they'd inadvertently stumbled across an splendid antispy technique. He was certain that not even his own mother would recognize him, done up in a foxy-colored wig as Mercutio.

Nevertheless, despite all of his other worries, the moment the curtain came up, somehow he forgot all of them. He watched raptly from the wings as Sampson and Gregory (who were Capulet servants) complained that they would not put up with insults from the Montague family. Then Abram and Balthasar (Montague servants) appeared and the four started quarreling. Benvolio (Lord Montague's nephew) appeared and tried to break up the quarrel, but Tybalt (Lady Capulet's nephew) appeared and picked a fight with Benvolio.

That was Pausert's first cue. Himbo Petey had enforced his will on Richard Cravan at least to this extent: he insisted on mêlées of the largest possible size whenever there was supposed to be a sword fight. So, the captain rushed onstage to join the action.

Here, Richard Cravan's cleverness showed itself. Every pair of fighters had only four moves to memorize: two attacks and two parries. The secret was that each pair had *different* combinations, so that it looked like an amazingly complex and very realistic fight. In fact, out in the audience, Pausert could hear cheering and bets being placed. Every actor who knew how to handle a sword was doing so—everyone else was waving or wielding foam batons disguised as clubs or singlesticks. Even Goth, the Leewit, and Hantis were doing so, while Pul put in his bit by lunging into the mêlée and—carefully!—seizing the leg of one of the actors. It was a well-rehearsed bit of business. Pul dragged the fellow offstage while he screamed at the top of his lungs.

At length, officers tried to break up the fight, even while Lord Capulet (played by Cravan) and Lord Montague (played by Himbo Petey) began to fight one another. The Prince of Verona finally appeared and stopped the fighting, proclaiming sentences of death to any that dared to break the peace of the city again.

Pausert could then retire from the stage with everyone else— and to his amazement, he found himself shaking with excitement. The cheers of the crowd had acted on him like a drug, and it was a drug he wanted more of!

But he could not have any just then, for the curtain fell and came back up on Montague's house, and there were two more scenes before his next entrance in Scene Four.

He got to observe Hulik, then, in her first real stage appearance as Juliet. Even though he had watched her in rehearsals, her full performance left him blinking. He would have sworn on his life that she was hardly more than a young girl, in her mid-teens at most. Maybe some of that was makeup, but the rest was acting. He'd seen her act the seductress often enough, but it was a revelation to see her play the complete innocent, and do so convincingly.

Her performance left him vowing to make his Mercutio alive and real to those people out there. So when he swaggered onstage, he threw himself into his part with everything he had.

He had to stay onstage, in the background, for the rest of the party scene. And, great Patham, if he wasn't half in love with "young Juliet" himself before it was over. And he *knew* her!

When he finally made his exit, to gratifying applause, he felt almost drunk. It was wonderful! Wonderful! Who would have guessed that he had the makings of an actor in him? Who would have guessed that it was so intensely satisfying? He began to wonder if perhaps when this was all over, maybe he could come back to the *Petey B* and resume his place here. . . .

And that was when he relled vatch.

"Oh no—" he breathed, and looked frantically about for it.

But it was not his nemesis, the little silver-eyed one. It was another big one, and he didn't even wait for it to announce itself or start in on mischief. While Juliet and Romeo played out their first love scene, he closed his eyes and made klatha hooks and tore into the thing.

OW! STOP! OW! It shouted at him, shocked and dismayed. STOP IT, DREAM THING! THIS IS MY DREAM! STOP IT RIGHT NOW!

Go away! he thought back at it, *This isn't your dream, it's mine, and I don't want you in it.*

OW! SPOILSPORT! the vatch whined. VICIOUS BEAST! SEE IF I EVER DREAM ABOUT YOU AGAIN!

It took itself off to wherever vatches went, leaving behind little black patches of vatch stuff. Pausert collected it all up, and that was when he relled vatch—again.

This time it *was* the little silver-eyed vatch.

Hee hee! it crowed with glee. **You got him good!**

Suddenly he smelled a rat, a vatchy-rat. *You lured that vatch here, didn't you?* he thought at it, suspiciously. *You* wanted *me to beat him up!*

Sure. I want to get bigger and you can help me. And you know what? I'm not sure you're a dream thing at all. I think you might be a real thing, coming into my dreams, like another vatch.

Suddenly, Pausert felt very cold all over. Here was something he had worried about for a long time, staring him in the face. The vatches were some sort of interdimensional beings who thought of Pausert's universe as nothing more than a dream, and good only for entertainment value. So they were inclined to meddle and make trouble for the amusement of it, but that also meant that they didn't take any of what they saw and did too seriously. But if they actually realized that all of this was as real as their own universe, what would they do? Try and destroy it, for instance?

Oh, don't be such a fraidy, the vatchlet said scornfully. I won't tell. You help me, Big Maybe-Real Thing, and I'll help you!

How? he asked skeptically.

Give me that vatch stuff, so I can get bigger. I'm tired of being little. They pick on the little ones.

I'm not sure that's a good idea. Pausert reminded himself forcefully that he couldn't actually control this sort of vatch, only distract it. Even as little as it was, the thing had been something of a nightmare. Grown big and powerful . . .

I'll help you, the vatchlet countered. I promise! If you give me the pieces of vatch stuff, I'll only do what you ask me to. Well, pretty much. Please?

He wanted to ask Goth for advice, but there wasn't time.

And this vatch, while full of mischief, had never actually done anything malicious . . .

Unlike the Big Windy, for instance. Now there was a vatch that could stand having a few more bits pulled out of it!

All right, he agreed, pulling the vatch stuff out of his pocket. *But you have to ask me before you go luring any more vatches here for me to beat up. And if I don't have the time right then, you'll just have to wait.*

It absorbed the shadowy patch of vatch stuff before it answered, and even as it grew bigger, it also seemed to become a little more serious.

All right, I promise. You *must* be a real thing. I finally figured out this place has linear time. I wouldn't dream something as silly as linear time, so you've got to be real. Anything you want me to do?

Oh my, he thought. *Not only more serious, but more intelligent!* It made him wonder just what the vatches actually were. And how they normally "got big."

Not right now, he said hastily. His next cue was coming up. *Just, er, watch, and enjoy the show. This is—is—kind of awake-dreaming that we real-things do, to tell a story to each other.*

Is it? What fun! Oooo— Pausert sensed it somehow looking over the audience. **It's just a story? Like a dream? But they're excited like it's all real!**

Yes, and some of them already know what the ending will be, but they're still excited. He was pleased to have given it a new sort of diversion. *Watch them watching us, and you'll see.*

Then his cue came, and he swaggered back onstage.

By now the audience had decided that they liked him, especially when he played his bawdy tricks on Juliet's Nurse. They were laughing at the slapstick humor of it, and even though half of his attention was on the vatch, he thought he had completed the job that Richard Cravan had set him—to make the audience care about him, so that when Tybalt killed him—

Well, that was for later. He took his exit, and realized that the little vatch was gone. He heaved a sigh of relief. One less thing to worry about.

For now.

"—and that was when it stopped, well, acting like a vatch," he concluded, as Goth and the Leewit stared at him. "Or at least, like the vatches I've run into before."

"We always knew there were some vatches that couldn't be controlled, even by a really good vatch-handler like you. What I'm wondering now is whether that's just because the vatches we usually run into are just, well, vatch-style village idiots?"

The Leewit scowled, but it was her thinking sort of scowl. "You did all right, Captain," she said, finally. "I think maybe Goth's right. It's not a new sort of vatch, but just one you don't run across too often. You think if it eats vatch stuff and keeps getting smarter, maybe someday it'll get smart enough to leave us alone?"

Pausert shrugged. "As long as it's willing to play nice, I don't care. I'm not going to give it too much vatch stuff, though. What if it gets smart and big, then decides to really mess with us? By that point it'd be so big I couldn't distract it anymore by tickling it with klatha hooks."

"Good thinking," the Leewit agreed, just as her chrono chimed.

"Oops! Got to get to the Big Top!" She scampered out of the dressing room so fast she might just as well have teleported to the circus side of the ship. Pausert glanced at his own chrono; she had about half an hour to get into her clown costume and makeup before the Entrance Parade. It was the first time he'd ever seen the Leewit making sure she was on time for anything.

That worried him. She was enjoying her role in the circus; maybe enjoying it too much.

"We're fitting in here entirely too well," said Goth, in an echo of his own thoughts.

Pul shouldered his way into the dressing room, growling back over his shoulder at the Nartheby Sprite and Hulik, who were following him. "—and you're liking this too much!" he said. "What about our mission? What about the Nanite plague? What about the Empress?"

Hulik, smiling faintly, leaned back against a wall, and started removing the long wig she wore as Juliet. Hantis folded herself into a chair. "I am liking this, but I haven't forgotten, Pul," she said seriously. "The trouble is, there are entirely too many people trying to find us. The Agandar's pirates, not to mention the ISS. For all I know, the Sedmons might even be looking for us! One at a time we could evade, but until we shake some of the hunters off, every time we start to run, we're only going to run into someone else. And the only way we can shake them is by doing what we're doing: going to ground, not poking our noses up until we've lost some or all of them."

"We're going to ground?" the grik-dog said, blinking. "I thought we were earning fuel-money, repair-money, our passage and buying the *Venture* free."

"We're also in hiding, in the best way possible way," said Hulik. "We're *not* hiding."

Pul shook his head rapidly, his ears flapping like a pair of frantic wings. "Hiding? Not in hiding? You two are making my head hurt!"

"Mine too," said Pausert, "And I have to agree with Pul—I think you all like this life too much."

"If we tried to actually hide anywhere, chances are that we'd be found," Hulik insisted. "Believe me, it's the hardest thing in the world, trying to stay underground. You have to eat, you have to drink, and sooner or later, you nearly go crazy for a bit of open space around you. And people will always be looking for you and looking *at* you if you act as if you don't want to be seen. But if you do what we're doing—why, we're not in hiding, are we? We're some of the most visible people on the *Petey B*! Three shows a day, for most of us, two shows in the Freak Show or the Big Top and one on stage, out in front of thousands and thousands of people. Obviously we're not trying to hide! But—!"

She held up a finger, as Hantis nodded. "Do we *look* like the people that the ISS and the pirates are trying to find? Do we *act* like them?"

"Well, no," admitted Pul.

Goth was apparently rethinking the matter. "If we do witchery here, people will just assume it's tricks," she admitted. "And they'll figure we're working on something new for the acts. Nobody believes in Karres witches on the *Petey B*—I know; I've nosed around. They think it's all misdirection and mirrors!"

Hulik spread her hands. "You see?" she said to Pul and Pausert. "There's something else I don't think you've noticed. Outside— people are always asking personal questions about you—who are you, where are you from, where are you going, who do you know, what's your business? Hadn't you noticed, not even Himbo Petey asked very much about us."

"Well . . ." said Pausert slowly, his brow wrinkling as he thought back. "I guess you're right."

"I've been monitoring his data-access, Captain," said Goth. "He just did superficial checking on us, to make sure we weren't well-known violent criminals or something. After that, he didn't seem to care."

"He *doesn't* care," Hulik said firmly. "Showboat people are often people hiding something, or running from something, trying to live something down, or trying to forget something. That's why nobody goes poking their noses in where they're not invited. I expect if I ran full security checks on everyone on the *Petey B*, there wouldn't be more than a handful of people who would pass. Everybody has a secret, and in order to keep their own secrets, they protect the secrets of everyone else in the family. We're part of the family now, and if any outsiders come poking around, asking questions, they'll get as many stories about us as there are people they ask, and not one of those stories will be anything like the truth."

At that, Goth started to chuckle. "That explains why Mannicholo was telling the Clown Master that the captain and the Leewit and me are all cousins that Ethulassia talked Himbo Petey into hiring away from a big, important theater company on Rellart where we were all stars!"

Hulik echoed Goth's chuckle. "And last I heard, *you*, Pul, are actually a were-dog from Kolatte—and you're the real ventriloquist, because Hantis is a mute!" She smiled, and began to comb out her wig. "The stories will only get wilder and less believable. Everyone will make a up a different one, to help protect us, without any of us even hinting that we need protecting. So we're as safe here as we could be anywhere outside of the Empress' palace."

"That may be true," Pausert said grudgingly. "But what about our mission?"

"The mission is only going to end badly if we get caught," pointed out Hantis. "So we'll just have to be patient, and do what we can, when we can, until we can break away without being chased."

"And right now, I think that means doing your escapist show over on Sideshow Alley," said Goth, looking meaningfully at his chrono.

Pausert left, shaking his head. They were probably right, but he didn't like it. If anything, he was even more worried, because the longer they stayed here, the harder it would be to leave. After all, wasn't this a dream come true? Didn't everyone want to run away to join the circus? The trouble was, running away was the last thing he wanted to do.

Pausert woke up in the darkness, and relled vatch. **Hello, Big Real Thing!** it saluted him cheerfully.

For once, he was happy to salute it back. *Hello, Silver-eyes*, he thought at it. *I have a question for you.*

Oh, a question! Now I know you're a real thing. Dream things don't ask questions.

He thought about asking the vatch if it was different from other vatches, but realized that was a stupid question and would deserve a stupid answer. After all, if the vatch had asked him if he was different from other humans, he'd answer "yes," of course. Any human would.

Do all vatches get bigger and smarter when they eat vatch stuff? he asked instead.

Silver-eyes laughed—a new difference. It used to giggle. **Bigger, sure. Not always smarter, though. A lot of the big ones are really stupid.**

But you do get smarter and bigger?

Of course. That's why I want more vatch stuff. Being smarter is a lot more fun than being stupider.

Are there more vatches who can do that? If he was going to run into a plague of uncontrollable vatches, he wanted to know about it.

Not many. And when we get smart enough, we can go to the (*) place.

The thought of (*) seemed untranslatable. But the clear sense Pausert got was that it was a place that was very desirable—and very much "not *here*." He decided not to ask Silver-eyes any more questions about it. It probably wouldn't mean anything to him, and it just might be one of those strange klatha things that would turn his head inside out if he did understand it.

I've thought about something you can do for me, then. I'd like it if you can make trouble for the dream things that start to make trouble for us. Not the ones that only pretend to make trouble, he added hastily, *like the ones in that show-story that the others and I play in, or the way the clowns toss the Leewit around. I mean real trouble.*

Like when you were trying to hide Little and Teeth? That was a neat trick, the way you twisted light around! I never would have thought of it myself until I saw you do it.

What Pausert got along with the words "Little" and "Teeth" were impressions of Hantis and Pul that concentrated on the Nartheby Sprite's relative height and Pul's formidable jaws. Pausert thought about trying to get the vatch to identify them by their names, but it was probably a lost cause.

Yes. If that sort of person is going to make trouble, I'd like you to make their lives as difficult for them as possible. For once, he reflected, he was not going to have to worry about people seeing impossible things. This was a circus, and anything that appeared impossible would, without a doubt, be chalked up to smoke and mirrors and stage-trickery.

I might, agreed the vatchlet. Since that was probably the most he was going to get out of the creature, the captain left it at that. It had already promised not to make trouble for *them,* which was more than he had ever gotten out of a vatch before this.

Feed me?

Can you bring me something to feed you with? he countered.

Think so.

Its presence faded away, and he started to drift back to sleep again, when he suddenly relled something *big*, and right on top of him!

With a muffled, startled yell, he formed klatha hooks and sank them into the thing. The vatch was almost as startled as he was, even more so when it knew it had been caught. It literally ripped itself off his hooks and vanished.

Silver-eyes appeared the instant it was gone, and he sensed it dancing with impatience when it "saw" the bits of vatch stuff clinging to his hooks. **Feed me!**

Once again, Pausert realized, Silver-eyes had lured a big vatch into the area. He was irritated at the little vatch—it could have at least given some warning!—but he gave it what it wanted. And, once again, saw it growing just a tiny bit bigger.

I'll watch, it said then, in a "voice" that seemed a bit more mentally resonant. Then it faded away again. Unable to make up his mind if he had done a good or a bad thing, Pausert turned over, and finally got back to sleep.

There seemed to be no immediate fallout from the agreement the next day. Which was just as well, since the theatrical company was now in rehearsal for a second play in the morning, while continuing the performances of *Romeo and Juliet* in the evening, and one of the works they'd already had in their repertoire in the late afternoon. That one was called *Twelfth Night* and required a much smaller cast.

Contrary to Himbo Petey's glum predictions, the audiences here seemed to have no objections to a play that ended in tragedy, but Richard Cravan decided that the second play put into performance with his augmented cast should be a comedy. He chose *A Midsummer Night's Dream* in order to use Hantis and Pul. Pul, Goth and the Leewit were creatures called Fairies with fairly extensive speaking roles; Hantis was the Puck-creature that Cravan had mentioned by name, and Hulik played one of the two romantic parts, a girl by the name of Helen. As usual, Cravan himself acted as well as directed, playing King Oberon; Ethulassia was Titania, his Queen.

Even Vezzarn was pressed into service this time. This was a play with an enormous cast, even bigger than *Romeo and Juliet*, and Cravan recruited people from all over the showboat for non-speaking roles. If they were able to come in on cues and "hit their spots," had interesting faces or could dance a little, they would find themselves filling a place in crowd scenes.

And Pausert found himself playing the clown Bottom against Dame Ethulassia.

Now that put him in an extremely uncomfortable position, for

Ethulassia was supposed to fall in love with him thanks to a magical love potion administered by Puck. He couldn't tell if her flirtatious manner onstage was part of her act, or some not-so-subtle attempt to get his attention offstage. Maybe he was enjoying his performances as Mercutio a little too much, and this was the Fates' way of getting back at him. And the more he, as Bottom, tried to evade Ethulassia's cooing caresses, the more she pursued him.

Cravan found this interpretation to be hilariously funny. So, evidently, did almost everyone else in the company, for many of the cast members congratulated him on an original "take" on the character. Goth simply gave him sidelong, opaque looks, saying nothing. The Leewit, on the other hand, taunted him with scathing remarks under her breath whenever he was just within earshot. Hantis and Hulik were amused; Vezzarn couldn't understand why he wasn't following up on Ethulassia's flirtations. Only Pul seemed to sympathize with him.

And he had not forgotten Silver-eyes, either. Though, if the little vatch was around, it was staying so far out of his way that he couldn't rell it at all. He finally cornered both the girls, and told them what had happened the last time it had come around.

"So now I think maybe I've gotten us deeper in trouble than we were before," he said worriedly.

The Leewit shook her head. "I don't know—" she began, but Goth let out her breath in a hiss.

"Huh," she said. "I just thought of something, Captain. What if the vatches we see are all—oh, in a coma or something. They aren't stupid, they're just brain-damaged. That's why they think we're dreams. And the ones like Silver-eyes are the ones that are going to wake up, if they can just get enough vatch stuff put together. Maybe they need it to get their brains back on-line."

Now Pausert felt guilty as well as worried. "That's horrible!" he replied. "If that's true, then I'm beating up on—"

Goth waved her hand at him. "We don't know that," she reminded him. "We don't really know anything much about vatches. And anyway, they don't have any guilt over making *our* lives miserable, so I don't see why you should feel guilty about what you're doing. Maybe it'll teach some of them not to mess us up."

"Besides," the Leewit said firmly. "Silver-eyes is one of the kind that you can't control. The sooner you get it out of our universe and into some place else, the better!"

Well, he could agree with that, but it just didn't make him feel any better.

CHAPTER 15

Sedmon the Sixth, Daal of feared and blood-soaked Uldune, looked at the exquisite little jewel box inset with chalcosites and pieces of peacock-blue Lepida Pua nacre. It was a pretty little trinket—not to mention a very expensive one. But would the intended recipient like it? With that person, it was hard to know.

And, more to the immediate point, where was she? Where were the rest of them, for that matter? He knew the *Venture* had had little air, a leaking airlock, and very little fuel when it had evaded destruction at the hands of the Imperial Navy off Pidoon.

Despite these rather unpromising circumstances, he was fairly certain they'd have gotten away. In the hexaperson's youth, Sedmon had once made the mistake of taking Karres lightly. Threbus and Toll had given the Daal—and a goodly portion of his space fleet—a polite but firm lesson. Two witches . . . and he almost hadn't had much of a fleet left. Ever since, Uldune had bent over backwards not to irritate the witches. And, ever since, Sedmon had been careful not to underestimate them and to wear his telepathy disturbing skullcap when they were around.

It had been made abundantly plain to him that if worse came to worst, the witches could do without spaceships or even space-suits.

Hulik do Eldel couldn't. Neither could his former spy, Vezzarn, though that did not trouble him much.

And, he privately suspected—although he had no proof—neither could Captain Pausert. But Pausert *might* be one of the Karres witches. You never could be absolutely sure. Sedmon hoped not—because he was very sure that the little Wisdom with Pausert would not abandon him, which would probably mean keeping Hulik alive too.

But there was no trace of the blasted ship! If they'd only used the drives inside an atmospheric envelope, the detectors wouldn't have picked that up. Unless they were dead, or had used some form of Karres witchery.

Light-years away on Uldune, the other Sedmons concurred. They used the House of Thunders' elaborate astrography equipment to look for possible destinations for ships low on air and fuel.

Vaudevillia came up on top of the probability list. Since they had no better leads, the *Thunderbird* left for the planet—on the same day, as it happened, when the Pidoon vidcasts were trumpeting the demise of the infamous Nairdoo Sheyan, pirate murderer of Coolum's World, along with two of her criminal associates.

The trail might have run cold on Vaudevillia—except that a lucrative offer got a freighter captain to remember that someone had been trying to scrounge fuel and air. The captain also recalled some radio-squalling about a vagabond hitching a ride on a very unwilling lattice ship.

For the first time in many days, the Sedmons smiled. They were aware of the habit of lattice ships of using old hulks for airtight holds. Such a maneuver would confound most of the people pursuing the *Venture*, sure enough. For a time, at least.

Sedmon nodded to Sedmon. "Pausert. He's a cunning one. We'll need a trace on as many lattice ships as possible."

Uldune and her operations had many agents. And subradio meant the news could be sent, fast.

Two days later, the Sedmons were in pursuit of the *Petey B.*

CHAPTER 16

By the time that Cravan had all four of the new plays in production, most of the free money on Hanson's Reach had found its
way into the coffers of Petey, Byrum, and Keep. The silver-eyed
vatch had lured two more victims within the reach of Pausert's
klatha hooks and had gotten fed twice more, despite Pausert's
feelings of lingering guilt. Then the *Petey B* took to space again,
and Pausert felt that he was finally going to be able to relax for
a while.

Well . . . from having to look for spies and agents around every
corner, at any rate. He suspected that with more free time on her
hands, Dame Ethulassia was going to become a bit of a problem.

As, indeed, she did. But Pausert was able to evade that danger
in a generally satisfactory manner. Although, on one occasion, he
apparently didn't extract himself from her company quite quickly
and smoothly enough. At least, the captain assumed that it had
been Goth who teleported a still alive and wriggling jellysnail into
his soup.

They set down again on another agro-world, this time not quite
as primitive as the last—which was not, in Pausert's opinion, an
advantage. Tornam was not backwards and isolated. It had a real
spaceport that saw more than the occasional slow-freighter and
desperate trader. There were five other spaceships already on the
field when the *Petey B* set down on it.

Tornam also had an ISS office.

Hulik tried to reassure him that it was just a little backwater of a place; and that, even if the agents in charge had even heard of the *Venture* and its crew, they would hardly look for them snugged into a showboat. They would expect such desperate criminals to be trying to hide, not starring in a play.

It didn't help. In truth, the only reason Pausert wasn't starting at every sound and looking over his shoulder constantly was that, irrational as it was, he had begun to *trust* the little Silver-eyes. Or, perhaps, he just trusted that the vatch had come to realize that there was great deal more amusement to be had from helping Pausert and his crew than from trying to trip them up at every turn. But he still had the nervous certainty that disaster of some sort was just around the corner, a feeling of a metaphorical storm just below the horizon.

Yet, when disaster came, it had nothing to do with Pausert and the others. It didn't even happen in or around the showboat itself.

It happened when the second lead of Cravan's company, Ken Kanchen, was in Bevenford, the largest town on the planet. Kanchen took the part of Tybalt in *Romeo and Juliet,* of Horatio in *Hamlet*— pretty much any male part that required a handsome face, athletic ability, solid if not inspired acting, and the ability to memorize a part in two days,

He wasn't even there to do anything that could have conceivably gotten him into trouble. He was running a simple errand, visiting a local bookshop. Unfortunately, he stepped back into the street just at the wrong time. Traffic laws on Tornam were haphazard. Kanchen ended up under a floater, and then in a hospital, with more broken bones than anyone wanted to think about. He was just lucky that he was still alive—and that his handsome face was still untouched.

Not even Sir Richard could manage to act the part of Tybalt in a full body cast.

Himbo Petey had Kanchen brought back aboard the *Petey B* as soon as possible, of course. A ship the size of a showboat usually had a sick bay as good or better than anything a provincial planet could provide, and the *Petey B* was no exception to that. Besides, the showboats had a long tradition of taking care of their own—even people not as well-liked as Kanchen was by virtually everyone in the company and crew. The poor man was guaranteed better round-the-clock nursing as well as superior medical care; his problem would not be a lack of care and company, but a surfeit of it.

But the thespians were without their Second Male Lead. They were stretched so thin now that there was no understudy. Cravan was beside himself.

"There's no help for it," he said at last, after a meeting of the full company determined that there wasn't anyone able or ready to step into Ken's shoes. "I'll have to call for outside auditions. You'll all have to help me; otherwise we'll never find someone we can lick into shape in any reasonable period of time."

A groan went up. "Dick!" cried Alton. "You're going to kill us! The last time we had to hold a cattle call, on Plankelm, I was ready to slit my wrists before it was over!"

"Yes, but that cattle call netted us Trudi," Cravan countered, "and she's the best Female Character I've seen in—well, longer than I care to think."

Pausert glanced over at the plump, middle-aged woman who played Juliet's Nurse; she shrugged, but smiled.

"Tornam is more populous than Plankelm," Trudi commented. "A lot. Double the population in this city alone."

"Double the number of clueless idiots who think they can act," Alton groaned.

"It could be worse," Cravan pointed out ruthlessly. "We could be looking for a Juvenile. Then we'd have stage-mothers to contend with."

"If you dare inflict that on us, I *will* slit my wrists!" Alton started clawing at the prop dagger at his waist.

"Right. I want panels of four," Cravan continued, ignoring him. "Each one headed by an *experienced* Lead, which, Miss Hulik, I regret to say does not include you. Alton, Lassia, Trudi, myself, Hembert, Doeen, and Killary. That's six for initial auditions, with my panel making final judgment. Panel heads, pick your teams— you newcomers, please do not be offended if we don't select you. We need people who are dedicated thespians who are going to be living with this actor for a very long time, and we all know very well," here he bestowed a kindly smile on Pausert, Hulik, and Hantis, "that as soon as you can, barring that you decide differently, you are leaving us."

Was it that obvious? Pausert sighed. Not that he wanted to be on any blasted panels, listening to people stumble their way through speeches—not after the way that Alton had been carrying on.

✳   ✳   ✳

For two days, during which the theater was dark, the panels held nonstop auditions in any little space that would hold a table and four chairs. The pickings were thin, though the applicants were legion—in two days, only three candidates were passed up to Cravan's panel waiting in the theater. At the end of the two days, however, about the time that the panel members were beginning to look haggard and despairing, Vonard Kleesp appeared.

Trudi's panel passed him on to Cravan after only five minutes of audition. By the time he took his place on the stage in front of Cravan's panel, rumor had spread through the showboat like wildfire in pure oxygen. Everyone who could get away was trying to get into the theater to see him. Pausert was no exception, though, by the time he got there, Vonard had already gone through two major soliloquies with impressive ease.

What he saw up on the stage as he squeezed in between Hulik and Vezzarn was a man who, like Cravan, had a very memorable face. It was not, strictly speaking, handsome. The face was too saturnine for that, there was too much of an ironic lift to his eyebrows, and a cynical twist to his lips. But it was memorable, which was what a Second Lead needed. And the man moved like a cat. Just as Pausert got there, he was demonstrating that he even knew how to use a sword properly.

"Well, Master Vonard," said Cravan after a moment. "Familiarity with the very plays we are putting on, acting experience, something of a swordsman. You seem almost too good to be true."

"Well, Sir Richard, under most circumstances, I would agree with you," said Vonard, with a lift of his lip that was not quite a sneer. "Except that I come to you laden with some personal baggage, which is the reason why I am here on this backwater dirtball in the first place."

"Ah," Cravan said. "Weaknesses?"

"Near-fatal ones, I'm afraid. The first, the one that all too many of our profession are prey to—" Here he mimed a man pouring and drinking. "Not to put too fine a point on it, I drink to excess, I'm a very devil when drunk, and I never drink *without* getting drunk."

Cravan leaned forwards over his steepled hands. "And why do you drink?" he all but purred.

Vonard laughed. "My other weakness, sir, and the one that sent me here, putting all of the distance between us that my pocket could bear, here to drink until what was left in my pocket was gone."

"Ah," Cravan said, leaning back in his chair. "The female of the species?"

"Deadlier than the male," agreed Vonard. "Insofar as I was thinking at all, which was not a great deal between the madness and the wine, I had intended to commit slow suicide. Fortunately, both my money and my resolve ran out at the same time."

"Surely not *just* when we arrived?" asked Himbo Petey.

Vonard laughed. "Of course not. I have been driving produce floaters. The local—*thespians*"—here his lip curled—"were not inclined to welcome an outsider into their ranks, especially not one who, by this time, had the reputation as an ugly drunk. I was attempting to budget my drinking to allow me to put enough away to get me off this benighted rock. I didn't even know there was a showboat on-planet until one of my employers told me. I took a two-day leave to get here, hoping I could sign on for anything like an acting job. I didn't even know about the cattle call until I walked through the gate."

"And can we trust you to stay off the bottle if we take you on?" That was Trudi; Pausert recognized her voice.

"While I'm working, yes. I have never missed a rehearsal, a gig, or a line because of drink, and I don't intend to start now. When I am not working, however . . ." He shrugged. "I can't promise. Or at least, I can promise only that I will confine myself to quarters so that no one is inconvenienced but me."

Pausert watched as the panel—with the additions of Trudi and Petey—put their heads together. It seemed that they spoke together for a very long time, and it if seemed long to him, surely it seemed even longer to Vonard.

Finally they all sat back in their chairs. "Master Vonard," said Sir Richard, "pending completion of a three-planet probationary period, I believe you can consider yourself one of us."

Vonard bowed, and most of the company, including Pausert, broke into applause. And if there was as much relief as acceptance, well, that was only to be expected.

Whatever else, Vonard Kleesp's joining of the thespian troupe solved one problem for Pausert. Ethulassia left off her aggressive flirtation with the captain. The Dame's enthusiasms in that direction became entirely diverted onto the newcomer in their midst.

"Sure," sniffed Goth, after Pausert made it a point to mention it to her. "You don't stand a chance, Captain. You're not a romantic alcoholic, drowning his romantic woes in a bottle—and only to be saved by an even greater romance."

Pausert was relieved. And decided to say nothing when, the next day, he spotted Goth examining the level of the bottles in the *Venture*'s liquor cabinet.

"It's a day for new crewmates, it seems," said Vezzarn, when they caught up with him at dinner and told him about the audition. "In addition to the usual run of locals looking for adventure, Himbo Petey just snugged in a new tramp freighter that ran out of luck. Four-man crew, already assigned; a new roustabout who's doubling as a barker, a wiring tech—and you can bet *he*'ll be all over the ship—a new cook, and a cargomaster."

Goth looked up sharply, and Hulik and Pausert exchanged a glance. Every planet a showboat visited invariably produced a few local people who hired on. But the crew of a tramp freighter supposedly down on their luck...

That seemed oddly coincidental.

"I don't like it," growled Pul. "Think I'll go sniff them over."

Hantis nodded, and raised an eyebrow at Hulik and Pausert. "It does seem a bit too convenient, doesn't it?"

"Very," said Hulik. "I believe I'll go do some of my own sniffing."

"What do you think?" Pausert asked the girls.

The Leewit scowled. "*Might* be coincidence," she said, very grudgingly. "I suppose ships come up short of fuel and cash pretty often in ports like this."

"But you don't like it," said Pausert.

Both the Leewit and Goth shook their heads.

"Good. That makes it unanimous. So as soon as I rell a certain something—"

"And in the meantime," said Goth, looking innocent as a flower, "girls can get *awfully* hungry when we're still growing. We'll just see how good a cook the new one is." And she and the Leewit strolled off, hand in hand.

Hulik looked after them with an expression of reluctant admiration. "Ah, to be young and reckless again," she said.

"Now Hulik," said Pausert, daring to reach out and pat the back of her hand. "You were never that young."

His theater training was paying off; he managed to duck, just in time.

＊　　＊　　＊

"All of them!" growled Pul. "All four of them! I could smell 'spy' from yards off. You ought to let me bite them, Hantis."

When you were being spied on, it was always better to keep on doing things that you'd made habitual. The crew of the *Venture* always got together for breakfast and supper. Everybody knew they'd arrived together, and still intended to leave together if they ever could, so nobody thought anything of the habit. You ate with your friends; nothing mysterious about that. And the noisy mess tent provided plenty of chatter to cover anything they were talking about.

Pausert shook his head. "Much as I sympathize, Pul, it's better to know who your enemies are and have them under your eye. If we get rid of these four, whoever their boss is will only send new agents, and this time we might not spot them."

"We ought to find out who their boss *is*, don't you think, Captain?" asked Goth.

He nodded. "Do you think, if we got into the *Venture*'s control cabin, you might be able to find out if they're communicating with someone?"

"Believe so. They're not real bright—they're all even on the same shift. Which means I only need to listen when they're off-shift."

"They'll probably use a code, though."

She shrugged. "A code's a language, too, Captain. We may not have tried it, but I bet the Leewit can use klatha to translate a code."

"You think?" asked the Leewit, looking suddenly alert.

"We haven't anything to lose by trying," Pausert agreed.

"And the *Venture*'s still *our* ship," Vezzarn said, a little aggressively. "We still use our staterooms, don't we? We've a right to get into everything there but the holds. No reason why a couple of us couldn't be tinkering with the com to see if we can't get it working, either."

It wasn't as if they weren't still living in the *Venture*. After brief forays into the accommodations provided for the unmarried players and workers on the *Petey B*—which were, essentially, bunkhouses—they'd all decided they wanted their own cabins back. Even if that meant having their sleep interrupted by props heaving and bumping bits and bobs in and out of the holds at all hours.

"Hmm," said Pausert. "Vezzarn, how are your scrounging skills?"

The old spacer grinned. "The best, of course! And I think I know where you're going. You want me to start scrounging com parts, so it looks like we're trying to repair on the cheap and slow."

"Which will give us a good reason to be in the cabin, and even monitoring chatter if somebody walks in at the wrong time!" said the Leewit with enthusiasm. "Clumping *brilliant!*"

Hulik smiled. "He has his moments. And so do I; if our watchers happen to be ISS, I'll probably know their code anyway." She sniffed. "This far out, they're probably still using codes cracked and abandoned a long time ago."

The only problem with the plan was that it left everyone but Hantis and Pul with exactly no spare time—and Hantis and Pul were watching the agents in their own ways. Pausert rapidly began to feel like a man holding down three jobs, which, in point of fact, he was. He was an actor, a sideshow operator, and now a com-tinkerer, because it was possible that the agents wouldn't be using standard channels to talk to their boss.

The young witches were doing just as much, if not more, but at least they seemed to be buoyed up on the excitement of it all. That was a good thing, because the Leewit in particular was difficult to manage if she began to get the least bit bored.

The silvery-eyed little vatch elected at this point to be absent, which was aggravating. Pausert could have used the help, even from a vatch.

Or maybe, especially from a vatch. That one big vatch Pausert had half-shredded had neatly translocated the ship and everyone in it not once, but twice, when they were caught between the ISS and the pirates. It hadn't been hugely far, but then, he hadn't specified where he wanted to be. What were a vatch's upper limits on teleporting, he wondered? If he found a vatch big enough—or Silver-eyes got big enough—could he torment or talk the vatch into taking them all the way to the Empress?

On the other hand, would a vatch even understand time and space as Pausert was used to it? He recalled, belatedly, Silver-eyes being intrigued by the notion of linear time—which it apparently considered "silly." Pausert shuddered to think that even the best-intentioned vatch might teleport them into the distant past or future—or, what might be even worse, into the recent past where they already existed.

Probably not a good idea. He had a vague impression of being told—perhaps on Karres—that if you violated time and space by being two places at the same time, something very bad would happen to you. He made a mental note to ask Goth about it at some point when they weren't heavily involved in keeping their own skins intact. The captain had come to have a great deal of trust in the girl's judgment, and no longer undertook any major change in plans without consulting her.

In the meantime, it was moderately amusing to be watching their watchers.

"I'm sure they haven't yet decided if we're the ones they're looking for," Hulik said, on the day that *A Midsummer Night's Dream* went into the repertory and they started rotating it with *Romeo and Juliet.*

That had made a welcome change for Hulik. She hadn't nearly the pressure on her as Third Romantic Lead that she had as First Romantic Lead. Helena was an easy part, really. "Mostly confusion and hysteria," she opined. "And a cat-fight, of course." There *wasn't* a "cat-fight" in the original script, or at least, not the mud-wrestling match that Hulik and Meren Dall were required to perform. The cat-fight was Himbo Petey's idea. Sir Richard had put it in, but not without a fight of his own.

But like the extended sword fights, the public loved it.

"There's no *fights* in this thing, so you are *going* to have to have something in place of a mêlée!" Himbo had shouted. "I say mud-wrestling, and mud-wrestling it is! Just because your precious Bird—Bart, whatever—didn't put in mud-wrestling in the first place, that doesn't mean he wouldn't have if he'd known there was such a thing! I mean! It even fits the script!"

"And I suppose you want me to put a Blythe gun battle in the Scottish Play?" Sir Richard had shouted back—and had then gone pale with horror at the speculative look on Himbo Petey's face. "No! Forget I said that! You can *have* your wretched mud-wrestling, just do *not* ask me for one more change! Not one!"

Hulik didn't mind; she thought it was funny. And Meren was enough of a trouper that she would have mud-wrestled the entire female cast if that was what the part had called for.

"Why are you so sure they haven't spotted us?" Pausert asked. There were bits of what appeared to be the com strewn all over the floor in front of the unit, and he was pretending to repair it. Pretending, because the com was working just fine, and the bits were nothing more than the results of Vezzarn's scrounging, acting as camouflage, while the Leewit listened to chatter on headphones and Goth worked out whether the chatter was coming from inside the *Petey B* or was just the usual sorts of traffic outside of it.

"Because they're spreading themselves too thin," Hulik said

firmly. "And I'll tell you something else—even if they have our descriptions, or some of us, anyway, that doesn't mean they're going to trust those descriptions. *I* wouldn't. Because I would know that any smart quarry would have already changed as much about himself as he could."

"So they are basically looking at everyone." Well, that was comforting. "Hmm. So a really smart quarry wouldn't change himself at all?"

"Or would do exactly what we've done: put ourselves into a position where our appearances change constantly." She nodded at him. Pausert was still wearing his Mercutio hair because it was perfectly comfortable to wear—quite natural-seeming, really, but a royal pain to take off and put on. Tomorrow the makeup specialist would take off the foxy hair and replace it with Bottom's unruly haystack, and he'd wear *that* all day, for the same reason. Rehearsals had just started for play number three, the Scottish Play, and as King Duncan he'd have gray hair that worked for both the part of the King and of the King's ghost.

Most of the other actors did the same. Only when they doubled a part, as Alton did with Romeo and the Prince of Verona, did they use true old-fashioned wigs that could be put on and taken off quickly, but were horrible and itchy to wear.

"Great Patham, we must be driving them mad!" he exclaimed gleefully.

Hulik nodded. "We couldn't have picked a better place. Even if they're looking for two young Karres-witch girls, they can't be sure that they have the right girls, or even that they should be looking for girls at all. There are dozens of families here with children the right age. The little Wisdoms could be posing as boys, as midgets, or as even as something in the Freak Show."

The "little Wisdoms" were freakish enough as it was anyway, he thought. He didn't say it out loud, though.

"Well, good. I want them as confused as possible; that can only be to our benefit." He thought of something else. "So, how are *they* fitting in?"

It would be very awkward if these people were used to being with a showboat. The tall tales spun about every member of a showboat crew would not distract them too much, and once they got themselves oriented, it wouldn't be long before they got onto the truth—or figured out that if nothing else, sign-on dates and the identity of the ships welded to the frame would be found in Himbo Petey's own records.

"According to Pul, like desert-cats in a swamp. Which argues for them being ISS agents. I would think that the pirates would know better—or would have operatives that spent time on a showboat in the past."

"The ISS isn't stupid—"

"No, but this far out in the hinterland, what you get are agents that were put out here because they weren't good enough to be entrusted with truly important postings, or were stupid enough to do something that made it necessary to transfer them where they couldn't do much harm. If they aren't ambitious, they're going to be unhappy because their comfortable paper-pushing existence has been interrupted by a tedious, possibly dangerous job. If they are ambitious, they're going to be blundering about doing plenty of wrong things, because they don't know that what they need to be good undercover agents won't be found in a book." Hulik sighed. "They get posted out to places like this because at least there's a smaller chance that they'll get themselves killed or do something to anger someone important."

Pausert hesitated, then asked the question that had been lurking in the back of his mind ever since Hantis told them about the plague. "Hulik, what are the odds, do you think, that someone high up in the ISS is infected by Hantis' Nanites?"

She leaned back in her chair, and licked her lips. "You do know how to ask the nasty ones, don't you? Truth to be told, I think it's quite likely, odds of up to fifty percent. I've thought that ever since that ISS goon overrode your safe-conduct from the Empress."

She began ticking things off on her fingers. "Whoever it is knows about Karres witches, believes in them, and wants them. Whoever it is does not have the Empress' best interests at heart, and does not want whatever information it is that we carry to get to the Empress. Whoever it is knows about Hantis and Pul, and possibly wants them disposed of as well." She shrugged. "Now, that could cover both someone high up in court circles who has ambitions for becoming Emperor himself or working for someone who does—but it covers someone in the ISS infected by the plague equally well."

Pausert's heart sank; but then he, too, shrugged. "I suppose it doesn't make much difference at this point, does it?"

"No. Whoever is behind this is high enough up in ISS circles that if Hantis can't do anything, we're on our own for the moment."

She looked pensively at a poster on the wall advertising romantic getaways on Beta Caeleen. Goth had been sticking them up to cover the paint splatters from the first appearance of the little silver-eyed vatch. It seemed an eternity ago.

"I used to like being a lone operative," she said, sounding oddly plaintive. "In fact, I used to like being an *operative,* period. I must be getting old. It isn't fun anymore. I find myself wishing I had a lot of people at my back, and that I was doing things using my brain rather than a gun, things with a lower chance of getting me killed. A desk has begun to look a lot more attractive than it used to."

Pausert stared at her. "You aren't actually thinking about *settling down,* are you?"

"It has its merits," she said wistfully. Then she shook her head. "No, not really. You know how it is. Everyone wants what they don't have, and then, if they get it, half the time they discover they don't want it after all."

Pausert wasn't fooled. She *was* thinking about it! He tried to imagine it. Hulik do Eldel, in a little house, behind a desk. Maybe even married, and with children!

Great Patham! What would any children *she* raised be like? Worse than young witches, even, probably wreaking havoc on their kindergarten, playing "pirates and hostages" with real Blythe guns, breaking into the crèche offices at night to rifle through the teacher's desk, looking for blackmail material . . .

"It wouldn't suit you," he said firmly. "You'd be bored before the first day was over."

"You're probably right," she replied, still sounding wistful. "Still, with the right set of circumstances, the right job, and the right partner . . ."

CHAPTER 17

"We're getting closer," said Sedmon to Sedmon. "At Hanson's Reach we missed them by weeks. Maybe we can catch up finally on Tornam."

"Provided we don't have to clean up any more messes along the way," cautioned the second Sedmon. "Eliminating Imperial agents is a dangerous pastime."

The first Sedmon shrugged. "He was too curious as to why we wanted descriptions of the cast of the Petey Byrum and Keep. The lattice ships do get watched. They're good cover, mind you. I think we need to look into investing in one, someday."

The Sedmons back on Uldune nodded. "The records here indicate that several of them are considerably indebted to our bank. And the one we're following is in financial difficulty."

"The records we've looked at indicate this to be the norm. They're potentially profitable, of course, but it's usually the debt load that cripples them. And a lot of the showmen seem to have the financial acumen of a Humpity. But this Himbo Petey seems a cut above most. Our contact with the Imperial Bank of Credit and Commercial Ventures does indicate that he's been trying to bring it under control."

All of the Sedmons knew they were avoiding thinking about how they would deal with meeting up with Hulik do Eldel. Like almost all of the Daal's citizens, she was blissfully unaware that she'd actually met, physically, four different bodies. The same mind, of course.

At one stage, when they'd first begun considering a personal liaison with the Imperial agent, the hexaperson had assumed they would conduct it the same way as they dealt with the people of Uldune—with one of them on display and the rest in reserve, in hiding. But as time went on, and the do Eldel grew more central to their thoughts, the thought of deceiving her became distasteful. Besides, as intelligent and capable as Hulik was, it would probably be futile as well. Even though the Daal had kept a certain distance from her in the past, he suspected that she had already guessed at least part of the truth.

But they'd deal with that issue once they caught up with her. First, they had to do that.

CHAPTER 18

At long last, Pausert relled vatch. And he could tell that this was a vatch that he had relled before. Goth relled it at the same time, and looked up sharply. "Is that our old friend, Captain?"

A patch of misty black blinked silver-slitted eyes at him. "I believe it is."

Hello, Real Thing. Are you going off to be stories for the waking-dreamers now?

As a matter of fact, we are. He did not ask where the vatch had been. Truth to tell, he wasn't sure he really wanted to know.

Good.

Are you planning on luring more victims here? he asked cautiously.

Not now.

"Time, Goth," he said, and Goth put away her headphones with a sigh. They looked as if they were plugged into her personal player; they were, and they weren't, because one of the channels on her personal player was set to scan all the com that was coming from inside the *Petey B* as relayed from the *Venture*.

"Still nothing," she complained.

"Cheer up. After this show, we lift—and even if they've been reporting to someone in person, they won't be able to do that anymore." They now had the third of their plays, the Scottish Play, in production, and Sir Richard had elected to put off beginning rehearsal for the fourth until they were back in space.

The new man was working out well enough. True to his word,

Vonard Kleesp was awake and ready for first rehearsal and he never showed the least bit of unsteadiness from that moment until final curtain. Though, as Vezzarn said with reluctant admiration, "what he drinks in a night would kill five men." Presumably he'd gotten to that stage of alcoholism where the alcoholic could not function without liquor in his system.

Besides, Pausert had overheard Cravan saying to Ethulassia one night they only needed Vonard Kleesp until Ken Kanchen was all healed up.

"You won't fire him?" Ethulassia had asked anxiously. "He's a superb actor, whatever else." Her voice seemed to get a little dreamy. "Quite a charming and handsome man, too, for that matter. And he doesn't really drink as much as people think. With my personal intervention . . ."

"No, I certainly won't fire him," Cravan had replied. "He'll be useful if Pausert leaves us. He can take those roles; for that matter, he could double and stand-in on just about every male lead we do. But he won't be indispensable, and when something happens to him, it won't leave us short."

When . . .

Well, Cravan was right to use that word. Drinking like that, a man's liver would only last so long and his heart would probably go even sooner. Medics could give you artificial organs, but if you collapsed with heart or liver failure out in space or some backwater world in the middle of nowhere, you might not live to make it to a place where they could install one.

"Well, little Wisdom," Pausert said teasingly, "time to go be a Witch."

"Very well, Your Majesty," she mocked him back.

Oh, good. A story I haven't seen!

It was a good thing that Pausert's time on stage as King Duncan was limited; the vatch was full of questions. Some of them Pausert couldn't answer, such as the very reasonable question of, if the Witches were so powerful, why didn't Macbeth keep them around to show him the future all the time? "I don't know; I guess it's just the way the story-maker wanted it," was all he could say. The vatch didn't seem to mind that he didn't know, and best of all, it behaved like a mannerly child at a grown-up party.

But as the play hurtled towards its conclusion, he began to get a prickling at the back of his neck. Then Vonard Kleesp appeared at his side, coming from the direction of the dressing rooms.

"Something's amiss, I think," he whispered into Pausert's ear.

"I was just coming out of my dressing room and saw a man I don't recognize going into yours. I don't believe he was alone, either. I notified some of the stagehands, but you might want to look into it yourself."

Trouble! said the vatch suddenly, and with great glee. **This'll be fun!**

And it vanished.

Standing backstage as he was, Pausert could hear the vatch's "fun" as a series of crashes and muffled shouts. Things were falling over— or being knocked over—onto several people who had been, he suspected, trying to sneak around backstage. The vatch had put paid to that particular plan, though. And now, even as the shouts got louder, Pausert saw several burly stagehands converging on the area.

Fortunately, by that point, the final sword fight between Macbeth and Macduff was in full swing. You could probably have staged a barfight backstage without anyone in the audience noticing.

The noises stopped at the point where Macduff killed Macbeth, and the stagehands returned, dusting their hands in satisfaction.

So did the vatch.

The altercation had not escaped the notice of Sir Richard, however. As soon as the last of the curtain calls was over, he came striding backstage with fire in his eye. The first thing his eye lit on was Pausert. "What was the meaning of that ruckus?" he began, but the chief rigger interrupted him.

"He didn't have nothing to do with it, boss," the rigger said. "We caught those four new guys trying to sneak into the dressing rooms. Kleesp gave us the warning."

"Sneak!" Sir Richard snorted. "That didn't sound like sneaking to me!"

One of the lighting techs sniggered. "They had some bad luck, boss," the old man told Sir Richard gleefully. "Bad luck and lots of it, and if I find out what they was smoking before they got here, I'm buyin' a pound. Swore up and down that the props and stuff was getting thrown at 'em and jumpin on 'em. That's what most of the noise was."

"Huh." Sir Richard lost most of his wrath. "And the rest of the noise?"

"Oh," said the chief rigger, attempting to look innocent and failing utterly, "that was them falling down a lot while we was helping 'em find their way out."

"Helping who find their way out?" Himbo Petey asked, having

arrived with the rest of the cast. The rigger helpfully explained, while the techs snickered.

"Trying to get into the dressing rooms, hmm?" asked Petey, his jaw tightening. "*Which* dressing rooms?"

"Well," the rigger said, with a shake of his head. "I almost feel sorry for 'em. Normally fans try to get to the leading lady's room, and thieves too. These guys were such losers they were trying his." He pointed at Pausert.

Cravan blinked. "Have you got something in there you're not telling us about, Aron?"

Pausert shook his head. "Not that I can think of." He'd have to think quickly here and just hope the girls could ad-lib along with whatever story he came up with.

"Unless..." He rubbed his jaw. "Well, someone might have been prepared to pay someone to take my older niece back to her step-father. There's a pretty large family estate involved and nothing much Dani or anyone can do about it until she's of age to sign the documents. Tregger—that's her stepfather—would undoubt-edly like to have her back under his eye. I'm the girls' guardian—and I have the papers to prove it. But if I had an *accident*... then they'd go back to Tregger. Ask the girls how they'd like that."

"Please don't let the captain get hurt," said the Leewit, sniff-ing. "Tregger's *mean*. He used to beat us. And momma. She died and the captain took us away."

"Huh," said Goth. "The captain'd have dealt with them just like he did with the last one."

It was a superb piece of acting.

"What did these guys tell you?" growled Petey to the riggers.

"Some cock-and-bull story about being friends from way back, and wanting to give the new show-folk a surprise," the rigger said. "We didn't buy it. You don't need a pry-bar for that. Or a cosh and forcecuffs. That was why they fell down a lot on the way out."

Petey turned to Goth and the Leewit, who were wide-eyed. "Just for the record, do you and your sister know any of the new people? Any sausage sellers from way back?"

They both shook their heads vigorously. "Only people I'm friends with outside of the company and my uncle's crew are the fellows in Clown Alley," the Leewit said, in a very small voice.

Goth shook her head. "Don't even know what the new guys look like, sir."

"I don't tolerate people interfering with *my* thespians!" said Cravan stormily.

"You get no argument from me, Sir Richard. They're working members of the *Petey B*'s company. We look after own, girls." Petey's face was flushed. He looked to the techs. "You can identify them, of course?"

"Huh. We marked 'em good," said the rigger with satisfaction. "Uh, that is, they got marked pretty good falling down a lot."

Petey reached inside the huge sleeve of his doublet, and pulled out a wrist-com. He tapped out a sequence, and spoke into it. "*Hey, rube!* Backstage. Theater."

The thespians all seemed to know what was coming, for they cleared back against the walls and scrims. Dame Ethulassia grabbed Pausert's elbow and pulled him back along with the rest, while some of the others did the same for Hulik, Goth, and the Leewit.

Suddenly there was a thunder of running feet, and backstage became very, very crowded as the biggest, meanest-looking, and strongest members of the circus converged on Cravan and Petey. If Goth's and the Leewit's eyes had been big before, they were dinner-plate-size now.

Himbo Petey spoke to them in a very low, very angry voice, explaining what had just happened. An animal growl arose from several of the throats, and postures went rather beyond "tense."

"These boys will help you identify them," he finished, gesturing to the riggers and the techs. "I want them off the ship, off the grounds, bag and baggage. Keep 'em off. And spread the word: we're lifting early. I want us derigged, packed up, and gone. We've got most of the loose money on this planet anyway."

Before Pausert could blink, they were gone. Petey looked around, his eyes lighting on the little witches. "We take care of our own," he said again, reassuring them in a surprisingly gentle voice. They nodded, though their eyes were still enormous. "Good. Miss Hulik? Would you and the rest of your crew take them to their cabins on your old ship? And when you get there, close and dog down the airlock. Don't come out until we're out of orbit. Girls, don't bother to change out of your costumes until you're in your own cabins; just bring them back at rehearsal tomorrow."

"Yessir," they said in chorus.

Cravan looked around as well. "You heard the Showmaster," he said firmly. "Break and stow, we're lifting early. Quicktime!"

Pausert joined the girls, and they all started to move away. Cravan shot a look at them.

"*Quicktime*, Mister Pausert!" he barked.

They ran.

*   *   *

"Are we in trouble?" asked Goth quietly, when the lock had been secured. "With the show, I mean."

"Oh no," Hulik replied. "No, not at all. However, your would-be kidnappers are."

"You think they were going to kidnap us?" the Leewit asked, looking more interested than frightened.

Hulik shrugged. "It's what I would do, if I were the kind of wretched scum that they are," she replied. "Kidnap you, and use you to get the rest of us without a fight. That is, if I hadn't bothered to look into the reports of the last lot of ISS agents who tried to take us."

"Do you think we should tell Himbo Petey what's really going on?" Pausert asked, feeling guilty again.

"*No!*" said Hulik and Hantis at once, and very vehemently.

They exchanged a look, and Hulik elaborated. "Look, Captain, Petey has a perfectly good explanation for what those men were going to do. Those men can claim to be ISS until they're blue in the face, and it won't do them any good, because you and the little Wisdoms would have convinced me. And I know the truth."

Goth blushed a little. The Leewit looked so innocent that it seemed as if a halo might descend on her head at any moment. Pausert rubbed his jaw. "Well, yes," he said. "But they weren't—"

"If you can explain to me how planning to kidnap two children and use them to get their friends and guardians to surrender, possibly torturing one or both girls to make us frantic to do what they asked is any different, I'd like to hear it." There was more than a touch of frost in Hantis' voice.

"Anyway, it's all done with now," said Hulik. She turned to Pausert. "You know, we might as well go open all the com channels and find out what's going on."

"That sounds like a good idea."

What was going on was a lot of frantic work, apparently. When Petey said *quicktime,* he meant it. All of the decorations, the bunting and banners and synthasilk sheathing, were already stowed away, and the full breakdown was, impossible though it seemed, half over. Goth put the viewscreen on channel-flick, so they could see what every camera that was broadcasting was showing.

"Look!" said Goth, suddenly, freezing the view.

The four "new men" were being ungently escorted to the other side of the showboat's gates, with some of their escorts carrying what must have been everything the men owned. Once they were

tossed beyond the perimeter, their belongings were unceremoni-
ously dumped—a fair amount of it on them. There was no sound
on this particular camera, but it was obvious from the gesticula-
tions that there was a lot of angry shouting going on. But the
escort-party wasn't moving, and those who hadn't been carrying
baggage were handing out clubs to those who had been.

The four men seemed to come to their senses. Sullenly, they shut
up and began loading themselves with their baggage, then dragged
it out of the camera's view.

"What about their ship?" the Leewit asked. "I mean, Petey's still
got their ship! Won't the law come after him for that?"

Goth unexpectedly grinned. "Nope. I'm the one that worked our
contracts, remember? There's a clause in there that says that if any
of us break the Code of Conduct, Petey can throw all of us off
and take our ship. Bet that's in their contract, too. And I betcha
Petey's transmitting the contracts to the police right this minute.
If they want the law after us, they'll have to break cover—and
remember, they got no proof that we're anything but what we say
we are, so I betcha the law won't move until they can *prove* they're
ISS, and then it'll be too late."

"But what if we break the Code?" Pausert asked, now more
worried than ever.

Goth rolled her eyes. "Oh please, Captain! It's all *heavy* stuff!
Murder or attempted murder, theft or attempted theft, kidnap or
attempted kidnap. That kind of thing. Believe me, I *looked* at it,
hard. Petey'll call it 'attempted kidnapping,' and the local law'll
probably agree."

"It's a bit rough on four incompetents," said Pausert. "The
Empire's judges don't look kindly on the kidnapping of minors."

"I don't know if it is that harsh," Hulik said, grimly. "ISS agents
can be cashiered to the hinterlands for other reasons than just sheer
incompetence. And it would take a certain sort of mind to think
that kidnapping and torturing a little girl is a good way to get a
job done."

"You should have let me bite them," growled Pul from the floor.

CHAPTER 19

Whoever the would-be kidnappers had been working for, they were either unsuccessful in persuading the authorities of their wrongs, or else they decided not to even try involving the locals, for there was no pursuit and not even a query from the law. The *Petey B* lifted and got into and out of orbit with no more trouble than usual, and things went back to normal.

Pausert was left to ponder something remarkable: their little silver-eyed vatch, of the untamable sort, was not only behaving itself, it was cooperating and making itself very useful. He was not at all used to thinking of a vatch as useful.

The *Petey B* was well out of orbit and into interstellar space when Silver-eyes caught up with them again. Pausert just had time to notice it was there, when it announced itself.

I deserve feeding! it said cheerfully.

That you do! Pausert agreed. *If you can lure something big, dumb, and juicy here—*

The vatchlet vanished, but it wasn't gone long. And the vatch it brought with it was exceedingly big, slow, and evidently not much brighter than a cow. Pausert felt not a trace of guilt over tearing a couple of head-sized chunks out of it before it fled, protesting. Silver-eyes feasted, growing a bit in size.

I like you, Silver-eyes announced. **I've decided that helping real things I like is more fun than playing tricks on dream things.**

149

Maybe that's because just playing tricks is too easy for you, Pausert suggested.

The vatchlet seemed to think that over for a while. It didn't go away, it just floated in the middle of the control cabin, like a puff of shadow, while its slitty eyes winked and blinked.

What are you doing? it finally asked.

I'm resting. And thinking.

No. I meant, you have something important to do, I can feel it. I think that's why you get in so much trouble. So what is it?

Should he tell the vatch? Well, why not? It wasn't as if it would be able to blab things to anyone else who didn't already know. Only a klatha practitioner would be able to even sense a vatch was there, much less hear it. On the other hand, if he told the vatch what was going on, it just might be more inclined to help because he'd answered its question.

So he explained it all. The Nanite plague. The disappearance of Karres. Needing to get the information to the Empress.

Then he had to explain what "the Empress" was. Traitors in the ISS—and then he had to explain what "the ISS" was. That the pirates who had followed the Agandar were inexplicably convinced that *they* had the Agandar's treasure and were also trying to find them. And, naturally, he had to explain what "pirates" were, and who "the Agandar" had been and so forth. There was a lot of explaining to do.

The vatch was quiet for a much longer time, then. Pausert had never really gotten the impression that vatches thought much about anything before this, but he sure got that feeling now.

I don't understand most of this, the vatch said finally. **I'd like to help anyway, but I'm not very big.**

You're bigger now than you were when we met you, Pausert pointed out.

True. That's because you feed me. I think that's a good thing.

I'd like to think so also, Pausert told it. *Believe me, I appreciate the help you've been giving us.*

The bigger I get, the more I can help you. And when I'm big enough, I will be able to go to the (*) place. I think that's probably a good thing too.

So do I, said Pausert, and he meant it. Not that it wasn't a grand thing, in some ways, having a vatch around that was making its business to be helpful. But, on the whole, Pausert would be relieved to know that the one vatch he couldn't actually control had gone somewhere else and wouldn't come back. *I wouldn't be a friend if I asked you to stay any longer than you have to.*

What is a "friend?" it asked, and then the captain had another long explanation to make. It was one he was very careful with, emphasizing that one of the things that friends *did not* do was to indulge in mischief that caused each other harm, and that the thing they tried to do all the time was to make each other happy and help each other.

Like feeding you, he finished. *And like you keeping those un-friends from hurting us. And no matter how far friends are from each other, they always remember what they did for each other, and they remember how good it was to be friends.*

I like that. Okay. I will be your friend, Big Real Thing, and you will be mine. And that will be true even after I go to the (*) place.

Goth came in then and the vatch vanished, as vatches were inclined to do. Goth stared at the place where it had been, and then at Pausert.

"All right, Captain," she said, putting her hands on her hips. "Just what have you been up to?"

When he finished telling her, Goth continued to stare at him. Now, that was not at all unusual; what *was* unusual was the kind of stare she was giving him.

"I'm not entirely sure you're a witch anymore, Captain," she said slowly. "You're doing things no witch I ever heard of can do, or has ever tried to do."

He felt himself flush. "Oh, come on!" he scoffed. "I can't use the Sheewash Drive—"

"Yet," Goth interrupted firmly.

"I can't use the Egger Route—"

"Yet. And you *are* a vatch-tamer, and now you're making friends with the things! You're no kind of a witch I ever heard of."

"All right," he replied. "Just what am I, then?"

He didn't really expect a reply, but he should have known better. This was Goth, after all.

She canted her head to the side. "A wizard, maybe," she said, rubbing the tip of her nose. "Hmm. Maybe that. A wizard of Karres."

"A vatch that wants to be friends." Hantis shook her head. "I've never heard of such a thing, but it certainly beats the alternative. You do have a way with the oddest creatures, Captain."

"He does," agreed Pul. "I only want to bite him a very little, now and again."

"I'll take that as a compliment, coming from you," Pausert replied. "Does anyone know where we're going next?"

"A mining world," Pul told him. "I overheard Cravan and Petey talking about it."

"Mining!" Pausert was surprised. "I wouldn't think miners would appreciate anything we do." And with that, he went to find one of the more experienced members of the troupe to get his opinion.

The first one he found was Mannicholo, who was trying out a new juggling act with glowing wands, which set off the reflective colors of his dermis wonderfully. Pausert didn't interrupt him, since it looked as if the chameleon man was finally getting some success with it. When Mannicholo caught all of the wands, he offered up some sincere applause.

"Thanks," the chameleon man said cheerfully. "By the time we hit ground again, it might even be ready to show. What can I do for you?"

"I've found out we're going to a mining world, and I wouldn't have thought that we'd have much of a chance of an audience there."

"Hmm. Depends on the world. One that's being mined by a major concern, no, you're right; most of the mining there is automated, and the big companies tend to keep their workers well fed and entertained, because working those machines is skilled and dangerous work. But there are plenty of worlds where the big deposits have been mined out. Even though there isn't enough left there to interest the big companies, there's plenty to go around for wildcatters." Mannicholo tossed one of his wands idly from hand to hand. "And you'd be surprised at what they like. Things that remind them of when they were kids and carefree—like the circus part of the show. And a lot of them are better educated than you'd guess. It's self-education, often as not, but they can be pretty bright boys and girls. Stupid wildcatters tend to die quickly, you see. The littler mining machines are powerful and tricky to run, and a wildcatter uses explosives nearly as often as he uses a mining machine, and you can't be stupid and know how to handle explosives properly."

"That still doesn't explain why they'd like the thespians."

"Well, they all tend to listen to stuff while they tend the mining machines," Mannicholo explained. "And here's kind of what happens. Everyone that comes out here has his own set of personal recordings. But it's expensive to bring in anything new, so when a miner gets tired of his own stuff, he starts trading around. Pretty soon he runs out of stuff he knows he likes, then he gets desperate, and starts trading for anything. So the longer a miner's been out here, the more different stuff he's tried, and he'll have listened to practically anything—every kind of music, lectures, plays, educational recordings, spoken books, you name it. So a miner can have a taste for things you wouldn't expect. Then there's the last thing— and that is that wildcat miners work alone for the most part, so the one thing they really crave is company, light, color, and sound, and lots of it all. So no matter how bad our acts were, chances are they'd come to see us for a while. But if the acts are really sad, it won't be for long."

"Oh." He hadn't considered that. "And—you said they aren't stupid—"

"That's right. So that's why, if a showboat wants to really make money, the acts have to be good. Funnily enough, *I* have always found that the one set of acts that consistently makes money on a mining world is the thespians and people like them; people who rely as much on what's heard as what's seen, and people who do things that open up the imagination." Mannicholo winked. "Which is why *I* am very grateful to you for tipping me off before anyone else. I've got a song-and-comedy act I'd better dust off before we hit ground. Believe me, Pausert, when miners like you, they *really* like you, and when they *really* like you, they've got some fine ways of showing it!"

All right, he had one set of questions answered, only to give rise to another set—because what Mannicholo could have meant, he had no clue.

Until he got to rehearsal, that is.

"Ladies and gentlemen," said Cravan, summoning them all to the stage. "Our next destination is the mining world, Altim Four."

There was much excited murmuring among the older members of the thespians. Cravan waved his hand. "My old troupers, please allow me to explain what this means to the newer members."

The murmuring died.

"We have done some investigation," Cravan said, with satisfaction. "The last time a showboat passed this way, Altim Four, a world with nothing more sophisticated than lower vertebrates, was being mined by one of the major mining companies. They have since taken what they wanted—which was heavy radioactives—and left. That was five years ago. The wildcatters moved in immediately, and as those of you who are familiar with heavy-metal worlds know, Altim Four would have been rich in—"

"Gold!" shouted someone.

Cravan nodded graciously. "And other precious metals. The consortium didn't even bother to look for gemstones. Needless to say, since it was a heavy-metal world, the conditions are hazardous, and everything needs to go through decontamination, which has meant there was no 'rush' to speak of when it was opened to wildcatters. Nevertheless, those who dared are profiting richly. What this means to us, my friends, is that if these people decide that they like us, they are going to give ample evidence of that. And what that means is that if these miners wish to offer an accolade beyond applause, there probably will not be flowers thrown on stage at the end of a performance—there probably will be pouches of gold dust and rough gemstones."

For a moment, Pausert was not sure he'd heard that correctly. But Dame Ethulassia's eyes shone with enthusiasm.

Pausert sucked in a breath, while one of the other cast members whistled. Why, if something like that happened—they could all get enough extra to buy the *Venture* free and get her fixed and fueled!

Cravan interrupted the buzz. "Now, before we ever make planetfall, I want it understood that this sort of thing is provided for in your contracts. It probably isn't anything you even looked at too closely at the time, but I want the terms understood from the beginning. Provision one: for accolades that are tossed onto the stage, no matter who is the assumed person being rewarded, one third goes to the general fund for the *Petey B* along with ticket receipts, and two thirds is shared out among all the members of the company on an equal basis—one share each, no matter how junior or senior you are." He looked quite stern, but Pausert could not help but notice that the techs and riggers brightened up considerably at that. No doubt why, either; otherwise, they'd have had no chance at getting such bonuses.

"Provision two: for gifts delivered backstage to a specific artist: one half the artist may keep for his or herself, and one half is shared out among all the members of the company. While I realize that this may not seem fair to those of you who are Leads, let me remind you that although you are the apex of a pyramid of talent, without those beneath you, you would swiftly find yourself plummeting. Ask yourself if you could have earned such accolades without the carpenters and techs, good lighting, good sound, makeup, hair and costuming, and the support of all of the extras, before you feel yourself wronged."

"I'm grateful, Sir Richard, not complaining!" said Hulik into the silence. "On any other world, we'd get a bunch of flowers and applause and be happy for that. And we're lucky to have Himbo Petey for our Showmaster, smart enough to find this place before anyone else did!"

"Here here!" said Alton, and "I'm with you, sweetheart!" said Trudi, and that seemed to settle it for everyone. Rehearsal went forward in a cheerful glow.

Afterwards, Pausert caught up with Goth. "What's on the contract for solo acts?" he asked in an undertone.

"Half to the general fund, half to you," she replied, without needing to think about it. "And the circus side is similar to the thespians. So you betcha there's going to be a lot of extra stalls and people trying to think up a hot solo or small ensemble act to run on the side."

She was right, of course, which led Himbo Petey to insist that all such solo acts pass an audition if they weren't already on the bill. Just as well that he did, or Sideshow Alley would have been neck-deep in exotic dancers. Furthermore, Petey would not permit anyone to have an act in direct competition with someone who had an established stall. If, for instance, someone wanted to set up an exotic dance turn, they had better not only be good, they had better have a different theme than anyone else. Pausert was the comedy escape-artist, which meant that anyone new had to go for the dangerous and hazardous escapes. Not surprisingly, no one did. The thrill-escapes needed someone who was a superb athlete and very, very practiced in his art. Anything less got people killed.

"Not in my show! You're smart, you can do better than that!" was the roar often heard coming from Petey's office. And it was Ethulassia, surprisingly, who met the crestfallen at the door, took them off for tea and sympathy in her stateroom, and usually was able to suggest something that Petey would approve.

Or, if she couldn't, Vonard Kleesp usually could. Kleesp was often to be found in the Dame's stateroom, these days, lounging on one of her overstuffed divans. Dame Ethulassia's campaign of "personal intervention" seemed to have succeeded, at least to some extent. The man had become Ethulassia's paramour, in a manner of speaking. Pausert suspected the Dame's passion for the fellow was a considerably more casual thing than she professed—she *was* an actress, after all, given to public flamboyance—but he was simply relieved to be spared her aggressive flirtations himself.

For all of Vonard's self-professed reputation as a mean drunk, he was actually never more than moderately pickled these days and seemed rather inclined to sardonic humor than anything nastier. And his checkered past had given him insight into a thousand clever little scams and hustles, any number of which could be adapted to these circumstances.

If Pausert hadn't had that little discussion with Mannicholo, he probably would have been surprised by some of the acts that people came up with. There were several singing acts, for instance, ranging from opera to folk ballads, several solo instrumental musicians and four different instrumental groups. Among all of the exotic dancers, there was a ballet act, adagio dancers, staged by two of the acrobats. Mannicholo wasn't the only one doing comedy. There were three fortune-tellers, each one doing a different sort of supposed divination, and a mentalist act.

"But *no* one, absolutely *no one,* is going to run a clairvoyant act," Petey decreed in a company-wide meeting. "I am not having anyone duping these poor people by pretending to speak to their dead. That's not only fraud, it's obscene. I won't have it under my tent!"

And no games of chance, either—though without a doubt, members of the company were going to run covert card games anyway. But if they ran a dirty game and got caught, well, it would be their own skin they risked, and nothing to do with the company as a whole. It wasn't that Himbo Petey objected to gambling, nor to fleecing the miners with the usual house edge—it was just that miners were generally large, strong people with short tempers, and they had a habit of wrecking places and people that they thought were cheating them. Soon enough, someone would come and set up a casino here, and take that chance. Petey was too conservative to risk it.

Goth and the Leewit decided to perform a variation on Pausert's comedic escape-act, by putting together a comedy magic-act. Goth would fumble the tricks, and her assistant, the Leewit, would, in the process of putting the equipment away or getting it ready on stage, do them flawlessly. And with just enough exasperation to make it funnier.

When they presented the idea to Petey for his approval, the Showmaster hesitated. There was already a comedy-magic act—Alton's, whose persona was a gentlemanly drunk. Assisted by a pretty little acrobat in a scanty maid's costume, he would produce all manner of unlikely objects from hat, coat, pocket, and thin air, seeming as baffled and surprised by their appearance as the audience was. But Petey decided that the novelty of having two young sisters work together, along with the sibling-rivalry theme, was sufficiently original to let them go ahead.

Even Vezzarn got into the mix with a novelty target act—throwing everything from styluses to meat cleavers, and doing so well at it that Pausert was glad that the little spacer was on *their* side.

"How did you get so good at this?" he asked in surprise.

Vezzarn shrugged, and lobbed another fork into the target. "When you're as short as I am, and as puny, and you find you've gotten into a fight, you don't want to get too close to the other guy if you can help it. It's a good thing if you can stick him full of things from the other side of the room and make him think about something other than hitting you. And when you're *in* that situation, you usually don't have a lot of time to choose what you're going to use to throw at him."

Hulik alone among their group wasn't going to have a solo act—but then, she was hardly going to need one. If there were going to be pouches of gold dust being sent backstage, thought Pausert, she was going to be the person most likely to receive them. He just hoped that she would at least think about contributing some of it to getting the *Venture* back and spaceworthy.

He thought about asking her directly about that. But she seemed to have something else on her mind altogether, and as far as he could tell, it didn't have anything to do with the potentials of this next planetfall. He caught her, more and more often, gazing off into space with a puzzled and wistful expression, and he wasn't the only one.

In fact, she was acting *very* oddly, one minute her old self, then the next, someone softer, and so unlike her normal self that he wouldn't have recognized her. But it was Dame Ethulassia who finally put an end to his bemusement with what—he was sure—was the right answer.

They were both offstage, waiting for their cues, during a rehearsal of *Romeo and Juliet,* watching Hulik pour out her feelings into the waiting ears of Romeo. Ethulassia said suddenly: "That woman is in love with someone—and she hasn't even realized it for herself yet."

"What?" he replied. "But who?"

Not me! he thought, in half a panic. Not that Hulik wasn't stunningly beautiful—but he really didn't want anyone that dangerous in love with him!

"Oh, no one in your crew, or even on the *Petey B*, I don't think. Which is why she hasn't yet realized that she's in love with whoever it is." Ethulassia rubbed her finger along the side of her nose and continued to watch Hulik with narrowed eyes. "If I know that young woman at all, and I think I do, she's the kind that gets what she goes after. And she would leave Hulik-shaped holes in anything that got between her and the one she loved. Whoever he is, he may be the luckiest, or the unluckiest, man in the universe—depending on how he feels about her."

Since that was a perfectly accurate description of the former ISS agent, Pausert nodded agreement. And he was quite relieved to hear that the object of her affections was someone other than himself.

But of course, that left the question open—who was it?

And what was Hulik going to do when *she* figured it out?

CHAPTER 20

The judge facing Sedmon pursed his lips. "I've had a well-placed official request to dismiss the case. The witnesses have left. The charges may not stand up to a serious perusal. Attempted kidnapping is a vague sort of thing, after all."

Sedmon smiled at him. "On the other hand, Your Honor, fraud is usually not a vague sort of thing. Certain people might be very interested in the Arimann Trust."

The judge went absolutely white. Sedmon continued breezily. "And I do have certain knowledge that, if not child kidnapping, all of the prisoners have potential murder dockets. The evidence will be with you this afternoon. I trust the case will be handled then?"

The Daal had some of the best forgers in galaxy on his staff. But it had proved unnecessary to use them. ISS agents were used to being above the law. Breaking it was just too easy. On sensitive cases like this, the Daal knew, they didn't carry ID, just a communicator number in their heads. And with a little leaning he'd have that senior officer. "And just who did this well-placed official request come from, Your Honor?"

"Uh, a certain Colonel Pasker. He's a part of the Imperial Governor's staff," said the judge, nervously. "Er. About the Arimann Trust. It was just to tide me over . . ."

"And so it shall," said Sedmon. "Just as soon as these cases are dealt with." Then he left, to go and arrange an accident—of reasonably long duration—for a certain Colonel Pasker. And then to get aboard the *Thunderbird* and head, finally, towards Altim Four.

"I do wish that Pausert was tidier about these things," said Sedmon, plaintively.

CHAPTER 21

Vaudevillia had been, in Pausert's opinion, one of the ugliest mud-balls in the universe. Altim Four made Vaudevillia look like a pleasure-planet.

At least it wasn't a swamp. The vegetation was limited to the local versions of mosses and lichens; the local fauna was lower reptiles and whatever was swimming in the oceans, and a lot of insects. Fortunately, none of them found any of the invaders at all tasty, but they were a nuisance, anyway. All the heavy metals made it dangerous to drink the water without a lot of processing. Eating anything grown here, except what was grown hydroponically, was out of the question. The water was a curious green color—copper salts, Pausert thought. And while the air was breathable, it left a faintly bitter taste in the back of the throat.

If Altim wasn't a swamp, it was nonetheless warm, humid, and overcast most of the time. That was above ground, of course, a place where the miners mostly weren't. Every man, woman and neuter among them was spending most waking hours trying to dig out a fortune without poisoning themselves.

The ones who had it easiest were the ones who had staked their claims to EmCorp's tailings. That ore was already out of the ground and processed. It didn't need mining equipment to dig it out again, it just needed more processing to extract whatever else was lurking in there—and a decontamination unit to clean out residual radioactives. Those machines could run themselves. The hard part of their job was that in return for the stakes, by the terms of their charter these miners also served as reclamation techs, turning poisonous tailings into something benign and restoring the landscape. What there was of it.

Still, no telling what might evolve. Or what might turn up one day to take them to task for ruining the place. Better to be safe than sorry.

The spaceport was huge, built to take EmCorp's enormous freighters, and lots of them. Now it was mostly empty, which meant the *Petey B* was able to come in, set down, and set up on real tarmac without inconveniencing anyone. Better yet, since Altim Four was still officially EmCorp's private property, that meant that there was *not* an ISS presence. What passed for law around here was EmCorp's security service. They acted pretty much like local police, and enforced what little law there was. Lawbreakers were brought up in front of a magistrate and either fined or booted off the planet. Since being booted off the planet was the last thing any of the miners wanted, it was a simple, but effective, form of justice. The miners were all rugged individualists who didn't give a damn about government, anyway. They paid EmCorp for their stake, EmCorp kept the spaceport running and utter mayhem from breaking loose, and everyone seemed reasonably satisfied with the arrangement. EmCorp didn't even try the usual heavy-handed tactics of unrestrained giant corporations. Dealing with wildcat miners, that . . . could be risky.

Himbo Petey did not do a leaflet drop as they came in; with most of the miners underground, that would have been a wasted effort. And for the same reason, few people saw the showboat come in to land. Instead, he did something that a showboat almost never did: he bought advertising time on the news com-channel.

There was only one, and probably all of the miners listened to it at least once a day; it was just about the only way these far-scattered and reclusive people could keep track of what was going on with the rest of the universe. And there wasn't much else here that needed to purchase advertising; everyone knew every single bar, eatery, and entertainment-parlor there was. That would change, of course, as other merchants got wind of the place and decided it was worth the chance of poisoning to set up shop here. But, for now, Port-town was the only center of population, and it was pretty much as it had been when EmCorp moved out.

Only four locals appeared to watch the setup, and they were all viding for the local newsfeed. Pausert was surprised. Usually there were lots of folk turning out for what amounted to a free show. But miners, he was told by other members of the slowship's company, were always an odd bunch. It would be like them to figure they could get a better view on the vid during their downtime, and meanwhile, they could be making money.

Himbo Petey realized that this amounted to free advertising, of course, and immediately sent out Mannicholo (for the exotic look), the most articulate of the clowns (for the comedic aspect) and the prettiest of the female aerialists to give the vid-crew the full tour and the best shots of the setup. Mannicholo extolled the wonders of Sideshow Alley and acted as the clown's straight-man, the clown cracked some excellent jokes, and the girl waxed eloquent over the delights under the Big Top and on the stage of the Theater. Pausert watched some of it himself; it *was* a good show, and if the cameraman spent a lot of time with the lens focused on the aerialist, well, that was hardly a shock since the population ran to seventy-five percent male. And given the usual programming available—mostly "educational" programs, which the station could get for free—it wasn't surprising that the show got a major chunk of the broadcasting day, with one initial play and two replays to cover all three work-shifts.

No doubt about it, the *Petey B* was Big News so far as Altim Four was concerned.

Pausert expected that, given all the coverage, Himbo Petey would want things up and running immediately, if not sooner. But, no. The whole first day, the showboat was dark, running extra dress rehearsals for every act, even the sideshows. Pausert learned later from Mannicholo that this was for two reasons: Petey wanted the chance for *every* miner to have seen the 'cast, and he wanted anticipation to build on both sides of the equation.

It was smart thinking; as Pausert had long since realized, just one more example of Himbo Petey's shrewd business sense, which lurked beneath his sometimes buffoonish exterior appearance.

All four of the new plays were now in production: *Macbeth, Romeo and Juliet, A Midsummer Night's Dream,* and *The Merchant of Venice.* For the moment, the previous four, *Hamlet, Othello, Twelfth Night,* and *As You Like It* were out. Although Dame Ethulassia told Pausert confidentially that if the miners responded with enthusiasm to these plays from Old Yarthe, Cravan would probably put all four of the old ones back in performance, and have the *Venture's* crew understudy for parts already held by the original cast.

Maybe being a witch—or a wizard—made memorization a lot easier than it was for most people. Pausert was mildly surprised to realize that the idea of memorizing four parts (or more, if he was going to understudy more than one in each play) didn't bother him that much.

Before the *Petey B* set down, Himbo Petey had delivered a cautionary speech to the entire crew, warning them not to *expect* that the miners had made fabulous strikes and were laden with wealth. Even though the conditions were right for such a thing, that did not mean it had happened. But when the first of the crew actually made it into town and saw the hideously inflated prices— set out in weights and karats, rather than maels—there was no mistaking the feverish look in the eyes of anyone with an act.

And that was when Pausert got an idea.

He went into the bowels of the ship, looking for engineers. He had the feeling that these, the people who kept the ship and not the show running, might be the forgotten ones in all of the hurly-burly. And that although they were getting crew-share of the new profits, they were probably feeling a bit resentful that they were not going to be able to make more.

"How many of you *don't* have an act?" he asked the chief engineer bluntly.

The grizzled old man rubbed the back of his head thoughtfully. "Most of us," he admitted.

"Good. I have a proposition for you, then. There's no rule that stalls can't sell things. In fact, there are souvenir stalls salted all through Sideshow Alley, and I have a hold full of tinklewood fishing poles and allweather cloaks. There's fish here, you know. Even if you can't eat them, there's still sport in catching them, and it certainly rains here plenty enough. All you have to do is make them into *souvenir* fishing poles and allweather cloaks. Just slap '*Petey, Byrum and Keep, the Greatest Show In the Galaxy*' on them, and you lot can take turns off-shift in the stall selling them."

The chief engineer brightened. He'd seen the prices of merely ordinary objects here. A souvenir of the showboat could be marked up a bit more than that. Still, he was cautious. "So—what do you get out of this?"

"I need my ship fixed," Pausert said bluntly. "I know you patched her to keep her from leaking too much, but I need her fixed right. You boys get the poles and the cloaks and anything else that used to be in the holds to peddle as souvenirs, and in your off-shift time, you fix my ship right and tight. But—oh, you'd better not try to do anything with those educational toys," he added hastily. "They tend to explode."

"Can we take 'em apart and do something with the bits?" the chief engineer asked.

"So long as you don't get blown up, you're welcome to," Pausert replied, wondering if he was finally going to get rid of the wretched things after all. "Is it a deal?"

"Let me get the crew together and you can put it to them," the chief said. "But on the surface of it, I like it."

"And I'll get my niece."

With Goth doing the negotiating, an agreement was soon reached that was satisfactory for both sides. Even Himbo Petey approved when he was approached for permission.

"That's a cut above fluffy clown-dog toys and whirligigs," he said, rubbing his hands with pleasure. "With no children on this planet, I was wondering what we were going to do for souvenirs. In fact, I ought to canvas the rest of the ship to see if anyone has any more ideas, besides programs."

They did. Recordings of the circus music. Banners to brighten up Spartan quarters, cut from spare synthasilk and printed with the same images as the posters and fliers. Badges for coveralls, of animals and clown-faces. Carryalls and cups and drink-bottles with *"Petey, Byrum and Keep"* blazoned across them. Copies of the scripts of the plays, with holos of the performers in costume. The showboat began to buzz with frenzied activity as those who hadn't come up with acts, or whose acts were marginal at best, began working frantically to produce souvenirs aimed at adult pockets, rather than children's. And in the meantime, there was a showboat crammed full of things—unused or duplicate personal items, stuff that was still in the holds of the ships that had been bought and incorporated into the frame, forgotten bits and bobs that people had brought aboard and discovered they didn't need—much of which could be branded with the showboat name and logo and put into a stall until the real souvenirs were ready. Himbo Petey beamed with approval upon it all, for the ship got a cut of the profits from every stall, and he got a cut of the ship's portion.

In fact, he elected to keep the show dark for an unprecedented second day to allow the merchandise stalls to take the place of those who decided that they would rather peddle souvenirs than compete on talent alone.

Meanwhile, the rumors outside the gates continued to swell. Curious and increasingly impatient miners began to show up at the ticket office to demand schedules and ask about advance tickets for particular shows. So when the gates did open at last, at dawn on the third day, there was a gratifyingly large crowd.

Which Pausert didn't see, of course, because he was in morning rehearsal. But when the cast broke for lunch, he was gratified to see several of his allweather cloaks and one or two of those dratted fishing poles going past in the possession of new owners.

He inhaled his food, and headed for Sideshow Alley. The stalls were never actually empty. The morning shift in his stall was being maintained by one of the aerial contortionists from the Big Top who was part of the curtain act and the Spanish web ensemble. Here she performed solo contortion and balancing on the tiny stage. As Pausert entered the stall from the back, she passed him, dressed in her street clothes, with a friendly wave. "No accolades yet," she said cheerfully. "But I'm getting a full house every turn."

"Excellent," he replied, and ducked inside.

There was just enough room behind the stage for him to change into his Escapist costume—in his case, a skin-tight shirt in silvery synthasilk and looser breeches in electric blue. As he put his own props up on the stage, he heard the talker outside, running his pitch, talking up the act. Sometimes, when things were slow, acts would come out in front for a free-see. Pausert had the feeling that would not be the case here.

Then he relled vatch.

Do you need me? asked Silver-eyes.

Are you willing to be my assistant, the way Second Littlest is usually?

Sure. You don't even need to feed me.

Unbelievable. A cooperative vatch; at least, for as long as it wasn't bored. But maybe the reactions of the audience would keep it from being bored. He could hope, anyway.

The persona he had cooked up for this act was, in truth, based a bit on the way he used to think of himself, and a lot on some of the overinflated egos of his superiors on Nikkeldepain. He waited a bit nervously behind the curtain for the talker to give him the signal that the stall was as full as it was going to get—a flashing red light just above his head. Then it was his turn to toe the control that set the automated lights and his recorded music going and the curtain to rise.

Then he struck a pose. As the curtain came up, the stage lights brightened and the house lights dimmed, the audience of miners saw a fellow in flamboyant costume in an exaggerated "strong-man" pose. He took a couple more—equally exaggerated—poses, while his recorded music played, until the audience began to chuckle, realizing that he was "playing" someone who was altogether too full of himself.

Then his talker came in, and began doing the spiel, and he went into his act.

The first couple of escapes were done "straight," though with a ridiculous amount of flourish. Then came the comic sequence.

He wasn't altogether certain that the vatch was going to help—until, practically on cue!—he felt the cool breath of air on his hands that told him that Silver-eyes was doing Goth's job exactly. The roar of laughter as he struggled, while the talker pretended consternation, came as a relief and a surprise. There were a *lot* of people in here!

He finished the act exactly as scripted, and went into the "blow-off" poses to gales of laughter as the curtain went down.

Perfect! he thought at the vatch.

That was fun! replied Silver-eyes with enthusiasm. **I like the watchers! But what was that noise they were making?**

It's called laughing, and it means that they are having fun, too.

Will the next ones laugh too?

As long as we do the act right. Pausert kept part of his attention on the barker outside as he cleaned up and replaced all of his props. For a while, he had been unhappy with this act, until he'd hit on the idea of creating a kind of character to play. It might have been silly, but once the audience was laughing at the pompous character, rather than at him, it became a lot more enjoyable to put on the shows.

Then we have to do the act right. The vatch sounded quite determined on that score. **Can we change it when we get tired of doing the same thing?**

I think that's a good idea, he told it, cautiously. *But you need to talk to me beforehand about the changes you want to make, or they might not laugh when you do them.*

He sensed its agreement, and then the light flashed and it was time to do the show again.

Three shows an hour, with a break for fifteen minutes, for four hours; that was his shift in the stall, and every show was full up. The tent stall held fifteen or twenty people at a time—probably fifteen the size of the miners he'd been seeing—and it seemed as if the audience was completely new each time. It was astonishing.

Even without tips or accolades, he was earning a good pile of cash this afternoon. His talker (with whom he split the take, since the talker was as important in a way as the act) had never, ever been able to fill the stall at every show before!

Every time the audience laughed, the vatch giggled with pleasure; the little thing was actually enjoying performing! By the third hour it was suggesting small, cosmetic changes—like holding the drape down when he'd freed his hands so that he had to "fight" his way out of it—that increased the comedic impact of the blow-off. When his turn in the stall was finally over, and he made way for an exotic dancer who was one of the glamour-riders with the fanderbag act, the vatch was practically glowing with happiness as it popped away.

And it was a little—just a little—bigger.

Now that was interesting. He hadn't fed it. So how had it gotten bigger? Could it be that something about strong human emotions also fed it?

He was going to ask Goth about that when they met for dinner, but the four little, heavy knots of scrap cloth that the Leewit *thunked* down on the table in front of him drove the question right out of his head. "Lookee here, Captain!" she crowed. "Tips!"

"We aren't the first to get them—the dancers are starting to get a lot," Goth added, judiciously. "But a couple of the miners got all sentimental about our sibling-rivalry business. I guess sentimental will work, if you don't have a pair of big—"

"Fewmets!" exclaimed Hantis, plopping herself down in her usual place at the table. "And here I thought I was going to be the one to surprise you!" She added a couple of knots of her own to the small pile. "The buzz is that the merchants are doing all right, and that those benighted fishing poles and cloaks are about half gone already. What passes for fish around here concentrates metal in its skeleton! It's only copper, iron, and some sulfur, but it's pretty, like peacock ore. Some of the engineers are trying to figure out how to clean the meat from the bones and use the things for jewelry. No point in trying to peddle it here, but maybe our next stop."

"The Big Top was full, and everybody seemed to be enjoying the show a lot," said Goth. "Makes me wonder what these miners are going to think about the play."

Pausert had been wondering that, too. Were their tastes as sophisticated and eclectic as Mannicholo seemed to think? Or would the Old Yarthe plays be beyond them?

But as he opened his mouth to ponder the question aloud, Hulik appeared—

And her agitation caught the attention of everyone around their table.

Pausert couldn't recall *ever* having seen her look this way—it wasn't "upset," exactly, but it was disturbed, and excited, and—unsettled.

Enough so that everyone stared at her, until Hantis broke the little pool of silence at their table by asking the obvious.

"Hulik!" she said, urgently. "What's happened?"

"It's the Daal!" she whispered. "Sedmon! He's here!"

"Are you sure?" was all Pausert could think of to say, and he knew it was a stupid thing the moment the words were out of his mouth. Hulik gave him a withering glance.

"Of course, I'm sure, Captain!" she said. "I talked to him!"

"You *what*?" That came out of several mouths simultaneously, and Hulik waved at them frantically to keep them from all talking at once.

"It's all right, he's not chasing us, not exactly, but—oh, let me begin at the beginning!" She paused, took a deep breath, and settled herself. "I had no idea he was here until I got a message asking if I would meet with him, just before lunch. I wouldn't have believed it was Sedmon except that the message came with certain recognition signs."

Pausert nodded; that was only the smart thing to do.

"And I agreed to meet him at one of the public food stalls, anyway." She was regaining her composure, and now, in contrast, Pausert realized just *how* flustered she had looked. "We didn't have a lot of time to talk, but we both agreed that the meeting was more for the purpose of identifying ourselves. He says he has a lot of information for us, and a lot of warnings. I told him we'd already figured that virtually everyone in known space is after us again, and that our safe-conducts were worth exactly nothing right now. And we agreed to meet again after the play tonight, at the *Venture*."

"You think there's any chance he's setting us up?" asked Goth.

"No!" Hulik replied, indignantly. Then, as if trying to cover her vehemence, said, more calmly, "No. Firstly, he doesn't really have anything to gain by turning us over to anyone who's after us. What could they offer the Daal? He already rules an entire system!"

"That's a point," Goth acknowledged.

"And secondly, I've never known Sedmon to be in the least inclined to do anything to aggravate the witches of Karres, and I can't see that starting now. You all must admit that interfering with us and what we're doing would *seriously* aggravate Karres—" Hulik raised an eyebrow, and the Leewit laughed.

"Have to admit you're right there, too," Goth agreed. "But it must be something pretty pressing for the Daal of Uldune to have come after us personally!"

Hulik didn't say anything, but Pausert thought she seemed to be a little flushed. And she was staring off into the distance as if her eyes weren't focused.

A sudden, wild surmise came to him. Goth started pounding him on the back, with a look of concern.

"Are you okay, Captain?" she asked.

"Clumping stupid!" scoffed the Leewit. "Choking to death on this goop! Hadn't got a bone in it!"

CHAPTER 22

Sir Richard had debated long and hard about which of the new plays to present first. *Romeo and Juliet* had a strong story, of course, and was full of both action and pathos. The Scottish Play—odd, how even Pausert now could hardly bring himself to even think of it by its proper title—had plenty of fighting too, not to mention the added attraction of the magic and all those murders. *Twelfth Night,* on the other hand, though a "comedy," wasn't really all that funny. Of the four, it was probably the one least likely for a new audience to appreciate, which was why Cravan had added it into the repertoire last. *A Midsummer Night's Dream* was a lot funnier, even if you didn't altogether understand the language, and there was that ladies' mud-wrestling scene . . .

In the end, that was what had decided Cravan. Of all of the plays, *A Midsummer Night's Dream* was probably the most accessible. And with the mining population heavily weighted in favor of men, the mud-wrestling, much though he abhorred it himself, was probably going to please even the densest of them.

The miners proved just as pleasantly intelligent and appreciative as had been suggested. They laughed at most of the right places, oooh'd and ah'd at the fairy-lights provided by the Leewit and Goth; and, yes, were very enthusiastic about the mud-wrestling scene. Enough so that when the curtain came down and the cast came out for final bows, there was a pleasant pattering of those little knots of gold-dust on the stage at Hulik's feet and those of her co-star.

171

Dame Ethulassia got a share of them, too, interestingly enough. Pausert had to admit that she was a regal figure in the Elven Queen's elaborate costume, and if she was more than a few years Hulik's senior, the exaggerated makeup that went with the costume went a fair way to hiding that. Mostly, though, Pausert suspected that it was The Incredible Bosom which did the trick.

Even Hantis got a knot or two. Under other circumstances, Pausert would have been the first to suggest staying to find out just how much had been collected. Not tonight, though. Hulik managed to put on a veneer of graceful modesty when Cravan asked if she wanted to stay on with the company accountant and shook her head. "If I can't trust you and Himbo Petey to deal fairly with us all, I doubt my being there in person would make much difference. Besides, it's been a very long day, and there are going to be a lot more of them ahead of us! I'd rather stare at the inside of my eyelids than an accounting page."

"And speaking of accounting," Pausert said in a low voice, as they all hurried towards the *Venture*, "I for one would like to find out just why our bank account was frozen. If it hadn't been for that, we might be at our destination right now!"

"I'm sure he'll have a good explanation," Hulik said, though she sounded uncertain.

"I clumping well hope so," the Leewit said ominously. "Or it just might be Sedmon of the Five Lives pretty soon."

The Daal of Uldune chose that moment to step out from the *Venture*'s airlock—just in time to hear that pint-sized bloodcurdling threat. He smiled serenely. "Please, Little Wisdom, have mercy. That ploy was never meant to do more than create a day or two's delay, in order that we could catch up with you. You were all in grave danger, and heading into still more."

From her scowl, the Leewit was not much mollified. Neither was Pausert. "Well, by the time the trouble your 'delaying tactic' caused us was over," he said with some heat, "we'd been shot at, thrown into prison, kidnapped, shot at again, sunk into ferroplast, shot at some more, and were running short on air *and* fuel. With 'help' like that, who needs enemies?"

"I can explain," said the Sedmon smoothly. He gestured regally, inviting them to enter their spaceship as if it was his own palace. Oddly . . . he managed to pull it off—even after introducing his twin, once they reached the ship's salon.

Hulik looked a little smug. More than a little, in fact.

✳   ✳   ✳

"You are not entirely surprised, I gather?" one of the Sedmons asked her, cocking his head. His twin's head was also cocked, although in the opposite direction. To Pausert, the look both of them were giving the do Eldel seemed oddly intense.

"No, not really." Hulik looked back and forth from one to the other. "I was always curious about that 'of the Six Lives' business and did a little discreet investigation on my own. The timing of your public appearances is not, I'm afraid, always up to professional standards. Quite good, mind you, for a monarch. But from my vantage point, a bit on the sloppy side. There have been occasional reports of these odd overlaps. Not many, and I doubt if anyone except me has ever really put it together. Perhaps, in the future . . . a little expert advice . . ."

"Indeed," said both of the Sedmons simultaneously, almost eagerly.

The Leewit interrupted. She was almost cross-eyed, staring at them. "You mean you're—you're—?" She gave her older sister an exasperated glance. "What's the word, Goth?"

"Sextuplets. But I don't think that's it. Here, I mean. I think they're clones."

The Sedmons nodded, again simultaneously. "That is correct. Although, even that does not fully encompass the reality. The witches of Karres are not the only ones who have delved into the mysteries of klatha."

Hantis nodded. "You were birthed by the Hospitalers of Ghrauth, then." She made a face. "Risky business, dealing with them."

Pausert had never heard of "the Hospitalers of Ghrauth." But he noticed that both Goth and the Leewit's eyes were wider than they had been.

"Clumping crazy," muttered the Leewit.

The Sedmons shrugged. "It is an old arrangement," said one of them, "dating back through the last four Daals of Uldune. A bit dangerous, I suppose, but . . . let us say that my forefathers not only paid extremely well but had certain methods of ensuring that the Hospitalers stuck to their side of the bargain."

Goth seemed to suppress a snort. "No fooling! Burn their moonlet down to bedrock."

"Well, yes, that too," said the other Sedmon modestly. "Though, of course, that would only be an inconvenience to the monsters. But the Daals have other longstanding arrangements, you know. The Hospitalers have always been considerably more impressed by our friendly relations with the Nemode Cluster."

So was Goth, from the way her eyes kept widening. The Leewit's eyes bore a fair resemblance to saucers. "Clumping *insane!*" she choked.

Hulik, on the other hand, simply looked intrigued. Very intrigued.

Pausert cleared his throat forcefully. He didn't understand anything they were talking about, and had more pressing concerns anyway.

"You were going to explain why you had our account frozen . . ."

The Sedmons knew about the Nanite plague. They had known about the Agandar's fleet *and* the ISS being in pursuit of the *Venture* and its crew. This, according to the two that were here, was why they had put a hold—"a hold *only,* and then only with the instructions to verify with us before authorizing payment"— on the account with the Daal's Bank on Uldune.

"The hold was on the *account,*" the right-hand Sedmon said crossly. "It wasn't an order to hold the captain who tried to use it! All that was supposed to happen was that the person verifying the information was supposed to call us, and we would release the account. It seemed a perfectly reasonable and quiet way to find out where you were without sending out messages that would have revealed you, and us, to enemies! Our instructions were *not* carried out, and we are most aggrieved."

"Hmph. Not half as aggrieved as we were," Pausert replied, but he was privately feeling a lot less angry. When Sedmon of the Six Lives was "most aggrieved," heads usually began to roll.

"Your instructions may have been subverted and contaminated, Excellency," said Hantis. "When the ISS fails to honor a safe-conduct in the Empress' own hand, such a thing is not unlikely."

Both Sedmons nodded somberly, like a pair of souvenir bobble-heads. "All the more reason to be aggrieved," the left-hand one said, this time very grimly indeed. Pausert could practically hear the echo of a falling ax behind his words. "And our sources give us three reasons why such things could have happened to you and to us. One—that someone high in the Empress' government has been infected with the plague, or is jockeying to make himself Regent or Emperor. We think the former is the more likely possibility, otherwise why try to stop you? You only bring word of the Nanite plague—this could not help or harm someone who is merely engaging in cutthroat politics, so there would be no reason to try to intercept you."

Pausert nodded, and so did the Nartheby Sprite.

"Two—someone high in the ISS is the infected entity."

"We thought of both of those ourselves," said Goth evenly.

Unlike the Leewit, she was not scowling—had not scowled once, in fact—but there was always something rather unsettling about that expressionless face on a girl who was still only twelve standard years old. For a moment, the Sedmons almost seemed to flinch a little.

"Ah, but there is a third possibility." The right-hand Sedmon raised a finger. "The Agandar's followers pursue you, under the assumption that you have the Agandar's treasure, or at least, the key to it."

"I don't—" Pausert began with some heat, but the Sedmons both waved him to silence. He might not have obeyed, except that seeing both of them move and act as one was oddly compelling and a bit creepy.

"Whether you do or not is irrelevant," the left-hand Sedmon said. "The point is, that they *believe* that you do. And so, perhaps, does someone in the ISS."

"Eh?" said Pausert, and "Oh!" said Goth and the Leewit together. The older sister's face now had an expression, and the Leewit had left off scowling.

"Captain! Someone in the ISS might be looking to make himself rich on the Agandar's treasure," said the Leewit. "And that's a *lot* of treasure."

Hantis and Pul stared at each other. "Reason enough," Pul agreed. "Even for ignoring the Empress' safe-conduct."

"Personally, of all three reasons, this is the one that is the most likely, we think," the right-hand Sedmon said. "Greed is a more reliable motivator than anything else."

Pausert didn't agree with him, although he wished he did. The Daal's third alternative was the least frightening. A corrupt ISS official was somehow easier to deal with in his mind than someone who—well—wasn't "himself" anymore. *That* just made the hair on the back of his neck stand up, and worse, made him want to shut himself in his stateroom and weld the door closed.

"Now, we have unlocked your account, but it may not be safe to use it," the left-hand Sedmon continued. "Clearly, someone has a watch on it. We underwent some difficulties ourselves in the course of finding you, that lead us to believe that our own safeguards off Uldune are not as secure as we had thought. We have access to other accounts to pay off your ship and refuel it, of course, but it might be best not to touch them until you have lost pursuit. So—it may be that *this* is your best and safest means of travel for some time."

"But the *Petey B* won't be going anywhere near the core worlds," Pausert protested.

Both Sedmons raised their eyebrows. "Oh?" said the right-hand one. "The ship goes where the profit is, does it not? And if the Daal's Bank on Uldune elects to sponsor this ship on a goodwill cultural tour spiraling towards the core?"

"There might even be some profit in it," the left-hand Sedmon added, thoughtfully. "These Old-Yartheian plays are strangely compelling. Especially the one with the mud-wrestling scene—"

"Sponsoring the showboat would certainly guarantee that it went where you wanted," Pausert interjected hastily. "But Sedmon—uh, or is it 'Sedmons'?—you aren't dealing with some back-country yokel here. Himbo Petey is shrewd. So are Richard Cravan and Dame Ethulassia—and Himbo won't do anything like this without consulting with them. They're all going to be curious about *why* the Daal's Bank is suddenly sponsoring cultural tours, and they probably won't stop looking for an answer until they find one."

"And in the process, they may reveal us to more than just the cast and crew of the showboat," Hulik cautioned.

The Sedmons pursed their lips. "Just 'Sedmon,' please, whichever of us you are addressing—or however many at once," murmured the one on the right. A moment later, his clone said, a bit reluctantly, "In that case, I believe we are going to have to tell them the truth. Most of it, at least. My identity will have to be fudged, of course, beyond what's needed to make the offer of payment believable. But I think we can leave the specific details regarding the Nanite plague on the vague side. As well as your exact identities, beyond being agents for the Empress. I see no reason to mention Karres at all."

The proposal should have made Pausert very unhappy. In fact, it did the opposite. Logic and cunning maneuver be damned. His instincts told him that Himbo Petey, Richard Cravan, and Dame Ethulassia were to be trusted in a matter of this sort. Besides, the duplicity they had been engaged in was chafing at him more and more. "I'm for it," he said immediately.

Hulik sighed. "It goes entirely against all my training," she said, "But I feel the same."

Hantis shrugged. "At this point, there is danger either way. But Himbo might order us off his ship, and keep ours!"

"This is a mining world," retorted the left-hand Sedmon. "If we cannot buy an old freighter, I would be very much surprised."

Pausert winced. He had grown very attached to the *Venture*. "Well, we could probably buy our way off, though that much activity might alert the people we're trying to hide from."

"I don't think he'll dump us," the Leewit said suddenly. "Himbo Petey, I mean. And I'd feel better telling him, too."

Goth nodded, Vezzarn shrugged, and the grik-dog simply grunted.

"It seems unanimous," said the right-hand Sedmon. "I suggest, then, that you tell him. Now, if possible."

"Me?" Pausert asked. "What about you?"

"It seems prudent that we remain an unknown," the Sedmons said together. "In fact," added the left-hand one, "we intend to send one of us back to our own ship to remain there for the duration. It is not a wise idea for us both to be seen at the same time."

"It didn't ever occur to you to pass yourself off as perfectly ordinary twins, did it?" Goth asked, sardonically. "I don't know, sometimes. All that supposed intelligence—"

The Sedmons looked stricken. "Twins?" they said together. "But do twins—"

"Sort of," said Vezzarn thoughtfully, tapping his finger against his glass. "Not a real psionic bond, like the Hospitalers seem to have given you. But twins sometimes do act together, talk together—know when each other's in trouble. Why, I remember a couple of girls in a social-club back on Nardis that—"

Hulik coughed; Vezzarn flushed, and cut off whatever he was going to say.

"Very well, then," the Sedmons said. "We will come with you— but *not* as ourselves. Agents for the bank, perhaps."

"I don't care how you come," said Pausert flatly, "so long as you have some way of proving to Himbo Petey that you have access to enough money to commission his ship for this 'cultural cruise.' Because if you can't do that, you might as well unlock our account so we can cut loose and take our chances."

"That," said the Sedmons, "would be a bad idea."

Himbo Petey looked from Hantis to Pausert and back again, his eyes narrowed. Pausert expected an explosion, but he wasn't getting one. He wasn't sure whether to be relieved or more worried.

"Well," Petey said at last. "If that doesn't beat anything I've ever heard."

"But it certainly explains some otherwise inexplicable things, Himbo," said Richard Cravan thoughtfully. "Mind you, I am less than pleased with their lack of candor up to this point. On the other hand, I can understand why they prevaricated."

"Sure, so can I," growled Petey, "But I still don't like it, not one bit. 'Gainst my showboat principles."

"You have to admit that *not* knowing hasn't harmed you or the showboat," Hulik pointed out reasonably.

"And you're serious about paying the *Petey B* to go on this inner-system tour, are you?" Himbo Petey licked his lips. "I dunno. I just don't know. It'd mean guaranteed pay, no matter what the box office took in, and that's not to be sneezed at. But I dunno . . ."

"Himbie!" cried Ethulassia, seizing his arm urgently and drawing him close. "I like the idea!" She and Cravan exchanged a quick glance, and Ethulassia nodded slightly. As she did so—the Dame was no mean magician herself—The Incredible Bosom seemed to expand still further.

"Himbo," Cravan said, his eyes taking on something of an unholy glow. "You *know* how my one dream has been to take my company and these plays to the central worlds. You *know* how sure I've been that we could hold our own against any other theatrical company there. This is our chance! This is our chance to prove what we can do, who we are, and at no risk at all to you, financial or otherwise. Please, Himbo! Please! I have never truly begged you for anything before this, but I am begging you now—please let us do this!"

Himbo Petey looked from Ethulassia to Cravan, then to Pausert, then the Sedmons, then back to Cravan. "Well—"

Cravan seized his hand and pumped it. "Thank you, Himbo! Thank you! You are making my dream come true!"

Petey hemmed and hawed a little, looking pleased but embarrassed. "But we don't leave here until we've earned everything there *is* to earn here," he added hastily. "Damned if I will! Showboat principles are showboat principles."

"We do not disagree," said the right-hand Sedmon earnestly. "It would seem odd if we did. And ah—er—" he coughed. "Our own disguise—perhaps 'bona fides' is a more salubrious term—needs to be established. We think perhaps our ship should be added to the frame, and a job found for us. Temporarily, of course."

"Of course," Himbo agreed. He cocked an eyebrow at Pausert and Hulik. "Suggestions?"

"Mentalist act," said Hulik instantly.

"Cage-sweeper," said Pausert, just as quickly.

The Sedmons gave the captain a look which did not bode well for Pausert's fate and fortune, should he ever find himself back on Uldune again. But he couldn't pass up the opportunity. Once in a lifetime, that was. Besides, he was still a little peeved about the episode on Pidoon.

CHAPTER 23

Of course, the Sedmons were not made into cage-sweepers. They would have been entirely useless at the job, for one thing. They were accustomed to having people following *them* about, picking up what they absentmindedly dropped, not cleaning up other creatures' messes. Old habits are too hard to break. Much as Pausert would have enjoyed watching the Sedmons try to cope, even he had to admit that.

No, as Hulik had suggested, the Sedmons got a mentalist act; it was easy enough for them to do, and a good talker made up for their inexperience.

They also got a make-work job as Dame Ethulassia's assistants in wardrobe. Not that they were any good at sewing and the like, but they could at least check in the costumes that needed repairs and cleaning, and check out the ones to replace them. "Wardrobe" covered, not only the thespians, but the entire company, so there was enough work to make them look busy, at least.

The Sedmons had agreed initially to the plan not to leave until every last mael had been milked from the miners, simply to resolve the initial situation. But they had always assumed they could, eventually, persuade the Showmaster otherwise.

They were wrong. Absolutely and completely wrong. No argument, no persuasion, not all of the Sedmons' diplomatic experience served. Himbo Petey was not going to budge from this planet as long as there was money to be made there, and no matter what the Sedmons said to him, he was adamant on that score. It seemed—the Sedmons were quite astonished, actually—that the man took his ridiculous "showboat principles" in deadly earnest. It was like dealing with a religious zealot!

The Sedmons were left with the depressing feeling that receipts were never going to drop off, that the *Petey B* would be here forever. They had to get out of here! Somewhere out there the Nanite plague had started, they were sure of it. Too many things were going wrong out there, and it chafed at the Sedmons that although the other four had the best information services in the galaxy at their disposal, there just was not enough information coming in. Why else would Karres have disappeared again? They had to leave, and yet, it seemed that Himbo Petey's people would never want to.

And, for a while, it looked as if their worst fears might be right. Miners continued to pack the stalls, the Big Top, and the theater, and accolades continued to come in. Hulik was the recipient of quite a few of those, especially when she played Juliet or Helene.

And that was another source of fretting, for the Daal. When that happened, when the gifts and inevitable marriage proposals appeared backstage . . . The emotions stirred up were something the Sedmons were ill equipped to handle.

But Hulik always sent the same answer to the proposals, a politely, even kindly worded refusal, and the Sedmons relaxed. There was time, apparently.

Time, yes—and now time spent in Hulik's company. The experience only confirmed what had sent them across the galaxy in the first place. It hadn't been the danger of the Nanite plague. Not really.

The Sedmons were in love. Hulik do Eldel was, impossibly enough, the most important person in the universe to them, as important as any one of their six selves.

Maybe more.

The only problem was, they hadn't the faintest idea what to do about it.

How could they propose any sort of alliance with a woman, *any* woman? What sort of woman would consider such a thing? What had always seemed to be their greatest strength, their very nature, now seemed to be the greatest of curses.

Nevertheless, they could not, would not leave. Aside from any other considerations, this mad longing for her kept them at her side.

Surely, with enough time, they would think of something.

Or Hulik would accept one of those proposals.

Or they would fall out of love. Such things could happen . . . however unlikely it seemed.

And it seemed more and more unlikely with every passing day. Before long, the Sedmons were in a perpetual agony of indecision. What to do? What to do?

After two weeks, however, audiences for the sideshow acts finally began to drop down to more normal levels, and some acts stopped getting any attention at all. The exotic dancers—in fact, any act featuring a pretty female—remained popular, but some of the rest began to cut back or close. It was obvious why it was happening, of course; you could only watch a comedic escapism act so many times before you got tired of it.

But the theater stayed packed, and Cravan made up for the drop-off in attendance at the sideshows by putting all four of the old plays back into production. Those who had closed their sideshow acts quickly found places to fill there. Even the Sedmons were recruited for nonspeaking roles.

Two weeks became four. The Sedmons still had not thought of a way to approach Hulik.

They began to think that they never would. And in all of their lives, they could not remember feeling such despair.

They actually indulged in daydreams, imagining scenarios in which they rescued Hulik and her companions from thugs of varying design. The costumes changed, though the scenes remained pretty much the same. They even dreamed such things at night, and in fact, almost came to long for such a thing to happen. At least it would give an opportunity to speak!

It became worse when new ships arrived, bearing new miners. Would one of *them* win Hulik's heart? Or had it already been given? Perhaps to one of the thespians?

That last thought was the worst of all.

Pausert went through his limbering exercises as he had done so many times, although by now he was no longer nervous about that part of his role as Mercutio. His body knew every choreographed movement so thoroughly that he could have done his fight scenes blindfolded or drunk. So all that mattered was his own preparation, warming up his muscles so that he wouldn't injure himself.

Himbo Petey had confided to the thespians that it was getting to be time to move along, he knew the signs, and Cravan agreed with him. The advertisements would go out tonight: *Last four days onplanet! See your favorites again for the final time!* There were several potential problems, not the least of which was the possibility of developing jealousy between those whose acts had lasted past the novelty stage, and those whose acts had not.

But even the thespians were beginning to see signs of the contempt bred by familiarity. Early in the run, the audiences had been forgiving. But now, if someone fumbled a line or a prop, there was a subtle grumbling; even, on occasion, outright raspberries.

So there it was. Time to go. The announcement of last days would bring a final influx of customers and cash, and then they would lift. And now they would be heading in the direction where they needed to go. Hubwards. Towards the Empress, to deliver their message. And what then? Pausert only wished he knew. He could not imagine how even the Empress could do anything about the Nanite plague, but who was he to assume he knew anything at all?

He heard the start of the music for Act Three, and swaggered onto the stage as the curtain rose.

Benvolio fanned himself with his hand, and spoke the first lines of Act 3. "I pray thee, good Mercutio, let's retire: The day is hot, the Capulets abroad, and, if we meet, we shall not scape a brawl; for now, these hot days, is the mad blood stirring."

Pausert made a face and waggled his finger in Benvolio's face. "Thou art like one of those fellows that when he enters the confines of a tavern claps me his sword upon the table and says 'God send me no need of thee!' and by the operation of the second cup draws it on the drawer, when indeed there is no need." He raised his eyes heavenward, as if asking for patience.

They traded jibes until Tybalt entered, Vonard Kleesp playing the role with his usual swaggering panache. Benvolio exclaimed: "By my head, here come the Capulets!" He flung himself down on the steps of a prop-fountain, right in their way. "By my heel, I care not."

And that was when Pausert relled vatch.

Not that Silver-eyes hadn't been around, quite faithfully. It was just that the vatch hadn't made its presence known during one of the plays for quite some time. It had been quite scrupulous, in fact, about not making itself a nuisance.

Suddenly, from the aura the vatch was emitting, Pausert realized that Silver-eyes had not come here in play or jest.

Trouble! Trouble! Trouble! shrilled the vatch.

A sudden commotion erupted backstage.

Vonard Kleesp's eyes narrowed.

There is one sound that no fencer every forgets, if he's heard it once. It is the sudden *snap* of the protected tip of a fencing blade being broken off. It is the sound that says: someone has a deadly blade in his hands now, a length of steel that can kill you.

It was the sound that Pausert—and everyone else—heard at that moment.

"Move, and you die," said Kleesp softly.

So, of course, Pausert moved.

He rolled out of immediate striking distance, desperately trying to get his own blade free at the same time. It got tangled up in his cloak, though, and as he shot to his feet, he saw Kleesp coming at him and he thought it was all over—

But like a miracle—vatch-style miracle, he realized—the cloak flung itself off his blade, wrapped itself around his free hand, giving him a "shield" of the sort that street-fencers would use.

And there was a lot more noise going on backstage. Pausert didn't have time to think much about it, but his initial assumption that Vonard Kleesp had simply gone mad due to the effects of his alcoholism vanished. This was foul play of some sort, not lunacy.

Kleesp lunged. The tip ripped cloth on his hose and Pausert felt warm wetness on his thigh. Then the blade licked across his upper arm. Penetrating, and being pulled free.

The captain tried to get into the most sensible position which a man with a buttoned foil can take when facing a murderer with a naked blade. That position was somewhere a long way off.

Unfortunately, short of jumping into the audience, Pausert had run out of space to go to. So, he parried the next lunge, wishing desperately it was really as easy to convert a foil into a live blade as the three-dee made it out to be. It wasn't, or there would have been a lot of dead fencers every year. Kleesp had obviously prepared his sword ahead of time. Pausert had no such advantage. Standing on the tip and giving it a sharp jerk upwards was a futile pastime—unless you had a handy metal vise under your shoes. The soft rubber sole on the buskins he was wearing certainly wouldn't do the job.

So he did what the sword could do—parry. He managed to force Kleesp's blade up, so he could grapple the man. Pausert dropped the foil, and, snatching at the base of the naked blade with his cloaked hand, clung to Kleesp's shirtfront with the other.

It was the last thing the murderous actor had expected.

"What in the name of Patham's Seventh Hell are you playing at, damn you?" Pausert hissed into his ear. "Drop the sword and back off."

Kleesp wrestled with manic strength. "I'm going to kill you and be a wealthy man, Pausert," he hissed back. "The Agandar's fortune belongs to *me*, since I was his lieutenant. You think I spent this much time tracking it down and setting my trap just to walk away? Not a chance."

He managed to wrench his blade free, but he was still too close to use it effectively. And before he could back away, Pausert had him in a bear hug. Whatever else, the captain wasn't letting his armed opponent go.

Kleesp tried to headbutt the captain, but Pausert had been in too many brawls as a junior naval officer. He met the headbutt with one of his own—harder and better placed. Kleesp grunted softly and, for a moment, seemed to weaken. Off-balance, they stumbled against the one of the prop pillars at the edge of the stage. The prop, never intended to withstand such impact, promptly collapsed.

They fell to the floor together. Kleesp's foil was jarred out of his hand when they hit the stage, skittering a few feet away.

Pausert felt a momentary surge of elation. Then—somehow—Kleesp managed to break the captain's bear hug and roll clear. The actor-assassin scrabbled for his foil and came back to his feet, weapon in hand. He lunged at Pausert in a single smooth motion. Pausert dove out of the way and landed, painfully, on another foil. He'd barely managed to take it in hand before Kleesp was onto him again.

The captain parried successfully and took a step back. And then he learned the lesson all good actors do: If you are retreating, don't do so towards the edge of the stage.

He tumbled over and fell against the front row seats.

With a leap, Kleesp followed him. "Give them space!" yelled someone. "Move the chairs!"

To Pausert's astonishment, the audience was cheering wildly. This was entertainment! They thought the play was still on!

The cheers grew to a deafening roar, as the captain's sword and

Kleesp's clashed in a flurry of thrusts and parries. Alas, not all the chairs had been moved out of the way. Pausert stumbled over one, bringing it down in his fall.

Luckily, Kleesp fell also. The captain's sudden fall caused his lunge to miss wildly and the assassin lost his balance. Pausert snatched up the chair he'd fallen over and slammed it down on Kleesp's back. Unfortunately, it was one of the flimsy folding chairs used for the front seats of overflow crowds. It couldn't do any real damage—though it bought Pausert enough time to vault back onto the stage.

Kleesp followed relentlessly. "You'll pay for that," he snarled. Another flurry of lunges and parries—alas, all lunges by Kleesp and parries by Pausert. What else could he do with a tipped sword?

Steadily, the captain was forced back towards the wings. He stumbled over the fallen prop pillar again, and rolled backstage under the curtains.

Kleesp followed instantly, sensing the kill, using his free hand to thrust aside the curtains. He arrived backstage so quickly that the captain was just getting back onto his feet. Kleesp lunged at Pausert. Hard.

Knowing it was useless, Pausert tried to hold him off with the foil, but Kleesp's blade struck the captain neatly on the middle of the left breast.

His powerful lunge also carried Kleesp forward with his full weight pressed against Pausert's foil, which the captain had held up stiffly in that last futile gesture.

The buttoned tip bent, as intended.

The other blade, carefully weakened with an acute-angled cut so it would snap to a sharp point, did not bend at all. It slid with sickening ease right through the ribs and into the chest cavity.

Kleesp looked down, gaping. Blood suddenly gushed out of his open mouth. "You've killed me!" he coughed. The words were spoken more in chagrin than anger.

That was quite understandable, Pausert thought wildly. He didn't know much about the mentality involved, but he was quite sure that dying because you'd grabbed the wrong blade . . . was not going to make for bragging rights in whatever afterlife pirates enjoyed.

Or didn't.

Another cough; another gush of blood. It was obvious the sword had pierced the assassin's heart. Kleesp clawed at the blade, but his eyes were already rolling. Horrified, Pausert released the hilt of the sword.

Some strange last surge of effort kept Kleesp on his feet for a few stumbling backwards steps—just long enough for him to collapse through the curtains and back onto the stage. His impromptu and quite unplanned reentrance produced a veritable hurricane of applause.

Pausert shook his head. And then realized that his troubles were far from over. Something hard and narrow was now pressing into his lower spine. The way something presses which is being made to do so.

"That's an M9 blaster you're feeling," growled a voice in his ear. "Now move—slowly—back onto the stage."

Seeing no alternative, Pausert obeyed.

As soon as he came through the curtains, Pausert realized that his earlier premonition was quite correct—Kleesp had been no madman, suddenly unhinged. He'd planned everything as part of a coordinated effort. There were three men standing on the stage who constituted no part of the thespian troupe. The captain vaguely recognized two of them—some of the locals hired on by the showboat during its stop at Tornam, the same planet where Vonard Kleesp had joined the company. Four men, in all, counting the one still prodding Pausert forward. And all of them were armed with M9s. Not a handgun any military force would favor, due to its short range, but one that was quite in demand in criminal circles. Whatever that model blaster lacked in range, it made up for in destructive power.

The actors were also on the stage, but they all had their hands raised. And it wasn't just the actors, either. However they'd managed it, Kleesp's cohorts had rounded up Vezzarn as well—along with one of the Sedmons.

"No funny stuff, Pausert," growled the voice in his ear, "or we'll kill all the actors. Starting with the women. Don't think we won't. We're the Agandar's pirates and you know our reputation. Now. We need those two kids also, and then we're all out of here. You figure out how to get them, or we start the killing."

In the odd way that one notices details at this sort of time, Pausert's eyes fell on one of the blaster-holding men on the stage. The one nearest to him, except for the one at his back that he still hadn't seen. Something about the man's stance made it clear that he was now the one in charge. The burly pirate grinned sardonically. "You might have killed the boss, but I guess that just means more money for the rest of us once we get our hands on the Agandar's account. So where are the two witch kids?"

"I really have no idea," said Pausert slowly. His arm was now beginning to hurt. He needed time to think.

He wasn't going to get it.

The pirate turned to one of his associates, and pointed at Hulik. "Shoot her in the head. It'll help his memory."

And then things started happening very fast, and all at once.

Somebody kicked the backstage door off its hinges.

A flat came hissing down onto one of the assassins, knocking him off his feet. Unseen hands—or vatch ones—had apparently untied a rope.

A whistle like a punch on the jaw felled another, the pirate leader.

One Sedmon came through the door he'd just kicked in. The other, the one already on the stage, dove at the pirate who was bringing his blaster to bear on Hulik. He never would have made it in time, except that something—a pen? Pausert couldn't quite tell—went sailing from Vezzarn's hand and struck the assassin. Whatever it was, it was sharp enough to gash the man's face and completely distract him. An instant later, the Sedmon's tackle had the pirate on the floor and the two of them fell to wrestling for control of the weapon.

That left the still-unseen man holding the blaster against Pausert's spine. Old naval training came back to the captain. Holding a weapon pressed directly against a trained fighter is the trick of an amateur—or a thug grown overconfident. A quick twist and an elbow strike knocked the weapon aside. The same elbow came back up in a forearm smash to the jaw that drove the man backward. The captain followed, raising his hand for a very nasty strike at the throat.

The strike never landed. The fellow, already staggering, flipped onto his back as if he'd tripped over something unseen. The unseen something emitted a very Goth-like "Ow!" and the assassin's head made an even louder "thunk!" as it smashed against the floor of the stage.

Pausert pounced on him. He hit the man once, with his fist. A nasty temple smash. But he did so more out of anger and general principle than from any real need. The fellow had obviously been knocked cold from the impact of his head against the stage.

The captain pried the blaster out of a limp hand and rose to his feet, ready to use it. But—

There was no need.

Vezzarn had apparently joined the Sedmon's tackle on the man who started to shoot Hulik. Between the two of them . . . especially since Vezzarn had retrieved whatever missile he'd thrown so accurately and had then used it to . . .

Pausert winced. He winced again when he caught sight of the pirate who'd been floored by the falling flat. In and of itself, the flat hadn't done much more than knock the man down. What had kept him down thereafter was Pul's jaws, clamped on his leg.

Well. At one time, clamped on his leg. Right now the leg itself was no longer attached. Mentally, the captain shrugged. If the thug didn't bleed to death before medical help arrived, modern prosthetics were quite miraculous. And although Pausert wasn't any more familiar with the ethos of maximum security prisons than he was of the pecking order in the pirate afterworld, he suspected that "Stumpy" was a better monicker than "the Goof Who Picked Up The Wrong Sword."

Not that he cared anyway. *Live by the growl, die by the growl.* So be it.

Besides, Pausert had other problems that were far more pressing.

First, the applause from the audience was so deafening he could hardly think. The exuberant miners *still* thought it was all part of the act. Apparently, they ascribed such minor details as a severed leg and several quarts of spilled blood to "smoke and mirrors."

Secondly, the accolades now showering the stage—no, raining on it—were a positive menace. Gold is *heavy,* even in small pouches. Pausert found himself wondering for a moment if he and his fellow thespians were about to undergo an ancient form of death by torture. "Stoning," he thought it was called.

Then he spotted the person he was looking for, off in a corner, and forgot about everything else. Pausert felt almost dizzy with relief. Goth was holding the Leewit, both of the sisters shaking a little in the aftermath of using a lot of klatha power. They'd need to be fed, a lot, and quickly.

But he'd deal with that later. Goth had been looking for him also, and the moment his eyes fell on that expressionless face he knew she would be okay for a while. Something in her eyes told him so. He wasn't sure what it was, but he didn't doubt the knowledge.

Deal with the rest first, then. He saw that Dame Ethulassia was binding up a bleeding gash on Vezzarn's forehead. Hantis and Pul were mounting guard on the pirate whom the Sedmon and Vezzarn had grappled. The man looked to be badly beaten up, but he was not unconscious. It hardly mattered. His gaze was flicking back and forth from his cohort's severed leg to the instrument that had severed it. Pul in Full Gape Mode was . . . an utterly paralyzing sight.

As for Hulik, who'd almost been killed—

Hulik was cradling one of the Sedmons in her lap, while the other hovered over her. "Sedmon! Sedmon! Speak to me!" she was pleading.

Why is she doing that, Big Real Thing? There is nothing wrong with the Divided Thing.

The vatch was sorely puzzled, and Pausert didn't blame it. The captain was quite sure there was nothing seriously wrong with the Sedmon, beyond a few bruises. He wasn't breathing the way someone would if he was knocked out. Nor—the real tip-off—was his clone acting at all anxious. In fact, he seemed immensely pleased.

"Please, Sedmon!" Hulik whimpered. "Please!"

Slowly, theatrically, the Sedmon opened his eyes. "What—happened?" he asked, putting on such an act of being dazed and confused that Pausert had to fight down a laugh.

"You saved us, Sedmon! Both of you, you saved us all!"

"Hey!" the Leewit interjected from the corner, annoyed enough to come out of her own shock. "Other people had something to do with that too!"

Hulik ignored her. "You were amazing!" she said. "Can you move?"

"I don't know," said the Sedmon, who started to sit up, then groaned. "My head!"

"Here, I'll get you both back to your ship," said Hulik tenderly, helping the prone one to his feet. "I'll take care of you until you feel better."

"Oh—thank you, lovely lady," the Sedmon breathed.

She blushed. *Hulik* blushed. Pausert could see Vezzarn's jaw sagging. His own jaw was pretty loose, too.

"We need to get you both lying down," she told them. "You might have gotten hurt somewhere else—"

Pausert felt a gentle tug on his sleeve. "Come over here, Captain, and we'll see to that," said Dame Ethulassia, tugging on his good elbow and pointing to the wound on his other arm. "I realize that the do Eldel is normally your ship's medic. But—ha! No use trying to get *her* attention right now."

She coaxed Pausert over to sit down beside Vezzarn, and began cutting his shirtsleeve away. He yelled as she pulled the cloth out of the wound. She ignored him just as resolutely as she ignored the corpse of her former paramour Vonard Kleesp.

"Here, Captain," said someone—Richard Cravan, from the rich-sounding voice—handing him a cup of something. He drank it, and felt a pleasant numbness begin immediately.

"What—" he asked, thickly, "What happened to *Hulik*?"

"Remember that I said she was in love, but hadn't realized it yet?" asked Ethulassia. "Well, she just realized it. So did he. They, I mean. Hence the act." One corner of her mouth came up in a sardonic little smile. "I'm glad we never gave either man a speaking role—I've never seen such a terrible bit of overacting."

Pausert blinked. He'd already deduced as much himself, but now that he really thought about it . . .

"Hulik? But—" his mind grappled feebly with the ramifications involved. "There's six of them!"

Ethulassia raised her eyebrow. "Sextuplets? Must be clones, I think. Either way . . ." Her other eyebrow raised. "Adventurous lass!"

"And one of her. And that's not our problem, Captain," said Vezzarn. "Somehow, I doubt it's much of a problem for her, either."

"Besides," rolled the rich tones of Cravan's voice, sounding enthusiastic, "think of the dramatic possibilities for future thespians! A modern update on the venerable Hindu epic, the *Mahabharata*—whose heroine Draupati, I'm sure I needn't remind you, married all five of the Pandava brothers."

Pausert has never heard of the Mahaba—whatever it was called. He mumbled as much.

"How unstudied of you, Captain," reproved Cravan. "You really should, you know. Draupati and her husbands had *such* a lot of adventures. Oh, volumes and volumes and volumes worth."

Speaking of volumes . . .

Pausert looked for Goth, and saw that other members of the cast were now providing her and the Leewit with something to eat. A lot of something to eat. He didn't know where they'd found so much food on such short notice, but he wasn't really surprised. Thespians, he'd come to learn, were nothing if not adaptable and expert at improvisation. Especially with the Leewit's scolds to spur them on.

Nothing left to worry about, then. The drug Cravan had given him was definitely taking effect. The audience's applause now sounded like a waterfall, heard dimly at a distance. The pitterpat of the accolades still showering the stage, like a gentle rain.

"I think I'd like to lie down and sleep," Pausert said weakly. And did.

CHAPTER 24

"I think we're probably done with the Agandar's pirates," said Captain Pausert, as they sat around the mess table in the *Venture*. "Their leader—his name turns out to be Juhta—confessed that Kleesp was the Agandar's lieutenant although he still refuses to explain why they've been chasing us so relentlessly. But what's worrying me is the fact that we haven't seen any more of the ISS. I mean, by now they should have talked their way out of prison on Tornam. Subradio should have carried the news ahead."

Goth yawned. She'd had a hard day practicing their roles in the latest thespian production, and some cage mucking-out, and bit of practice at their act. "The Sedmons said they'd done some covering of our tracks. Besides, Captain, the *Venture* is ready to fly again. We can run if they come looking."

"And all for the cost of some tinklewood fishing poles," said the Leewit. "You ought to be ashamed of yourself."

Captain Pausert was getting the measure of the littlest witch by now. "I kept one as a switch," he said, calmly. "You never know when you might need it."

"Huh," said the Leewit. "You and which army?" But it was quite cheerfully said. "So does anyone know where we're going next?"

"Yes. The Sedmons have set the itinerary along with Himbo. We're going to Yin Bauh. It's at least a place we should be safe from the ISS."

"I thought," said Goth, biting the end of a strand of her brown hair, "that Hulik said no place in the Empire was really safe from the ISS."

"Ah. But Yin Bauh isn't really part of the Empire, missy," said Vezzarn, looking very cheerful. "It's an independent principality. Within the Empire's borders, true enough—but the sultan doesn't like competition with his secret police, and has some pretty abrupt ways of making that clear."

"What do they do there, Vezzarn?" asked the Leewit, just an edge of greed in her voice. The witches didn't, strictly speaking, need gold dust. But the Leewit had enjoyed collecting it anyway. "Is it another mining world like the last one?"

"Yin Bauh? No." The old spacer laughed and pointed at the dishcleaning unit. "If you want to know what they do there, look on the base of half the cheap trade goods in the Galaxy. 'YB made.'"

The Leewit looked astounded. "I thought that stood for 'why be made?' You mean it's a *planet*?"

"It's a planet, all right. A tax haven, without the labor laws of most of the rest of the Empire. All the big companies have manufacturing plants there. It's a pretty grim sort of place, mind you. But it is nice and inconspicuously on our way to the Imperial Capital, eh, Captain?"

Pausert nodded. "So it is. And you girls should be nice and inconspicuously on your way to bath and bed. And remember to wash behind your ears," he said sternly to the Leewit.

She stuck her tongue out at him. "I'm going to talk the little vatch into putting baking soda in your bubble-bath."

"Don't have any, child," said Pausert with a grin. Bubble bath was a newly discovered chink in the Leewit antiwashing armor. Actually, Goth had privately told the captain, most of that was for show these days. But the Leewit liked to resist baths. She felt it was something she ought to do just as a matter of principle. The Mistress of the Universe shouldn't even be subjected to getting dirty in the first place.

Goth rolled her eyes, but her shoulders shook slightly as she led the Leewit off to that fate worse than death, hot water. "And don't *you* forget to wash behind your ears either, Captain," she called back sternly.

"I won't. Good night, girls."

Three days later, the lattice ship drifted her way downward to a landing on Yin Bauh. They were making a night-side landing and it was plain to see that this world was heavily populated.

"We going to get audiences?" wondered Goth, with all the scornful skepticism of a new-converted thespian. "This looks like the sort of planet full of holo-theaters and threedee parlors, with wall-to-wall vidscreens in every house."

Vezzarn snorted. "Not likely, missy. Those lights are either factories or dormitories. Mostly factories. The dormitory towns are the bleakest places you'll see this side of prison. I was here to look over the potential for a smuggling route, once, since it's an independent state and nice and free of official Imperial customs. The sultan's customs are worse, unfortunately. And it's a bad place for anything except murder—they don't worry about corpses much." He seemed to shudder a little. "Those dormitories are full of debt-prisoners whose prison contracts are sold off by various Imperial worlds. The people don't get paid much at all, other than production bonuses. But food and your bunk are free, and there's not much to spend money on. The poor beggars are mostly desperate enough for any kind of entertainment. Any showboat that's down on her luck comes here—it's not great money, but it's reliable."

"It seems a bit like robbery, taking it from them," said Hantis. "It's one of the things we Sprites find strange about you humans."

"It's in character for the *Petey B*, though," said the captain. "It's on our way, and there's nothing suspicious about us setting down here. Lattice ships aren't cheap to operate, and most of the showboats get into financial trouble sooner or later." He rubbed the back of his neck, wincing. "Still, reliable as it might be, Yin Bauh is a frightening place for a Showmaster. A threat of where he might end up, with the *Petey B* sold off and him still in debt."

The Leewit was horrified. "Ol' Himby belongs with the show! And the *Petey B* is going to go for ever and ever and ever. You couldn't let that happen to him, could you, Captain?"

Touched by her faith—most unusual, that, coming from the Leewit—the captain smiled. "I'll do my best." Privately he suspected the *Petey B*'s debts might easily be enough to give the Sedmons pause. And he didn't see them coming to the *Petey B*'s rescue, anyway, in the event the showboat fell on hard times. Over the centuries, the Daals of Uldune had been famous for many things— a very long list of things, in fact, including most capital crimes. But neither altruism nor generosity had ever been on the list once.

✳   ✳   ✳

The setup on an expensive piece of wasteland hired from the sultan's factor didn't even draw the four reporters that Altim Four had.

"Where is everybody?"

"They work long shifts here. And you have to get a pass to travel anywhere outside your official place of residence and work."

"So how do they get to know we're here, Mannicholo?"

The chameleon man stopped hauling on the banner rope for a moment. His colors rippled. "Word gets through the dormitory towns like lightning, the sultan's rules be damned. That's why the sultan's satraps don't let ships set down too close to the last spot a showboat visited. It'll be a year or so since these people have had anything more than a game of cards to entertain them. When the next shift ends we'll have 'em in droves. We only sell cheap tickets when we come here. Himbo says it's too close to the bone to exploit these poor devils."

"At least it'll be short shows," said Timblay grumpily. "All we'll get out of this place is refueling money, you watch and see."

"Maybe so," said the chameleon man tersely. "But at least we'll give them something to forget about this dump for a while."

"Dump" was certainly the right word. The place was an industrial garbage heap. The air burned in the captain's lungs. The sky was a brown color, and the rows of factory chimneys belched out more of it. He was glad they wouldn't be staying.

Sure enough, that evening was a full house. It was also one of the most depressing crowds that Pausert had ever seen. There was a beaten look about the people buying the one-price special-offer tickets.

It even infected the actors. The first scene of *A Midsummer Night's Dream* was, Pausert thought, completely flat. But the audience still drank it up as if it were the honeydew of paradise.

Never had Helena's "How happy some o'er other some can be!" seemed more appropriate.

Cravan was backstage, snapping like an irate turtle. "They paid to be lifted up from this misery—not have you join them! Now, scene change is coming. You"—he pointed—"Bottom, Snug, Flute, Quince, Snout and Starveling. You go out there and give the punters the show of their lives."

So Pausert, AKA Bottom the passionately pursued . . . did. So did his fellow actors. The audience loved it.

Well, *most* of them loved it. But there were some people sitting in the front row who didn't seem to be enjoying anything.

That worried Pausert. Pausert, the new thespian, because members of an audience who don't enjoy the show are always worrisome. Pausert, the captain entrusted with a vital mission, was a lot more worried.

So, as he changed costumes in the dressing room, Pausert wasn't surprised at all when Silver-eyes showed up and echoed his own anxieties.

I think there's more trouble, Big Real Thing, squeaked the little vatch inside his head. **There are some strange dream things here— or maybe real things. It's hard to tell. They're like not-things. Like those tiny bits of klatha stuff you feed me, except different.**

That was confusing, although . . .

Now that he thought about it, it struck Pausert that "not things" was a fairly accurate description of the oddly impassive bunch of people sitting in the front of the house tonight.

They are waiting back at your ship, too.

That was another unpleasant report.

Like the ones in the front rows out there?

The vatch disappeared briefly, before returning to the dressing rooms. **Yes. But there are more than that at the ship. And some more still at the edge of the lattice. Digging.**

Digging what? Well, whatever they were up to, it would be no good. He didn't need Pul's Nanite-sniffing nose to tell him the Nanite-infected ISS had almost certainly caught up with them. Thoughtfully, Pausert sucked his teeth.

You feel like some mischief, Silver-eyes?

I always feel like mischief. I'm like the littlest witch.

That was true enough. The vatch had grown but it was still barely a hand-sized creature. Obviously the thing's mental age was still preteen, even if it could think. The Leewit certainly could, whenever she chose to, and Goth's ability to think was sometimes downright scary.

Mischief's fun! What do you want me to do to them? I'm still little, though. I can't do big stuff yet.

Pausert went over to the store cupboard in the props section. He found some of the luminous virulent yellow-green paint they'd used for the posters a few days earlier. *Here.* He pointed. *Can you put a big splash of this on all of the "not-things"? Maybe on the back of their heads or something.*

Sure! Big fun! The little vatch vanished. Pausert went off in hasty search of the others. He still had a few minutes before he was due onstage again, and that would be the last show for the night.

The captain was willing to bet that whatever the Nanites had planned was supposed to happen after the punters had gone . . . one couldn't exactly say "home," but back to their miserable bunks. Both Vezzarn and Hulik had assured him that the sultan did not take kindly to the ISS sticking its nose into his territory, so Pausert had thought them safe enough here. But the Nanite-infected agents apparently ignored the conventional bounds.

He found the Leewit first. Or rather she found him. She'd just come backstage. "We got troubles, Captain," she said quietly. "Vezzarn sent me to tell you. The *Petey B*'s engine room is in a shambles. Old Vezzarn found one of the engineers unconscious, the drive control boxes trashed, and whole lot of other stuff busted."

Someone intended to make sure the *Petey B* didn't do a hasty retreat, obviously. Pausert winced. "There are also a bunch of them waiting for us at the *Venture*, and some in the audience. And they're digging at the perimeter struts for some reason. I've got the little vatch tagging them with some of that lime-green luminous paint."

The Leewit grinned. That was the kind of trick she adored.

"See if you can get the others together here," the captain said. "I'm due onstage in a minute. Where's Vezzarn?"

"Reporting the incident to Himbo. He's coming down here next." The littlest witch shivered. The captain gave her brief squeeze. "The show's got to go on. But stay here, backstage."

The curtain call was enthusiastic. But Pausert noticed that the "not things" had already left.

A few minutes later, as the factory workers streamed hastily into the night to get a few hours sleep before returning to work, Pausert came backstage and unobtrusively joined the rest of *Venture*'s crew and the Sedmons.

"I think we need to head for the *Thunderbird*," said one of the Sedmons. "She's well enough armored and armed to hold off a fairly serious assault."

"We could flee in her too, if need be," said the other Sedmon. "It'd be crowded, but we could manage."

Himbo Petey arrived on the scene then, looking grim. "I need to talk to you about—"

Something exploded.

The lattice pole the captain was leaning against shivered. One of the main lattice legs caved in with the terrible sound of shredding synthasilk; the stage canted sideways, spilling screaming people and terrified animals.

In a flash, Pausert understood why the Nanites had been digging. The entire exercise was designed to cause maximum chaos and send the *Venture*'s crew scurrying for shelter in their ship. The Sedmons were right.

"Come on. To the *Thunderbird*!" he yelled.

He had to yell. With the destruction of one of her main struts, the old *Petey B*'s structure was under terrific stress. Things were breaking loose, and falling everywhere. Some of the power-cables snapped, plunging the tented area into darkness except for showers of sparks and cascading and exploding lights. And the din produced by the people and animals was even worse than that produced by the inanimate objects.

In a tight-knit bunch, they left the chaos of the dressing rooms and headed out.

The first thing that Pausert saw was that the vatch had exceeded its mandate. The bunch of people shooting at them should not have been able to fire anything at all, since their heads had been doused in luminous lime-green paint. The vatchlet must have raided the *Petey B*'s main store, not just the little props-room cupboard.

But the Nanites, it seemed, didn't need human eyes to see well enough to shoot. A blaster bolt seared above them, hitting another strut, bringing down a large banner.

"They're between us and the *Thunderbird*," said Hulik, drawing her own elegant little blaster from an outfit that Pausert would have thought couldn't hide a toothpick. She started returning the fire.

Another paint-head tried a flanking shot. His paint-soaked blaster exploded, just as the Leewit gave a shattering whistle. Whether it was the paint or the whistle that caused that was a matter for later academic discussion.

Goth narrowed her eyes and looked intently at a surviving speaker-bank above another group of painted heads. It began, slowly, to totter, as an already off-balance pile will when an extra wedge is teleported under its base. Moments later, tumbling tons of electronic speakers were hurtling down on the painted heads.

Another group found they'd made a mistake with their target. Timblay folded neatly, avoiding the blaster fire with a contortionist's skill, and started shooting back with a Blythe rifle.

"Keep going towards the *Thunderbird*," said Sedmon. "The other Sedmons are controlling her computer system remotely. They activated blaster tracking. Whatever you do, Hulik, don't fire again."

Blaster tracking meant that the *Thunderbird*'s weapons systems responded with automatic ship-fire to any active weapon in the vicinity. Pausert could only hope that the *Petey B*'s own defenses didn't get manned. He had a feeling there wouldn't be much left of the old showboat if the *Thunderbird* really cut loose.

A trio of painted heads appeared from behind a tumble of flats. Pul bit one of them as the captain cold-cocked another. A flying paint-pot materialized in the face of the third attacker and did for him.

In the background, the *Thunderbird*'s guns vaporized steel and a Nanite-carrier. The Nanites didn't seem to have realized yet that firing immediately made them a target. It suddenly occurred to Pausert that while the Nanites were clearly able to think, the diffuse form of their intelligence made them relatively slow witted.

They had no sense of macrocosmic scale, clearly enough! The Nanites themselves were micrometers in size, and didn't seem to be able to gauge proportions properly in their human hosts. Mannicholo and Master Himbo came charging through, mounted on pair of fanderbags—and several of the Nanite-carriers raced up to stop them. With the pancake-flat results you'd expect.

The tide had turned. Still, the Nanites kept shooting—and being vaporized almost instantly by the *Thunderbird*'s deadly guns every time they did. They seemed incapable of learning the lesson.

Within minutes, it was no longer a case of retreating to the *Thunderbird*. It was a case of mopping up.

But as the sun came up over Yin Bauh district 323, one thing was plain.

When the next shift came off-duty, there would be no show.

CHAPTER 25

Himbo Petey looked at the chaos which had once bragged the name "The Greatest Show in the Galaxy." He sighed, reflexively twirled his mustachios, and then uncharacteristically stopped and sat down. His shoulders drooped. He shook his head. There was a small tear in the corner of his eye.

Dame Ethulassia came and sat next to him, putting an arm around his shoulders. "We'll get it all back together again, Himbo," she said in a quiet voice, quite unlike her usual brassy contralto.

"No. Not this time, Ethy," he replied quietly, sadly. "The old show is over. What is left of the lattice ship will be broken up for scrap. We could have afforded to get off-world, since there's enough money for fuel. But there's nothing extra for repairs. Not repairs on this scale, anyway. And with this wreckage, we can't even put on a show to earn any more."

He sighed. "No, we'll have to sell the old girl off for scrap and pay off the artistes as best we can. This is the end of the Petey, Byrum and Keep."

Mannicholo's colors turned a melancholy blue. The other show-people looked silently at the walls and scuffed shoes.

"Ahem." One of the two Sedmons cleared his throat, stepping forward from where the clones stood with the *Venture*'s crew. "Perhaps we can be of assistance?"

Himbo looked at him and laughed bitterly. "I think you've assisted me to ruin well enough already, thank you."

"Quite." The Sedmons nodded in unison, looking just a trace embarrassed. "And thus it seems only fair that we should attempt to make amends. I think we may safely assume that Messrs. Byrum and Keep are long dead?"

Himbo Petey shrugged. "Legend traces the show all the way back to Old Yarthe. The lattice ship is at least fifteen centuries old. She's held together with hull-metal welds on hull-metal welds. I presume there must once have been a Byrum and a Keep. Like the name Petey: All gone now." He picked up a handful of premier deluxe-box tickets and flung them like confetti up into the air.

"So, you, Himbo Petey, are the sole owner?" continued the other Sedmon, ignoring the theatricals.

Himbo looked at the still smoldering remains of the bright lattice awnings. "Of this ruin? Yes. It would be a waste of effort suing me, though. By the time my creditors are finished, there won't even be a square inch of skin for you to auction off at the slave market."

The Sedmons frowned, again in that uncanny unison. "We have no intention of suing you. How would you feel about another partner?" His clone cleared his throat. "One with, ah, capital to invest."

The Showmaster blinked at them. "Invest in what? This wreckage? Where would I find such a fool?"

The Sedmons smiled sardonically. "It seems likely to me, Showmaster, that you might find at least two right here," said the one.

"Has it not occurred to you that such destruction and such expense would only be incurred for very high stakes?" continued the other.

Himbo shook his head, refusing to allow any trace of hope to trickle into his mind. "Your 'high stakes,' Mister Twins-or-Clones, are very small compared to the debts we've racked up. I leave aside the cost of getting the lattice ship into space again. I'm sorry, but you just don't have any idea what repairing the Petey, Byrum and Keep would cost."

"On the contrary," said one Sedmon. "This estimate is child's play."

His eyes and those of his clone flicked here and there, assessing the damage. Very expert eyes, they seemed. Not surprising, thought Pausert. The Daals of Uldune *would* be experts at assessing havoc and ruin.

"Repairs would cost approximately seven million, three hundred thousand maels. Not more than eight million, for a certainty."

The other Sedmon chimed in. "Simply say the word, and you will find that the Petey, Byrum and Keep account has been credited with ten million maels."

"Which will mean your account would be in the black, for a change."

They each raised one eyebrow. "For the first time in generations, actually."

Pausert's conscience started tugging at his sleeve. While it went against the captain's grain to disrupt the dawning look of amazed hope on Himbo Petey's face, he also felt that it was only fair to explain to the Showmaster exactly who he was dealing with. Pausert had seen enough of Sedmon's operations to be very sure that Uldune had not moved *that* far from its piratical past. The Daal was—were? dealing with a six-way person was confusing—still neck-deep in smuggling and had certainly taken the lead over the Empire in some fields of weaponry, to judge by the latest display of firepower. The Showmaster might just prefer bankruptcy to being indebted to Uldune. The captain cleared his throat.

The Sedmons continued without a pause for breath—easy for them, of course, since they could speak in turns. "I suspect, although I would have preferred them not to be involved, that their Wisdoms of Karres will match that in the near future."

That threw Pausert right off his moral stride. *Match ten million maels?*

"I've lately gotten the feeling," said the second Sedmon, looking pointedly at Captain Pausert, "that they don't entirely trust the Daal of Uldune, though I can't imagine why. That's me, by the way. So we propose one-third ownership."

"Of course you will retain day-to-day control," said Sedmon, smoothly.

Pausert was still mentally stumbling. Even cut in half . . . *Match five million maels? HOW?*

Himbo Petey stared at the Sedmons, his eyes resembling the proverbial saucers. Then, turned his very wide, blue-eyed gaze on the others. "Uldune . . . *and* Karres! I should have guessed. It wasn't stage magic at all, was it?"

Goth was still-faced. The Leewit fidgeted. Then, the little blond witch half-wailed: "It's not cheating to use the real thing!" She glared about, the surface belligerence in her eyes covering not-so-veiled anxiety. "Well, it's *not*. I don't think."

Ethulassia barked a laugh. "Ha! An interesting question, that.

Our magicians will probably spend a year wrangling over the professional ethics involved." The Dame bestowed a fond and approving look upon the Leewit. "Never you mind, dearie. Even if those cranky magicians crab and complain, you'll *always* have a place in the thespians' company."

The Leewit beamed. Goth's face still held no expression, but her brown eyes seemed to lighten a bit.

Pausert kept his mouth shut. *Five millions maels? HOW?*

If didn't occur to him until some time later that, in addition to his—their?—other talents, the Daal of Uldune would be a superb card player. And he had just bluffed the captain right out of the hand by simply cranking up the stakes.

For the first time since the disastrous fight, Himbo Petey let his round face slip into the creases of his familiar smile. "It *is* against magicians' union rules, as a matter of fact. Says so right there in Section III, Article 1, Clause 3(f): 'no use of exotic mental powers to imitate stage magic and fakery.'" He glanced about the area. "But since there are no members of the magicians' union here . . . Well, if you don't tell them, I won't."

He did something totally unlike himself, then. He took the waxed end of one of his proud mustachios and chewed it.

Everyone was silent, waiting. Then he pulled it out and twirled it in a familiar manner. Nodded abruptly. Took a deep breath, knelt on the floor and began picking up the premier deluxe-box tickets he'd scattered about.

"Well, come on. All of you! We'll be needing these. Collect them up before someone stands on them. We can't waste funds by throwing tickets on the floor." He turned to Pausert and waved a handful of tickets at him. "I'll be looking to Karres to provide us with a counter-weight to Uldune. They're notorious criminals, you know, the lot of them." Then he waved the tickets at the two Daals. "And *you* will have to keep an eye on the witches. Their reputation is no more savory than yours."

"We have been trying to do that."

"It's less easy than we would like," said the other. "Do we have a deal, then?"

Pausert was uncomfortably aware that the *Venture*'s account stood at four hundred thousand maels in credit. That once-magnificent amount seemed measly now, when compared to the resources the Daal of Uldune had on call. "Well . . ."

Goth interrupted him smoothly. "I reckon Karres will buy in, Sedmon—*if* we can get through to the Imperial Capital in time for the Winter Carnival. But you'll just have to wait for our share of the money until then. And help us get there."

Pausert knew that if they didn't get there, it wouldn't matter if Karres agreed or not.

Himbo Petey nodded. "I think we have a deal."

"You're undervaluing the Petey, Byrum and Keep," said Dame Ethulassia, her brassy voice miraculously returning. "She's more than just a lattice ship. More than a mere showboat. She's a body of Artistes!"

The Incredible Bosom made a grand entrance. Ethulassia put a hand on Himbo's shoulder, as he knelt and gathered tickets. "The Greatest Show in the Galaxy, with real dramatic and artistic merit. She's worth at least twice that!"

The two Sedmons looked at Hulik do Eldel. Looked at the hand on Himbo Petey's shoulder. The nails were red, and there were a number of rings studded with improbable diamonds on the fingers, and a vast clatter of gold-in-appearance bracelets on the plump wrist. But the grip was a firm one.

"A point," one of them acknowledged, "but only valid so long as the component parts of the show are kept solidly together." He cocked an eye at his clone, who picked up the train of thought flawlessly.

"Precisely. So I think—a matter of simple fiscal prudence—that our offer should be contingent on Petey, Byrum and Keep being maintained as a family enterprise."

The eyes of the two Sedmons, like gun barrels on a single turret, swiveled back and forth from Himbo to Ethulassia. "The deal hinges on an imminent marriage. A young Petey to take over the reins one day. Otherwise who knows what we might get?"

"The sooner the better," agreed Hulik, doing her best—not entirely successfully—to disguise her glee. "Starship captains are empowered to perform marriages, aren't they, Captain Pausert?"

Pausert nodded. "Indeed," he said sententiously. "We're often called on to perform the rite. It is legally binding."

It was a pleasure to see Dame Ethulassia doing a very good imitation of a fish suddenly pulled from the water. For once in her life, she wasn't acting.

Himbo Petey got up from his ticket collecting. He was quite a lot shorter than the Leading Lady. "Ethy is married to her Art," he said, in a tone which was an odd combination of humility and sarcasm. "I don't even understand it half the time."

Ethulassia's gaping mouth snapped shut. She bestowed upon

Himbo a look that was its own peculiar combination: indignation, calculation, amusement, and . . .

Something else. Something quite warm, in fact, if Pausert didn't miss his guess.

"Just as I don't understand the mystical significance of that mustache of yours," she said, a bit acidly. "However—"

She struck a truly dramatic pose. The Incredible Bosom soared to impossible heights. "We must all make sacrifices for the common good."

The tone was tragic—but Pausert noticed that the bejeweled hand never left Himbo's shoulder. Never even twitched.

"He's not such a bad old dope," the Leewit said gruffly. "You could do worse."

For a moment, there was an awkward pause. Everyone did their best to look somewhere else, sure and certain that the brash little witch would continue the thought: *You DID do worse—recently.*

Whether she would have said it or not, would never be known. The Dame, after all, was a lady of many parts.

Ethulassia laughed, easily and throatily. "Oh, sweetie, you can say that again! I hate to say it, but that bum Vonard probably wasn't even the worst."

The Incredible Bosom vanished magically. There stood before them, now, just a quite attractive woman of middle years—still with a most impressive bust—her pleasant face lined with much experience. The look she gave Himbo was a fond one, and her hand squeezed his shoulder.

"We'll consider it a marriage of convenience, Himbo, how's that?"

He nodded solemnly, though his eyes seemed to twinkle a bit.

The same twinkle that was in the Dame's eye, in fact. "Of course," she mused, "we'll have to figure out how a marriage of convenience manages to produce the heir our ruthless financial backers demand. A desperate situation. But . . . I dare say two experienced and stalwart troupers like you and me can manage to pull it off."

"Imagine so," huffed Himbo, rising to his feet. "In fact, a notion has already come to me."

He glanced towards that section of the wreckage which had once—and might still—contained his stateroom. "This clever witchly trick of faking fakery . . . it has possibilities applied elsewhere, you know?"

*   *   *

Hulik do Eldel was the maid of honor. Mannicholo, the best man, in a face of startling pinkness. And the Leewit would have been a flower girl, except that she had a newly broken collarbone from trying to ride Mannicholo's unicycle for the occasion. She was going to have to endure strapping and an hour a day in the bone-growth-promoter for the next two weeks.

She was very grumpy about it. "Back on Karres someone coulda done a bone-meld."

Goth spoke the usual serene, philosophical phrases spoken in the presence of those recuperating from injury and illness. The Leewit glared at her.

"You!" She slapped her hands on the rim of the growth-promoter. "Just happy that she won't be sniffing around the captain any more! Can't fool me."

Goth's serenity seemed untouched. "Don't be silly. Though, now that you bring it up, I notice that Himbo and Ethulassia disappeared right after the wedding."

"Course!" sniffed the Leewit. "They're sweet on each other. I always knew. Probably been for years. People are stupid."

CHAPTER 26

"This is all very well, Captain," said Hantis worriedly. "But the lattice ship will take weeks to repair, at best. We need to move on if we're to get to the Empress in time."

The captain tried to focus his thoughts on the business at hand. He'd been completely preoccupied making sure his part of the wedding went off satisfactorily. Despite his public boast, Pausert had never had any occasion to perform a captain's marriage before. He was just grateful that the little vatch hadn't showed up to amuse itself at his expense. It been active enough in the last fight, but it had disappeared since.

"Well, what I had in mind," said Pausert slowly, "was getting the *Venture* free from the lattice and heading onward on our own. All the old ship needs now is some fuel. And it looks like we have the credit to fuel her up, and to replace her with a hulk. Maybe we can talk Himbo into faking our presence here for a while. The ISS will come looking again, even if I think we've dealt with the Agandar's pirates once and for all."

Goth nodded. "Be good to have our own ship again, Captain."

The Leewit looked across at the hive of activity that was the repair program on the lattices of the PBK. "I guess," she said, at least half-regretfully. "Nice to be in the circus for a while, but home is best. I guess."

It was curious, thought Pausert, as they walked over to talk to Himbo Petey, that the little fair-haired scrap of a gray-eyed witch

209

should regard the old *Venture* as "home." Her real home was Karres, after all, along with Toll and Pausert's great uncle Threbus. The captain had stayed at her parents' house when he'd made his one and only visit to the world of Karres.

True, Goth and the Leewit's world wasn't the easiest place to find, let alone visit, the way it hopped around the Galaxy. A bit like the *Venture* in that way. And it was a very witchy place. Very like the *Venture* in that way, these days! Now that he thought about it.

Himbo Petey was visibly shocked at the news. He glanced at Ethulassia, lounging nearby on a divan, and tugged at his mustachios. "You can't leave! We agreed to take you all the way to the Imperial Capital. And I'm a man of my word, Captain Pausert. Besides, the act of the Great Escapologist Aron is famous! You're one of our most popular shows. People expect to see you. You're a star. I could stretch to a bigger contract . . ."

Pausert got the distinct feeling that most of that little speech was spoken by rote, while Himbo gathered his thoughts. Just for starters, while the captain's escapologist act was certainly no financial drain on Petey, Byrum & Keep, it was hardly "one of our most popular shows."

Himbo paused, looking at them with a considering eye. "But there's more to this than just money, isn't there?" he said abruptly. "I suppose money doesn't matter that much to people who can buy into the PB and K to the tune of ten million maels. There's something big going on that I'm not part of, and not supposed to know about."

He looked at them like an expectant bird. No one said anything, so he went on. "You know, all the kids in the galaxy dream of running away to Vaudevillia. I was born on Vaudevillia, and I couldn't wait for the Petey Byrum and Keep to take off for anywhere else. I dreamed of going to Karres, because there is supposed to be real magic there." He sighed. "Well. I can't stop you. I wish I could, to be honest. You've paid off your debts. Actually, I think I owe you a little. Ethy'll have to check the books. We're going on to the Capital anyway."

He stood up from his cluttered desk, and patted the two girls awkwardly on the shoulder. "Remember: if your uncle the captain is nasty to you two, there is always a place for you on the old *Petey B.*" He looked sternly at the Leewit. "But no more riding unicycles."

She stuck her tongue out at him. But there was a quiver in her chin. The Leewit loved the Greatest Show in the Galaxy.

"Make you a deal, Showmaster," said Goth, looking at the Leewit. "If everything works out, we'll arrange for the *Petey B* to do a show on Karres. You'd be the first ever."

Himbo smiled from ear to ear and put out a plump hand. "It's a deal, lady."

"Huh. Lady," muttered the Leewit. But she also stuck out a hand and shook the Showmaster's hand. She didn't even squirm too much when Ethulassia hugged and kissed her.

"I'm sure Karres can't wait for a dose of culture," said the Dame. "It will be a great day for them."

Privately, Captain Pausert thought that the people of Karres, living in their tranquil houses in the forest, with their wonderful music, might just show the statuesque leading lady another side of culture. But he thought that the witches would probably like the circus side. A lot of the witch-children might like it *too* much, in fact. He could foresee a lot of runaways.

He said as much to Goth and the Leewit on the way back to the *Venture*.

The Leewit glanced at him as if he were an imbecile who'd just issued an especially mindless statement.

"Well, sure. What you expect."

Goth shrugged. "It's really a lot safer than most adventures young witches get into. Remember where you found us?"

Pausert grunted. "Um. Point."

The Leewit giggled. "Half of the younger ones will want to go on a trip with the *Petey B*. Old Ethy will be pulling her hair out, never mind her wig off, after a week or two."

"I wouldn't worry, Captain," said Goth. "Witches can look after themselves. Besides, Himbo is good people. So's the Dame and Richard Cravan. And it *is* good cover. Witchy stuff on a showboat doesn't stand out. That's why I reckon Karres will be happy to buy into the lattice ship. You don't look for the real thing in a ship-load of fake magicians and trickery merchants." She rubbed the tip of her nose. "Have to reach a private understanding with the magicians' union, of course. We don't want *them* mad at us. Some of their skills aren't all that fake."

Pausert thought about it, then nodded. "I guess you're right. It would be a good way to do a lot of Karres' work in future."

"What I thought," said Goth, looking up at him with those big brown eyes.

"Goth is sweet on the captain!" jibed the Leewit. Then the little witch scampered off.

"You just wait," said Goth. But Pausert noticed that she didn't bother to run after the Leewit to chastise her. And it occurred to him that "you just wait" wasn't necessarily a threat aimed at the younger sister. It hadn't been spoken like a threat, certainly; just stated in that serene tone of voice that came so naturally to Goth, when she contemplated the workings of fate.

The captain's estimate of just how seriously he ought to take Goth's assumption they'd eventually get married cranked up another notch. He was beginning to understand how his great uncle Threbus must have felt, many years before, when Toll made the same confident prediction.

Pausert chewed on the matter for a time, as they walked together in silence, for the first time giving it some serious thought. It wasn't as if the prospect bothered him, after all. In fact . . . he was beginning to find himself sharing Goth's opinion that there ought to be *some* way klatha could affect the aging process.

But, if there was, he'd never heard of any. So, since they were nearing the ship, he just dismissed the whole matter from his mind. Whatever happened, it was a matter for the future.

At the ship they met up with the Sedmons. "Well?" said one of the two. They both had their arms around Hulik do Eldel. That was something Captain Pausert was still getting used to. He always felt as if he were seeing double around the cloned Sedmons. Hulik seemed to accept it, though. She'd once told the captain that she didn't think she'd ever meet a man she would love enough to marry. Apparently, in her own inimitable style, the do Eldel had found a solution to the problem.

"We're going to have to split up and each try to reach the Empress Hailie," he announced, "since we're running out of time. I think, Hulik, you'd better travel with the Daal. If you get through, at least you can get the Imperial Navy pulled off our back."

The Sedmons nodded, clearly not inclined to argue the point.

Hulik nodded also. "I don't want to desert you, Captain. But I was going to ask if you'd mind if we did that. I think I should keep an eye on him. Both of him," she added impishly.

The *Venture* and the Daal's *Thunderbird* made quiet, low-fuss departures that night. Darkness would not shield them from watching instrumentation, but it might hide their departure from human spies. Even instruments might not spot the *Thunderbird*, actually. The Daal's ship was equipped with the very best anti-detection gear available.

The best that they'd been able to do for the *Venture*, on the other hand, was adding a few mock-ups from the Dame's props, which slightly changed the outline of the ship. If whatever watchers there were—and by now the captain was sure that there must be some—didn't see Pausert's trademark wobbly take off, and didn't have instruments tracking, then they were away, at least until daybreak.

No atmospheric revolt-ships rose after them, at least. The Leewit left off manning the rear turret of the nova guns and came back to the *Venture*'s control room. She was rubbing her shoulder. "You'll kill us all yet with these take offs, Captain," she complained. "My shoulder hurts. And I'm bored already and we've only just left the circus."

"Tell you what," said Goth. "You fish out those cards you found in the Agandar's kit and I'll play you snap."

"Don't feel like snap," snapped the Leewit. But she pulled the pack from an inner pocket anyway.

She always seemed to have them with her, Pausert noticed. The hand-painted cards had been found in the Agandar's personal kit after the pirate's death, and the Leewit had expropriated them. The cards were probably valuable antiques, given that the pirate lord had been fabulously wealthy and successful. Pausert had occasionally wondered if he should try to keep them safe from the Leewit, but it hadn't seemed worth the fight it would entail. Money was only worth its face value, but a contented Leewit was a jewel past price. And she was mostly pretty happy playing endless games of snap or patience.

But it appeared she'd been broadening her horizons. "Let's play poker," she piped.

Pausert raised an eyebrow. "Where did you learn that game?"

"Vezzarn taught me."

"I should have guessed. Well," said the captain, setting the course for Gentian's Star and clicking on the long-range detectors, "we'll play for spillikins. Every ten you win, I'll buy you a packet of candy at the next spaceport. Every ten I win, you bathe without a fight. And wash behind your ears."

She looked darkly at him. "Twenty."

"Fifteen."

"S'a deal. But I'm not too sure how you play poker, really."

The captain had been around the witches too long to fall for

214 *Mercedes Lackey, Eric Flint & Dave Freer*

that one. He was a lucky gambler because of klatha, and as soon as he heard that statement he knew he'd need to be.

"Deal me in," said Goth, sliding bonelessly into the chair next to the chart table they used for cards. "I'm not too old for candy."

"But you wash behind your ears, anyway!" protested the Leewit.

"I'm not planning to lose, so what does it matter?"

"Huh!" said the Leewit scornfully. "You're getting to be just like Maleen."

"Deal," said the captain, before this well-used argument could get any more exercise.

A few minutes later Vezzarn came up from the engine room and joined the game. And the captain soon realized that he had fallen among thieves, or at least cardsharps. If the witches or Vezzarn ever needed money, they had a profession lined up already. Pausert was quite relieved when the ship-detector alarm went off.

CHAPTER 27

Here, near the Empire's center, ship traffic was much heavier. There was virtually no way to keep out of detection range of all of them. And it very soon became evident that the ISS was searching hard, and that the Imperial Space Navy now had orders: destroy the *Venture* on sight.

Twice now their ship had come within detector range of ISN vessels and had not even been given the chance to try deception. She'd been pursued and fired on—despite being within hailing distance.

"Communicator chatter indicates we've been fingered as a plague carrier, Captain," said Vezzarn indignantly. Aft of the *Venture,* space was lit up again by the blue lightnings of Imperial guns.

"It's more like the other way around," grunted Pausert. "We're the antibiotic and this is the disease trying to keep us away."

Goth stared at the ship detectors. "Guess we'll have to use the Sheewash Drive, Captain. Those Space Navy jobs are gaining on us."

Pausert nodded. "I'd rather not have to, because it gives them a definite fix on where we are, again. But I don't think we have a choice. We're certainly not going to win a battle with that many Imperial cruisers." Seeing the littlest witch glaring, he added diplomatically: "Not even with the Leewit at the nova guns."

That seemed to satisfy the Leewit's touchy sense of honor. So, once again, she and Goth made orange fire dance over the twisted pattern of black wires. Pausert found himself staring so hard at the pattern that his eyes felt as if they'd crossed. It was *almost* making sense.

The *Venture* leapt away from the Imperial Space Navy ships. The acceleration was fantastic—except . . .

Looking at his instruments, Pausert knew that it wasn't what the ship could do, or used to do, when the witches of Karres pushed her along with Sheewash Drive. They used to move faster than his instruments could cope with measuring. Now the *Venture* merely ambled along at about double her normal top speed. Enough to shake pursuit, certainly, but not enough to break through the cordon that the Imperial Space Navy was putting around the heart of the Empire.

"I'm sorry, Captain," said Goth tiredly. "That pushing through jelly feeling is back."

"I wish I could help," said Pausert, apologetically. "I've almost got that klatha pattern."

Goth shook her head. "You can't force klatha, Captain. It'll come when you're ready. I've got an idea that may work. They obviously know what the *Venture* looks like. But I could do a light-shift on her external appearance. Make her look like . . . say a Sirian passenger liner."

"Could work," said the Leewit. "They wouldn't fire on a passenger liner. Not a Sirian one, anyway."

"And we could get you to talk to them in Sirian, missy," said Vezzarn, "before you switch to Universum."

"Let's try it," said Pausert, decisively.

Hantis looked a little uncertain. "It's going to put a lot of strain on you, Goth," she pointed out.

The slim brown-haired witch shrugged. "I think I can do it, and you're supposed to be there before another fifteen ship's-days pass, Hantis. We've got to do something."

So they moved slowly forward, towards the globe of ships that the ISN seemed to have clustered around the spaceways to the inner worlds of the Empire.

"I don't see that the Nanites have very much left to take over," grumbled Pausert, as they came within detector range of yet another flotilla of Imperial Space Navy ships.

"You're *quite* wrong," said Hantis, coolly. "All they've done is to infiltrate the ISS and probably taken over one or two admirals. That gives them leverage but not control—and certainly not ownership. If they had full control over the Empire, they wouldn't bother to try to stop us at all. In a queer, backhanded sort of way, Captain, this is hugely encouraging."

Pausert decided she was probably right. However, if so . . .

"It also means," he said, "that we have to fight shy of actual shooting combat, even if we might win."

Hantis looked thoughtfully at Captain Pausert, as if looking right into him. The Nartheby Sprite was supposed to be a truth-hearer.

At length, she said, "Yes, Captain, I know you don't want to kill innocents. But the stakes here are very high."

"We'll try to avoid it," said Pausert, tersely. That issue had been worrying him for a while now.

A few minutes later he had other things to worry about.

The Leewit was giving the commodore of the Imperial Space ships some lip. In Sirian, fortunately, which they recognized but didn't understand. Then she switched to Universum. "Syrian registered passenger liner, *Pride of Vorvian*. What ship?"

"Ah. *Pride of Vorvian*. This is the ISN *Huntinglea*. Slow your acceleration. Please give us more details on your registry and port of origin."

"There are two ships peeling off into flanking position," hissed Goth.

"We're out of Shebreith's World, of course, registered on Lepper," said the Leewit, imitating perfectly the typical arrogance of Sirians. "That's in the Regency of Sirius, if your knowledge of astrography is up to the usual Imperial standards. Why do you wish to know?"

The ISN commodore ignored the implied insult. Wisely, Pausert thought. The Regency of Sirius was powerful enough—and certainly belligerent enough—to give pause even to the Empire.

"Ah. Administrative details," he said, his voice smooth as swanhawk grease. "I'm afraid we still need some more information, *Pride of Vorvian*. This will only take a few minutes. Please continue to slow your thrust."

"He's lying," said Hantis abruptly, looking at the officer on the screen.

Captain Pausert grit his teeth. "We're going to need the Sheewash Drive, then. We'll have to turn and run again. We can't possibly break through."

He took the microphone from the Leewit, who hurried to join Goth at the tangle of wires. "We've just discovered we have an outbreak of severe gaspartis on board. We are going to have to return to our last port."

"Wait, *Pride of Vorvian*. We have medics on board . . ." The

Imperial smoothness disappeared. "Halt or be fired on! Pirate vessel *Venture*. Halt or be fired on!"

But the *Venture* was already heading away, back where she'd come from, before the two flanking cruisers could come within range.

"They must have our engine's signature keyed into their detectors, Captain," said Vezzarn. "I don't know how they managed that, though. These engines were installed on Uldune, and the Daal certainly didn't pass along the information to them. But I can't see any other explanation."

Pausert sighed. "If that's the case, short of hauling the *Venture*'s engines out and putting new engines in—which we just don't have the time for—the Imperial Navy will spot us no matter what we do with the light-shift."

"I guess it'll have to be the Egger Route, then," said Goth, her face even more expressionless than usual.

The Leewit scowled, bit her thumb. "Guess so. But—" She jerked a nod at the captain, the grik-dog and the Nartheby Sprite. "Can *they* do it? Old Vezzarn can't, that's for sure."

Hantis shook her head. "Alas, no. It is not a klatha power that Sprites can harness."

"Well, I suppose it doesn't matter then, that I can't do it either," said Pausert. "As the point is to get Hantis and Pul through to the Empress before the Winter Carnival, we'll have to try some other form of disguise. Maybe we can sneak past on the Sheewash Drive."

"No good," said the old spacer, who was still very uncomfortable about the Sheewash Drive he'd tried so hard to steal—until he found out what it actually was. "At the speed the little Wisdoms can manage now, Captain, they're still going to detect us."

"True," agreed the captain, glumly. "And now that we've tried the light-shift, I don't think that's going to fool them anywhere."

This is not as much fun as the circus, Big Real Thing, tinkled a vatchy voice.

"Get that stinkin' little thing out of here!" said the Leewit, wrinkling her nose. You could hear the girl's tiredness and hunger in her peevish tones. Doing the Sheewash Drive had taken it out of the littlest witch. Besides, Pausert didn't doubt, she was missing the circus and the people there badly. She'd been rather spoiled by them.

The little vatch simply danced around the room, levitating things.

Captain Pausert raised his eyes to heaven. He could chase it with hooks of klatha force . . . and tickle it. Lately he'd found that the best answer was to humor it. Much the same way as he did with the Leewit, actually.

Where have you been for so long, little-bit?

Got sick. The dream-candy from the one the dog-thing bit was sour. Got to go, now. I'll find you again. G'bye.

It disappeared as quickly as it had come.

Dream-candy . . . from the Nanite-infected pirate? The universe as the vatches saw it was rather different from the universe as perceived by humans. Distance and time were fairly meaningless concepts to them. So what did they find in here that was "candy" to them?

Pausert was sure that many of the words that the vatch put into his mind were not strict translations but merely the nearest human equivalent. Well, there'd be time enough to puzzle over what was candy to a vatch, once they'd solved their present problems. The captain turned his mind back to that. "So just what is the Egger Route?"

"The way I came here, stupid," said the Leewit crossly. "Do you forget everything?"

Of course Pausert remembered the droning sound—in space, where there was nothing to transmit sound—and the abrupt and inexplicable arrival of the Leewit, and the way they'd had to wrap her in blankets because of the shaking.

He also remembered that she'd been . . . well, not breathing.

"Kind of hard to explain," said Goth. "I asked Threbus that question once, and he said that I'd have to get to understand n-dimensional math first. It's . . . well, there is a place outside this place, and times and distances aren't the same there. There's billions of Egger-spaces, and they relate to the person going into them. Even if the Leewit and I went home to Karres by the Egger Route, we wouldn't be in the same Egger Space."

"You can take someone else through your Egger Space. Or even send them through it. But that takes big power," scowled the Leewit. "Toll and Maleen could do it. Maleen could make us swim. Her Egger Space was wet. Don't know about Goth."

"Uh-huh," said Goth. "I do it pretty good, Maleen says. I can push quite a lot with me too. Or I could last time I tried. It's not something you try too often, although all Karres witches have to learn how."

Inwardly, Pausert sighed. The trouble with the Karres witches was that just as soon as you thought you had a handle on it all, they introduced new things. "If I've got this straight, the Egger Route goes through Egger Space, and Egger Space is different depending on who goes on the Egger Route. So what exactly is in this 'Egger Space'? Is it totally non-physical? What is there?"

The Leewit shrugged. "Everything."

"Anything," said Goth. "All the things you never want to meet. The details kind of blur up, Captain. It's like a defense that your mind has got against it."

"It's safe enough," said the Leewit. "Just horrid. So long as you don't meet any stinkin' vatches."

Involuntarily, Pausert looked around the room. No vatch in sight. "Why? We seem to have one we can't shake off."

By the way Goth looked around, she was also trying to rell if there were any vatches in the area. "Because vatches make what you find there real . . . here. When you come back. Threbus says they think that's where the Megair cannibals originally came from. From beyond the divide. From some Karres witch's trip through Egger Space. That's why, unless there is a real emergency we don't send any witches into Egger Space, except in a trance. That way they're protected. You still see stuff, but it's more like a nightmare than reality. If you send yourself through . . . well, it's just impossible to tell that it isn't real."

"So it's a sort of extradimensional dreamworld?" persisted the captain. He felt that if he could understand this, then he could do it. He just knew he could.

"I suppose so. It's a place. A little bit of everything in our universe is there too, and you've just got to sort of push and twist and align everything. That's what the vibration is about. You kind of bounce around until your body is back in the same dimensions as the rest of our universe. And then you come back. It's pretty bruising. But that's not the worst part of the Egger Route."

"Yeah," said the Leewit, shuddering a little. "It's bad enough when you go through someone else's Egger Space. Mostly that's just hard to remember."

"We've got another problem, Captain," interrupted Vezzarn, who had been gazing at the detector screens while all this had been going on. "I reckon those Imperials have done some calculations on our possible course, and got on the subradio. There are seven ships incoming. Looks like they're spreading out for an englobement."

They all rushed to the screens. Looking at them, Pausert thought there could be little doubt that Vezzarn was correct.

"Going to have to try and run again, then." Captain Pausert dropped himself into the control chair. "Goth, the Leewit—you two go and eat and get some rest. We may need to use the Sheewash Drive again."

Soon, Pausert started worrying that even the Sheewash Drive wouldn't get them out of the fix they were in. The fancy ship detectors they'd had fitted on Uldune were registering a second layer of ships—an outer englobement pattern. The captain handed control over to Vezzarn while he wrestled with the computations. After a few minutes, he clicked the trajectory calculation screen off and bit his knuckle.

"What is wrong, Captain?" asked Hantis, coming in with a tray of food.

Captain Pausert looked at the elfin alien woman that the Nanites were so desperate to kill. "They've deployed a lot of ships. They've obviously been tracking us and coordinating their efforts by subradio. The formation out there is big and elaborate. At the best speed we can manage with the Sheewash Drive at the moment . . . we're going to have to come under fire from at least one Imperial Space Navy ship. And I'm not at all sure we're heavily enough armored to survive that."

"I see," said Hantis. "How much time have we got?"

"The longest I can gain for us is half an hour."

"We'll have to try the Egger Route, after all. I'll get Goth and the Leewit." The Nartheby Sprite hesitated a moment; then, said softly: "I'm afraid it may mean abandoning the *Venture*, Captain."

Pausert patted the console awkwardly. The *Venture* was old, but she was his ship. He hated the idea of losing her. "It's the ship or our lives, Hantis."

But when she came into the control room, Goth had other ideas. "Me and the Leewit can work together. We'll just have to take a chance on not being in a trance, the two of us. We should be able to bring the *Venture* into Egger Space with us. The only trouble is that we'll have to go somewhere we've been or to someone we know. Otherwise—well, you can come out anywhere."

Vezzarn looked nervously at the screens. "I reckon, Your little Wisdom. Anywhere would be better than right here."

Pausert still had a mission to complete. "Can you take us anywhere closer to the Imperial Capital? Or at least on the other side of this cordon?"

The two little witches looked at each other. "Well. There's always Porlumma. You know, the world where we met you."

Pausert nodded. "That would probably be close enough. But it's on the opposite side of the Capital."

Goth shrugged. "Distance doesn't really matter much in Egger Space, Captain."

Pausert looked at the screens. The Imperial warships were closing steadily. "Okay, Porlumma it is. Anything I can do?"

"We'll need a clear piece of floor space. And some chalk, if you've got it. It helps to draw the klatha pattern for this one. And then I guess we'd better all strap in and pad ourselves. There'll be no one to wrap us up on the far side."

"Is the ship going to shake the way you did?"

The Leewit nodded. "Threbus and Toll did it with a house once. You can move pretty well anything over the Egger Route. But when they got there . . . the house was a real shambles. Didn't have a roof left at all." She seemed to find this very funny.

Pausert didn't. "We'd better secure everything we can then, Vezzarn. Set that course and come and join me. It doesn't matter exactly where the *Venture* goes for now. We're going elsewhere soon."

"I hope," muttered the old spacer.

Twenty minutes later, with the first Imperial cruisers sending probing fire towards the *Venture*, they were all strapped in.

And then the shaking began. At first it felt as if a herd of fanderbags was thundering past in the distance, but the intensity began to build. Pausert tried to move, but could not. He felt as if his body was strapped to a gigantic drumhead and the drummer was picking up both the volume and the tempo. The droning noise was like thunder.

Then it began to die away. "It's no use," said Goth. "That swimming through jelly feeling is back. We need more power."

The hull vibrated for an entirely different reason. "Near miss, Captain," said Vezzarn. "Can't you help the little Wisdoms?"

The Leewit looked at Goth. Goth stared back at the Leewit. "Going to have to try it I guess," said Goth. "Captain. Follow the pattern with us."

Captain Pausert realized that he had been staring at it while they'd tried. Now he did his best to mesh in with Goth and Leewit. Suddenly, the mesh came into being.

It was like being plugged into an electrical outlet. The Egger

Route was grinding away at him, and shaking everything. He found himself twisting parts of the pattern that now burned as if outlined in fire. Tweaking this, flicking that over. Gradually the shaking lessened and died away.

But the darkness that enveloped them was complete.

"Are we dead?" asked Vezzarn, nervously.

CHAPTER 28

"No, I don't think so," said Goth's voice, out of the darkness.

"But don't ask us where we are . . . because we don't know," said the Leewit. The Leewit didn't sound grumpy, as she usually did when things went wrong. Just a little scared.

"What I do finally know," said Goth, "is what caused that swimming-though-jelly feeling, Captain. It went away just as soon as you joined us. But the power you poured into that pattern and the changes—it was like riding a runaway bollem. I got no idea what happened or even where we are."

Embarrassment flooded the captain. The other Karres witches had grown up with witch magic. They had instructor patterns in their minds to guide their development. Pausert, a one time citizen of the stuffy and conservative little Republic of Nikkeldepain, had no such special advantages. He just had to muddle along with klatha. He did achieve some spectacular results, some time to time, though they were rarely the results trained operatives would achieve. But his uncontrolled klatha pooling had disturbed all the adult witches when he'd been on Karres, and even the adolescents.

"You mean *I* might have been causing the problems with the Sheewash Drive?"

"Pretty sure, Captain. The feeling was the same."

Hantis spoke from the darkness. "Have you been concentrating on the patterns for the drive, all this time?" she asked.

"Er. Yes. I felt I nearly had them . . ." Pausert heard his own voice trail off.

"Foolish churl," growled Pul. "Haven't you been told that klatha powers come in their own time?"

If the darkness had been mere absence of light, then Pausert was sure the others could have seen the dull red glow he was sure that his face was putting out. "Yes. But, well . . . I thought I could help. And I felt I nearly had it."

"Instead you were dragging like a dead weight at those who did have it," said Hantis. "At least we understand what was wrong, then."

"Yeah," said the Leewit. "Now all we need to know is what went wrong with the Egger Route. And where we are."

"This isn't the Egger Route, then?" asked Pausert.

"Nope," said the Leewit. "Not like it at all." In a small voice: "Can you get us out of here, Captain?"

"Well," said the captain. "I'd like to. But how? Like I did with those shields? Tracing it backwards?"

"If that worked at all, we'd be right back under fire from Imperial cruisers," pointed out Goth.

"Anyway, I don't know if I can," admitted Pausert. "The pattern. Well. I sort of changed things as I went along, because it was hurting, and I'm not sure I can visualize it."

Then suddenly he relled vatch.

So there you went! said a cross little voice. **How did you get here, Big Real Thing? And why did you run away from me? Did you think I wouldn't find you?** There was a trace of plaintiveness in the voice.

For the first time ever, Captain Pausert was truly glad to see those tiny, slitty silver eyes peering at him. One of the reasons he was so glad about it was that they could be seen at all. There appeared to be no other form of light, and his attempts at moving hadn't succeeded. He wasn't really sure if they were actually talking with sound and words. It didn't feel as if his lips were moving. Actually it didn't feel at all.

"I never thought I'd be glad to see a vatch," said the Leewit. "Hey! Leggo, you little beast!"

Where are we, little vatch? asked Pausert.

You mean you don't know?

Tell us. Please?

Might. If I feel like it. What are you going to do now, Big Real Thing?

Pausert didn't tell it that what he really wanted to do right now was wring the little silvery-eyed vatch's neck, if it had a neck and if he could have come to grips with it. *Nothing interesting*, he said. *Sit here and be boring.*

The vatch made a rude noise. **Can't do that. The wave of everything is coming.**

Wave of everything? Pausert wondered if it was worth fashioning klatha hooks. Of course he could only tickle this one, but maybe he could tickle it into telling them. Tickling was not that far removed from torture, after all.

Yes. You're outside of everything. The only thing that's here is your ship. Even time hasn't got here yet. It's a strange place to come.

Well, can you get us out of here? Or tell us how to get out of here?

I don't think I will, said the vatchlet petulantly. **Last time I did something for you I got sick. And then when I went to play in all the other ships so they'd leave you alone, you ran away.**

Inwardly, Pausert groaned. If there had been any doubts in the minds of the captains of Imperial Space Navy ships that the *Venture* was indeed chock full of the notorious witches of Karres and should definitely be destroyed on sight, he was sure it wasn't there anymore.

But here, outside of everything, that seemed a minor problem. *Oh, well. I suppose you can't do anything, anyway.*

Can too! snapped the little vatch, and vanished.

Sitting in the darkness, Captain Pausert had time to wonder if he'd handled it right. And time to try to reconstruct the pattern he had used, inside his head. He was sure if he could just get up and redraw it, he'd have it.

"I've been thinking, Captain," said Goth.

"Careful! You know what happened last time you did that," said the Leewit, snippily.

"You're lucky I can't move," grumbled Goth.

In the interests of peace, Pausert intervened. "What, Goth? Have you some idea of how we can get out of here?"

"Well, no. But I think I have some idea of how we got in here. You remember you said you had changed some things in the pattern?"

"Yes," admitted the captain. "They . . . well, they just didn't seem right. It felt as if my changes would stop all the vibrations."

"And it did," said Goth, thoughtfully. "Never heard of that with the Egger Route, before. But we—the Leewit and me—were also using that same klatha pattern. And so I think we didn't end up where any of us were heading."

"So you mean we could just do it again?" asked the Leewit.

"Doubt it," answered Goth. "It might do something else entirely. Anyway, I've tried all sorts of klatha stuff. It doesn't work. There is just nothing here, except us. Or nothing here yet. Looks like only vatches can handle this place, though I don't know why that should be true."

Goth was sounding very like her mother, Toll, now. The captain wondered whether it was her Toll-pattern speaking, and wished, yet again, that he could have such an instructor.

"It also means," she continued, "that to reverse it we'd probably have to work together."

"Uh-oh!" interjected the Leewit. "I'm relling vatch again. *Big* vatch."

It *was* a big vatch. A huge one—and it was in hot pursuit of little Silver-eyes, who didn't seem in the least bit amused about anything. Downright scared, in fact.

The huge eyes were green, at the top of a mountain of tumbling black energy, roiling and twisting klatha force. The vatch paused abruptly in its chase, its eyes fixed on Pausert and his crew. HOW DID THEY GET HERE? HOW ODD. The big vatch laughed thunderously. NO—HOW DELIGHTFUL! WELL, I'M GLAD I FOLLOWED YOU AFTER ALL, YOU LITTLE NUISANCE.

Pausert hastily began fashioning klatha hooks in his mind.

They're mine! All mine! hissed the little one, buzzing around the big vatch and then hastily retreating.

Before Captain Pausert could react, he was plucked, no, hurtled, out of the *Venture*. He was dimly aware of the passage of enormities of time and space. And then of sitting down, hard, onto blue-green spongy stuff.

His first realization was that he'd actually *felt* that landing. The next was that, far from the darkness of a few moments before, his senses were almost drowning in colors. The horizon was pricked by towers. Improbably slim towers, elfin and beautiful, and very white against a sky that was definitely a shade of primrose. Somewhere in the middle distance a waterfall splashed.

He glanced around hastily. To his immense relief, he saw that the whole crew of the *Venture* had come with him and were sitting on the same spongy material. Above them, parasol-like trees stretched feathery red leaves towards an alien sun. The air was full of strange but almost intoxicating scents.

"Where are we?" asked Vezzarn, warily. "Boy, I really *hate* this witchy stuff."

Hantis answered, in an almost dreamy voice. "We're on Nartheby. Nartheby in her golden age." She pointed to the towers on the horizon. "The towers of fabled Delaron were destroyed during the final phase of the quarantine wars. We lacked the skills needed to rebuild them. They are partly creations of klatha force."

Pausert knew that time and space were not limiting to vatches, particularly large ones. He was also grimly aware that this was a game to them, an entertainment played with what they considered to be phantasms of their minds. And that a vatch loved to test its phantasms, to see if the pieces in its mind-games had a role in the dream-drama.

True, there was usually a way out for pieces of quality. Although not always—the vatch who had placed them on the Worm World had fully expected them to be destroyed. The immensely powerful and capricious living klatha creatures were quite capable of maneuvering players into hopeless situations, just to watch the drama of their doomed efforts to escape.

And even if there was a way out, there was usually only one. Not for the first time, the captain wished that vatches would just leave him alone. Of course, that wasn't likely. Klatha use attracted the creatures; the *Venture* must have stood out like a lighthouse.

"What do we do now, Captain?" asked Vezzarn, looking nervously around.

Pausert did rather wish that people wouldn't keep asking him that. He really had no idea. This vatch was undoubtedly watching, but from beyond the range at which the Karres witches could rell it.

And there seemed to be a more immediate problem, anyway. By the deep-throated rumble issuing from Pul, there was something else watching them too. Pausert felt the hairs on his neck rising the way they had when the Sheem war robot had been stalking up behind them. He stood up, turning as he did so.

Of course. The vatch would not have chosen a safe, comfortable place to deposit its play pieces.

No. They just *had* to be in trouble.

Hantis had turned from her rapt contemplation of the towers and was now looking in horror at what Pul was growling at. *"Gnyarl!"*

The creatures that were staring at them from the fernlike

undergrowth were sinuous, reptilian and gray. Their eyes, how-ever, flamed a particularly disquieting shade of orange.

"Hantis," said the captain quietly, warily watching the statue-still creatures. "What are they? What do we do about them?"

"We are on some High Sprite's lands. These beasts are his guard. We can do nothing, so far as I know. They have been extinct on Nartheby for many centuries, but I have been told gnyarl were nearly impossible to kill and equally difficult to shake off. We can split up. Maybe they won't get all of us."

"How do they do on direct blaster fire?" asked Pausert grimly. Of course it would help if he had a blaster snugged to his hip. Hulik always carried her slimline Mark 7 model. But the captain's weapons were safely locked up in the *Venture*. And the *Venture* was somewhere beyond the edge of nowhere.

Vezzarn proved that once a rogue . . . always a weapon-carrier. The little thief had a military RV special, out and at the ready. "I don't know, Captain. But I can try them on this."

One of the gray reptilian forms darted forward, snaking its long neck towards them. Vezzarn fired. The gnyarl's head was engulfed in flame. The creature blinked, shook its long beak-nose, and spat a gout of fire back at Vezzarn. Only being nimble on his pins saved the old spacer.

The other three gnyarl had taken advantage of the distraction to split up and begin flanking them.

The Leewit looked hard at the advancing creatures—and whistled. The sound was like a wet finger being skimmed around the edge of a delicate wine glass, but many times as loud.

Everybody, from Pausert to the grik-dog, cringed. The gnyarl backed off a bit, rubbing their ears with black-taloned paws, blink-ing those flame-orange eyes. They looked puzzled. Obviously, nothing much had ever given them pause, before.

"Right, let's head out," said Pausert. "Keep together. And the Leewit had better be ready to whistle again."

Watching the gnyarl, they began moving away up the hill. Silently, keeping to the cover, the creatures followed. Sometimes all they saw was a sinuous streak of gray through a gap in the undergrowth. The clearing they'd landed in, with its distant pros-pects, had narrowed into a path that wound upwards through a defile. The way grew ever steeper and narrower.

"I don't like this," said Goth, who was an accomplished hunt-ress herself. "It's almost as if we're being herded."

"I guess we should just be grateful they're not eating us," said

Vezzarn, who had tucked away his RV and was looking to be on the edge of panicky flight.

Very distantly, just on the edge of perception, Pausert could rell vatch. If he could get klatha hooks into the creature . . .

"Stinkin' vatch," said the Leewit.

Pausert agreed this time. But the big one was keeping out of range.

The feathery trees had thinned. Ahead stood a stalked building. That was the best way Pausert could describe it. It looked rather like a giant piece of broccoli, though it was plainly stone. There were high, round windows looking down on them. Flicking a glance at her, Pausert could see that Hantis was biting her lower lip with those slightly odd-shaped, very white teeth of hers. She looked to be almost in pain.

Behind them, one of the dragonish gnyarl hissed.

The Leewit must have been waiting for the slightest provocation from them. She turned around immediately and whistled again. The pitch was too high to hear. But not too high to feel! The captain felt his teeth ringing.

The gnyarl had a lot more teeth—and they were on the directional receiving end of that whistle. The Leewit could target things rather precisely.

The lead gnyarl yowled like a cat that had had its tail stood on. Then, scrambled back hastily, wrinkling its long nose-snout, and attempting to squint at its snaggled teeth. The other three also retreated.

Goth took Hantis' elbow. "Should we go somewhere else? It doesn't look like you like this place much."

Hantis gave a low, musical laugh. "It's no use going anywhere else, my dear. This is where we were meant to go. And it's not that I don't like this place. I love it, as does Pul. We know it well. But seeing it like this hurts."

"We'll make them fix whatever it is they've done wrong, then," said the Leewit, using her Mistress of the Universe tone.

"Nothing is wrong, children. This is my home. This is where I was born. But Castle Aloorn, in our time, has few inhabitants. And I am afraid it is not in the best repair. This is the golden age of Nartheby, when our star-empire was at its height and the Sprites' culture was in full flower."

A swinging platform was being lowered slowly down from the broccoli-head of the building. The platform looked as if it were glass, and made by some Old Yarthe baroque-style glass-smith. It was transparent yet ornate, full of gilt and green curlicues and spikes. On top of it, on an angular throne, was a statue. A haughty-looking perfectly realistic male Sprite, but only half Hantis' size.

Captain Pausert had assumed it was a statue, because it was all one color, even the hat—a pearly white. And then, it moved. He was no statue. He'd just been sitting as still as one.

The captain looked at Hantis to see her reaction. And suddenly realized that she was no longer next to them. She was using her klatha powers now, to levitate. And she was speaking, but not in Universum.

"What's she saying?" whispered Goth to the Leewit.

"She's just greeted the Lord of Castle Aloorn. Real flowery stuff. Huh! Never heard Hantis talk like that before!"

The half-pint Sprite spoke.

"He wants to know who she is that dares to trespass on the lands of house Aloorn."

Hantis replied.

"She said she has the hereditary right to visit her own lands and home. She said some words that I don't think mean anything."

The haughty looking Sprite looked as if he was about to fall off his throne. He raised his hands and began jabbering furiously.

"Oh. They must be like a password or something. He says . . . he wants to know who betrayed his house. Oh, that's nasty, what he just said! You oughta wash his mouth out with soap, Captain."

By the widening of the Leewit's eyes, Hantis' reply was even more educational. "Oh, boy. I think we are in trouble. The two of them are mad clear though. I've never heard anyone say anything like that. Not even the Agandar's pirates."

Somewhere in the distance was a hint of huge vatchy laughter. The captain didn't like this situation at all. Other glassy platforms were beginning to be lowered down from the bulbous castle above. Behind, the dragonish gnyarl still hemmed them in. The Leewit's whistle had put them off, true, but would it stop them in a truly determined rush? And this was definitely playing the game the way the vatch wanted. They had to break out of its pattern.

The small Sprite's earlier cool and haughty air was gone. His face-color no longer matched his attire. He'd have had to change into purple robes to do that. And Pausert did not need the Leewit to understand that the next words out of the half-pint's mouth were something along the order of: *Guards! Seize them!*

The furious Lord of Castle Aloorn wasn't prepared for one of the Leewit's shattering whistles, though. The small Sprite's glassy platform exploded in a very satisfying shower of bright-colored shards and spilled the Sprite onto the ground fifteen feet below.

But the Sprite Lord displayed that he too had klatha skills. He caught himself, just before an undignified landing, and levitated—straight for Hantis. It was plain that he thought that she had done it to him.

Pausert realized just how lucky he'd been that Hantis had simply been amused when, thinking it was Goth playing a light-shift trick, he'd lifted the Sprite's hat and veil. The red-maned Sprite's grass green eyes were narrowed with fury. A nimbuslike halo of energy hung around the two of them as they dueled. The issue, however was not decided by klatha powers. Hantis doubled her elegant six-fingered hand into a fist and punched the other Sprite in the gut. His hat flew off, revealing hair as flame-red as hers.

But the captain had no time to watch any more. Battle was joined. The Sprites might be small, but they were inhumanly strong. There were also an awful lot of them. And the gnyarl were charging.

When Pausert woke up, he noticed that his bed had become very lumpy. And whatever he'd drunk the night before had given him a splitting headache.

Gradually, he realized it wasn't anything he'd drunk the night before, and that the ache in his head was probably related to the bumps it had acquired. He opened his eyes, cautiously. He was lying on the floor . . . trussed up like a roast. Looking around, he could see that the others were also lying around the room. All of them were virtually wrapped from head to foot in silky looking cord. It was an oddly bulbous room, but very elegant and beautifully proportioned—for a prison. The mirrors on the wall were odd too, as were the huge convex butterfly-shaped windows.

Not like the last prison he'd been in, but still a prison. Associating with the witches of Karres seemed to result in the captain spending a lot of time in durance vile. To think he'd once been a respectable person, not a wanted criminal—as he seemed to end up being these days, no matter how respectably he tried to behave.

Right now he could use some of the escapology skills of the Great Aron, even if it got him laughed at. But his little silver-eyed assistant wasn't around, and the big vatch was staying out of reach. This Big Windy enjoyed playing with humans, but was lot more wary than the last one had been. Maybe it had encountered a vatch-handler before.

Pausert settled for rolling over and trying to sit up against the wall. His Lambidian iguana boots had great traction, so it was not impossible, just very awkward.

The Leewit was gagged but conscious. She was making frantic squirmings towards him. The other four—Goth, Vezzarn, Hantis and Pul—were trussed up and still. For a grim moment, Pausert knew fear bordering on panic. Goth had long since made her way into his heart. Well, the Leewit too. But surely they wouldn't have tied them up if they were dead. Last he'd seen, Goth had been fighting off a small sea of Sprites, and giving a good account of herself.

The Leewit managed to wriggle herself close to him. The captain was upset to see just how pale she looked. Pale and very small. He set to work on her gag with his teeth. While he was busy, both Goth and Vezzarn stirred. Just those little movements were very comforting, but someone was going to pay for this. Witches didn't take kindly to captivity, and he *especially* didn't take kindly to anyone beating up these particular witches.

He'd just gotten the cloth to start tearing, when Hantis sat up.

She blinked as if trying to get her eyes to focus. Then she looked around. The strange elfin face looked thoroughly woebegone.

Pausert went on tearing at the fabric of the gag, and was rewarded by an "Ow!" The cloth gave and the Leewit's mouth was free again.

Which, of course, was a mixed blessing. "You! Clumping cud-chewer!"

But her ill-temper was brief. "Where are we, Captain?" asked the Leewit, after licking her lips.

Hantis answered in a kind of dreamy, singsong voice. "In the hall of the crystals, which is also called *Imnbriahn-des-sahrissa*—the place of heavenly late afternoon lights. It is, or was, Castle Aloorn's execution chamber. It was largely destroyed during the rule of an ancestor of mine, he who came to be called Arvin Warmaker, the destroyer of the Golden Age." She shuddered. "The blame for the fall of the towers of fabled Delaron has been laid at his feet as well as much of the destruction done to Castle Aloorn. Many other evils, also."

Hantis sighed. "I am afraid that the vatch served us a truly nasty turn, Captain. It sent us back in time to meet one of the greatest villains in Nartheby's history. I am sorry. When I realized whom I was dealing with . . . I let my anger overpower me. I have been brought up to hate this man, hate and despise him for what he did not only to Nartheby, but also the shame he brought to the Clan Aloorn. I should have been more tactful. Now we are trapped."

"Not for long," said the youngest witch. "The captain can do his shield trick on us. I never thought I'd ask him to do that, but it'll deal with these ropes all right."

Hantis grimaced. "Not these ropes, dear. Remember that klatha skills are quite common among the Sprites. The captain can make a shield cocoon around you, and that would work, but the ropes would remain inside it."

Hantis looked out of the windows. "No. All we can do is wait for the sun to go over the zenith. And then the sun will shine in through the windows and we will all die."

"Why?" asked Pausert, wriggling across the floor to Goth. She was stirring now, and groaning softly.

"Because of the crystals and the mirrors. When the sunlight shines in through those windows the facets inside the crystals will shatter it into prisms. This will become a place of hundreds of rainbows, and then, as the sun gets into line and the outer facets focus the light—a place of death. The ropes will burn away and this beautiful place will become a place for us to dance. You see, the crystals and the mirrors act as focus-devices and accumulative multipliers. As the heat builds up inside them they change facets. The light will blast from one, then another, in a pattern which is supposed to have been unique each time . . . a terrible choreography of laser-lights."

Looking at the floor now, the captain could see that what he'd taken for lumps in his bed when he had been coming to, were actually crystals. Multifaceted crystals. Thousands of them.

Goth groaned again. "There. It's all right, Goth," comforted the captain. She quieted at his voice and burrowed against him. Moaned as she hit a bruised spot, lay still for a bit and then opened her eyes.

One eye, rather. She could only open the other a crack—she'd have a magnificent black eye if she lived through the afternoon.

Since he'd promised that it would be all right, he'd better get free of these bonds. He strained. He noticed that Vezzarn was also trying to sit up.

"What's happened, Captain?" asked Goth, muzzily.

He explained.

She tried to sit up, and managed on the second attempt. "I guess you'd better get whistling," she said to the Leewit. "You won't get a chance to break this many things again." She looked at the

Nartheby Sprite. "Sorry, Hantis. I can't see any other way to deal with it."

"It is the one place in Castle Aloorn that I was glad that Arvin Warmaker destroyed," said Hantis, grimly. "The windows and mirrors are not true glass though. They are strong but flexible organics, like the castle itself."

"I'm not so good on things that bend," admitted the Leewit.

"But the crystals aren't flexible. Arvin destroyed many of them."

"Well, he'll have to make them again first if he's going to destroy them this time," said Goth. She nodded at the Leewit. "Go to it. Break as much as you like."

The Leewit scowled. "It's not as much fun when you've got permission."

"I promise you that the current owner is going to be as mad as a wet desert bollem about it," said the captain firmly.

The Leewit cheered up immediately. "Okay, then." She pursed her lips, focused her gray eyes on one of the larger crystals. There was a thin high-pitched sound and a series of little clinking noises, rather like the hull metal around a cooling spacedrive.

The crystal fell slowly in on itself.

The Leewit picked out another.

Vezzarn groaned and rolled over. By the time the littlest witch was onto her twenty-third crystal, the little spaceman, safe-cracker and spy was awake. "Captain," he asked weakly, "is there any reason we have to stay tied up?"

Pausert shook his head. "Other than the fact I can't get loose, no."

"I've got a small vibro-razor hidden in my bootheel, Captain. Along with lockpicks and some electronic gear. If I could get to it . . ."

Pausert smiled for the first time in quite a while. "Hantis—these ropes. They're klatha proof. But can you cut them?"

Hantis blinked. "Possibly. They muzzled poor Pul. That could be why."

Captain Pausert thought they probably did that to stop the grik-dog biting them, but he held his tongue. Instead he said: "Goth, do you think you could 'port that razor into my mouth? As we can't even use our fingers?"

"Sure, Captain." She smiled wickedly. "Open wide."

He did. And the tiny tool arrived neatly between his lips like a little cigar. And abruptly disappeared. "Sorry, Captain. Wrong way round. If you'd clicked it on then you could have taken out your tonsils."

A moment later, the hilt was held by his teeth. He felt around the ported vibro-razor with his tongue until he found the click-switch. The vibro-razor starting buzzing like an angry gnat under his nose. Very cautiously, he touched it to Goth's silky rope-wrapping. It frayed. He went on, trying not to cut her. The rope might resist klatha, but it was no match for Imperial technology. By the time that the Leewit had dealt with nine more crystals, Goth was shrugging off her rope-cocoon.

After that, freeing all of them was a quick job.

The sun had moved directly above Castle Aloorn and the room was already full of dancing rainbows. Vezzarn got awkwardly to his feet, rubbing life back into his arms and hands. "Let me see if I can master an alien lock, Captain. If I can find the door, that is."

"It is there, behind the mirrors in the corner," said Hantis, pointing. "But it isn't intended to be opened from the inside."

"Milady, I've even dealt with a safe like that," said Vezzarn with a lopsided grin. He walked over to the far corner and began examining the smooth surface with the tiniest folding magneto-calipers the captain had ever seen.

"What about guards?" asked the captain. "Where would they be?"

Hantis waved her slim elfin hands. "In my day there was no need for guards. Aloorn is a peaceful, friendly place where any visitor would be welcome."

The captain grimaced. "Well, this kind of welcome I could skip. What about a way out, Hantis?"

The Sprite wrinkled her sharp nose. "That . . . could be difficult. Of course it is not a problem if you can levitate. But there is no walkway down. And we are about one hundred and twenty of your feet off the ground."

"What about those platform things?" asked Goth.

Hantis shrugged. "Every set of chambers has a hoist. Most of our people use them rather than levitating, which takes a great deal of effort. In my time we could have gone to an unoccupied chamber, swung the hoist arm out and dropped down. But it would appear to me that Castle Aloorn is very well populated right now. To get to a hoist you would have to break into some Sprite's home. And we are, as a species, able to scream telepathically. Someone has been trying to probe me since we have been trapped in here. Fortunately, I have very good shields."

"Haven't felt anything," said Goth, warily.

"That is not surprising," said Hantis. "I am a better-than-average telepath among my own kind, and I can barely pick up the general drift of human thoughts. Our minds are very differently constructed. That is why the captain's klatha use does not affect me the way it does other adults."

Over in the corner, Vezzarn sighed. "Sorry, Captain. But it's not working. The mechanism itself is simple enough. But there is something else there. It's not mechanical and not hyperelectronic. It's some kind of energy construct. I can't budge it. The door is open except for that."

"Klatha lock," said Hantis.

"Can you do anything about it?" asked Captain Pausert. The Leewit was still crumbling crystals, but there were a lot of them, and the mirrors were full of rainbows. All of them were bathed in the multicolored light. It made the Nartheby Sprite look even more alien.

Hantis shook her head. "No."

Then, the mirrored door swung open. They all stared at it. Even the Leewit stopped her whistling. Peering cautiously back at them was a wizened Sprite, a knife in his hand. He put his finger to his lips. Some gestures obviously crossed both species and time lines. He beckoned and said something.

"He'd come to cut us loose. He wants us to go with him," said the Leewit. "He has the hoist ready back in his master's chambers. He will help us to escape, he says."

"Something about this smells wrong to me," said Goth.

Pausert felt the same way. He remembered Hantis' klatha skills. "Is he telling the truth?"

Hantis nodded. "But you need to remember, Captain, that truth-hearing only extends to the limits of what the speaker knows. He might not be aware that he is lying. Some of the great truth-hearers of our history have been fooled thus."

"We better chance it anyway, Captain," said Vezzarn nervously. "We need to get out of here, before these folks see what the little Wisdom has done to their precious crystals. I reckon they're not going to be pleased."

The captain could see his point. Even if the Sprites of Castle Aloorn had been planning to kill them, they were going to be mad about the destruction the Leewit had wrought. They might as well go and find trouble as wait for it. And the Leewit was looking tired. "Come on, brat," he said, snagging her and hoisting her up onto his back.

"Don't need to be carried," she said, peevishly.

"But I need you to have lots of spare breath for whistling."

The Leewit thought about that. " 'Kay," she said and wrapped her arms around his neck.

The party walked towards the beckoning Sprite . . . and Pul paused. "Nanites," he growled. "He's been near Nanites."

Hantis stopped too. "Is he possessed?"

Pul sniffed. "No. He's just touched something that had their exudates on it. But there is a trace of Nanite in these corridors."

Pausert wasn't aware of the Nanite smell, but he could just rell that big vatch again, along with a feeling of being laughed at. "Even more reason to get out of here," he said. "Come on. Our guide is getting nervous."

They swung the door to click shut behind them. The Sprites were in for something of a shock when they opened their execution chamber. The destruction, and the absence of dead bodies, would give them something to think about. All the captain could hope was that it frightened them out of pursuit. Not that he was too sure where he was going, except that it should be somewhere else. Then, somehow, he must try to catch that wary vatch, get back to the *Venture* and back to their mission.

They went past numerous round doors. The passage was empty, which seemed a little odd, seeing that it was mid-afternoon. Perhaps the Sprites slept during the daytime. Hantis didn't, herself, but she had spent a lot of time among humans. The captain enquired about it, as they hurried after their scurrying guide.

Hantis shook her head. "It *is* a little odd. I'll ask our guide." She did so, in a quick exchange.

"He says they are at a council-of-war meeting. His master sent him to rescue us now as everyone would be there. He would have come earlier, otherwise."

They went up several spiral ramps, very steep and difficult to climb, and came at last to a larger round door, covered in ornate embossed-work—a pattern that looked like complex multipetaled flowers. Their guide touched one of these with a wide open palm.

"I wonder whose rooms these are? It's a pretty posh door," said the Leewit, who still had breath for talking. The captain would have asked too, except that his lungs were gasping from the climb.

"This . . . part . . . of the castle had been destroyed, in my day," said Hantis, trying to catch her breath. There was something reassuring about the fact that even the alien had found the climb hard going.

Inside, the room was still more ornate. In what Pausert was now beginning to realize was typical Sprite taste, there was a great deal of translucent and different colored glass. There was a table made of a thin section cut through an enormous amethyst crystal. It had been delicately fractured and the myriad cracks infiltrated with gold.

And, by the frantic wrinkling of Pul's nose, the place was rotten with the stench of Nanite.

"Whose chambers are these?" growled the grik-dog at the wizened little Sprite-servant.

The servitor looked puzzled. The grik-dog spoke again, but remembered this time to do so in the Sprite tongue.

The wizened little man drew himself up proudly, and answered.

"He says Lord Nalin, the advisor of young Lord Arvin. And he says we must go quickly. The hoist is through there. His master says we should head for Delaron."

Hantis, however, had stopped dead in her tracks. "You smell Nanites here, my Pul?"

The grik-dog pawed its snout. "The place reeks!"

Hantis turned to the others. "You should all flee. But my duty is clear. I must remain. I think," she said grimly, "I have made a great and grave mistake. History is not always as accurate as we would like it to be. I began to get that feeling when I saw just what the Leewit had destroyed in the hall of the crystals." She looked at the Leewit. "You will be glad to know that you never got the blame for that."

"Oh. You mean . . ."

Hantis nodded. "History was wrong about that. This period was a violent and much disrupted one. Records are poor. But there is no record that Nanites made it to the surface of my world. They certainly never survived through the troubles. So: I am going to the great council chamber of Aloorn—the Hall of Stars, it is called—to try to take steps to eliminate this plague." She smiled impishly. "I am less afraid of Arvin than I was. He was always described as a giant among my kind, instead of a vain little shrimp."

In the distance, the captain could rell vatch. Still far off, but closer and more intense than before. This, he suddenly realized, was why they'd been brought here. This was the vatch's game. "I think we should all stay. I think the Nanite smell in here was why things smelled wrong when the wrinkled retainer offered to let us out—but I don't think it was just the smell of Nanites."

The little man jabbered something in Sprite, again, and pointed frantically.

Captain Pausert shook his head. "I don't think so, old fellow. I think what you're saying is hurry and go. I also suspect you'd get killed, pretty soon after our escape, to hide your boss' Nanite tracks. Come on, Hantis. Let's all go to your great council chamber."

Hantis nodded. "I don't think we need a guide for that, either. I can find our way."

It was just as well. The terrified servitor had obviously worked out that they weren't going, and had bolted.

CHAPTER 29

As she led them towards the Great Council Chamber, Hantis found herself trying again to deal with the conflicting emotions that had overwhelmed her since she'd found herself back on the mother-world. She'd traveled far and dealt extensively with humans. She and the witches of Karres had found much common ground. But . . . this was Nartheby, Aloorn. The place in her heart of hearts. And Castle Aloorn, to see it like this, lit with faerie-lights, gleaming and glorious—that was a treasure beyond her wildest dreams.

She understood now that she might have come to destroy it. Or, at least, to lead to its destruction.

The council chamber, the Hall of Stars, was the highest and largest room in Castle Aloorn. They came in through an upper door—the door of the accused, which, as she had been sure it would be, was open and led to an empty gallery. Looking out, she could see that the many tiers of the chamber were full, fuller than she had ever seen it.

On *her* chair, the judgment seat of Aloorn, sat Arvin War-maker. His head was bandaged, and he did not look particularly warlike. Actually, now that she was able to look at him slightly more dispassionately, he looked both sore and a little afraid.

They had arrived at an interesting moment. A gold-clad Sprite was just giving Arvin the news that the prisoners had escaped from the *Imnbriahn-des-sahrissa*.

"The destruction, my lord, is terrible! More than half of the precious crystals are shattered into dust."

"My lord," said a Sprite standing at the side of the judgment seat. "Have patrols sent out! Release the gnyarl! We must capture these miscreants before they get back to Delaron."

Arvin waved a hand in irritation. "Enough, Lord Nalin. I can deal with some things myself. Angbar. See to it."

The gold-clad Sprite bowed and scurried out. Nalin spoke again. "Do you see how right I was now, my lord, to have them sent to the *Imnbriahn-des-sahrissa*? Delaron will stop at nothing to see our precious Aloorn destroyed."

"Nonetheless, Nalin, it is customary for the accused to come before the seat of judgment before they are executed." Looking at him now, her fury gone, Hantis could see that Arvin was a very young Sprite. Young and probably unsure of himself.

There was nothing unsure about Nalin. "My lord, it was necessary to take swift and decisive action against these criminals. You were incapacitated and their guilt was established beyond all doubt. They were spies from Delaron. Murderers and assassins."

An elderly Sprite from one of the front galleries stood up. "My Lord Arvin. What rubbish is this? Assassins come in darkness, in secret and with stealth. They do not arrive at midmorning with a group of aliens and give the greeting words of the Clan Aloorn."

"Treachery in our very midst!" proclaimed Nalin, pointing at the Sprite. "Now, my Lord Arvin, we know who betrayed the passphrase of the great Clan Aloorn! Look no further than Lord Laar, of sept-clan Aloorn-Taro."

Lord Laar looked as if he might just leap over the edge of the gallery and seize the Lord Nalin by the throat. But young Arvin raised his hand. "Enough! There will be time enough for accusations and counteraccusation, when the prisoners are recaptured."

Hantis decided this was as good a chance as she was going to get. "We are here, Lord Arvin! In the gallery of the accused, where we should have been brought to begin with. We await our hearing."

Pandemonium was the right word for what followed.

Captain Pausert wished he could understand what was being said. The huge hall that Hantis had led them to was an amazing place. It was several hundred feet from the floor to the ceiling, for a start. The ceiling itself was a semitransparent dome-roof. Pausert could now understand why the council chamber was called "the Hall of Stars." Around each star in the night-sky the ceiling glowed, as if magnifying their light. Although he could see no other form of lighting, the chamber was nonetheless quite bright. Perhaps the light came from hidden globes in the hanging translucent galleries that studded the walls like so many bracket-funguses. All of the galleries, but for the one they stood in, were jam-packed with Sprites.

Until Hantis spoke, that is—when, like great flocks of angry birds, they all headed for the hanging balcony.

"Don't do anything. Don't fight!" said Hantis, urgently, as the Sprites levitated towards them. With the numbers of Sprites coming up, Pausert realized a fight would have been futile, anyway.

So, for the second time that day, but this time with his cooperation, the captain allowed himself to be bound. He consoled himself with the thought that, after all, he could always get loose again. Vezzarn still had his vibro-razor and Goth could still teleport objects.

Hantis said something, and the Leewit squawked. "I am *not* a little child! Come closer, you! I'll pull your pointy Sprite nose!" She then said something that caused the Sprites to gape. Pausert was glad he didn't understand. It saved him having to go through the fight to wash her mouth out with soap, again, and he had enough trouble already.

Besides, he wouldn't have minded saying it himself, whatever it was, if the Leewit and Goth hadn't been listening.

Soon Pausert found himself being carried away. This time the chamber he was taken to had a far greater resemblance to a prison cell. At least it was clean.

He was also alone in it.

He had plenty of time to examine the bare room, he decided, and to wonder just why Hantis had told them not to resist.

Eventually the door would open.

While she waited in her own prison chamber, Hantis had plenty of time to doubt the wisdom of her actions. She'd had time to realize that perhaps she'd been a bit too imperious herself. It was indeed her castle. But how would she have felt if some stranger had turned up, without warning and without an appropriate escort, and used the words she had?

But she would put it right, and somehow she would deal with the plague that had infected her people. After all, she knew the laws and customs of Aloorn: none better. She would be taken back to the Hall of Stars and would address the seat of judgment and explain.

Then the door to her holding room opened and she realized that she'd missed one possible scenario. The Sprite who stood there was not going to listen. That would not suit Lord Nalin, advisor to High Lord Arvin. Or, rather, it would not suit the Nanites that populated him, who had taken over his body and mind.

Her flesh crawled with horror, realizing he had probably *not* come to kill her. Killing her would serve his purposes less well than infecting her.

Hantis screamed. And screamed with her mind too.

And this time that was enough. A group of seven Sprites came running into the room.

"What is it, My Lord Nalin?" one of them asked.

Lord Nalin gestured in irritation. "Nothing. Go. I wish to question the prisoner alone."

If the Nanites could lie, so could she. "He assaulted me! Look at my face." She knew that her face was bruised from the earlier encounter. "Is this how the people of Aloorn use prisoners?"

The leader of her guards drew himself up. "My lord, I cannot allow you to assault the prisoner," he said stiffly.

"What nonsense," said the High Lord's Advisor haughtily. "I did nothing to her!"

The guard looked doubtfully at Hantis, who cowered away into the corner. There was no need for her to pretend fear. That was real enough. "Don't let him touch me," she whimpered.

The guard commander nodded reassuringly. "We do not allow prisoners to be tortured or hurt, lady. You will face High Lord Arvin for justice. He is good and fair, if young."

"Did High Lord Arvin order us killed without a hearing?" demanded Hantis, forgetting to be humble and cower.

The guard commander gave a hard look at her, then at Lord Nalin. "No," he said. "As a matter of fact, the order was issued by Lord Nalin. My lord, I shall have to ask you to leave. And do not attempt to visit the prisoners again. Escort Lord Nalin away, Fotri."

As the Nanite-controlled Sprite was ushered away—politely, but the guards were making very clear that they'd brook no nonsense—Hantis relaxed. "I am willing to talk to anyone, as long as the guard watches, except for Lord Nalin." The news of the Nanite plague had plainly not reached Nartheby. "I think he is in the pay of Delaron."

The guard blinked. "But he is advisor to the High Lord himself!"

"Exactly. Now, can I explain why we are here and from whence we have come? We traveled far and in great peril to bring this word to the Clan Aloorn."

The guard commander shook his head. "The High Lord himself will hear you. You must wait for him."

"Will you at least keep Lord Nalin away from me—and my companions?"

"The order will be given," said the guard commander.

And with that, Hantis had to be content.

But a little later her door was opened by a very worried looking guard. "The prisoner that you told us was a young girl child, of a species from the outworlds. She has disappeared!"

Hantis felt herself go cold with fear. The Nanites would take some hours to assume control, and in the meantime the victim's body would be wracked with spasms and rigors. Once the Nanite infection had begun, all you could do for the victim was to incinerate them. The only thing that slowed the plague at all was that after taking over a new victim the Nanites required several weeks to build up their numbers to the point where they could send out breeding colonies. But the mind of the victim was destroyed within the first hour.

Hantis had known Goth and the Leewit since their birth. Now she was desperately afraid for the littlest witch.

"How?" she croaked.

"A hole was cut from storage chambers through the wall and into her holding chamber. Or the other way around. We are not sure if she cut her own way out."

Hantis shook her head. "I doubt it. She wouldn't leave us. She is still very young. Please. Put us all together and set loose my grik-dog Pul. He will defend us."

The guard looked worried. "I cannot do that. I have strict orders to keep you apart."

"Well, then, please put Pul in with Goth. The next youngest alien."

The guard considered, then nodded. "I suppose, precisely speaking, the grik-dog is not a prisoner, but more in the way of a caged animal. The High Lord has several. He breeds them. Very well, I will do as you wish." He smiled thinly. "I have heard they have a nasty bite to them."

Hantis realized that grik-dogs, in the here and now, had not yet been bred to sniff out Nanites. Their toxin was simply a general one. They weren't very intelligent yet, either. "And tell the others to scream if anyone comes in. Oh. They won't understand you.

Only the littlest one can speak our language." She sighed. "I don't suppose you'd let me speak to them."

"No, milady," said the guard. "Not without asking the High Lord."

"Can he be asked? You must send word that the Leewit is missing."

"He has already been told. Extra guards have been detailed."

CHAPTER 30

The Leewit had been a good three parts asleep when she saw the blade coming through the wall. It was a blur of blue-white energy, and was steadily cutting a circle out of the back wall of the room where she was confined. She'd had a long, tiring day—more exhausting than she'd been willing to admit. She'd been very glad of the piggy-back on the captain's back.

She wished that he were here now. Was this a dream? Was this a rescue or was it more trouble? She wanted Goth, or she wanted the captain or, preferably, both. Her older sister could be annoying, although Goth didn't fuss the way Maleen did. And the captain made her wash her neck and behind her ears. But she liked having them around, especially when things were unfamiliar, although she'd never have admitted that to anyone.

The shimmering light-blade finished cutting its circle out of the wall. Long slim fingers pulled the piece of wall backwards into the darkness and three furtive-looking Sprites came through the hole. Before the sleepy Leewit had a chance to even whistle, one of them clapped his hand over her mouth. She was carried to the hole and out, into the darkness beyond. A hand was kept firmly clamped over her mouth, as they carried her away. The Leewit was unsure if she was being rescued or kidnapped. If it was a rescue, she wished they'd tell her so.

They wrapped her in a heavy, smelly cloth. Now, the Leewit was sure she was being kidnapped. So she bit the fingers, hard.

"Yeeow!"

"Be still. Keep her mouth shut."

"She bit me!"

Another hand clamped over her mouth. "Bite me and I will stick a knife into you." This person sounded like he meant it. After a moment, she was picked up and carried off.

When they removed the heavy cloth, the Leewit found herself in a small chamber with a large balcony. Like all the Sprite places she'd seen, it was full of translucent glass.

The hand was pulled away from her mouth. She finally got to that scream she'd been saving up.

"Scream all you like," said the Sprite that had had his hand clapped over her mouth. "No one can hear you here, alien thing. Although Luwis may decide to punish you for biting his fingers."

"Who are you?" demanded the Leewit, looking around the room. It had a very high ceiling and was full of beautiful and delicate ornaments.

The Sprite's slanted eyebrows went up. "I would have thought it was quite obvious, small alien. We are spies from Delaron. We want to know what you're doing here, and just where you're from."

The Leewit rolled her eyes. "Clumping stupid!" She gave the Sprite an accusing glare. He seemed a bit befuddled.

That mollified the Leewit. A bit.

Of course, it didn't mollify her enough to be cooperative. She was *the* Leewit, after all.

So she did what she normally did when she was in trouble. Went straight up. She still weighed a lot less than the Sprites, and she'd spotted a high shelf full of obviously very precious bric-a-bracs. Before her three captors knew quite what was going on, she was on the shelf. Of course, most Sprites could levitate also. But there wasn't going to be any of that fragile glass and crystal stuff left by the time they caught her.

"Hey! Come down! Come down or you'll be sorry!" said the one with the bitten fingers. "Here, Wellpo. Make her come down before she bumps anything off there."

The Leewit shaped her lips into a whistle. One of her best and favorite.

It worked even better on the Sprites than on the people she'd tried it on before. Bones in the ears weren't . . . what was the word—flexible. They wouldn't shatter in there, but they did hurt.

The three doubled up, holding their ears. Just to keep in practice, she blew a beautiful shatterer at a display of rose and amethyst crystals on the table. It exploded very nicely.

But when the Leewit saw the look of fury on the face of the one who had threatened to stick a knife into her, she realized she wasn't high enough. There was a narrow chimneylike opening in one corner of the ceiling. It was made up of mirrors and had a skylight, and there was a small sill at the top that she could perch on. Best of all, even if they could levitate, none of the Sprites were going to fit into the mirror-chimney.

The Leewit scooted up. It was a tight fit even for her and it wasn't very comfortable. But then, from the angry sounds the Sprites were making, it would be a lot less comfortable down there.

A questing arm came feeling upwards. When it found the ledge, the Leewit stepped on the fingers as hard as she could.

"Oww!" The fingers vanished.

"Leave her, Luwis," said one of the other kidnappers. "She'll have to come down sooner or later."

"That's well enough for you, Wellpo. Why did we not take her to your chambers? You don't have skylighting."

"For two reasons, as I already explained to you. First, it's too far away. Secondly, it is near that stiff-necked old Laar's chambers. Given what that ass Nalin accused Laar of, that area of Aloorn is almost bound to be searched."

"But she has smashed my precious crystal sculpture-work. Smashed it!"

"She'll come down in time."

"I'll murder her!"

The Leewit giggled and whistled again. It was hard to be directional from here, but by the howl of anguish . . . she'd gotten lucky. And once the howl died away, she could hear the tinkling sounds of a glass ornament raining little pieces of its former self onto the floor.

Still, they were quite right. She couldn't stay up here forever. She was pretty tired, and starting to get hungry. She looked at the tiny chimneylike space she was wedged in. It was nothing more than a long tube with a window at the top. She peered out the window, but there wasn't much that she could see. It was dark out there.

But she knew they must be high up. Going out, this high off the ground, was scary. But . . . not as scary as going down, or trying to stay here until she fell.

So she whistled at the window.

All that did was make her ears ring. Angrily, the Leewit struck the window with her little fist.

The skylight opened right up, as neatly as you please. She must have hit a release of some kind that she hadn't even noticed.

Sticking her head out, she could see much better. It was less dark outside than she'd thought. The window must have been filtered. Best of all, this wasn't an opening over a sheer drop to the ground below—the window opened onto the roof. In an scrambling instant, the Leewit was out of the hole and onto the rooftops.

Someone else would have started their escape immediately. Not the Leewit. She turned, stuck her face back though the skylight window, and sent a real crystal-shattering whistle down into the chamber. Then, her shrill and powerful voice overrode the howls and splintering sounds below. The Leewit bestowed upon the Sprites any number of descriptions of themselves, using terms she'd picked up since their voyage began. Most of them were in the Sprites' own language, selected from the terms Hantis had bestowed on the little Sprite muck-a-muck. But the term *beelzit* was scattered freely throughout.

Then she closed the skylight and started crawling away across the steep rooftops.

"Boy, I hope the captain doesn't find out," she muttered. "I'll be eating soap for a clumping *year*."

She stopped crawling after a while, since the rooftops were very steep and scary and there seemed no end to them. No rhyme or reason, either, that she could see, to the Sprite notion of architecture.

When she came across a little cluster of skylights that formed something like a nest, she decided to stop. She was very tired and felt very alone, and the rooftops were very high and very steep and she was very scared—and, now, night was falling.

"It's not clumping fair!" the Leewit protested to the universe.

The universe gave no reply. Grumbling with indignation, the Leewit crept into the cluster of skylights and curled up among them. It wasn't the warmest or most comfortable place to sleep; but, in a tucked away corner, the littlest witch slept all the same.

Sleep was far from Hantis. She knew what danger they were in, and she was terribly worried about the Leewit. The worry steadily built into anger. By the time Arvin Warmaker finally walked into her room of confinement, she was quite ready to start her brawl with him all over again.

But . . . the High Lord looked even smaller than he had when she first met him—and a lot younger. All the Sprites she'd seen seemed much smaller than her people, which was something of the opposite to the way history had painted the matter.

He also looked very worried. "I had planned to leave this until the gathering tomorrow. But now the littlest of your band has escaped or been seized. Why are you trying to push us into this war with Delaron? I have tried very hard to avoid it. We've had generations of war. Surely that is enough?" His tone was plaintive.

The wind was taken out of Hantis' sails. *"Avoid . . ."*

"Despite what Nalin and his cohorts say, I am not convinced that it would be wise," said Arvin. "Or that we would win anyway, even if it were."

Hantis took a deep breath. She could tell that he spoke the truth.

So, it was history that had lied. Well, it wouldn't be the first time.

"High Lord Arvin, do you have a truth-speaker among your councilors?"

He shook his head. "Such klatha powers are rare. It is a pity, because they are useful to a ruler."

"Very," she said dryly. "You see, I *am* one. And despite everything I was raised to believe, I know you to be speaking the truth of your heart."

He looked at her, extremely suspiciously. "You say 'despite everything you were raised to believe.' So, you *are* one of our ancient foes, after all. I had wondered. Will you make peace with us, then? Is this an overture that has been terribly misunderstood?"

Hantis wished that, like humans, she could weep for this boyman. "I am not one of those you term 'our ancient foes,' but, yes, this has been a terrible misunderstanding." She sighed. "But I fear I have not come make a peace with Delaron. I fear, I fear terribly, that I may have come to make you go to war with them."

It was his turn to gape at her. "What? If you are not from Delaron, then where have you come from? And how did you know the kin-words of Clan Aloorn?"

"I was taught them," said Hantis calmly. "They were among the first things I was ever taught. Even in my cradle they were sung to me. I know how the flame walls are triggered. I know where the tooth-traps lie. I know the portal songs for each and every of the inner chambers."

He looked fearfully around. "You must indeed be a spy!"

"Why would a spy come here if they already knew all of our defenses?" asked Hantis.

He drew back between his two guards. "You are an assassin!"

She issued a small, wry laugh. "Why would I admit to knowing all of our ancient secrets, High Lord, if I were an assassin? No, I am one who would know these things by right. The only one who could know all of the secrets of Aloorn, besides yourself. *Think*, High Lord Arvin. Who has the right to know as much as you do . . . except one born to the inner Clan? I am of Aloorn, but I am from your distant future."

"That is not possible."

She shrugged. "Nonetheless, it is true. I am a distant descendant of yours. You are one of the most . . . well-known Sprites from the era of the Nanite plague wars. The most ill-famed and notorious, to be precise."

His eyes nearly popped out of his head. "Leave," he said to both of his guards.

"But, High-Lord . . ."

"Go! You may remain in the passage."

Reluctantly, the bodyguards obeyed.

The High Lord of Aloorn waited until they were out of earshot. "You know something that is secret from all but the High Lords. This is either a very cunning trap . . . or the truth. Prove to me that it not a trap."

"I can show you the secret exit to your chamber, which is activated by placing your palm on the points of the tsaritsa flower in the middle of the window-wall. And I can tell you that the early secret quarantine will fail. It has already failed."

He blinked, his double lids covering his violet eyes. "Who are you? I mean who are you where you come from?"

"I told you. I am your direct descendant. I am named High Lady Hantis des Shaharissa of Clan Aloorn."

"Why have you come here? How have you come here?"

"A vatch." As Hantis recalled, there had always been vatches. They had just become more numerous around humanity. Klatha wielded by humans seemed attractive to them and, to creatures to whom time and space were equally insubstantive, they could congregate where they willed.

He bit his thin lips. "It is possible, I suppose. We know the vatches sometimes use their power to play Sprites as pieces in great dramas. But what test have you and your companions come to Nartheby to perform? Aloorn is no place for such deeds."

"I think," said Hantis carefully, "that I was brought here as part of a vatch joke. I was supposed to kill you, and thereby—having destroyed my own progenitor—destroy myself. This vatch seems more malicious than most. But you are wrong about the role of Aloorn. Aloorn played a great and central part in the plague wars. And there is need. The Nanites are here already."

Arvin, he who would be called the Warmaker, the destroyer of Delaron whose infamy for the burning alive of those in the towers lived on through centuries . . . looked horrified.

"But—we'll contain them! A cure will be found. There'll be no need for violence. The problem can never spread as far as Nartheby."

Hantis shook her head, sadly. "This is an intelligent plague. I should have realized before that the historical accounts made no sense. They came here to Nartheby first. We always believed the plague started in the outer realms and was fought, planet by planet, inward to Nartheby. But why would they act in such a mindless manner? Of course the Nanites would have struck for Nartheby first! If they could decapitate the Sprite dominium, the rest would be theirs for the taking."

She did not say, but did realize, that the strategy she sketched was exactly what the reemergent Nanites had set out to do in the Empire, centuries in the future.

"But . . . do you not know how the plague was fought?" demanded Arvin.

"The records from the plague years are very confused. What I do know—what I was taught, rather—is that High Lord Arvin, he who was called the Warmaker, brutally took control of all Nartheby and isolated her."

The young High Lord gaped at her. "I did what?"

"Took control of all Nartheby and isolated her. You went to the council of High Lords and in the Hall of Truce, killed three of the High Lords and their advisors and kinsmen. The three who, besides yourself, were the most powerful. Then made the rest bow to your will."

"That is mad!"

"I wish it were," said Hantis sadly. "I conclude that you must have taken Pul with you, and sniffed out those of the High Lords and those who were Nanite infected, and killed them."

"Pul?"

"My grik-dog. I believe you breed them." She raised her eyebrows at him. "It is one thing history gives you great credit for:

breeding grik-dogs that could sniff out Nanite infection. That was how the plague was eventually dealt with, other than in open warfare."

For the first time there was a slight smile on the face of High Lord Arvin. "My grik-dogs are bred to smell out truffle-fungus. Their noses are fantastically keen. I've been trying to reduce the toxicity of their bite to make them easier to handle. They're far more intelligent than most people realize." It was obviously a subject dear to his heart and one he'd rather talk about than the Nanite plague or the domination of all Nartheby.

She smiled at him, too. It appeared that being besotted with the yellow-furred creatures was a hereditary trait. "Intelligent and loyal, High Lord. My grik-dog is with one of my human companions. Why don't you go and ask Pul to confirm my story?"

He was plainly quite taken with this idea. "Their speech is a bit limited. It's one of the things I've been working on."

"I think you will be pleasantly surprised at how well Pul speaks," said Hantis graciously.

When High Lord Arvin returned a few minutes later, he had Goth and Pul with him. He bowed. "High Lady Hantis. First, I must give you my apologies for having treated you like this in your own home."

"Will you tell him to stop talking?" said Goth, crossly. "Let's get the captain and go and look for the Leewit."

"What did the little alien say?" asked Arvin.

"She is very worried about her younger sister. The humans are good klatha operatives, but this is a young one to be off on her own. She wants you to free the other human, who is something of a guardian to both of them, and to start looking. If I may suggest, we could use Pul to track her down. Pul knows her scent, don't you, my clever one?"

Pul growled. "Can't miss it. It's the soapy teeth."

"He is a magnificent male," said Arvin enviously, petting Pul. The grik-dog gave the High Lord a none-too-friendly glance, but, to Hantis' relief, didn't even bare his fangs.

"Yes," Arvin said decisively. "Let us do it." He snapped orders. Hantis could see that, once he grew up a little more, this would indeed be the ruthless and effective Arvin of legend. It was also plain that, although he might doubt Hantis, Pul had the High Lord under his paw.

Together, they went to Pausert's holding chamber. The captain was very pleased to see them. And, Hantis realized at the same time, in a very dangerous state because of his worry about the Leewit. Toll and Threbus had not put their children's welfare lightly in the care of just anyone. He took his responsibilities very, very seriously. The captain was probably unaware of the klatha energies surging around him. Hantis wasn't.

But all he said was: "Let's get onto the trail, quick."

Pul sniffed around the storage chamber and found the trail of three, mixed in with the smell of the Leewit. He set off at a run along the curving corridors of Castle Aloorn. They had to race to keep up with him.

They caught up with the grik-dog at a beautifully inlaid door, covered in an intricate knotted pattern in strings of opaque glass. Hantis had no chance to ask Pul, privately, if he smelled the odor of Nanites. All she had time for was fear.

"Luwis. Luwis crystal-crafter!" said the High Lord incredulously. Captain Pausert shoulder-charged the door. It didn't break.

"Open the door," said Arvin to his guards.

They added their slighter weight to the captain's, but to no avail.

"Stand aside," commanded Arvin. Pausert might not have understood the words, but he understood the tone of voice and the behavior of the guards. He stepped aside, and the door imploded into dust and a wash of heat that frizzed the hairs on the captain's hands.

From the moment the captain had shoulder-charged the door to its disintegration had taken at least a minute. By the time they got into the chambers, the last of the room's three occupants were leaving into the predawn, via the balcony and the stairs leading downward.

They rushed after them, out onto the balcony. Hantis caught sight of the fugitives far below. She could see no sign of the Leewit, either accompanying them or bundled in any way. But the light was poor, and the shreds of morning mist soon obscured them completely.

"Shall we pursue, my lord?" asked one of the guards.

The High Lord shook his head. "No. Give the order to release the gnyarl. Let them hunt. The flight of Luwis proclaims his guilt."

"So does this." Hantis pointed to the mauve powdery remains on the table, and the little piles of fine dust on the carefully placed and lit shelves. "She was here."

"If they've so much as hurt a hair on her head . . ." The captain balled his fists.

A worried Hantis wondered why the Leewit had not been taken by those who fled. Had she been infected? Nanite infection patterns were well known. The invaders immobilized the victim within minutes; then, over a period of several days, reproduced and gradually took control. It took roughly a week before full control was established. They wouldn't have had to take her along, if they could hide her well enough.

"Any sign of Nanites, Pul?" Hantis tried to keep her voice casual. She sensed Pausert's gathering fury, and the immense klatha energies that fury could unleash. If the captain realized what Hantis would have to do if the littlest witch had been infected . . .

"No," growled Pul. "Not a trace."

Relief washed her. Pul sniffed the floor, and rose onto his hind legs, sniffing upwards.

"She went up," the grik-dog said, pointing with his nose to the mirrored-chimney skylight that was catching the first rays of dawn.

Goth might not have understood the words but she understood the gesture. She levitated towards the chimney, with a scant regard for what remained of Luwis crystal-crafter's prized creations. The upper end of the chimney-skylight was nearly too narrow for her, but she managed to force herself in. She got to the top and called down. "This window does open, huh?"

CHAPTER 31

The Leewit woke, shivering and hungry. It was bad enough that it was cold, and dark, and that she was alone, but the thin rain that had started to fall seemed just too much to her. No one could hear her snuffle, so she did. But she wasn't going to stay out here in the rain. So she started trying to find a way off the roof of Castle Aloorn, that didn't involve going straight down a long, long way. As worn out and hungry as she was, she was afraid to try levitating even for a short distance, much less that great drop to the ground below. Levitation was a new klatha skill for the Leewit, and she still wasn't as good at it as her sister Goth.

The answer seemed to be to climb into a skylight. A different skylight.

The problem was that most of them seemed to be shut from the inside. It took her a long time to find one that wasn't. And then to climb in with her hands so cold they were almost numb.

Inside it was gloriously warm. The ledge up here wasn't as narrow and uncomfortable as the last one, but there was no point in staying on it. Carefully, the Leewit started climbing down. As usual, there were loads of shelves on the walls, full of glass and crystal. She had a very difficult time descending without kicking something off, especially since she was sorely tempted to smash everything in sight anyway. But the room she'd climbed into seemed to be empty, and it wouldn't be smart to make any noise.

When she finally reached the floor and looked around, dim light filtering from panels left the whole place a rather ghostly blue. Kind of eerie, in fact. But the Leewit decided that the place was as good as any to hide out. It was warm and dry, if nothing else, and there might just be some food somewhere.

"Maybe in one of those jars or bottles," she murmured to herself. "Clumping stuff has to be good for *something.*"

"The night-rain has washed away the scent," growled Pul. "And I do not like being up here."

Pausert could see why. The roof of the castle sloped steeply, and the slope was treacherous in places. The thought of the Leewit wandering around up here in the dark made his blood run cold. Blessedly, the High Lord's guards hadn't found Pausert's worst fear, a small broken body on the ground far below. And they'd now searched everywhere she might have fallen, so apparently she hadn't.

The Leewit was just missing. She wasn't responding to their shouts, either. But there were any number of the chimneylike skylights and odd towers sprouting from the top of the castle.

"She could be hiding anywhere," said Goth tiredly, leaning against him. "When Hantis said those skylight things opened for ventilation, I was pretty happy. Now, I almost wish they didn't. The Leewit can get herself into impossible places."

Despite his simmering anger, the captain had to fight down a smile at the cross tone in Goth's voice. As if *she* never got into any such predicaments!

Hantis came across to them. "Come. We must go within. The High Lord Arvin will call a council and get everyone to help look for her. And, besides, you look all in. You both need food."

"You're pretty chummy with this High Lord Arvin now," said Goth, eyeing the Sprite. "He tried to kill all of us, remember?"

"It was a misunderstanding," said Hantis, quietly. "We fell over our mutual pride. I assumed too much. And High Lord Arvin did not send us to the *Imnbriahn-des-sahrissa.* That was his advisor, Lord Nalin."

"But that was the name of the boss of the little old guy who came to rescue us!"

"Yes." Hantis' eyes were cold. "The same Lord Nalin. Who also claimed that we were assassins from Delaron. In whose apartments Pul smelled Nanite exudates. While Arvin was unconscious, Lord Nalin ordered us executed as spies and murderers because that would help to fan the fires he's trying to start. When objections were raised in the council, Nalin sent his servant to free us and send us fleeing to Delaron. The High Lord is actually the only one who can pass the death sentence, so Arvin sent his guards for us. Only we'd escaped, which made us look guilty and Lord Nalin seem to have been correct. That was why I put us in the position of honorable prisoners."

"So what's all this got to do with the Leewit's kidnapping?" asked Goth.

"We don't know," admitted the Sprite woman. "Come. Let us eat and contemplate our next move. Good Sprite food may help me to think properly, anyway. I've had to reassess my ideas about history."

"Apparently so," said the captain wryly. "I thought you said that this Arvin was the greatest villain in your history?"

"It appears that history blamed the wrong person. It appears that the greatest villain in the history of Nartheby may be . . . me. Come. I will explain while we eat. The High Lord needs to marshal his soldiers. Nalin has gathered many adherents, some of whom may be Nanite controlled."

Down inside the castle, sitting at a construction of glass and silver on velvety upholstered translucent chairs, Pausert realized that the holding chambers they'd been put in were probably the Sprite equivalent of the cell he'd been put into on Pidoon. The food wasn't the usual breakfast fare for humans. The ice-crystal layers of sweet and tart and definitely alcoholic stuff wasn't anything Pausert had encountered. Neither, really, were the thin nutty-tasting pancakes and deep purple jelly. But they were very welcome, nonetheless, and they were certainly easier to digest than Hantis' explanations.

"Don't you see? The Nanites are doing precisely what they are trying to do in the Empire in our time: decapitate. At this stage, their numbers are probably very few. They take control of key individuals. Ones like Lord Nalin, whose position makes them powerful but whom few people really know well. The Nanites can take over the body of the victim, but the behavior and mannerisms change. So: the Nanites must either take over a whole group, which is difficult for them at this stage, or someone like Nalin. He has been away from Castle Aloorn for some twenty years, as a governor of one of the outlying dominions."

"You think this is what we're facing in the Empire too, then," said the captain, spooning the fragrant purple jelly onto yet another pancake. "So why are we trying to reach the Empress Hailie? She's a well-known recluse. The Empire only sees her twice a year. I would have thought that she would be the perfect Nanite victim. She still wields a lot of power."

"That would be correct, except that Hailie disappears. Between official engagements, the Empress goes . . . somewhere. She tours her Regency anonymously. She's been the unofficial friend of Karres for some years now. The best premote-teams on Karres predicted that the only chance of defeating the Nanite plague was to reach Hailie first, and provide her with information and protection. If necessary I am empowered to call for certain drastic steps."

Hantis looked grim. "I've never explained the details, Captain, but the plague wars were the worst episode in our history. High Lord Arvin destroyed any ship incoming to Nartheby—even when they appeared to be full of refugees."

She took a deep breath. "He was renowned for his brutal efficiency in disposing of enemies here on Nartheby. They were always incinerated, as were their homes. It was a technique he put to use against the Nanite-possessed in the later phases of the war, when we Sprites set out to destroy the Nanites."

"Is there any other way?"

"Not a really effective one, no," admitted Hantis. "Grik-dog venom affects all those in the host. But the environment they are found in should still burn. A colony of several thousand could be hiding behind a grain of sugar on the floor. But we did not know . . . I suppose—it makes sense, now—that it was always kept secret that Nanites had reached Nartheby's surface. I am afraid that Arvin did what was necessary, and shouldered the blame. He is a braver and better Sprite than I could ever be, but I must have been the one who told him it was the right method to use, and that it had to be done. He's young and scared; and, in truth, quite gentle. He wants nothing more than peace with his neighbors. He has to act the part of the arrogant High Lord to hide the fact."

The captain struggled to absorb it all. "So, this all happened in your history. Arvin, the shrimpy little Sprite, turned into what you thought of as a monster and dealt with the problem. Is that why the vatch brought you here?"

"No. I think vatches understand humans and time imperfectly. The vatch brought me here because Arvin was the worst thing in my mind. He is also an ancestor of mine. The vatch, I think, thought it would be funny if I killed him. Because then I would not have existed either. In which case, how could I have killed him?"

"Great Patham!" exclaimed Goth. "A sort of impossible loop. Stinking critter! It just wanted to see what would happen."

Hantis smiled. "Yes. Unfortunately, I don't know exactly what I did in history because records from that time are very poor. But if you want loops . . . well, I think the vatch outsmarted itself. An impossible loop is, after all, impossible. So it will be replaced by loops which aren't. Just to name one: I believe Pul is off fraternizing with High Lord Arvin's lady grik-dogs. The origin of grik-dogs with anti-Nanite venom and the ability to smell out Nanites comes from Arvin's breeding program, you know."

"You mean Pul's his own great-grandfather?" demanded Goth, laughing. "That's not exactly 'fraternizing.'"

Hantis nodded and smiled. "It's quite a bit further removed than that. But, yes."

"And Pul is the end product of a long breeding program. It does beg the question of where the first Nanite-killing grik-dog came from," said Pausert. "But right now I am more interested in finding the Leewit, and somehow getting back to our own mission and own Nanite fight."

"If we can get her back at all," said Hantis, biting her lip. "The gnyarl caught one of those who kidnapped her. A Sprite called Luwis who owned the apartment. Unfortunately, he won't be talking to anyone. But the Leewit definitely wasn't with him. They think the other two may have dodged back into the castle."

Captain Pausert rubbed his temples thoughtfully. "So they're still on the loose, the Nanites are here and can only be destroyed, with difficulty, and the Leewit is still missing."

He rose abruptly to his feet. "At least we've had a good breakfast. And I can still rell a hint of that blasted big vatch. If it would get closer . . ."

Goth stood up from the elegant table. "Old Nasty-Vatch has been caught before, I reckon. He's not going to come close enough, Captain. He's watching us from a distance."

"Then we'll have to go vatch hunting," said the captain grimly. "In the meantime, we have a Leewit hunt to organize."

Goth grinned. "Catching a vatch might be easier."

Her confidence cheered Pausert up. His worst fear, now that it was clear the Leewit hadn't fallen to her death, was that her abductors might have murdered her and hidden the body somewhere. But that dark thought was difficult to maintain in the presence of Goth. The girl had a way of projecting serenity, somehow.

As his greatest worry faded, a smaller one finally had the chance to push its way forward.

"Oh," said the captain guiltily. "We'd better ask our hosts to release old Vezzarn."

"Oops. Hadn't thought of that either, Captain," admitted Goth.

Pausert yawned. "Well, at least he got some sleep last night, even if I'll bet his breakfast wasn't as good as ours."

The Leewit, however, was enjoying a far more varied and even bigger breakfast. Moreover, she had two new . . . well, friends was the wrong word. Young Sprites who had the delusion that a fascinating new pet had wandered into their chambers. It could even talk! Far better than their dolls, although it was the oddest looking creature they'd ever seen. And it could play games and do all sorts of tricks!

They'd successfully hidden her from their nursebeast and their parents, so far. And then they'd raided the larder to see what their new pet would eat.

Now that the Leewit had a full stomach, she was beginning to think about how she could get out of here. And it was going to be less easy than just getting out of prison had been. It was not that the two little Sprites were cruel. Well, not on purpose. They were just a great deal stronger than humans of that size would be. Stronger than she was, for sure, and quite happy to tug at their new toy, now that they'd fed it. The worst part was when they insisted on dressing her in Sprite clothes.

They would be adamant that she wasn't going out of their sight, obviously.

"Look," said the Leewit in desperation, "Let's play cards."

"What's 'cards'?" demanded the two little Sprites, almost in unison.

So the Leewit had to fish out the Agandar's cards, have them peered at, and examined. Fortunately, she always carried them with her. The Leewit considered boredom the worst peril in the universe, but as long as you had cards you could always fend off the monster by playing solitaire.

"Hey! You can't eat them. You play with them. Here I'll show you. Do you know Snap? No of course you don't. Look, here, I'll deal them."

Their names turned out to be Lisol and Ta'himmin. Fortunately, they were quick to learn the rules of the game. Mostly, though, they just seemed to love the cards themselves. The Leewit had looked at the pictures on the cards, of course. But the Sprites noticed the tiniest details. They picked up the patterns around the edges, and Ta'himmin was scathing about the fact that each had an error.

"My father makes inlays," said the littler Sprite proudly. "*His* edge-patterns are *always* the same *all* the way around!"

"Play," said his sister. "The thing's cards are thing-made, little brother. 'Course they won't be as good as papa's."

The game was noisy, cheerful and did not manage to distract the Leewit from the fact that she had to somehow get out of here and rescue Goth and the captain. And old Vezzarn, Hantis and Pul, of course. At least, in the hooded Sprite cloak and tunic, she could pretend that she was a Sprite. Even if Lisol and Ta'himmin thought blond hair was hilarious, the Sprites couldn't see it under the hood.

The young High Lord Arvin had underestimated two things. First, the depth of support that Nalin had gathered around him. And secondly, just how effective Lord Nalin's spy network was.

There was no element of surprise on their side, when they marched up, with Pul in the lead, towards the wing that Lord Nalin had made his own. Actually, it was High Lord Arvin who walked into an ambush. The High Lord had been still-doubtful and had been beginning to question his own judgment. The small band of his guard that accompanied him were not really prepared to fight.

The firefight turned nasty almost immediately, as Nalin's team of ambushers had the advantage of a good solid barricade. Then Arvin stood up and traced a pattern on the air . . . and part of the barricade burst into flame and then fell into dust. Before the dust had settled Arvin's troops were sprinting forward, firing at their now unprotected and shocked foes.

"Push on hard and fast!" yelled the captain, without thinking that the High Lord's troops would not understand a word he said, or take orders from someone who had been a prisoner until the middle of the previous night. He ran forward and picked up one of the fallen Sprites' projectile weapons, trying to figure out just how it worked.

But Arvin, who had looked doubtful about the entire exercise a few moments before, was giving orders himself. He was only a shrimp-size Sprite, but he could do a giant-size job of bellowing, thought the captain.

Instead of chasing after Lord Nalin's fleeing loyalists, the guards began taking up defensive positions. One of them roughly hauled the captain down beside him. Pausert turned and was surprised to see the High Lord was striding back the way they'd come, accompanied by half a dozen of the guards.

"He has gone to raise the alarm," Hantis explained quietly. "To sound the Warcall of Aloorn. Only the High Lord himself can do that. History reached many inaccurate conclusions about Arvin: But one thing no one ever accused him of was personal coward-ice. There will be more resistance ahead. Fierce fighting. We are too few for that. Arvin will be back soon, at the head of his soldiers. He had a reputation for remaining calm in battles, although he had a terrible temper. I see that much at least was true."

Things were relatively quiet for a time, with occasional prob-ing shots coming from further up. Then they heard a horn blowing. A sort of wild tantivity which seemed to echo through the very material of the castle itself. The captain saw that Hantis' back straightened as it sounded. And then, within a moment, the attack came from the Nanites. There were several hundred of them fir-ing on the handful of Arvin's guards that had been left to hold this place.

"What made them attack?" asked Goth.

"That was the Warcall of Aloorn," said Hantis. "The shutters have come down with it. Now, the enemy cannot flee the castle. Their only chance is to fight."

"Well, they're doing that all right." The captain looked specu-latively at Goth. "I think I need to shield you again, child."

Goth looked speculatively back at him. "Sure, Captain. If you stand behind me."

Pausert suddenly had an idea. "Hantis. Are these men armed with some form of grenade?"

She nodded and pointed to things that looked like Indian clubs on the belt of the nearest guard.

"Could you 'port those, Goth? I'll shield you and you 'port those around the far corner up there."

Now Goth grinned. "Sure, Captain. You can even push me for-ward like a screen while I do it."

Pausert traced the klatha patterns with his mind. "I think we'll settle for just holding this place until Hantis' nasty ancestor gets back."

"He's not so bad, Captain. Pul likes hi . . ." Goth was in her shield. A grenade vanished from the guard's belt. Nothing happened.

"I think they have to be armed first," explained Hantis, speaking hastily to one of the guards. He took a Sprite-grenade off his belt and twisted the base, and held it up. It vanished from his grip. An explosion occurred further up the passage. The other Sprites began doing the same for Goth.

Deep in the castle, the Leewit was getting desperate to get out of her new quasi-captivity when a strange wild horn-call sounded, echoing through the walls. The Sprite children dropped the cards, and their green catlike eyes widened. "What's that?" asked the Leewit warily. There were distant clanging noises, now.

"The Warcall!" said Lisol, looking terrified. "It means the castle is being attacked."

"Great Patham!" said the Leewit, irritably collecting her precious cards and stowing them in a pocket. "Stupid clumping place—can't even play cards in peace. I think I'd better go, little 'uns."

"You can't," said Ta'himmin. "Shutters are down. We're all supposed to go to the Star-hall, now. With Mamma and Pappa if they are here or else with the nursebeast."

Sure enough, the nursebeast arrived. There was no time for the Leewit to hide, and besides there seemed little point. The creature looked about as dangerous as belly-button fluff. It was big, furry and distinctly cuddly. The two little Sprites flung themselves on it and clutched it.

"Come, Leewit," commanded Lisol. "We must go."

The huge fluffy beast didn't seem worried by an extra person in with its charges. It just fussed them towards the door, snuffling anxiously to itself.

Out in the passage, where she'd been trying to get for the last hour, the Leewit realized things were even more serious than she'd realized. The passage was occupied by several armed and nasty looking Sprites. "Get back! Get back into your chambers!" yelled one. Further down the passage something exploded.

But the nursebeast was determined to see her charges through to the right place, no matter what explosions happened or orders anyone gave. She hooted mournfully and ambled forward.

One of the Sprites shot her. The nursebeast squealed in surprise and pain.

The two little Sprites shrieked and clung to her.

"Get out of here!" yelled the shooter. "Go. Back to your chambers, before I shoot you too!"

A moment before the Leewit had been really frightened. Now

she was just mad clear through. She didn't even think about which whistle to use. *That* one busted up machinery something awful.

And . . . that gun would never fire again. The Sprite who'd been holding it was hopping around, clutching his hand and hissing. "Quick," said the Leewit. "Hold my hands, you two. Let's get them under nursebeast and carry her back."

Scared, the two little ones did their best. But the big fluffy creature was heavy, and bleeding. And there were more Sprites coming. The Leewit whistled again.

Behind the remains of the barricade, Pausert heard a familiar high-pitched whistle. It was like having his ears pricked with a hot needle. And it was on the wrong side of the barricade! Then the second whistle . . .

The captain seemed to detect a terrible urgency in that whistle. He reached into himself, knowing there was desperate need and knowing that klatha power came not when you wanted it, but when you were ready for it. He pictured the Leewit in his mind: a little blond waif, her cold gray eyes staring at him, and began to weave the klatha pattern around her. She seemed larger than he'd envisaged, so he made space. He didn't want to accidentally cut pieces of the Leewit off, so he made the pattern include all that was alive. And then, pattern completed, he picked up his Sprite-rifle and began running forward. He was unaware that the rest of the little outpost had followed him, or that more Sprites were coming up behind that, led by a shrimp with attitude. All the captain knew was that he wasn't going to be stopped short of the Leewit. Goth's 'porting of grenades had kept heads down ahead of them.

Now, as Lord Nalin's cohorts put their heads up, they found themselves facing what seemed to be a wave of fury. Sprites are more klatha-sensitive than most humans. The creature running towards them, one of the survivors later said, seemed at least fifteen feet tall and as unstoppable as an avalanche. And they were already rattled by the exploding grenades that had appeared from nowhere.

Afterwards the captain admitted that he'd even forgotten to fire, while he was running forward.

Those behind him made up for it.

Lord Nalin's loyalists were not all Nanite-infected. Few of them were, actually. These were just foot soldiers following their lord's orders, who really didn't want to be there at all, fighting the High Lord. They turned and fled. Some of them fell over the barrier of the large cocoon shielding Leewit, two little Sprites and a huge furry beast of some kind. The beast was wounded and bleating plaintively.

The captain got there, and, as he stopped, Arvin's Sprites surged past. There were several hundred of them, and High Lord Arvin was in the van. So was Hantis, accompanied by Pul. A panting Vezzarn and two other Sprites he'd co-opted came up with a makeshift stretcher—and Goth, still in her own shield cocoon.

Catching his breath, the captain decided that the Leewit could wait until he'd liberated Goth. If he could lipread she was saying some pretty awful things, and he didn't know if the Sprites had soap anyway.

Calming himself slowly and deliberately, the captain retraced the pattern that shielded Goth.

"What did you leave me behind for, Captain?" she demanded as she bounced to her feet. "You agreed to stay behind *me*." It was one of the few times he'd ever seen Goth hopping mad. She even stamped her foot. "What's the point of me staying around until I'm marriageable age if you're going to do STUPID things like that!"

"Er," said Pausert. "The Leewit was in trouble."

Goth was not mollified. "The Leewit's *always* in trouble." Crossly, Goth glanced at her little sister. "I'd say leave her in there, out of trouble for a change. Save us all some grief. Except those two Sprites seem to want to get to the others that are in with her." She pointed to two anxious Sprites who were trying reach into the shield cocoon.

Pausert realized they were trying to get to the two small Sprites in there, and that the Leewit was signing frantically at him.

He took a deep breath and retraced that pattern too.

Instantly the passage was overwhelmed by yelling.

"Captain!" The Leewit tugged at his sleeve. "The nursebeast's been shot!" She dragged him towards the fluffy thing.

It was definitely bleeding and in pain. He knelt beside it and parted the rich fur, looking for the wound. "Give me the vibro-razor, Vezzarn. Let me just cut the fur clear, here."

He did, exposing the entry-wound. The beast turned its long neck to try and peer at it. Its beery-brown eyes had a look of entreaty that made Pausert feel terribly helpless. Goth and the Leewit were kneeling beside him. So, on the other side of the fluffy creature, were two small Sprites and what were apparently their parents. Sprite soldiers streamed around them as the captain felt around the wound cautiously, wishing he knew more about first aid and more about alien physiology. At a guess, the creature had a bullet lodged in its lung—if it was built like the creatures he was familiar with.

"The bullet will have to come out."

Goth took a deep breath. "I can do that, I think." She closed her eyes, briefly. "Here, Captain." She held out a bloody metal fragment.

"I think I can still the pain and stop the bleeding," said a voice from the Leewit's mouth. It didn't sound like the Leewit, but more like her older sister Maleen. Captain Pausert realized that the Leewit was calling up her sister's pattern to guide her through some piece of unfamiliar klatha. "But I'll need to borrow from you two."

"Sure," said Goth, gruffly. "So long as you fix it. I ought to give you a good thumping later, you idiot. The captain and I have been worried stiff about you. And you nearly got him killed."

"You and what clumping army?" the Leewit jibed. "Just 'cause you're sweet on him! Take more than a few silly Sprites to hurt the captain, anyway. Now help me with the nursebeast. We can fight later."

Goth smiled mistily at her sister. "Just you wait. Now, draw away. This is what they premoted you'd be good at one day."

"What must I do?" asked the captain.

"Just hold her shoulders. And when she needs your strength, let her have it."

"I'll do my best," he said, a bit uncertainly. He knew it wasn't physical strength she wanted.

The Leewit began to glow. Her hands, wrapped in the nursebeast's fur, looked like little torches of warm redness that seemed to be sinking into the animal. The captain felt himself being drawn on . . . and gave. The nursebeast gave an odd sort of hooting whinny and stuck a long pink wet tongue out and licked the little Sprites and the Leewit. Then the fluffy head sank down. The little Sprites gave unmistakably heartbroken cries.

The Leewit said something, tiredly. Even if they weren't human, there was no mistaking the incredulity on the faces of the Sprite parents. And hope on the faces of the little ones.

"I told them she's going to be all right now, with some rest. I think we did the trick, Captain. I could use some rest myself. Can you give us a hand to carry her into their home?"

And then the littlest witch hugged him fiercely, and so did Goth, and Captain Pausert, once of the Republic of Nikkeldepain, suddenly felt very good about the universe and his place in it.

Pausert took one side, Vezzarn and the male Sprite the other; joining hands, they lifted the fluffy thing and carried it down the passage, while the little Sprites, the Leewit and the mother rushed ahead and opened a door into what the captain presumed was the Sprites' apartment. They three carried the nursebeast into a small entirely soft-upholstered room and put it down.

"I guess I'll skip whopping her," said Goth. Her little sister had flopped onto a chair, with the small Sprites on either side. The Leewit looked tired and pale. "This time, anyway."

The Leewit beckoned. "Hey. I've asked them for some food."

"Better make it something we can eat on the run," said Goth. "We've got to catch up with Hantis before *she* does something silly. She's very taken up with this High Lord Arvin. And we've *still* got a job to do for Karres, getting her and Pul to the Imperial court before the Winter Carnival."

The Leewit sighed. "I guess. I'll just ask for a few of the meat-roll things, then. They're pretty good and we can eat those while we go."

There followed a high speed exchange in the Sprite language. The two little Sprites were still clinging onto the Leewit, from whom they had to be pried away by their parents.

"I said we'd see them and explain later. And thanks for the food," said the Leewit. "Phew. I hadn't realized what hard work it is not to be the youngest."

Once they got back into the corridor, it was easy to work out where to go. There was a steady stream of armed Sprites heading in one direction. Word must have gotten around, too, because no one tried to stop the human party. They ate as they walked. The captain found he was both ravenous and tired and was grateful to his professional beggar "niece." She must have done a fair job of cleaning out the Sprite family's pantry, as well as expropriating some of their children's clothes.

Nalin had apparently retreated into the upper reaches of the castle. As they got higher, it became apparent that they were catching up on the fighting, and that it had been fierce. Burned areas showed that the High Lord had been forced to make his own path forward. The air stank of smoke, fear, and the coppery smell of Sprite blood.

Captain Pausert began to wonder if he should perhaps have left Goth and the Leewit with the grateful Sprite family. But the Leewit reassured him. "They say it's all over. A small party cut their way out through the shutters and the rest are dead or captive. And the High Lord and the foreign Lady are still alive. Oh. And Pul bit someone."

Pul had indeed bitten someone. Lord Nalin had not been one of those who got away. The Sprites moved aside to allow the captain through to Hantis and the High Lord Arvin.

"They say you're a hero, Captain," said Hantis. Her brown face had sooty smudges and a shallow scratch on it. "That you charged the barricades alone."

"You know the captain thinks he has to look after us . . ." Goth's voice trailed off, and it was hardly surprising. Lord Nalin was on the ground in a circle of nervous Sprite-soldiers. He was jerking and twitching, and something that looked like gray dust was spilling out of him.

"Poisoned Nanites," said Hantis grimly.

"And the others? Was he the only one infected?" asked the captain, both fascinated and revolted.

"No. At least seven of them got away. They fled in the direction of Delaron." There was no expression in Hantis' voice. "We also have the infected but not yet controlled ones."

She patted High Lord Arvin on the shoulder. "High Lord, this one is safe. But we must deal with the others. We must sterilize their nest." She turned back to Pausert, Goth, the Leewit and Vezzarn. "Come. See what we're up against."

They went through into an adjoining room. This did not look like it was a home—even a war-smashed home—of the detail and decor-conscious Sprites. Instead the glass and bric-a-brac with which the Sprites filled every spare corner had been carelessly swept together. Glass, gold, silver, gems and crystal lay broken and jumbled in a trash pile.

On the floor lay some twenty-seven Sprites. Males. Females. Even a child. Their bodies convulsed every now and again. Their eyes were open . . . and empty.

Hantis saw how the High Lord started when he saw the infected ones.

Then he gave a cry of horror and would have run into the room, if Hantis had not restrained him. "You don't understand," he said frantically, trying to pull away from her hands. "Hantis, that is Neirion there! We must help her! We are betrothed."

"No, my Lord Arvin," said Hantis. "It is you who do not

understand. That *was* your betrothed. Now she is just a crawling mass of Nanites."

"But we must get them out of her! We *must*."

"We can't. We have found no way of doing so. Not without killing the victim. Anyway, it is already too late." She spoke as gently as she could, knowing full well that it was this moment that had transformed the gentle young Arvin into Arvin Warmaker, who had half-destroyed Nartheby to save it. And been cursed by generations unborn for his goodness and greatness.

"You must destroy this with your klatha power. Destroy all of Lord Nalin's chambers. Sterilize everything with cleansing fire. It is the greatest—the only—mercy you can give to those infected."

Hantis saw the anguish in the young High Lord's face. "I can't!"

"High Lord Arvin. Unless you would see all Aloorn, and indeed all Nartheby like that, you must. Our dominions are already lost. Without you, we are, too." She paused. "And you do have the strength. Three thousand years later we still remember that you did."

CHAPTER 32

It had been a more comfortable rest than the last couple he'd had, Captain Pausert had to admit. The Sprites were treating them rather like royalty, even if Hantis said that they would still have to appear in the Hall of Stars before High Lord Arvin in the Seat of Judgment the next morning. Arvin was recovering from the immense amount of klatha energy he'd expended. If Hantis was right, he was also preparing to attack and destroy the neighboring principality, as part of saving his species and the galaxy from the Nanite plague

That was all very well, but the captain wanted to get back to saving his own species and the galaxy from the same plague—three thousand years from now. It was of course logical that it had to be saved earlier, in order to have it around to save later, but Arvin seemed to have the matter in hand. He was doing just fine, and didn't need them at all, other than some advice from Hantis and the loan of Pul as a stud. But Pausert was no nearer to solving his own problem of how to get them back. The vatch was still around, but it was keeping its distance.

The Hall of Stars was just as full as it had been the last time they had been there. And once again they were in the gallery reserved for the accused. But this time they were respectfully ushered into it.

"It's mostly a formality," said Hantis, with slight unease. "It was all something of a misunderstanding."

"But you did call the High Lord names," pointed out the Leewit, a bit self-righteously. "You punched him in the belly, too."

"And you, little lady, did willfully destroy precious crystals, some of which had been grown for more than five centuries in zero-gravity."

"Hey! The little squirts were going to fry us!" protested the Leewit.

"That takes some nerve—you, calling anyone else a little squirt." Hantis smiled impishly. "It's not that the High Lord wants to punish us, but Sprite law is quite inflexible. He'll have to go through the motions. If there are complainants, then he has to act. But now that the truth is being told, Arvin and the others are somewhat embarrassed. No one will complain."

But it soon became apparent that although High Lord Arvin was content to let bygones be bygones, some of the other Sprites were not. First, the accusers got to speak.

"They're saying," said the Leewit with a frown, "that misunderstanding or no, Hantis insulted Aloorn's honor. And we destroyed part of the ancient heritage of Aloorn. And that one is saying that the High Lord is taking a stranger's word and destroying part of— hey, wait a minute! I recognize him! That's the one they called Wellpo. He's one of those three that kidnapped me!"

"Ah," said Hantis. "I will ask the guard to take a message to the High Lord. I could tell he was lying, but I thought that it was merely politics, which is mostly lies. You don't remember the name of the third kidnapper?"

The Leewit shook her head. "No. She had a sharp chin and a pointy nose, that was all I noticed."

"Well, that means it could only be about any of the Sprites," said Goth with a yawn. The captain knew how she felt. The proceedings were long and the seats comfortable enough to encourage a nap. Below them the arguments went back and forth. And on and on, rather like a slow foreign play in which the dialogue was the only important part. Then, just as the captain was dropping off to sleep, things suddenly got more interesting.

"They're grabbing old Wellpo!" squeaked the Leewit with delight. "Said he'd stick a knife into me. Oh, look! He's hit one of the High Lord's guards over the head!"

Pausert sat up and peered over the edge of the gallery. There was quite a fracas going on in a gallery some ways down and further to his right. And, he noticed, one going on across to their left that the Leewit hadn't yet spotted.

He took her by the elbow and pointed. "That your lady with a pointy nose?"

The hat of the "lady" in question had just been knocked off. She was struggling with two of the High Lord's guards.

"Yep," said the Leewit in satisfaction. "I guess they got her, too." Then her eyes narrowed and she whistled. Several pieces of expensive crystal in the far gallery shattered, including a globe in the long-nosed woman's hand.

The Sprites in the gallery scattered. "Guess whatever was in there was pretty nasty," said the Leewit. "They've still got her though."

"She was one of those calling for retribution, too," said Hantis with satisfaction. "The guard I sent to tell Arvin about Wellpo said that the High Lord had instructed the guards to search his quarters. I think they must have found something that incriminated her. I think that this is all over, even before those who would speak for us have their turn."

"Vatch!" hissed Goth. "Captain, get ready."

Pausert began hastily shaping hooks of klatha force with his mind. And then realized that, unless Silver-eyes needed to be tickled, they wouldn't help.

Why didn't you catch the big one? it buzzed reproachfully. **I took a big chance teasing it, Big Real Thing. It nearly caught me, too— and then you let it get away!**

It was too quick for me, admitted the captain. *And I can't get close enough to it now. It's watching us, but keeping its distance. I've been trying to figure out how to either go after it, or to get it to come closer.*

The tiny vatch buzzed around, amusing itself by doing a quick light-shift and making the underside of the gallery where they stood transparent. **Why don't you hide where we can't see? Then the big one might come looking. Though it might just go away, I suppose.**

If the big vatch just went away they'd be stuck here in the past. But they had to try something. *Where can we hide, though? You seem to be able to find us across time and space.*

There's a no-place right here, Big Real Thing. Where they make the stuff for the lights. The place where up spins. You could hide there.

"Where 'up spins'?" The captain assumed Silver-eyes was talking about some kind of power plant. He thought about it for a while.

Where up spins. A generator? A spinning magnetic field? That might make some sort of sense to a creatures like a vatch.

The crowded galleries began cheering.

"What's going on out there?" asked the captain, irritated that his train of thought had been disturbed.

Hantis laughed. "We've got a lot more adherents than Sprites who wish us ill—especially as the chief detractor turned out to be a paid spy and possible murderer. The fact that the Leewit is a child and was kidnapped upset a lot of Sprites. The mother of young Lisol and Ta'himmin has just finished speaking. She was very eloquent on your behalf, Captain. We Sprites are protective of our young. They'll be yelling for war now, when they find out the infected ones have fled to Delaron."

"Huh. Child!" said the Leewit crossly. "I think I'll whistle at 'em. Lisol and Ta'himmin are children. Me, I'm—"

"An impossible brat," said the captain, with a smile. "A pint-sized disaster-in-motion. Other terms come to mind." He pressed on before the Leewit could do more than scowl. "Now, if they'll let us out of here, I want to try getting out of historical Nartheby before you go and destroy any more its ancient heritage. Is there a power-generator room we can get to, Hantis?"

She nodded. "But you will have to wait until High Lord Arvin rises from the Seat of Judgment. While this matter will, I think, be speedily settled, I believe there is a second item on the slate. A question of property. We Sprites believe in finders' keepers and there is a belief among a small party that you have expropriated their property, Captain. Property that they found, and should be entitled to keep."

"What's that?" asked Pausert warily, feeling in his pockets.

"Their pet," said Hantis, with a perfectly straight face. "Ta'himmin and Lisol Aloorn-Taro have prevailed on their grandfather to enter a plea for its return. They say it is skilled in playing games, and good for defense. Besides all that, it helped to fix their nursebeast. So they want it back, even if it does eat a lot."

" 'It'? A toy! Huh! I'll fix them." She began to purse her lips. Hastily, the captain clamped his hand over her mouth.

Hantis shook her head "The demand will be denied, of course. This is just their grandfather's way of raising a public vote of gratitude to you, Leewit. He is a powerful sub-clan head. This is how you gave rise to your own name, you know, as well as saving two great ones among my people. Ta'himmin Aloorn-Taro is credited with much of the restoration. And his sister is remembered as Lisol the Healer."

Hantis smiled oddly. "It is a bit strange to see my own distant and famous ancestor as a very little girl-Sprite. As you know, the youngest daughter of my house is always called 'the Leewit.' Toll and Threbus asked me for a good name for you, so I offered them one of ours. I never knew where it came from, until now. Ta'himmin and Lisol never forgot you."

The latest of the universe's Leewits dissolved into tears. The captain decided it was safe to remove his hand. But he still did so a bit warily. With the Leewit . . .

You never knew.

CHAPTER 33

The power rooms of Aloorn were hidden deep within the stalk of the castle.

They were heavily guarded both by ordinary and klatha means, but with the High Lord at their side those barriers were passed. Arvin had walked slowly, talking to Hantis, both of them looking sad and serious. From what the captain could work out, it would be a grim time and hard tasks ahead for the young Sprite Lord, for which he'd get much blame and little credit.

Down here, underneath the huge humming turbines, the captain hoped that they would be invisible to the vatches. Silver-eyes certainly hadn't followed them. The captain fashioned his hooks of klatha force for the big creature, with heat like a kiss of the sun. He put barbs on them, and not threads of force but broad ropes of it. This vatch wasn't going to get away, if he could catch it at all.

They waited. The Sprites also had folk who could rell vatch, and while the party from the *Venture* had to "disappear" to make the creature of klatha force curious, they could "reappear" in a hurry if the vatch came calling.

And it did.

The signal came down.

"All right, everybody onto the hoist. Go, go, go!" yelled the captain. They tumbled onto the hoist and rushed upwards. As they rose the captain became aware of the big vatch. He flung those hooks of force, flung them around and over the huge shifting cloud of vatch. They hooked into the black energy swirls, they hauled and tightened. *Tighten. More. As much as we need to immobilize this one. Pull in. Hold it. Hold hard.*

The vatch yowled. Green slitted eyes peered fearfully at him. NOT AGAIN! MONSTER, LET ME GO!

Not unless you do what I say—or I'll tear you apart and short out your innards! Playing with us! Take us back to our ship and our time right now! No. Wait. Let's finish things here properly. Let me see where those Nanite-possessed ones fled to.

The towers that Hantis had pointed out as "fabled Delaron" sprang into view from the grayness that was vatchspace. And then the elegant, slim towers shrank and broadened. The captain blinked. There weren't twenty of them. Just one. This tower looked like the others had—only this looked like it could be built with bricks and mortar. It was impressive but not impossibly tall. And looking in— somehow as if he had X-ray vision, he saw a group of Sprites in an upper chamber. Once again his vision shifted as if he was now seeing into the Sprites, and he saw them as a seething mass of myriad tiny klatha black energy points . . . all but three of those present in the upper chamber. The Nanites were klatha or klatha-using creatures too, and this was apparently what they looked like to a vatch.

Pausert directed a bolt of dark energy, torn from the mass of the great roiling thing that was the vatch, at each of the Nanite-creatures. It absorbed the little sparks of klatha energy that were billions of Nanites, and consumed the bodies in gouts of incandescent heat. He saw the three noninfected ones flee, and then he finished the business with a explosive bolt of raw energy that simply vaporized the now empty upper stories of the tower. That would do as a parting present for the safety of ancient Nartheby, if not Arvin's reputation—since he'd be the one blamed for the destruction in the historical records.

Now take us all back to our ship, and then take the ship where I tell you. Pausert had already decided that if he caught the vatch, he'd have it take them to within a few hours of the Imperial Capital. To Great Patham's Seventh Hell with all this mucking about in Egger Space!

The grayness whirled and surged. Even by the vatch standards of non-distance this place was far off. And dark . . . and then tumbling. Finally, they were back in the *Venture*.

But not the *Venture* in the stillness of the void: the *Venture* on

the expanding wild edge of matter. The *Venture* was being vio-
lently flung and rolled as a great tumbling tidal wave of energy
and existence picked her up. The ship was on the verge of breaking
up, torn between two states and sometimes existing in both. Her
engines roared at full throttle, and then cut out and then roared
again. Gravity surged in waves that almost made the captain black
out as he reached for the drive controls. The engines cut again . . .
then free lightnings danced through the ship. Sparks zipped and
sizzled. The *Venture* vibrated like some giant jaw's-harp.

Nothing could survive the front-wave of singularity for long.
Even the vatch was being battered and torn, and so were the cables
of pure force and the klatha hooks.

Suddenly, they were out of there.

The control panels were alive with flashing lights and the air
in the control room was thick with smoke and the sound of
damage alarms.

Pausert fought with the controls, realizing as he did so that his
grip on the vatch was literally being torn away. The vatch was so
desperate to leave that it was willing to part with large pieces of
itself in order to do so.

One of the control panels was actually on fire. Pausert just let
the vatch go, and focused all his attention on the damaged *Venture*. Vezzarn had managed to get out of his acceleration couch
and grab a fire extinguisher and spray the burning control panel.
But the power systems were running on emergency auxiliary now.
The lights dimmed and flickered. The *Venture*'s main drive engines
stuttered and hiccupped . . . and were still. Unfortunately, one
auxiliary lateral rocket still fired—even though the automatic
controls had it shut down—and it spun the *Venture* in a clumsy
spiral. The lights cut completely as the captain managed to shut
the lateral down with one of the manual override switches.

There was an eerie silence. A spaceship is never completely silent.
There is always some machinery running. There is always some
vibration, even at the subliminal level. Spacers became inured to
the roar of the main drive to the point where they just didn't notice
it. But when everything is still, the ship is dying or dead.

The *Venture* drifted like a derelict hulk. Inertia kept her on the
slow spiral that the misfiring lateral had caused. Then the standby
batteries cut in, lighting only the emergency glows and the instrument readouts. The air was thick with smoke, burning the captain's
eyes—though not as much as the readouts from the instrument
panel did.

Pausert knew sadness and despair. His ship was in no state to go anywhere. The old *Venture* would be lucky if it ever made another planetfall.

But he didn't let any of that show in his voice. "Vezzarn, better check the engine room. Give me a damage assessment as soon as possible. Goth, check the air recycler. Hantis, you and the Leewit start collecting suits, and get yourselves suited up. Then report back here." The captain was already examining the control panels. "A navigation readout would be good, too, if we've got anything still operating that will pick up beacons."

The captain himself had already taken the small atomic powered lamp from the worktable, and started undogging the access hatches to the control panel's electronics boards. The circuitry there was mostly solid-state, but there were various plug-in spares he could try.

"Ow." He burned his hand and sucked his fingers while trying to work out what was going on. The smoke didn't help. He waved it away and continued to examine the boards. He moved one and was rewarded with a shower of sparks. At least there was still power, even if Patham himself didn't know what was shorting out what.

He took a deep breath, coughed, and let klatha guide his hands. He pulled out one of the units. Part of it was melted and Pausert dropped it hastily with a word he hoped the Leewit wasn't near enough to hear. He plugged the replacement unit from the spares compartment into the panel. Luckily it was a J-83 and that was one of the modules the *Venture* carried in case of emergencies. He was rewarded by a buzzing sound and a red-flickering in the darkened control room. Hastily pulling his head out of the control panel, the captain was relieved to see that the flickering was caused by a bank of telltales, flashing red. The buzzing was stilled by flicking a switch or two, and the telltales at least told him where to start looking. There was life in the boards, and that in itself was reassuring. What wasn't, was the sheer number of faults being registered.

There was a sudden comforting hum, a vibration of machinery somewhere in the deepspace-silence of the *Venture*. The intercom crackled to life. "Captain, I've got the number two auxiliary running on manual. We can draw power for the air recycler off that, and some lights."

"Well done, Vezzarn. What's the status of the rest of the engine room?"

"Not good, Captain." There was a pause. "We had a burnback.

We've lost part of the aft tubes. The main drive . . . I don't know yet, Captain."

It was not what Pausert needed to hear. He studied the telltales, deciding what to do next.

Goth came in. "Got power to the air recycler again. They're working just fine, Captain. We'll at least have this smoke dealt with pretty soon." She went straight to the communicator and dialed the space beacon frequencies.

"Doesn't seem to be any life in the communicator system," she said.

"Hang on. You should have power now." Pausert pushed the module onto its pins and crossed his fingers. There were stars out there. The familiar river of light that was the Milky Way said that they were at least back in the right galaxy—but exactly where and when they were was another matter.

"The dials have lit up," announced Goth. "Still not getting anything, though."

"Try the general and Imperial ship-to-ship channels." The captain wrestled with a hot board that seemed to have soldered itself in place.

There was a vague crackly noise from the communicator. "Might almost have been someone saying something," said Goth.

The captain, more familiar with communicator problems, felt some relief. He'd definitely picked up a word there, in Universum. They were back in a familiar part of the galaxy, in human-occupied space. "I think we might also have lost our external aerials. It's a quick job to replace them."

"Uh-huh," said Goth. "Well, seeing as the Leewit's brought me a suit, I'll suit-up and see to it. You're busy and it's just plug-in, plug-out stuff." Since Goth had moved herself into the *Venture*, she'd taken on responsibility as naturally as a miffel grew winter fur to deal with the cold. The girl was a fair way to becoming a competent ship-handler, and her skill with navigation sometimes left the captain feeling embarrassed about his own ability.

"Anything else we can do, Captain?" asked the Leewit.

"A general check. Keep out of the engine room, but do a damage assessment of the rest."

The captain went back to his work. Some of the boards could be bypassed. Some could be replaced. It was a painstaking process that required him sticking his head under the console, and then getting out again, to check the readouts and displays.

" . . . proach on standard incoming lane three," squawked the communicator.

Goth must have replaced the aerials. And they had communications and they couldn't be too far from a planet or refuel space-station, with space traffic. That was a weight off his mind.

"Well, we've broken some furniture, and the electric butler's not working," said the Leewit. "Can't see any big damage so far though, Captain. And it's not so smoky any more."

Trust the Leewit to check out the electric butler first! That was the least of the captain's worries right now. The electric butler had always been a bit cranky and inclined to deliver ice cream when you asked for steak, and sometimes deliver it to the control room floor with a cackle, instead of to the small mess-room. He'd worry about starving to death once they'd reestablished control and engine function.

"Thanks. Try the communicators on the beacon channel again."

"What's the beam length?"

".02r00."

Less than half a minute later the captain heard the beep of the beacon signal. "You want the trans . . . transwatsisname, Captain?" asked the Leewit.

"Transcription. Yes, please. It's the green button on the right."

Two minutes later, the captain knew that he was back in his old stamping grounds. He could have been home in the stuffy Republic of Nikkeldepain within three weeks ship time. And the world of Porlumma, where he'd once rescued three witch-girls from slavery, lay just ahead.

Now the captain only had two problems. The first was simple enough to deal with. Certainly he, and probably Goth and the Leewit, were considered to be criminals on Porlumma, despite the fact that he'd sent Wansing's jewels back to him.

Well, the *Venture* could still travel under her Uldune-obtained false papers as the *Evening Bird*. He could go back to being Captain Aron of Mulm and Goth his niece, Dani. They could come up with a suitable alias for the Leewit and no papers would be needed, as long as she didn't leave the ship. But he wouldn't be surprised if there were "wanted" holovids all over the dock. He'd have to talk to Goth about doing a suitable light-shift, although he knew that was a tiring exercise to keep up.

The second problem was more immediate. Would the *Venture* make it to the surface of Porlumma at all? The captain got up and went to inspect the engines for himself. There was still several more hours work here on the control systems, but he needed some tools from the engine room to get into some of the panels. And besides, what was the use in fixing control and navigation systems if the engines weren't usable? At least they were within easy reach of Porlumma by lifeboat, if worse came to worst.

Down in the engine room the captain found Vezzarn hard at work on the main drive. "Might get three of her tubes functional, Captain. But they're none of them going to be calibrated right. I've adjusted the thrust settings as best I can for the situation. The main drive itself . . . well, she's working, but for how long I can't say. We'll be lucky if we get a light-year out of her, and I don't know if the damage can really be repaired at all. She'll need to be seen by the engineers. The tubes themselves are a write-off."

"Well," said the captain, comfortingly, "luckily enough we're within three light-hours of an Empire world. It's a backwater, but they'll have repair facilities. If I can get her down in this state, that is."

"Going to be tricky landing, Captain. But you'll pull it off." Vezzarn seemed more cheerful now that he knew there was an Empire world within reach.

"I'll do my best. Is there anything I can do for you down here? Otherwise, I need to get back to the navigation and control systems. There's a ton of work up there to make them operational, never mind fit to handle a dicey landing."

"I'll be fine, Captain. With respect, sir, I've probably worked on more tubes than you have. If you like you could send one of the girls down to pass me things. And it would make my day if I could have a cup of coffee with this job."

"The electric butler's on the fritz. But I'll ask the Leewit to come down here. I want Goth up there for navigation."

Vezzarn actually laughed, something that would have been unthinkable minutes before. "That electric butler is probably the one bit of this ship I wouldn't mind seeing in the state that these engines are in. They didn't like those surges, Captain. That's not going to happen again, is it?" he asked warily.

"Not if I can help it!" The captain went back up to the control room.

After several grueling and often frustrating hours of peering at manuals and working in awkward, confined spaces, Pausert had repaired or replaced what he could of the control system, and jury-rigged as best as possible whatever couldn't be repaired. Then Vezzarn and he went through an extremely cautious test firing of the main drive. At a very reduced capacity, the drive could push the *Venture* onwards to Porlumma. She began the slow limp to port. What would have taken hours would take her the better part of a ship-day, and, the captain knew, he'd have as tricky a landing as he'd ever managed to pull off at the end of it. It was nearly enough to get him to consider the Egger Route again. Nearly.

The captain went off to shower and returned to find that the now inevitable poker school had taken over the navigation table again. He was glad that he had the excuse of wanting to keep an eye on the instruments and do some calculations for the landing. He already owed the Leewit too much candy to be good for her. Goth said that his problem with playing with the Leewit was that he didn't really want to win. Pausert knew it was true enough. But using klatha powers on the two young witches would seem unfair, even if he was sure that the Leewit had somehow marked the Agandar's cards.

CHAPTER 34

Wiping the sweat from his brow, the captain exhaled long and slowly. If he could bottle that landing, he could sell it as the perfect instant diet. Pausert thought that he'd probably lost fifteen pounds on the way down. At least ten of them had simply melted away when one of the remaining tubes lost half its liner seconds before setdown.

And yet . . . he'd managed it. Near to a textbook perfect landing, in fact. Now, so long as Porlumma's authorities didn't recognize them, all they had to do was get the *Venture* repaired and get back into space again. Once they were out of detector range, they'd have to make use of the Sheewash Drive to get to the Imperial Capital in time. But, according to the calendar of the customs official who was coming to give the *"Evening Bird"* the once-over, they still had ten days.

The question, of course, was whether they could get the *Venture* repaired and space-borne before then. Even with the Sheewash Drive, it was going to be a close thing.

The engineer from Saltash & Gryfin, Ltd. was not encouraging. "The tubes will have to come out entirely, Captain Aron. They're just about completely shot. And half of the instrumentation needs to be junked. The fact that you managed to set your ship down without leaving a crater in the landing field fills me with admiration for your skill as a pilot, though I have grave doubts about

289

your common sense. I'll let you have a quote in the morning, but brace yourself for something steep. Frankly, if you could afford it, it would make more sense to haul your drive out and scrap it."

Captain Pausert sucked breath through his teeth. He was painfully aware that the *Venture*'s current bank balance was comfortable enough for regular running, but not really in good shape for massive repair bills. "How steep is 'something steep,' and how long is this going to take?" he asked warily. "I've got a contract to fulfill and it's got really harsh noncompletion clauses. We'll need to make this a rush job."

The engineer grimaced. "Captain, I've never seen engines or even control systems that have taken this kind of battering and still functioned, and I was once a Navy engineer. What'd you do? Pick a fight with a neutron star? I've seen craft towed in from battles that looked better. I'll give you a precise figure as soon as I can, but we're talking the better part of half a million maels, I'm guessing. And to reengineer and recalibrate the engine . . . call it three weeks. It's a big job."

"Oh." The captain sat down. So, by the sudden dent on the couch beside him, did Goth. She'd plainly been keeping an eye on the engineer while she was in no-shape. "Well," said the captain weakly, "will you get back to us with the exact quote?"

The engineer nodded. "As soon as I've done the calculations, Captain Aron. But as I said, it's a big job." He left the captain and Goth to stare at each other in despair.

"A half a million maels. And you know what these repair quotes are like," said the captain gloomily. "Never under."

Goth was already calculating. "We've got about three hundred and fifty thousand maels left in the account. And we can run into the red another fifty thousand or so. We'll be a long way short, Captain. And I just don't see how we can get Hantis and Pul to the Imperial Capital in time, if it's going to take them that long."

"It'd be quicker to haul the engines out and put a new drive in. They could do that in a couple of days."

"Well, then, that's what we need to do," said Goth, decisively.

The captain shook his head. "If we had a couple of spare million, we could do it. And stop thinking of Wansing's jewels, Goth. They'd catch us for sure. And besides, it's not right."

"It's an emergency, Captain," said Goth thoughtfully. By now her reserved manner fooled him not at all. The captain knew that she was thinking seriously about larceny.

Well, to be honest, so was he. They had a vital mission to complete, after all. But it still went against his grain.

He sighed. "Give me a few minutes to think. We must have some way of raising the money."

"I could go and play some poker," said the Leewit, appearing from behind the couch, the Agandar's cards in her hand.

"I suspect they might think that they were marked, child," said the captain, managing at least half a smile.

"Oh, they are," said the Leewit cheerfully. "Look. Here on the edges." She dealt a card out, face up. "See that pattern around the edge? It's different on some of them. Lisol and Ta'himmin spotted it back on Nartheby. Those Sprites have got sharp eyes."

"But that's on the face of the cards. That's no good. It's got to be on the edges or on the backs." Goth was betraying more knowledge of cardsharping than the captain would have expected.

The Leewit snorted. "So why is the royal flush marked then, smarty?"

The captain felt that odd scalp-crawling sensation that he got from klatha events. He reached slowly for the cards. "Not," he said in a hushed voice, "to enable the previous owner to cheat at cards."

"What?" said Goth, puzzled.

The captain looked at the two of them, and, dealing the cards out face up, separated out the suits. "Just who was the previous owner of this pack of cards?" he asked.

"The Agandar. Criminy! You mean . . . ?"

"Yes," said the captain, sorting the suits into order. "I think this pack of cards that the Leewit has been carrying around in her pocket is what the Agandar's pirates were looking for all along."

He drew the royal flush out of each suit and laid them out. "I think . . . I'm sure the answer is right here. Right in front of our eyes." He stared intently at the picture-cards. Patterns imported centuries ago from Old Yarthe, that had altered gradually over the centuries.

The Agandar had been on Uldune. Bloody-historied Uldune. The world whose pirate fleets had once spread fear and terror across a huge sector of the galaxy. The world that had turned from piracy and raiding to become the clearing house of half the dubious merchandise in the galaxy. A place that still welcomed pirates, at least successful ones.

Why had the Agandar been on Uldune? To follow up the rumor of a new spacedrive? Or had he been on Uldune anyway, for *another* purpose?—when his spies had brought him the rumor that the *Venture* was being renamed the *Evening Bird* by courtesy of the Daal's highly efficient staff of forgers.

Uldune still welcomed pirates. Successful pirates.

It provided, among other services, a fence for stolen goods and . . . banking. The pirates of ancient history hid their loot in secret hoards on desert islands, but the modern pirate was more likely to use a bank vault. Or a numbered private account. Kleesp's accomplice had actually said as much! Pausert was willing to bet that the cards in front of him held the key to just such a numbered account. But the question was: how? He studied the pattern on the edge of the cards. It was a simple repeat-pattern, hand-painted and skillfully so, but still nothing more than that, at least as far as he could see.

"I'll bet it's supposed to give us the numbers of the Agandar's bank accounts. Probably with the Daal's Bank. But for the life of me I can't see what the numbers could be. I suppose you could count which number of the repeat pattern was wrong, but what order would they go in?"

He picked up the four sets of marked suits. "See," he said, dealing them out again. "There are sixteen repeats of this pattern on the top margin. Each one of these cards has a different one of those repeats altered." He moved the cards around, arranging them in the order of the altered repeat pattern on the top edge. "We can make pretty patterns, but they don't . . . ulp."

As he laid the last card in the row, the altered patterns linked up. There was a brief hum and a small hyperelectronic screen and keypad appeared above the cards.

Letters began forming on the screen: **ENTER ACCESS CODE.**

"They aren't cards at all," whispered the captain. "It's a hyperelectronic computer. Those are circuits, not just patterns."

"And a mini-subradio!" said Goth. "No wonder the Agandar was able to keep in touch with his fleet."

The captain shook his head incredulously. "He even said he had a secret shielded transmitter! The Sheem robot was also hyperelectronic. We should have guessed."

"Only question is: what's the access code?" asked the Leewit." Then, a little plaintively: "And when do I get my cards back?"

"That's two questions," said the captain. "And I don't know either answer."

ENTER CODE WITHIN THE NEXT THIRTY SECONDS.

"Or . . . ? I guess we don't dare find out," muttered the captain.

"I need to be lucky. I need every ounce of klatha power." He took a deep breath and began to type a sequence of numbers.

Nothing happened.

FIVE SECONDS

"Hit ENTER," said Goth.

CODE ACCEPTED. DESTRUCT PROGRAM ABORTED.

A menu popped up. A very ordinary menu of choices, including subradio banking.

Pausert exhaled slowly. Then, accessed the subradio banking option.

"I think," he said, "the Leewit's cards have given us the jackpot. Let's see if we can transfer enough into my account to allow us to simply buy new engines, and forget about repairs. That'll be a lot faster."

When the figures came up, the Leewit whistled softly. "We could buy a whole new ship," said Goth.

"Buy a whole clumping fleet!" exclaimed her sister.

The captain shook his head. "The paperwork would take longer and attract more attention than a repair job. Besides, I like the old *Venture*. She's been places with us that no new ship would ever have coped with. But, when this is all over and we decide what to do with what's left of the Agandar's fortune—*after* we track down those of his victims we can trace—I will promise you both a refit and a redecoration of your cabins. And fifty decks of cards for the Leewit."

"Want *that* one," said the Leewit, pointing. "Always knew those were my lucky cards."

"Hmm. I was thinking about that share in the Petey Byrum and Keep," said Goth thoughtfully.

CHAPTER 35

Even spending money like water, it took three days to get the *"Evening Bird"* ready for space again. The captain was nervous every minute of that time, because he knew that the amount of money they were spending was sure to get someone from the ISS interested, before too long.

So, the minute the preflight checks were done, Pausert lifted the *Venture*. As if to make up for his brilliant landing on jury-rigged controls and with a mere three battered tubes, the takeoff was one of his worst. Still, they were space-borne before the authorities figured out just who had been spending rivers of money on little Porlumma. There were going to be some red faces if they ever they found out that they'd put in new engines for the infamous Captain Pausert, whose vid still graced Porlumma customs control offices. Still, in fairness, they could say that Captain Aron from far-off Mulm had looked nothing like the vid-picture. The stern-visaged, planar-faced Aron bore no resemblance at all to the images of the cheerful criminal Pausert.

"Right," said the captain to his two witches. "The time has come to show me how to work the Sheewash Drive. I feel I'm ready."

"Huh. Otherwise we'll have to hit you over the head or something," said the Leewit, cheekily. "I'm not going to do it with you dragging us back like a big rock, again, that's for sure."

"Only if you promise me you'll stick to the pattern exactly this time, Captain," said Goth sternly.

So Goth and Leewit talked the captain through the pattern. As it was developing, the captain thought he saw where it could be done differently. But this time he stuck exactly to the pattern as Goth and the Leewit presented it.

They kept it up for a mere fifteen seconds. The captain was sweating and beginning to feel as if the entire weight of the *Venture* was pressing onto his shoulders, when Goth said "Enough."

"Whew," said the captain. "It sure *does* take it out of you."

"Uh-huh. Come on. Let's eat."

They walked through to the mess. The captain found that Hantis had had the forethought to order the new electric butler to make them a substantial lunch. It was more reliable than the old electric butler, but he'd gotten used to the way the old one used to burn the eggs. "How did I do?" he asked.

"*We* did pretty good," said the Leewit, talking with her mouth half-full.

Goth swallowed and started loading up another huge forkful. She looked sideways at him with those big brown eyes. "Told you the captain is a hot witch."

Captain Pausert concentrated on adding food to a stomach that was telling him he'd been starving for a while. After he'd got to his third plateful he said, "You know, when we were doing the klatha pattern—the part where we sort of plait those strands of light—I thought, well, if we . . ."

Both witches started to giggle. In the Leewit's case, as she had a mouthful of juice, the captain had to pat her on the back while Goth fetched a pile of napkins. "Told you so," said Goth to the Leewit.

"Good thing you didn't try it," said the Leewit sternly.

The captain held up his hands. "But it felt like it would work. And I have worked out new klatha stuff that did."

Goth grinned at the Leewit. "Like our Egger trip."

"Or those clumping cocoon shields," said the Leewit, snorting. "Toll was so right, Goth."

The captain began to feel more than a little irritated. Sure, they'd had some misadventures here and there, but he didn't have a guiding pattern in his head. "I worked out how to do klatha hooks and the vatch-handling all by myself. And the cocoon shields might have been awkward to get you out of, but they worked. They worked pretty well."

"Oh, they work all right, Captain. Except," Goth scowled, "when you leave me behind and attack hundreds of Sprites on your own.

They just don't work the same way that most of the witches of Karres do things. That's what Toll said when Maleen suggested you'd need a pattern to teach you. She said you were better off learning to do them on your own and maybe seeing them in new ways. So Maleen and some of the other premotes did some work on it. Came out they agreed with Toll. Came out they thought we *wouldn't* survive if you were taught. So we've had to let you blunder along. Sometimes I wondered if we would survive because you weren't trained. But it seems like you're pretty lucky so far, Captain. It's hair-raising, though."

"But don't do any more 'sperimetal twists while we're linked," said the Leewit, shaking her finger at him.

The captain smiled at her. "Ex-pe-ri-men-tal. Not even little ones?"

"*No*," both of them said firmly.

It was somehow comforting to discover that Karres had not just turned him loose untrained without consideration of the matter. He could see the point, to some extent. A schooled witch would tend to approach things in the way in which they had been taught. Coming at it cold, he had a rather different perspective, and had come up with different but effective answers, even if some of them *had* been rather hair-raising.

Just that little burst of the three of them working together at the Sheewash Drive had shortened their journey by several weeks. The captain had added considerable power to the drive, as they saw when they picked up beacons on the communicator. The journey from Porlumma to the Imperial Capital would now take four days instead of nearly three weeks.

The trip wasn't entirely peaceful, though. The captain was awakened from his sleep by an intercom call from Goth. "Captain. You'd better get here, quick." She was laughing as she said it, but the Leewit was yelling in the background so he had a pretty good idea what the problem was.

He was quite right. It was Silver-eyes, who was, as usual, tormenting the Leewit. The little vatch gave up the moment the captain arrived and buzzed affectionately around him. **Hello, Big Dream Thing. Ooh, did you ever give that big bully a hiding! Can I bring some more big ones? They're scared of you.**

The thought was enough to make the captain shudder. Some vatches, like Silver-eyes itself, couldn't be handled. The next big one might be the same—only much more powerful. *Not right now. I don't want to frighten them all off.*

That seemed to amuse the little vatch. **Guess so. That last big one is making a lot of noise about it. The others are mostly laughing, though.**

There are a lot of others? Pausert felt weak at the thought.

Oh, sure. Little ones like me, lots and lots. Not so many big ones. But I'll be a big one too, some day. You wait and see! I'm already a little bigger now from eating that dream-candy.

Having seen the Nanites from a vatch perspective, the captain thought that he knew what Silver-eyes was talking about. *Lots of it? Inside dream-people?*

Yep. But they're dream-not-people. They're not there. Just the candy is. It sorts of thinks together to be a pretend-dream-people.

The vatch, obviously getting bored with all this conversation, went back to tormenting the Leewit. In the interests of peace, tranquility, and the noise levels in deep space, the captain had to tickle the vatch with klatha hooks to get it to go away.

When they entered the area around the capital planet, Pausert discovered that the new drive fitted on Porlumma had one other serious advantage: The signature of this engine was quite unlike the one that the ISS was hunting for. They passed unmolested through the cordon and went peacefully onward towards the great spaceport at the Empire's heart.

"What's the program, Hantis?" the captain asked, as they drifted in to land along with the thousands and thousands of other ships that were here for the Empire's biggest annual event.

The Sprite made a face. "The witches have cooperated for some time with Hailie. But the Empress is in quite a precarious position, as you know. Something like open contact with the witches of Karres could be the final straw to give her enemies the leverage to insist that she step down. Her stepson would jump at the opportunity. So the contacts are very secret. We have a rendezvous point at the Nenbutal Grill—it's an eatery on the portside of town. I give a certain password, and things will be taken from there."

"Hmm." The captain rubbed his chin thoughtfully. "I think we'd better all go along with you."

"An escort will be welcome. We can pretend to be a mere party of diners."

So, once the ship had docked and port formalities and customs had been dealt with, the entire crew of the *Venture* with her special passengers took a cab into the town, heading for the Nenbutal Grill. Pausert was relieved to think that his responsibilities were almost over. It had been a tougher mission than he'd anticipated when he'd cheerfully taken it on, back on Emris. But it was finally nearing completion.

However, when they stepped out of the cab into the cold evening air, Pul took a deep sniff of the warm steamy aromas coming out of the half-timbered restaurant and suddenly evinced a desire to visit a lamp-post further up the street. Hantis followed him, holding his leash.

Hantis came back a few moments later, trailing the stocky yellow grik-dog. "My dear Captain," she said, coolly, "I'm really not feeling at all well, and the smell of that Nenbutal food has quite put me off. I don't believe I'll dine after all. Will you call me another cab to take me back to my hotel?"

Captain Pausert fumbled for words. "Ah. Certainly ma'am. I think we'll accompany you. To tell the truth, I'm not all that fond of Nenbutal food myself." And he hailed a passing cab.

Back at the huge spaceport, the captain waited until he was sure they were quite alone. "What was wrong?"

"Pul smelled Nanites," said Hantis, worriedly. "I think that the rendezvous must have been discovered."

"Pretty sure, ma'am," said Vezzarn. "Something else smelled about that restaurant, too, and I don't mean the food or these Nanites. I looked in through the window, and those diners just didn't look right. You know why? No wine. You ever been to a Nenbutal place where they haven't served more wine than food?"

"I wonder what effect alcohol, or other drugs, would have on Nanite-controlled people?" said the captain. "I guess it might make those bodies harder to handle."

"Probably," Hantis agreed. "But what do I do now?"

A plump woman with gray hair and a rather frumpish uniform approached them. "Pardon me, sirs and ladies, but your coach has arrived."

The captain was about to point out that they'd not ordered a coach, when the woman continued. "You are the party I am waiting for from Nikkeldepain, I'd venture to guess, sir?"

The captain realized suddenly that it was Hulik do Eldel. Hulik made up as an older woman, and padded out to change her shape.

"Uh. That's us."

"If you would follow me, sir?"

❋   ❋   ❋

Ten minutes later, after a series of maneuvers designed to shake off any pursuit, they were sitting in the *Thunderbird*, with the Daal of Uldune. Or, rather, with two of the six Sedmons.

"Your ship is under surveillance. A large party of ISS operatives went out there shortly after you left. We've been monitoring all incoming ships of the right size-class, as we were pretty sure the vessel's appearance would be subtly altered."

"It took us a little time to get there—and we nearly ran into the ISS ourselves," continued the other. "They were probably mounting the same kind of operation."

"And the restaurant we were supposed to use as a rendezvous is full of Nanites," said Pausert. "I think there was a severe security leak. But the real question is: what do we do now? We've got no way of contacting the Empress."

One of the Sedmons coughed. "We have an official invitation to the Carnival ball. As usual, as part of the entertainment there is to be a cultural display from various planets in the Empire, organized by the Ministry for Arts and Cultures. Folk dances, traditional singing, apparently a display of fire-eating and stilt-fighting."

Goth was the first to catch on. "Is the *Petey B* in port?"

The Sedmons nodded in unison. "We have certain . . . associates in town. We believe a substitution could be arranged. The Ministry for Arts and Cultures is not terribly well organized."

"In the meanwhile, the ISS is searching for you," said Hulik. "We've arranged that you will disappear. We have a comfortably appointed warehouse on the northern edge of the port. Himbo Petey will be brought to see you. You may leave the arrangements to us."

"Better send Dame Ethulassia too," said Goth, thoughtfully. "We'll need to raid her wardrobe."

CHAPTER 36

So that was how the captain found himself sweating in the uniform of a Slalonican peasant festival dancer. The puffy sleeves would have been ideal to hide a Mark 20 in, but naturally they'd all been thoroughly scanned for weaponry before being allowed into the Imperial complex. Even here they were totally isolated from the actual guests and nobility of the Empire, and of course, the Imperial House themselves. The dances and displays took place on a stage, with an unobtrusive moat separating the mere entertainers from the jeweled and masked butterflies of the Imperial court. That moat, the Sedmons had explained, was actually a killzone. It had everything from spikes to detectors connected to sonic fibrilators, to several Imperial household bodyguards with heavy weapons, all to forestall a would-be folk dancer assassin. They were locked into their section—and the only official way out was through a long passage that led to gates outside the main compound. Emperor Koloth was taking no chances that the traditional Winter Carnival would lead to his death, the way it had to the death of his uncle, the Emperor Tarabian. There was, however, a door, which no one was supposed to know about. The Emperor Justino had had a secret way made to the dressing rooms, so that he could visit his mistress, who had been a tsling-dancer from Ambar's World.

It was, of course, securely locked.

The Empress Hailie would be at the ball, as would her stepson the Emperor. First there would be the dancing and the entertainments, and then the Imperial House would go out to the grand balcony for the people and the vids.

Outside in the Imperial city the revelry was noisy and cheerful, with music and dancing, fireworks and the drinking of loyal toasts. It wouldn't even pause until the Emperor and his retinue appeared on the stroke of midnight on the grand balcony, to accept the adulation of his people.

Inside the grand ballroom the royal orchestra played ancient music on traditional instruments—very badly, to the captain's ear. It didn't matter much, as the masked courtiers weren't letting appreciation of it spoil their cultivated languid boredom or their gossip.

"How is Vezzarn doing with that lock?"

Captain Pausert was living in mortal fear that he might have to dance. The pin-striped kilt and wooden shoes might be traditional dress on Slalonica, but as far as the captain was concerned, they made him feel very foolish. Not to mention clumsy.

"Fine. He said another five minutes," said a stilt dancer from Kota. She was a pretty little blonde with gray eyes.

"That's what he said five minutes ago," grumbled Pausert.

"Well, it still looks like you won't actually have to dance, Captain." Goth was dressed up in the red and green paint of the Mardaban fire-eaters. "I've got your evening-dress 'ported into the changing rooms, and a lovely mask."

Captain Pausert was going to accompany Hantis, who'd be wearing her fabulously expensive tozzami fur coat, lelaundel tippet, and a gorgeous beaked mask. The captain's costume, especially his own mask, was designed to match. The mask had jewels on it. Lots of them, and the captain didn't think any were fake. He decided not to ask where the jewels had come from. There'd be time enough later for his stern lectures on property and moral probity.

"Has anyone got the Empress picked out yet?" he asked.

"We think she's the one in the gold lamé with the feathers," said Hulik. "But that's the whole point of the masked ball, Captain. The idea is to let the Imperial House mingle with their courtiers."

"Stupid," grumbled Pul. "You can tell who anyone is by smell anyway. And that lot reek of Nanite. I'll tell you soon enough which one is the Empress. I was given her scarf to sniff, once."

"It's open," said the small spacer.

Lots of dream candy out there, said a little silver-eyed menace, suddenly.

Don't cause trouble now. Please, begged the captain hastily. Why did this vatch *have* to keep coming back?

"Let's go, Captain," said Hantis. He offered the Sprite his arm and she rested one elegant gloved hand on it. Pul had been decorated as much as possible to make the grik-dog appear to be a pampered lady's toy, not even to be left behind at a social occasion. The grik-dog looked more sour than usual about the pink bows and the jewel-encrusted leash.

They slipped out and were soon weaving their way between the Emperor's guests. The masked dancers were subjected to Pul's nasal enquiry. The feathered gold lamé, likewise. None of them were the person they were looking for.

At length they came to a small woman with a simply cut azure silk gown and a butterfly mask sitting quietly in an alcove. A couple of other guests lounged around nearby. Considerably bulkier ones.

Pul nodded and tugged at his leash. One of the two large men got up, ever so unobtrusively. Pausert knew then that they had the right person. "Your Imperial Highness," said Hantis quietly. "I have been sent to you by our mutual friends, of the house Serrak."

"Lady Hantis of Aloorn, I assume," said the woman in the butterfly mask. "It's all right, Jaime. These are our last remaining friends. Although, I think they have come too late. In a few minutes I will have to take my place on the dais with my stepson . . . or the thing that is pretending to be my stepson. And then the Nanites will have me at last."

"You know about the Nanites, Your Highness?" asked Pausert, puzzled.

She gave a low, sad laugh. "Why do you think I sent word to Karres that I needed help?"

"Oh." The captain felt rather stupid. "I wasn't told all the facts, ma'am."

She laughed again. "That old 'need to know' business. I wonder how many more disasters occur than are avoided, by keeping agents in the dark? I realize that Karres is in strict quarantine, but I have been hoping for rescue by witches coming thrumming down the Egger Route. But according to the last communication I had the only hope they had been able to come up with for the Empire was one 'Captain Pausert' and a companion by the name of 'Goth.' Their best premotors all agreed on that. They also agreed on there being a very low probability of success—less than a one in five chance that he would get here. But if he did, that he would have discovered how to deal with the plague. I don't suppose your companion would be Captain Pausert, Lady Hantis?"

"Er, yes," said the captain uncomfortably. "I am Captain Pausert, Your Highness. And Goth is with me."

He bowed. Now that he thought about it, it was all rather obvious. The witches could, if they'd wanted to, have reached the Empress via the Egger Route. Pul was indeed effective against Nanites . . . but there was a limited amount of venom in one grik-dog. And the Empress hadn't needed Hantis to tell her about the Nanites.

The Empress inclined her head at him. "And have you worked out how to deal with the Nanites, Captain?"

A number of pieces fell into place in the puzzle in Pausert's head. The mission hadn't been about Hantis and Pul, after all. It had been about Goth and himself.

"Then this was all a teaching device?" he demanded of Hantis.

"Say rather a learning device," she replied. "Threbus detected unusual klatha skills in you when he ran the tests. You affect adult witches enormously with your klatha gathering, but you don't appear to affect nonhumans or children—which is the reason I was sent on this mission as your minder. You are a klatha-force lighthouse, Captain. The best premotors on Karres worked on you—and found that you obscured their results. When fate said that you had to die . . . you changed the rules. They tried various future models. The predictors always came up with the same answer: allow him certain factors and allow him to evolve. Then they worked on what the best factors would be. Do not imagine that any of your companions are here by accident."

"Huh. They could have *told* us," said a voice close to his ear.

The Empress and her bodyguards jumped only slightly more than the captain. "Goth," he muttered. "I should have guessed. No-shape. And where is the Leewit?"

"The servant with the canapés," said Goth. "We couldn't let you out on your own, Captain."

The Empress' shoulders shook slightly. "Well, Captain, it appears that you inspire loyalty and great faith. So: Have you the answer we need? In less than twenty minutes I will need to take my seat among the Imperial House, who are, we believe, Nanite-invaded to the last person. If I fail to do so, I will undoubtedly be stripped of Amra's Regency. My influence and my daughter will disappear, and the Empire will slowly be devoured by the Nanites. Eventually, all humanity as well."

Knowing that what he needed desperately was to think, Captain Pausert felt as if his brain had turned into cheese. What *had* he learned? What klatha skills had he evolved? He suspected that he could use the Egger Route without the shaking. He'd learned how to do the Sheewash Drive. What else? Well. There was the cocoon shields. He'd bet they'd be proof against Nanites . . . or anything else.

And there was that, too. Betting itself. He'd *always* been a lucky gambler. Goth had put her finger on it: he always won if he really wanted to. When it came to the pinch, he'd gambled on the sequence of the cards being the access number for the Agandar's accounts. And he'd been right. He'd *known* he was right. And yet . . . it had needed Goth, too. To put the final key in to it. The predictors had said that it would take Goth *and* himself.

"Goth," he said quietly, "come and put your hand on my shoulder. Lend me your strength as we did for the Leewit when she helped the nursebeast. Be the key."

The moment he said it, the same hair-raising prickle that came with massive klatha use surged around him. This was right. He knew it. Knew it with a cast-iron certainty.

He felt Goth's hands—no, both arms—and not on his shoulder but around his neck, hugging him.

"So what is the answer, Goth? What can I do that Karres had to send us on this harebrained mission to learn?"

"It's got to be the vatches, Captain," Goth's voice whispered in his ear. "Or, at least, little Silver-eyes. I've never heard of anyone having a vatch that they play with instead of the other way around. Have you noticed that it always seems to come when you think of it?"

"I don't usually *want* the pesky critter."

"It likes you, Captain. Same as the Leewit does. And I think you do like Silver-eyes. Sort of, deep inside."

Silver-eyes *was* very like the Leewit, now that Pausert thought about it. Annoying, mischievous and capricious. Demanding, too. And, true enough, the captain had a soft spot for both of them. The vatchlet and the Leewit did things he'd often wished to do himself. "I suppose so. But I can't see why it would like *me*, Goth."

"You protect it. You frighten off the big ones."

The captain felt something dawn in him. "And it regards Nanites as dream-candy."

"Call Silver-eyes, Captain," said Goth with a calm, Toll-like certainty.

He did. And the little vatchlet came, like the sound of violets, like the smell of music.

Well, Big Real Thing, what do you want? Make that lady's mask disappear?

No. What I want you to do is to eat dream candy. All of it that's here. Every last piece.

The vatchlet emanated a definitely dubious feeling. **I don't know ... The last time I did that, I got sick.**

So much for that idea. The little vatch's worries were unwarranted, since Pausert was now sure that it had been Pul's venom which had made it feel ill, not the Nanites themselves. But how could he convince Silver-eyes of that?

The Leewit, too consumed with curiosity to stay away any longer, came over with her tray. "What are you doing here, stinkin' little thing?" she hissed.

Silver-eyes giggled. **Been playing with the others. But they're not as much fun as you are.**

The others ...

"You say," said the captain to Hantis, "that I'm like a klatha lighthouse. Threbus—Goth too—once said that would attract vatches to me."

"Yes, Captain," said the Sprite. "Threbus told me that you glowed."

"So call the vatches, Captain," said Goth.

The big ones are scared of him, said Silver-eyes, proudly and proprietarily, levitating a canapé to drop down a stately dancer's neck.

Ignoring the shriek, the captain asked, *Would the little ones come if I invited them? You said there were many of them.*

Sure. They only stay away from Dream Things because the big ones chase them. But it's like I said: the big ones are scared of you.

Captain Pausert felt that absolute gambler's certainty settling over him. *This* was the answer he'd been hunting for. He took a deep breath and concentrated on summoning them, across time and space.

Later, when she was called on to describe the event, the Leewit hit on it perfectly. "Imagine the biggest, messiest kids' party ever. Times ten."

❋   ❋   ❋

The captain was amazed at the number of little vatches who came. Still, there was enough dream-candy for all of them to gorge on. Which, they did, except for Silver-eyes. That little vatch—not quite so little, anymore—was too wary to do more than nibble a bit. So Silver-eyes amused itself with canapé bombing runs. There were entire buffets full of ammunition.

Only one of the Nanite-possessed came close to them. Pul bit him. It was not a pretty sight. One of the bodyguards dragged the writhing man away.

You could tell who the infected ones were, without Pul's help. They were the ones collapsing all over the place. The rest were screaming and running around in the food-fight and practical joke session to end all food fight and practical joke sessions. Admittedly, the victims weren't enjoying it much, but none of them was going to end up dead, which was what the captain had rather expected after the experiences in Nartheby. They just looked like the victims of canapé carpet bombing.

The Leewit stood it as long she could. Then she grabbed a platter of the stickiest canapés and announced to the captain that she was going to join in. "No fair that the stinkin' vatches have all the fun!"

The captain grinned. "Why not? You will never get such a chance again. Food fight at the Imperial gala event of the year."

Pul had walked cautiously over to one of the collapsed figures. Sniffed. "No live ones!" he growled in his gravel-crusher voice. "The human is still alive, though he won't be for long."

"They have to be alive!" said the Empress, turning pale. "If they don't appear on the balcony at midnight, we'll have panic across the Empire. Insurrections. War."

Why did it never get any simpler?

"Let's examine him," said the captain. "Maybe . . ." He and the bodyguard hauled the courtier into the alcove. He was breathing normally, although his pulse was racing.

He was also deeply unconscious. It was obvious to Pausert that there would be no way to simply prop him up on the balcony and fool anyone into thinking he was anything but comatose.

A man in evening dress walked over. "Good evening, Captain," said Sedmon. "Your Highness."

The Empress had retreated behind her two bodyguards. "Who is this, Captain?"

"The Daal of Uldune, ma'am," said the captain. He decided there was no point in explaining that it was actually one-sixth of the Daal.

Sedmon bowed. "Hulik wants to know whether you need assistance. The artistes of the *Petey B* are ready to intervene. Although, it appears that what is really being affronted out there is dignity." He looked at the chaos, and smiled wryly. "We've noted that Uldune wants no part in a fight with the witches of Karres, if this is what the three of you alone can do."

"Unless they want to get in the middle of this mess, I think not. Dame Ethy would never forgive us for getting pink turofish mousse on the costumes. We need to get these men back to their senses by midnight, Sedmon. Give that appearance, at least."

Sedmon looked thoughtful. "Or Uldune is in a remarkable position to possibly profit," said the descendant of the pirate overlords urbanely. "Not everyone will miss the Empire, Captain."

Captain Pausert realized it was up to him, again. But the gambler's certainty was back.

"I would," he said firmly. "Not the Empire as such, Sedmon. But the stability and peace it brings to ordinary people's lives. We're not going to start the war years, war *centuries* again. And before you think of taking advantage of the situation—I suggest you remember just who you are dealing with. Karres is not destroyed or even gone for long. I'll have your cooperation or Uldune will be fighting the witches of Karres. Look around you and be warned. This is what we do in mere play. Don't make us do things in earnest. Now, tell the other Sedmon that we need Dame Ethy to go through her wardrobes for regal gear. She and her troupe are about to play the role of their lives. In the case of Richard Cravan, an Imperial one."

Then he walked out onto the ballroom floor, accompanied by Goth. He clapped his hands. Vatches began swarming around him. All of them were tiny, but there were so many they seemed like a curtain of impossible blackness.

The party is over. Thank you all for coming. Please come again. Now go home.

The vatchlets squawked vehement protest. Pausert began forming vatch hooks. Great, big, glowing, terrible vatch hooks. That had the same salutary effect on the vatchlets as a father brandishing a great big terrible leather belt before his human brats.

Quickly, the blackness receded.

Silence settled over the ruined ballroom. And then the orchestra, those who still had whole instruments, began to play of all things, an ancient lullaby.

The Empress took off her mask and walked up onto the dais. She held up her hands to hush the crowd. The hysterical panic-filled babble subsided as they turned to stare at Empress Hailie.

"My lords and ladies. Control yourselves," she said, firmly. "We have an Empire to save. We have the Imperial appearance to make at midnight. If it doesn't happen, you know what the consequences are sure to be. So. Masks off, courtiers! And to work. If the Emperor himself isn't fit to appear on that balcony . . . I'll find someone else to stand in his shoes for the night, and wear the crown and wave to his people. But the people of the Empire will see what they expect to see. The Empire *will* go on. Then, when that is dealt with, we'll put things to rights here."

Dame Ethulassia finally got both the audience and the applause she'd always craved. Richard Cravan found himself wearing Imperial regalia, and playing the role of a lifetime. In later years it was said that was the Winter Canival when the Emperor had given his most regal speech ever.

Though the Leewit didn't think so. "Clumping stupid, you ask me! There wasn't any wind blowing at all. And even if there had been, he didn't have to say that crude stuff about wind cracking its cheeks." The Leewit was genuinely affronted. "Huh! It's not fair. If *I'd* said it, you'd be washing my mouth out with soap."

EPILOGUE

Things still had to carry on, and be finished off.

Hantis, however, wouldn't be part of it. She was dead keen to leave for Nartheby. "I have a great deal to rebuild. A great deal of history to see revisited. I made an arrangement with my ancestor before we left. He's hidden all his records in a secret chamber under the seat of Justice in Aloorn. Someone is finally about to receive the honor he deserved."

The captain realized just how closely they had been monitored—somehow, presumably with yet another branch of klatha he hadn't explored—when, a few minutes after the midnight ceremony, a delegation of witches arrived in the banquet hall. Pausert had no idea how they'd gotten there. There'd been none of the telltale signs of the Egger Route.

There was a lot of hugging as Toll was reunited with her daughters. Pausert was grateful to see that his great uncle Threbus had come to take control of the situation. Among those the witches had brought with them were a squad of healers, such as the Leewit would be one day. They took charge of the unconscious victims of the Nanite plague.

"It appears that the *Petey B*'s thespian troupe will have to remain here for some years," said Threbus later, as he and Pausert walked in the cool green gardens of the Empress-Regent's palace. "To keep the masquerade going until Amra is old enough to ascend the throne herself."

Pausert winced. "No hope of saving *any* of the people infected?"

Threbus shrugged. "A few—those who were infected at the carnival itself. But not all that many. It doesn't take long for the mind of the victim to be wrecked beyond repair."

Pausert wasn't really surprised. He tried to find what comfort there was. "Well, I guess that means Cravan and Ethy's troupe will have to be given official status. 'The Empress Players,' something like that. No other way to explain why a showboat would remain here for years. They'll like that, even if they'll complain constantly that they miss their wandering ways."

Threbus nodded. "And look on the bright side: the Empress has firmly cemented her position as the power behind the throne, since 'the throne' is now nothing more than an actor playing a role. And she's gained the respect and leverage she needs over the bulk of the nobility." He patted Pausert on the shoulder. "Karres is proud of you, Grandnephew. You came through at the end with flying colors."

"I wasn't inclined to forgive you at first, Threbus," said the captain heavily. "But I suppose you risked a great deal, too."

The Karres witch nodded. "Two of my daughters, Pausert. Two of those I love most dearly." He sighed. "It was a high-risk option, but all our predictors said it was the only alternative to a long and terrible war, just as the Sprites once fought. Now, we have an answer. You and the little vatches. We've bought time and can find other ways of dealing with the problem, without killing people."

Goth came to join them. As she drew alongside, she slid her arm around Pausert's waist and hugged him tightly. He placed his large hand on her little one and gave it an affectionate squeeze. There was a time when the captain would have been a little surprised at how easily and naturally that movement came to both of them. But . . . no longer. Again, he found himself wishing that klatha could somehow be used to affect aging.

Threbus was smiling. "Time passes, Nephew. Trust me."

The smug expression on his face, combined with the serene look on Goth's, aroused Pausert's natural contrariness.

"Ha! You two know-it-alls! I remind you that you *also* predicted something very good would happen to Goth if she spent the next year in my company. So? What is it?"

Alas, Threbus still looked every bit as smug. And Goth's serenity seemed completely unfazed. She gave Pausert that sidelong glance he'd come to know so well.

"The year isn't up yet, Captain," she murmured.

Pausert tried to think of a suitable reply, but couldn't. Then he caught sight of a pair of slitty silver eyes. And then another. And another. And more.

"The cure may just be worse than the disease, Threbus," he said with a grin. "Here we go again!"

3